COUNTING DOWN ELVIS

Counting Down

Counting Down is a unique series of titles designed to select the best songs or musical works from major performance artists and composers in an age of design-your-own-playlists. Contributors offer readers the reasons why some works stand out from others. The series is the ideal companion for music lovers.

Titles in the Series

COUNTING DOWN ELVIS

His 100 Finest Songs

Mark Duffett

ROWMAN & LITTLEFIELD
Lanham • Boulder • New York • London

Published by Rowman & Littlefield
An imprint of The Rowman & Littlefield Publishing Group, Inc.
4501 Forbes Boulevard, Suite 200, Lanham, Maryland 20706
www.rowman.com

Unit A, Whitacre Mews, 26-34 Stannary Street, London SE11 4AB

British Library Cataloguing in Publication Information Available

Library of Congress Cataloging-in-Publication Data

Names: Duffett, Mark.
Title: Counting down Elvis : his 100 finest songs / Mark Duffett.
Description: Lanham : Rowman & Littlefield, [2018] | Series: Counting down | Includes bibliographi-
  cal references and index.
Identifiers: LCCN 2017038499 (print) | LCCN 2017039831 (ebook) | ISBN 9781442248052 (elec-
  tronic) | ISBN 9781442248045 (cloth : alk. paper)
Subjects: LCSH: Presley, Elvis, 1935-1977—Criticism and interpretation. | Rock music—United
  States—History and criticism.
Classification: LCC ML420.P96 (ebook) | LCC ML420.P96 D72 2018 (print) | DDC
  782.42166092—dc23 LC record available at https://lccn.loc.gov/2017038499

Printed in the United States of America

CONTENTS

ACKNOWLEDGMENTS

Back in 1999, I completed a PhD examining the relationship between Elvis and his fans at what was then the University of Wales (Aberystwyth). Since then, I have taught at the University of Chester and published academic research on music fandom. Over the years, I amassed quite a library of Elvis material as part of my research process. This book had its origins in a visit to a famous London book emporium where I spotted another Rowman & Littlefield publication: Edward Komara and Greg Johnson's *100 Books Every Blues Fan Should Own* (2014). When I saw Komara and Johnson's volume, my first thought was that I might write a parallel tome on books about the Memphis singer. It was Bennett Graff, then a senior acquisitions editor, who steered me away from that idea and toward what you are now reading. First, I would therefore like to thank Bennett. Not only did he have faith that I could speak as a music critic and write something interesting, he also put the case to his editorial board that Elvis Presley made a *creative* contribution to popular music. As Bennett said, even though Elvis was not a songwriter, he was innovative in picking and interpreting material. I hope what I have written affirms Bennett's claim and celebrates some of Elvis's collaborators too. At Rowman & Littlefield, I'd also like to thank Natalie Mandziuk for her patience while I was finishing the manuscript.

I hope *Counting Down Elvis* will have at least two types of readers: recent fans, who want to get beyond the greatest hits and do not know quite where to start, and dedicated fans, who might use it as an inspirational day by day.

My thinking on Elvis would be impoverished if it were not for the support and friendship I've had over the years from many Elvis fans and colleagues. I'd like to thank Julie Mundy for giving me permission to visit the Official Elvis Fan Club of Great Britain annual convention at Hemsby in 1997 and the fans there for participating in my original research. I have fond memories from visiting several fan club conventions since then. In academia, I'd also like to thank colleagues at Chester and those beyond who have supported my research over the years. They have encouraged me to think in more detail about popular music and Elvis fandom. In no particular order, I would therefore like to thank the following: Tom Attah, Lucy Bennett, Michael Bertrand, Gary Burns, Claude Chastagner, Mark Goodwin, Jon Hackett, Ben Halligan, Anja Löbert, Richard Phillips, Paul Richardson, the late David Sanjek, Tim Wall, Eileen Weston, Jessica Wettasinghe, and Tim Wise.

To conclude this section, I will add a quick note on method. This book is my own interpretation, but existing thorough research has been invaluable in helping it come together. I was already aware of outstanding Elvis research by several authors—such as Peter Guralnick, Ernst Jørgensen, and Trevor Cajiao—who deserve great credit. Their work continues to be inspiring and invaluable. I also want to thank those who have pointed me away from myths or questionable sources—notably Richard Boussiron's 2004 volume *Elvis: A Musical Inventory 1939–55*—toward more reliable ones, especially Keith Flynn's excellent website: http://www.keithflynn.com/.

Finally, I would like to thank my parents, my brothers, and my partner, the wonderful Julie Burns. This book is dedicated to Julie, to Elvis, and to his family of fans.

INTRODUCTION

Picture the scene: a hot July night in Memphis, 1954. Up on the mezzanine level of the Hotel Chisca, in his WHBQ studio, the madcap DJ Dewey Phillips is talking to a shy, nineteen-year-old singer. Dewey starts asking him about a new and as-yet-unknown record called "That's All Right," a recording that seems to ignore age-old divisions between country and blues, just ripping them up for the sake of youthful abandon.

Track forward six decades. The universe has changed. Rock 'n' roll exploded. Rockabilly happened. Cliff Richard and the Beatles got all shook up. A new generation discovered blues, folk, and soul power. Rock was their baby. Elvis Presley spread his wings, inspired everyone who mattered, reclaimed his crown, lost his way, and died too young. Almost immediately, he was reborn like a phoenix. The world could not let him go. And we still can't.

Maybe it was the shake of a leg. Maybe it was that Southern accent, the hooded eyes, the curling lip. His deference, his charm, his wit. His grace. His voice. Whatever it was, we find ourselves walking back to Memphis, even if we have never been there before. As an icon, he was never quite with us, though we knew of his magic. Now he is never quite gone. The weight of his presence remains truly immense.

Those who don't know much about Elvis constantly ask things like: Wasn't he that guy who was hypnotized by his manager? Who did those bland movies? Didn't he just sing schlocky love songs, like all those bad-taste tribute artists? Aren't his followers a bit mad?

It's not obsession; it's dedication. It's not religion; it's appreciation. Profound appreciation.

Elvis's enchanting and timeless music ultimately stands on its own and speaks for itself. Listen again to the recordings, and Elvis amazes. Think about what they mean, and he astounds. Another person emerges. Not a dumb Southerner but someone who was magnetic, feral, funny, and knowing. Even if he was, at times, distinctly human, he inspired so many pretenders because his music was truly great. Therein lies the rub: Elvis was a mortal person who made immortal music.

More than seven hundred master recordings were released in Elvis Presley's lifetime.[1] In a career that stretched for more than two decades, he recorded many, many different songs. His story integrated his humble beginnings with the pinnacle of modern society. Equally, his studio music first relied on technologies of the 1950s—when a country double bass was known as a "bull fiddle"—and moved through an era of complex, multi-track consoles and mobile recording units. Along the way, Elvis worked with many musical collaborators. His albums sold in their millions, but ultimately Elvis was a *song* man. Songs were his medium, his focus, his art. Now we can get back to those songs.

The business of claiming to separate artistic wheat from the commercial chaff is a fraught one. There is an argument to be made that this should have been a much larger list, perhaps featuring almost as many songs as Elvis actually addressed.

Some fans will undoubtedly say: "Where was 'Mary in the Morning'? Why discount 'Money Honey'? How could you forget 'Clean Up Your Own Back Yard'?" In my defense, all I can say is that those are interesting recordings, but for different reasons, they never quite made my list. Some might be in the "100 more" section that finishes this account.

I was lucky to be asked to write this book. I had to skip a lot of gems and make some hard choices. I'm not going to pretend to claim some kind of superior status as a devotee or critic. There are always other ways to hear Elvis's music. There is much, much more to learn.

This is my personal 100 countdown. If you are a dedicated fan, part of the fun will be in deciding how much it resembles yours.

All I ask is that you listen.

THE COUNTDOWN

100. "Reconsider Baby" (from *Prince from Another Planet*, 2012)

One story about Elvis, just after he became famous, was that in the mid-1950s he showed up at Memphis's black radio station, WDIA. He carried an armful of records with him and made it his mission to get the charismatic DJ Nat D. Williams to expand his show's playlist. The WDIA story references Elvis's obsession with collecting records and his immense zeal as a kind of musical evangelist. Biographer Peter Guralnick said that Elvis was " as great an ethnomusicologist as anyone who'd been through college, gotten his or her degree, and done all of that—but he didn't."[1] The singer spent his life on a mission, asking us all to *listen again*. The trump card in his argument, of course, was his own music. According to Elvis's ex-wife Priscilla, "Music was never a mere interest but always an obsession."[2] At best, what he created sounded perfect consistently, but it was more than that. His music was always a team effort. Guitarist James Burton, for example, was one of the best studio players in Los Angeles and played on Dale Hawkins's "Susie Q," a single that came out in 1957 on the Chess subsidiary Checker Records. The *Louisiana Hayride* manager Horace Logan teamed him up with country singer Bob Luman after he left Hawkins. When Luman's band went to Hollywood to star in Roger Corman's exploitation feature *Carnival Rock*, Burton met Ricky Nelson. He backed Nelson in the long-running ABC television series *The Adventures of Ozzie and Harriet*. After a brief stint on *Shindig*, Burton's career as a session player exploded, to the extent that he even turned down Bob Dylan's offer to employ him as a touring musician.

Elvis told James Burton he had watched him play on *Ozzie and Harriet*. He tried to get him for the NBC TV special, which was known back then as *Elvis* and sponsored by Singer sewing machines (but will be referred to here as the *Comeback Special*). Burton was working for Sinatra at that point. The second time he got the request, though, he did not refuse. Elvis wanted him to form the foundation of his Las Vegas lineup. Burton accepted the position.[3] In "Reconsider Baby," his picking is every bit as gripping as Elvis's vocals.

It was the gift of music that allowed Elvis to transcend himself. In all its slinky, shimmering, fateful glory, "Reconsider Baby" presents that gift to listeners. As a singer, Elvis appears trapped by the ghosts of his own past. Yet he puts up a fight so spectacular that—just for a moment—his predicament is almost forgotten. Some detractors said he "stole" the blues. They were wrong. He lived them. He breathed them. From the porches in Shake Rag to the bars of Beale Street, the blues was just *there*. Elvis imbibed and inhabited the genre. He performed the blues. He blew them up. It's very hard to say he was a culture thief when he lived that musical form with such bravado, with such ease.

"Reconsider Baby" isn't Elvis's best track. It makes the cut, however, because it showcases exactly what made him so great. His music was news to mainstream America. His oeuvre was nothing short of a reconsideration of the tradition of genre separation. Walls could be heard coming down in those grooves. Elvis's recordings delivered the news that previously separate genre traditions had more in common than almost anyone—at least anyone who listened only to records or grew up outside the South—actually believed. Sure, he could do straight blues, and "Reconsider Baby" is as near as he gets, but he rarely did. More often there was just a hint of country, a nod to gospel, a self-knowing wink. By breaking down barriers, he made virtually all music his domain, creating a legacy that transcended race. His blues were loved by *both* white and African American fans. Rather than being inconsiderate, Elvis was *re-envisioning*, taking a new look at racial segregation as an old and outdated idea. Back in those days, it took a white performer to do it.

Elvis Presley had Lowell Fulson's 1954 original version of "Reconsider Baby" in his record collection.[4] The Checker Records single shows a certain humility and a muted, cabaret style. Presley's take positively glistens in comparison. His approach creates something more spectacular and less forgiving than Fulson's, bringing the material to life by making it more raunchy, glamorous, and existentially twisted.

Elvis tackled "Reconsider Baby" on 4 December 1956 during the Million Dollar Quartet jam session at Sun studio. The first version of it that he actually released appeared on the excellent 1960 studio album, *Elvis Is Back!* It is the live version that he performed at Madison Square Garden in the summer of 1972, however, that fully demonstrates the singer's intimate relation with the blues. Elvis is in teaching mode. His soulfulness sets him apart from the hacks. Musically, James Burton's guitar solo charts an extended course across the sky in a way that Boots Randolph's saxophone on the 1960 version never could. "Reconsider Baby" gets the "Steamroller Blues" treatment. Thematically, it became an ode to fate, a divorce song recorded not long after Priscilla departed, just before the couple filed for legal separation. The encircling vultures are almost audible. Elvis brings Fulson's number to life as a doomed exercise in persuasion.

99. "Early Mornin' Rain" (from *Elvis Now*, 1972)

When it comes to perceptions of Elvis Presley, it seems apt to borrow a question that one commentator asked of a well-known philosopher: "Ever since he became famous, has he ever been anything but an occasion for misunderstanding?"[5] Soon after the singer died, pop artist Andy Warhol lamented, "The people down there [in Memphis] really were dumb. Elvis never knew there were more interesting people."[6] Warhol was, in a sense, pondering his own views of small-town life. What his claim shows, nevertheless, is that the singer was often defined through prejudice against the South. Any attention paid to Elvis's entourage reveals that most were smart people. Many used their connections to create careers for themselves in the music industry. The musical side of the "dumb Southerner" stereotype has Elvis born singing country, making some blues, emerging with rockabilly, graduating to rock 'n' roll, calming down for ballads, getting lost in Hollywood, and fading in Vegas. It forgets diverse aspects of the singer, his life, and his music. Discerning fans know that Elvis fused different fields of music together. He had a deep engagement with gospel and flirted with quite a few other genres. Elvis had a knack that allowed him to sing everything from Neapolitan standards and children's rhymes to rustic ditties and "message" songs. He could even gesture toward jazz and disco. His most spectacular 1970s concert offerings—songs like "Hurt"—were, in effect, popular opera.

Contemporary folk was a field that Elvis entered and made his own, drawing it deep into his personal fusion of American music. Eschewing the harder-edged, "protest" side of the genre, he embraced its more gentle aspects. Folk artists made sounds that reflected early morning rides along misty highways; mature sounds that could present a side of Elvis's personality that was tender and wistful, yet courageous enough to express his loneliness. A spate of similar material emerged in the late 1960s and early 1970s. Elvis's personal collection contained Dion DiMucci's "Sit Down Old Friend" for instance, a breezy number with the kind of sound that might have nudged him in an appropriate direction.[7] As part of his extended affair with country folk, Elvis recorded two songs by the sagacious Canadian singer-songwriter Gordon Lightfoot.[8]

Back in the 1950s, Lightfoot was inspired to play guitar when he heard "Heartbreak Hotel." From the mid-1960s onward, he had a run of songs that reflected both manly vulnerability and a concern for social progress. Anchored by its regular, stomping foot beat, his Johnny Cash–like "Ribbon of Darkness" was a country hit for Marty Robbins. In 1968, Lightfoot's song "Black Day in July" painted a suspenseful word picture of civil disturbance in Detroit. "If You Could Read My Mind," from 1970, showcased the songwriter's ability to use life's smallest details and find poignancy in them as poetic expressions of heartbreak. "Early Mornin' Rain" reflected that gift. Though the idea came to Lightfoot much earlier, he captured it in 1964. Ian & Sylvia's consequent recording gently combined rodeo rider Ian Tyson's country voice with his wife's dignified warble. Judy Collins's version was more obtrusive, showcasing her strong, classically trained female voice against a mess of country picking. In 1965, Peter, Paul and Mary sent a new a cappella take climbing up the *Billboard* Hot 100.[9] The New York folk singers had already gone top ten with "If I Had a Hammer" and "Puff (The Magic Dragon)." By revealing the haunting, bittersweet center in Lightfoot's ballad, the trio set a new standard, but its recording only scraped the upper reaches of the *Billboard* Hot 100. George Hamilton IV—who began his career as a clean-cut teen pop balladeer—managed to have a hit on the country charts a year later with his own noble cover of the song. Five years after the release of Hamilton's country folk single, Elvis recorded "Early Mornin' Rain" in the four-song session at RCA's Studio B that also included the wonderful "Amazing Grace" and "The First Time Ever I Saw Your Face."

"Early Mornin' Rain" was unusual in Elvis's catalog; rather than expressing what he could do for it, the song's promise was much more reflected in what it did for him. It allowed a maturing singer to offer a new aspect of his personality to the audience. After one of the best investigations of the story of Elvis's version, Paul Simpson concluded:

> We don't know if he had heard Lightfoot's original. Peter, Paul and Mary alerted him to the song's quality without directly influencing him. His interpretation owes a lot to—but is no copy of—Dylan's cover. . . . Elvis had enough power and range to distinguish his version from Peter, Paul and Mary's and Dylan's with vocal histrionics. Shrewdly, he chose not to: his vocal is appropriately discreet. Instead, he adjusted the tempo, to create a sweet, natural flow that Peter, Paul and Mary's cover conspicuously lacked.[10]

Simpson was right. As soon as "Early Mornin' Rain" begins, Elvis's voice arrives like a warm caress. Although physically run-down, the singer manages to effortlessly coast through Lightfoot's song, leaving a quality performance behind. RCA released the end result on side two of its 1972 LP, *Elvis Now*, sandwiching it between the anthemic, yet rather gone-midnight, "We Can Make the Morning" and melodramatic "Sylvia."[11]

Elvis also made "Early Mornin' Rain" a frequent part of his 1970s set. Still in his American Eagle jumpsuit but with no live audience, in January 1973 he recorded a version in front of the TV cameras as additional material for the U.S. broadcast of *Elvis: Aloha from Hawaii*. While this version is, overall, passable, his ability to convincingly carry the song appears to waver a bit at the beginning. By the mid-1970s, Elvis established a concert version that began so subdued, its verse almost sounded mumbled. Strong country instrumentation and haunting backing vocals allowed him to come through, however, and to explore the number's uniquely rueful quality.

"Early Mornin' Rain" was included in the famous CBS TV curtain call, *Elvis in Concert*. The singer performed it both at the Omaha Civic Auditorium and at the Rushmore Plaza Civic Center in Rapid City; his posthumous double live album used the televised version taken from the second venue. Despite ailing health, Elvis maintained his usual humor for that show, saying, "Good evening, ladies and gentlemen. My name is Wayne Newton." Unfortunately, though, the *Elvis in Concert* version of "Early Mornin' Rain" sounds like something that has been sung just a little too often over the years.

In his final show, on 26 June 1977 at the Market Square Arena in Indianapolis, Elvis used "Early Mornin' Rain" to slip between the serene majesty of "Bridge over Troubled Water" and a goofy, breakneck-paced "What'd I Say." It is, though, the first released studio version that seems to best capture his vision.

98. "You Don't Have to Say You Love Me" (from *That's the Way It Is*, 1970)

It is a cliché to say that Italians feel everything with a passion, but clichés can sometimes have a ring of the truth. As his appreciation of Mario Lanza and versions of Neapolitan ballads indicate, Elvis was drawn to the operatic majesty of Italian music. There was something about its sense of high drama and capacity for emotional intensity that attracted him from the start. "You Don't Have to Say You Love Me" was concocted by the singer-songwriter Pino Donaggio and lyricist Vito Pallavinci as "Io che non vivo più di un ora (senza te)," which means "I, Who Can't Live (Without You)."[12] The pair entered it in the Festival di Sanremo in the mid-1960s. Showcasing the best unreleased songs in Italy, at that point the festival was broadcast by RAI television and used to select the Italian entry for the Eurovision Song Contest. Dusty Springfield performed a different number at the festival, but she was very moved by Pallavinci and Donaggio's song. After letting the fuss over it die down in Italy, Springfield commissioned English lyrics from her friends Vicky Wickham and Simon Napier-Bell.[13] Released as a single on Philips, her version was softer than Donaggio's and characterized by what Bette Midler called Dusty's trademark, "haunting and husky" voice.[14] Concluding with an immense and powerful climax, Dusty Springfield's version of "You Don't Have to Say You Love Me" combined gloriously lush orchestration with her great gift for expressing emotional loss and longing.

Dusty's English rendering of "You Don't Have to Say You Love Me" topped the UK singles chart and made the top five in the United States. As for the song's meaning, Napier-Bell himself said it as well as anyone:

> Great singers can take mundane lyrics and fill them with their own
> meaning. . . . Vicki and I had thought our lyric was about avoiding
> emotional commitment. Dusty stood it on its head and made it a pas-
> sionate lament of loneliness and love. [15]

Two and a half years after Springfield recorded the song in London, she
visited American Sound Studio to make the *Dusty in Memphis* album.

While Elvis's image was way too hot-blooded for him to be considered an easy listening artist in the traditional sense, he adopted many of
the same musical strategies: drawing on a full gamut of instrumentation,
engulfing a variety of different genres in a broad and unique style, refus-
ing to align with any obvious political side, and bringing together a wide
range of audiences on the center ground of good entertainment. Perhaps
that is why so many people loved him in a way that doesn't come close to
anyone before or since. To this day, what the star, his producer Felton
Jarvis, studio engineer Al Pachucki, and a range of talented musicians
created on "You Don't Have to Say You Love Me" stands as one of the
above-average moments in the 1960s and 1970s Presley catalog.

Elvis recorded "You Don't Have to Say You Love Me" one Saturday
night in June 1970, prior to tackling "Just Pretend." Located on the corner
of what was then 17th Avenue and Hawkins, Nashville's Studio B had,
by that point, gone sixteen track. Rather than supplying services across
the RCA roster, Jarvis focused his attention directly on Elvis. His charge
was in the middle of a five-day marathon that included a successful
attempt to record "Bridge over Troubled Water" the previous evening.

"You Don't Have to Say You Love Me" was put out as the B-side to
"Patch It Up." Nevertheless, it is hardly a wonder that Wickham and
Napier-Bell's number became a staple in Elvis's live set for the first half
of the 1970s. On Denis Sanders's feature documentary *That's the Way It
Is*, a lively version of "You Don't Have to Say You Love Me" is broken
down, like the performance by the Stones in the studio on Jean-Luc
Godard's *Sympathy for the Devil* (1968). Elvis goofs his way through the
rehearsal version before flinging out an impressively tight finish. On a
full Vegas performance from the same movie, he seems tired and a little
jittery as he shakes his leg all the way through. When the song reaches its
climax, however, the singer positively resonates with music. The 1972
performances that he offered at Madison Square Garden effortlessly combined lightness and authority—the Presley magic that was characteristic
of Elvis on his more confident days. His New York engagement was

special because he replicated the sound of his Vegas band by including a full orchestra, complete with reeds and strings, rather than just including a brass section.

One inspiration for Elvis's rendition of "You Don't Have to Say You Love Me" may have been the stately African American balladeer Arthur Prysock.[16] Formerly a star on Decca, Prysock was signed to Verve by the mid-1960s. He released a version of the number in 1967. Though Prysock's voice sounds bland at first, his approach wrings existential pain from the song. Elvis's rendition, meanwhile, is arranged to exploit its full power, with the performer asserting his role with a voice that is both dramatic and haunting. It is as if he is ripping up the map once again, alchemically combining a display of masculine petulance with an undertow that harks back to the delicious loss and longing of late 1950s and early 1960s girl groups. In that version, he is more than attached to his lover. He's bloodied, bowed . . . and just stung.

David Briggs started playing piano with Elvis in 1966 after Floyd Cramer was late for a Nashville session. He became a regular backing musician. When the keyboard player was interviewed in the mid-1990s, he did not hold back and severely criticized the quality of his former employer's output. Eventually, he conceded, "He was big *in spite* of the Colonel, *in spite* of the shitty musicians, *in spite* of the shitty producers, *in spite* of everybody."[17] In Briggs's view, it is clear that Elvis's music could have been much, much more. Asked in the same interview if there were any 1970s Elvis records that did actually rate, he said, "We only did one or two. 'You Don't Have to Say You Love Me'—we rehearsed that!"[18]

97. "I Can Help" (from *Today*, 1975)

By 1975, Elvis sat in the musical center of a diverse nation. He'd spoken for 1950s teenagers. He'd done his army duty. He had pleased the Colonel, Hollywood, and Uncle Sam. At his June 1972 New York press conference, a journalist suggested that the singer now "shied away" from rock 'n' roll. He replied, "It's very difficult to find that type of song. It's hard to find good material nowadays for everybody, for all of us, you know." He understood that his audience was now vast and multigenerational. It was hard to find one thing, musically, that could offer something for everyone. For all its faults, "I Can Help" could do that—though it is worth noting that Elvis may only have trifled with it, if at all, at one or two live shows.[19] The song is nowhere near "An American Trilogy," but it is no "Dominic" either.[20] With its easy, sing-along style and strolling bass line, some might say that "I Can Help"—beloved of fan club discos—epitomized the *worst* of Elvis's output: childish, pedestrian, predictable. Yet precisely like, say, Status Quo's version of "Rockin' All Over the World," those are the very attributes that end up, despite listeners' better judgments, drawing them to the music.

"I Can Help" was written and performed by the multitalented Billy Swan. Hailing from Missouri, Swan came to the attention of Elvis's former bass player Bill Black in the early 1960s. By that point, Black was making his way in the Memphis music business. As well as an extremely successful, tight little R&B outfit (The Bill Black Combo), he also started his own studio (Lyn Lou on Chelsea Street), a publishing firm (also called Lyn Lou), and record label (Louis Records). Under the name of Mirt Mirly and the Rhythm Steppers, Swan booked a recording session at a local precursor to Stax studio called Satellite. The famous producer Lincoln "Chips" Moman was his engineer. Bill Black released Swan's two-chord ditty "Lover Please" on Louis Records. Although the single was a commercial failure, Black gave the song to his friend Dennis Turner and put out another disc. That record started getting popular in St. Louis. Shelby Singleton offered to lease the master from Black through Mercury Records. When Black refused, Singleton persuaded the irrepressible Clyde McPhatter to take up "Lover Please." McPhatter supercharged Swan's composition with a smooth, snappy R&B delivery, and it entered the upper reaches of the pop charts. Decca Records released a swinging version in the United Kingdom by the fabulous Vernons Girls.

After the success of "Lover Please," Billy Swan moved to Memphis to work more closely with Black. In the first half of 1963, he boarded for a few months with Elvis's uncle Travis. Swan even tagged along when Elvis went to Libertyland and the movies. By the end of the decade, he gravitated to Nashville. His versatility as a writer, performer, and producer made him an attractive prospect in the country music scene. In 1974, he scored a hit on Monument Records with his new composition "I Can Help." Swan recorded the song's characteristic keyboard part using a Farfisa model borrowed from the session musician Bobby Emmons. He completed the recording in just two takes. "I Can Help" immediately became a crossover country-pop smash. By 1975, divorce rates were twice what they had been a decade earlier. Given such precipitous changes, the line about your child needing "a daddy" was topical. "I Can Help" topped the charts outside America, in places as far afield as Australia, and was even issued as a single in Yugoslavia. The bearded songwriter looked committed as he played it on Burt Sugarman's late-night NBC showcase, *The Midnight Special*. It was as if country had gone pop and was entering the family-friendly, easy listening mainstream. Swan immediately capitalized on his success and released a rock 'n' roll covers album.

By the mid-1970s, Elvis was working the same center ground carefully mined by Swan. A few years earlier, he had been at the head of a curve that was now folding back on itself. Taking advantage of the back-to-basics blues boom, he reminded America how to rock in the "new old-fashioned way" by adding the thrill of songs like "One Night" to the *Comeback Special*. "I Can Help" is not classic Elvis. Instead it's a kind of glorious self-parody of "Blue Suede Shoes" in which the King of Rock 'n' Roll hams it up, to the point where he triumphs over his own tribute artists, but only just. "I Can Help" is Elvis swinging straight into the 1970s nostalgia boom. It's *aggressively easy listening* with a slight nod to the fury of the genres it knows: country, funk, rock, and twelve-bar blues. Elvis recorded the number in the spring of 1975. The year got off to a difficult start: late in January, Presley was hospitalized to help address his medication. A few days later, his father, Vernon, had a heart attack and recuperated in the room next door at Baptist Memorial. In March, Elvis flew to California to make good on his commitment to a recording session that had been scheduled for the previous year. Most of the material from this three-day session would end up on the *Today* album. "I Can Help" was recorded in the early hours of a Tuesday morning, just after Elvis tackled the rousing "Green, Green Grass of Home."

As well as being an Elvis fan, Billy Swan was a friend of RCA house producer Felton Jarvis. Impressed by the universal appeal of "I Can Help," Jarvis offered it to Elvis, who jokingly moaned, "I'm tired of it. Billy Swan, my ass." As if to underscore his position, he only bothered with one take. Nevertheless, James Burton smoothly reproduced Reggie Young's original guitar pattern. The song came together.

Of course, "I Can Help" stays squarely on familiar musical territory, but listen to the way Elvis attacks the start of each verse and how well he pulls out all stops for the ending. As a unique memento of the session,

Jarvis gave Billy Swan the socks that Elvis wore in the studio. That was ironic in hindsight; the track was also released on a 1995 Elvis box set called *Walk a Mile in My Shoes*.

96. "Moody Blue" (from *Moody Blue*, 1977)

The Crown Convertible was a flagship model in Imperial's luxury brand, about as flashy as cars came in the 1950s. Chrysler's star designer, Virgil "Chrome-Plated" Exner, was a man famed for his gray silk suits. He gave his new model "Forward Look" styling: quad headlights, gun-sight tail-lights, and curved glass side windows. Elvis encountered the automobile during Paramount's *Loving You*—a 1957 feature that many say is as near as Hollywood got to a fictionalized Presley biopic. Country singer Deke Rivers rises to stardom in the movie. About two-thirds of the way through, on a country ranch, he accompanies himself on acoustic guitar as he sings the title tune to his belle, Susan Jessup. Their family picnic is disrupted, however, by the noisy arrival of sassy Ms. Glenda Markle, played by Lizabeth Scott, in a shiny, new $10,000 Crown Convertible. After standing up and staring, one of the family quips, "Wow! The flying saucers have landed at last!" Elvis exclaims, "Boy! Where did this come from?" Glenda replies, "Right off the drawing board and into your life. It's all yours!"

The Crown Convertible scene from *Loving You* captures something essential about Elvis Presley's image. He wasn't simply some country boy. Just as he became an ambassador for melting pot integration, he also represented a *bridge figure* that led American society from the hardships of the Dust Bowl era through to the chromium-plated peaks of high modernity. There was always a side to Elvis's image that connected him to the embrace of new technology—whether that was digital watches, TV remote controls, microwave ovens, or, alas, pharmaceutical pills. In other words, Elvis wasn't just *Wild in the Country*, he was also *It Happened at the World's Fair*. What mattered was the way that he brought the best of his roots with him—family, food, community, and compassion—while embracing the forefront of technological change. In some ways, part of his gift was his ability to effortlessly infuse modern life with *soul*.

"Moody Blue" is Elvis's most modern record. Its introduction is like a tribute to package holiday vacations and jumbo jet living. One of the interesting things about the song was the context in which it was recorded. Early in February 1976, producer Felton Jarvis used recording equipment in the Jungle Room to capture a series of mature and melancholic songs: from Fred Rose's tragic "Blue Eyes Crying in the Rain" to Larry Gatlin's sedate ode to divorce, "Bitter They Are, Harder They Fall"—a song that Gatlin performed like Glen Campbell. The day after he recorded Neil Sedaka's "Solitaire," Elvis addressed himself to "Moody Blue." The next day, the material got even heavier: "Hurt," "For the Heart," and "Danny Boy." In the midst of all those weepies, "Moody Blue" must have seemed like light relief. Mark James penned and recorded the original number for Mercury. His 1975 version had country vocals and the traditional genre style. Both James's version and Elvis's have similar arrangements and instrumentation. If Elvis's "Moody Blue" is a country record, however, it's country of the kind later heard on Dr. Hook's disco-friendly "When You're in Love with a Beautiful Woman"—slick and smooth, more Malibu than Memphis. Ten-gallon hats at the ready, but not for the ranch or rodeo; mixed instead with Hawaiian shirts and fitting the after-party of an extended, crazy vacation. Of course, "Moody Blue" doesn't stop there. Indeed, it never quite ends, or even fades; it ebbs away. If the main section affirms a woman's right to change her mind, the extended outro captures a feeling of indeterminacy that is familiar in both its musical shape and indecipherable emotional feel.

"Moody Blue" is the unending swan song of a singer who never quite left the building.

95. "Hi-Heel Sneakers" (from *Tomorrow Is a Long Time*, 1999)

It's easy, more than fifty years on, to look back at the early 1960s as a period in Elvis's career when, somehow, *King Creole* gave way to *Kissin' Cousins*, "Heartbreak Hotel" became "Ito Eats," and the singer of the century *lost his way*. That interpretation is partly true, but to reduce it to John Lennon's legendary dictum that "he died when he went in the army" slightly misses the point.[21] Lennon's words capture something about the rebelliousness of rock 'n' roll, but Elvis's talents were constantly in dialogue with changing times. In the early 1960s, things were different, not just for Elvis, but for the female fans that he served. Girl groups reflected romantic yearnings. Male teen angels offered safe courtship possibilities. If the excited fans of the 1950s made headway in putting the "good girl" stereotype to bed, a renewed rise of independent womanhood gave more people the choice of whether to break from constraints or follow traditional patterns. Widespread adoption of the Pill allowed young women to control their destinies without pregnancy taking them out of the workplace. Although Elvis continued to broaden his musical range, he had to move, to an extent, with the times. He rapidly found himself singing "The Hawaiian Wedding Song." Nothing in the decade, however, stood still for long. Beatlemania gave a new generation of fans permission to let their hair down—so far down, in fact, that for some the decade progressed into a helter skelter of free love and acid rock.

Elvis's conservative side seemed at odds with the louche lifestyles of the new breed of rock stars. Nevertheless, everyone who remembered rock 'n' roll knew that he still had a spark of male sensuality in him that could burn down Texas. The metaphorical panther leapt clean of its cage in Elvis's 1968 *Comeback Special*. In the early 1970s, it roared on a regular basis, but in 1967, the question was how its owner might be *allowed* to regain his mojo. One of the answers was through parody. Fooling around, after all, was a safe way to raise that dangerous issue of eroticism. "Hi-Heel Sneakers" is a *raunchy* record. It's not too much of a stretch of the imagination to think that it might just be Elvis's 1960s premonition of Rod Stewart's flimsy, slinky "Da Ya Think I'm Sexy?" as if Presley was saying, "Yeah—I'm sexy as hell, but, heck, I'm only kidding!"

The story of "Hi-Heel Sneakers" begins with Springfield, Ohio, native Robert Higginbotham, who released his own version in 1964 under the stage name of Tommy Tucker. He recorded a demo at first, hoping to shop the song to Jerry Reed. Higginbotham's manager, Herb Abramson, immediately saw the number's potential and leased it to Checker, a Chess Records subsidiary. With an acoustic guitar intro and jaunty organ sound, Tucker's bluesy rendition conquered the R&B charts and almost made the top ten of *Billboard*'s Hot 100. Elvis entered RCA's Studio B in September 1967, on a visit, in part, to cut new material for the *Clambake* soundtrack album. Chuck Berry's "Brown Eyed Handsome Man" had been dropped. The meat of the day was recording Jerry Reed's "Guitar Man."

One of the musicians at the session was a talented yet unassuming guitar player named Chip Young, a relatively unsung hero of the Southern country soul scene. After a brief spell in the army in the early 1960s, Young went on tour with Jerry Reed, then settled in the Nashville area.

He rapidly established himself as one of the region's hardest-working musician-engineer-producers. Young labored solidly in the studio with Elvis in the second half of the 1960s. He eventually converted the outbuildings of an antebellum farmhouse in Murfreesboro, Tennessee, into his own sixteen-track facility. At this new home, Young 'Un Sound, Chip produced Billy Swan's "I Can Help" and assisted Felton Jarvis in overdubbing and mixing tracks for the 1976 album *From Elvis Presley Boulevard*.

It was either Chip Young or his fellow guitarist Harold Bradley who suggested "Hi-Heel Sneakers" to Elvis at the September 1967 session, without thought for the Colonel's money-minded ban on using any material that Elvis's preferred publisher did not control.

The sitar made its way into Anglo American popular music in the mid-1960s through numbers like "Norwegian Wood (This Bird Has Flown)" by the Beatles and "Paint It Black" by the Stones. Although Bradley's electric sitar part on "Hi-Heel Sneakers" sounds a little dated now, Elvis's version transforms the number way beyond Tucker's original. Indeed, the Memphis Flash hammed it up to great effect. Captured on take seven, the result was a five-minute track that had to be edited down for radio. That Presley studio remake starts with Charlie McCoy's solid blues harp intro. What is amazing, however, is how far the singer's raw and almost shaking voice takes the song. In one way, he just lambasts the shallowness of girls' going-out rituals. "Hi-Heel Sneakers" is, after all, something hard to take seriously: a narrative about wigs, boxing gloves, and red dresses. With tongue firmly in cheek, Elvis finds the freedom to express more oomph that anyone should expect. Starting out as a parody of his own impersonators, he acquires the freedom necessary to pursue a certain raunchiness; something that, at length, ironically transforms into genuine eroticism.

Recorded several months before the *Comeback*, in hindsight "Hi-Heel Sneakers" suggests that Elvis already needed to start reining something in, if his audience was not to be knocked out by the thrill of it.

94. "I Can't Stop Loving You" (from *That's the Way It Is: Special Edition*, 2000)

Part of the *tao* of understanding Elvis as a public persona is acknowledging the way in which he mirrored the loving urgency and sincerity of his fans. Although he became increasingly confident in his role on stage as a sex symbol, he retained an appealing humility and periodic slight nervousness that positively informed his sexual chemistry. Where Frank Sinatra had it all together, the Hillbilly Cat was not so hard-boiled. Knowing that *Elvis was afraid of disappointing you* offered great relief to all those who might have felt scared to meet anyone quite so popular and important. Nowhere is Elvis Presley's gracious mirroring of his fans more apparent than in the choice of songs like "I Can't Stop Loving You." Its story starts with influential songwriter Don "The Sad Poet" Gibson.[22]

After his years with Sons of the Soil, in 1957 Gibson cut "I Can't Stop Loving You" for Chet Atkins. RCA Victor released it on 45rpm together with the more upbeat "Oh Lonesome Me." Gibson's A-side rendition sounds gentle and quaint, as if, during an evening's mandolin serenade, "Gentleman Jim" Reeves had embraced the style of Perry Como. Ray Charles's 1962 take was much more bluesy and assertive but maintained a Johnny Mathis–like grace. In both versions, the singers achieve a certain—almost waltz style—civility, as if to say that playing it straight and sedate is what really matters.

Elvis tackled "I Can't Stop Loving You" for the first time in February 1969 as a way to begin his second set of sessions at American Sound. That cool Monday evening, he practiced it at the end of an exploratory medley that featured country crooner Webb Pierce's "It's My Way" and producer Chips Moman's own "This Time." Eagerly twanging his guitar, he says, "I'm just jumping in whenever I can get a chance." Follow That Dream (FTD) is Sony Music's official specialist Elvis collector's label. A loose take found its way on the second disc of FTD's CD set *From Elvis at American Sound Studio*; the singer begins a little hesitantly but soon finds his feet, even laughing at his guitar accompaniment. He constantly explores the possibility of escaping from the phrasing set by Gibson's original arrangement. Elvis's next encounter with "I Can't Stop Loving You" came when he decided to work up the song as spectacular live material for his first Las Vegas engagements. Right from the off, it became a perennial favorite in his set, played regularly in the second half of shows performed in Las Vegas, Lake Tahoe, on tour, and in New York.[23] Ernst Jørgensen suggested that the song assumed "a new, in-your-face arrangement, hammered out with piano triplets, bulldozing right over its country origins and the seductively smooth Ray Charles version."[24] When "I Can't Stop Loving You" appeared on the January 1973 global telecast, *Aloha from Hawaii via Satellite*, its sound was gently nostalgic. It was also highly versatile, revealing an unusual intensity of feeling and offering relief from surrounding material. It can be read as Elvis's way of returning that deep sense of appreciation his fans felt for him being there for them.

93. "Where Could I Go But to the Lord" (from *How Great Thou Art*, 1967)

In Elvis's music, the traditional lines between artistic and commercial, sacred and secular, are often, in effect, erased. "Where Could I Go But to the Lord" was a song that he and his father sang at home after it became popular in the 1940s. Mississippi native and Louisiana State University graduate James B. Coates filed for its publishing in 1940. Coates was a schoolteacher by profession. He also had a strong Christian faith, eventually becoming a minister. He was a staff writer for Stamps-Baxter Music, a Southern publishing house that sponsored many of the gospel quartets. Stamps-Baxter was responsible for hits such as "A Little Talk with Jesus."[25] Coates's composition, which was simply titled "Where Could I Go?" was released in 1945 as a B-side by the Harmoneers, a folksy quartet from Knoxville who worked for RCA Victor.

"Where Could I Go But to the Lord" became a staple. Toward the end of the 1940s, a delightfully spirited New Orleans version, featuring Sister Ernestine Washington, was released by the early British independent label Melodisc. The good sister was accompanied by Bunk Johnson—a rather more secular trumpeter—and his jazz band. Many other recordings of the song appeared before Elvis's.[26] Chicago's Vee-Jay Records released the Harmonizing Four's swinging version on a 78rpm disc in 1958. Elvis loved that black gospel group's rendition of "Farther Along." He was taken with another of their songs, "Let's Go to That Land"; so taken that he even tried to recruit the group's bass singer, Jimmy Jones, to help with the gospel album *He Touched Me*.

Recorded during the early hours of Saturday, 28 May 1966, in Nashville's famous Studio B for the *How Great Thou Art* album, Elvis's version of "Where Could I Go But to the Lord" was uniquely collected. Set against Floyd Cramer's jazzy piano, the Jordanaires' vocal backing is so dark and low it almost purrs. Elvis Presley, meanwhile, injects some of his most ethereal vocals, creating a mood that is both sedate *and* gently rousing.

Perhaps the most memorable performance of "Where Could I Go But to the Lord" came during the gospel segment of Elvis's 1968 NBC *Comeback Special*. That version was laid down at Western Recorders in Burbank, with the singer backed by a black female trio called the Blossoms. When Elvis's gospel version of the track was recorded, despite all the racial turmoil that happened that year, a mild Herb Alpert instrumental topped the charts. The placement of "Where Could I Go But to the Lord" in the *Comeback Special*, between "Sometimes I Feel Like a Motherless Child" and "Up Above My Head" (followed by a gloriously frantic take on Leiber and Stoller's "Saved"), gave more than a nod to black struggle. In the first part of the sequence, the African American choreographer Claude Thompson offered a lyrical interpretation during a section of music that Elvis did not actually sing; it was as if Thompson showed—in a kind of premonition of "If I Can Dream"—that lyricism knew no racial barriers. Black performers could speak about their aspirations through the voice of high culture. For "Where Could I Go But to the Lord," Elvis donned a suave burgundy suit and took up the message with finger-clicking authority. His performance was so supremely smooth in its delivery that it was out of sight. Ultimately, then, it sounded as if—after faith smoothed all passage—the storm that is life had subsided. "Where Could I Go But to the Lord" proved that Elvis was comfortable as the King of Cool in both secular and sacred music settings.

92. "When It Rains, It Really Pours" (from *Elvis: A Legendary Performer Volume 4*, 1983)

"When It Rains, It Really Pours" is Elvis's unfinished symphony, stopped and restarted, a song that by some trick of fate frequently seems forgotten. The version Elvis recorded in November 1955 was sidelined after his Sun contract was sold to RCA; it never reached public ears until the 1980s. A second incarnation was recorded for RCA in 1957 but not released until 1965. By that point, Elvis's reputation was wavering. The song would have seemed dated. It didn't help that the LP sleeve of *Elvis for Everyone!* pictured its singer next to a cash register. Under the title of "When It Rains It Pours," the song was originally written and recorded by an associate of Ike Turner: the black Sun artist Billy "The Kid" Emerson.

When an R&B standard called "Move Baby Move" became his third single for the label early in 1955, Emerson's composition was included as the B-side. Its writer soon left Sam Phillips's orbit and graduated to Vee-Jay, then Chess Records, forming his own label a decade later. Emerson's version of "When It Rains, It Really Pours" was a swaggering black show tune delivered with vocals that were, for the most part, straight down the line.

To unappreciative ears, Elvis's Sun recording of "When It Rains, It Really Pours" might seem plodding or dated. Its singer was exploring the capability and range of his young voice. Where Emerson opted for a guitar break that sounded like a train crossing, Scotty Moore offered one of his classic, cryptic, noodling solos. He was, apparently, told to keep his approach simple by Sam Phillips. Together with Bill Black and session drummer Johnny Bernero, the guitarist and singer found enough spirit to bring the song to life within the space of its country blues heritage. There is a kind of quaintness, charm, excitement, and dramatized melancholy about this early take. According to Scotty, talking about Sam's method at Sun:

> He treated Elvis's voice like an instrument. . . . Everything you heard—country, pop or whatever—was ten miles out in front of the music, and he pulled Elvis's voice back where it was still—you could understand a word and everything—just above Bill and myself.[27]

"When It Rains, It Really Pours" was intended to be Elvis's sixth Sun single. One story has it that the recording session itself was cut short by the Colonel phoning Sam Phillips with an offer he just could not refuse.

The version of "When It Rains, It Really Pours" recorded at Radio Recorders in Hollywood for RCA, right after "Loving You," takes a quantum leap in comparison to the first. In a similar but more gentle way to "Hound Dog," Elvis's voice strains and pushes at its limits. Dudley Brooks provides some sultry piano fills and DJ Fontana adds his patent, burlesque-style drumming. Scotty's guitar solo sounds so weird that it is like he is translating some petulant alien. The collective result blows away the boyish youthfulness of the Sun version and replaces it with a knowing sensuality. This is a rendition more in tune with the South of Tennessee Williams than with *Hank Snow's All-Star Jamboree*.

"When It Rains, It Really Pours" was even considered for the NBC *Comeback Special* but dropped from the final recorded set. As Elvis tried it out for the show, he used something akin to the guitar pattern from "One Night" and evoked almost as much intensity. At one point he even quipped, "Goddamn, that's high!" His vocal for this version is so urgent that he resembles a man hanging on sandpaper, grasping for his very life. After the music appears to finish, he launches into scat for an impromptu coda, releasing what cannot be held down, and the song blooms again, as if of its own accord.

91. "Gentle on My Mind" (from *From Elvis in Memphis*, 1969)

Several highly skilled professionals contributed to Elvis's career, guiding his talent: Sam Phillips was one, Steve Binder another. As the 1960s drew to an end, the chief diamond polisher became music producer Lincoln "Chips" Moman. After helping to establish Stax, Moman used his $3,000 severance money from the label to set up American Sound Studio. He rapidly assembled a house band of session players from the best musicians in Memphis—ones Nashville publishers would use to help them create demos when they visited. With assistance from Tommy Cogbill, Chips led a team effort. In the late 1960s, the Memphis Boys, as they later became known, played together on a run of more than one hundred records that charted across an eighteen-month period. The Box Tops, Neil Diamond, BJ Thomas, Dionne Warwick, and many others recorded at the studio, with Chips usually producing their sessions.[28] Like Elvis, Moman was a perfectionist, willing to record multiple takes until he found the right feel. Like Elvis, when finding or shaping songs, he was not confined to any single genre. At Jerry Wexler's FAME Studios near Muscle Shoals, Chips had played guitar on Wilson Pickett's "Mustang Sally." He already had a great reputation in his own right, and he was not afraid to tell Elvis if he was singing off pitch. At that point, to Chips, the Memphis singer was another star artist on his own very busy schedule. The producer gave so much to his work, in fact, that he collapsed from exhaustion with the stress of everything he had been doing during the mixing of Elvis's material.[29]

One of the classics that Elvis recorded at his American Sound sessions with Chips was "Gentle on My Mind." As perhaps the most quietly mesmeric country song of the 1960s, John Hartford's sentimental ballad rests on a profound message about the nature of unconditional love. Almost everyone is an insecure lover, to some degree. "Leave the door open and they will feel free to come back" suggests that the most loving thing to do can sometimes be to offer a partner the option of his or her freedom.[30] Hartford was a master of stringed instruments: the guitar, banjo, fiddle, and mandolin.[31] Perhaps naturally, then, his own version of "Gentle on My Mind"—recorded for RCA in 1967—was peculiarly downhome and crackling. That original take was also supervised by Elvis's house producer, Felton Jarvis. It drew word pictures about the fantasies of a dreaming drifter, couched its message in confessional style, and used its accompaniment to convey a wry and wistful tone. Chock-full of country picking, Hartford's rendition offers a jaunty ride through back roads, emphasizing musical community and virtuosity as counterpoints to the song's lyrical theme.

After Hartford set the ball rolling, Glen Campbell made "Gentle on My Mind" the theme tune for his CBS TV show, *The Glen Campbell Goodtime Hour*. Although his version failed, at first, to make the top twenty singles chart, "Gentle on My Mind" was rereleased and soon received airplay as an audience favorite. Campbell's wonderfully mellow, gently capering cover struck a chord, to the extent that Hartford and Campbell each received two Grammy awards at the 1968 ceremony.

When Elvis tackled "Gentle on My Mind," it was already very well known. He pursued his version of the song in January 1969 at American Sound, straight after laying down a gloriously flowing cover of Hank Snow's country blues smash, "I'm Movin' On." Unusually, he returned to the song in the studio five days later to overdub the vocal. From the alternative takes, it is clear that Elvis addressed the material with considerable verve, but the accompaniment wasn't quite right. In his cover, Campbell did something Elvis later did in "Always on My Mind"—he exposed the vulnerable side of assertive manhood. Elvis's performance of Hartford's song is quite different. He delivers something less vulnerable and, paradoxically, more haunting, tackling the verses with bravado, then retreating, as each line ends into the kind of quivering "uh-huh-huh" style exaggerated by his many tribute artists. Although there were other similarities with Campbell's hit, without missing the sentimental magic summoned up by Hartford's arrangement, the result was uniquely Elvis. His genius was not necessarily picking songs that were obscure or morphing them out of all recognition. On some occasions, it was enough for him to acknowledge the appeal of popular material and make it his own.

90. "It's Only Love" (from *Elvis Aron Presley,* 1980)

"It's Only Love" was credited as a co-write between the hit maker Mark James and Steve Tyrell. The latter, who was born almost a decade after Elvis, worked in A&R for Scepter Records and was on his way to a long-running career as a songwriter, producer, and crooner of popular swing numbers, such as the Frank Sinatra classic "The Way You Look Tonight." According to arranger Glen Spreen—who worked with both parties when "It's Only Love" came together—Tyrell was based at a Holiday Inn next to the Mississippi in Memphis. It was there at one point in 1968 that Tyrell made a pitch to become Mark James's manager. On a piano in the suite, James revealed a piece he was working on about the exhilaration of falling in love. Tyrell gave him some options for the title. [32]

Born in Oklahoma but raised in Houston, BJ Thomas broke through in 1966 backed by the Triumphs with a cover of Hank Williams's "I'm So Lonesome I Could Cry." After that, Thomas moved to Scepter Records as a solo artist. At the end of 1968, he performed a twenty-minute set at Elvis's New Year's Eve bash. [33] Supported by the production skills of Chips Moman and talented musicians like Tommy Cogbill, in 1969 he also recorded a version of "It's Only Love" at American Sound, the same year that he released his signature tune, "Raindrops Keep Falling on My Head." The result was incredible. Although Thomas's contemporary country vocal still shines on the recording, a trendy electric sitar and eccentric percussive arrangement detract from its majesty.

Elvis tackled the song at a session in RCA's Studio B on 20 May 1971. He was reaching the end of a mammoth, almost weeklong stint, which produced diverse material for three future albums: *Elvis Now, Elvis (Fool)*, and *Elvis Sings the Wonderful World of Christmas.* That night, the team had already recorded the ghostly "I'm Leavin'" and heroic "We Can Make the Morning." The latter song worked as a prediction. "It's Only Love" was captured sometime approaching 4 a.m. The arrangement generally resembled BJ Thomas's interpretation. Kenneth Buttrey's drums and Norbert Putnam's bass offered the solid foundation upon which Elvis, his horn section, and female backing singers soared. There's a simultaneous jadedness and appealing vulnerability to Elvis's voice; it adds meaning in ways that bring extra dimensions to each line. The result is an overall performance that is both fluid and gentle but also able to build gradually in stature.

RCA Victor label released "It's Only Love" as a single in September 1971, backing it with "The Sound of Your Cry." Although the record had some success in easy listening circles, unfortunately it just missed the top half of *Billboard*'s Hot 100. Ernst Jørgensen suggested that the song was *too pop*: bereft of any vernacular music elements that might have redeemed it—whether from country, gospel, rock 'n' roll, or blues.[34] Nevertheless, "It's Only Love" has a smooth, rousing, almost gone-midnight quality. Compared with Elvis's rawer 1950s or late 1960s material, the song sounds tame and sanitized. Yet there is something that makes it way more organic and memorable than most of his movie soundtrack fodder.

"It's Only Love" does not so much start or end as flow its way through time. It never had the shape or punch of a single. Perhaps it should have been kept as an album track. Nevertheless, despite all that, it reaches the finish line with self-respect intact.

89. "Santa Claus Is Back in Town" (from *Elvis' Christmas Album*, 1957)

Almost everyone who writes commentary on Elvis at some time or another pays attention to his charismatic physical presence. He was not simply handsome in the rugged sense; he was beautiful. Perhaps it sprang from his particular combination of white, Jewish, and Cherokee ancestry. For commentator Camille Paglia, Elvis's beauty was set off by a kind of energetic dynamism that expressed inner turmoil. He was, like the dandy Lord Byron, both perfect and ruffled, immaculate and all shook up: a dangerous man of notorious charisma.[35] When the delightfully forward and wonderfully brassy Hollywood siren Mae West was asked for a comment in 1961, she placed him not as a new phenomenon or an update of Frank Sinatra, but instead in a lineage that included Rudolph Valentino and Cary Grant: "Presley is the sex personality of the times."[36]

Three years later, West was lined up for the role of the circus owner in *Roustabout*. Darwin Porter, a former *Miami Herald* bureau chief, claimed that Presley himself paid Mae West a visit during which she tried to seduce him.[37] He said that Elvis was also accompanied by his friend Nick Adams. The chronology is possible, as Adams died in 1968, but it is also highly unlikely. After Elvis went in the army, he seemed to lose touch with Nick. Their association was mainly in 1956. Some myths therefore matter more for their entertainment value than their actuality.[38] Jill Watts scaled back Porter's claim in her biographic portrait of West, saying that the Grande Dame met Paramount's executive Paul Nathan, not Elvis, but she still "insisted they discuss the proposition in her bedroom."[39] Unfortunately, the *Roustabout* role, which went to Barbara Stanwyck, was too serious for Mae and did not offer enough scope for comic reinvention. If the film had gone ahead, she would likely have maintained her crown as the queen of sexual innuendo, and she might well have relegated Elvis to the role of stooge—not something that was going to happen if the Colonel had any say in the matter. Still, the raising of a "what if" opens up a further question: How much did West's unique style inform the raunchy, sassy, playful *male* persona that Elvis developed during his singing career? Like Mae West, he could combine more than a hint of fun with seductive invitations that were shockingly direct.

"Santa Claus Is Back in Town" marked out the shared space in which both Mr. Presley and Ms. West could feel at home. Elvis, of course, knew how to tease. Though he was not a female impersonator, in such numbers he could flip the script and enjoy playing similar power games to those that very attractive girls could play; songs like "Santa Claus Is Back in Town" were perfect vehicles. Mae covered the number on her 1966 album *Wild Christmas*. She cooed, intoxicatedly, offering up the pleasure, in effect, of her own aural voluptuousness. Elvis, meanwhile, let loose in the *Comeback*, playing the song up as the raunchiest of blues. Even the introduction was an impromptu skit on his superstardom:

Elvis: "It being the time of year that it is—"

Charlie: "Hey—will you excuse me a minute?"

Elvis: "What?"

Charlie: "A piece of lint on your face."

Charlie Hodge reached over and plucked the speck of lint off Elvis's cheek, flicking it down on to the floor. A girl who sat at their feet grabbed it, folded it in a tissue, and snapped it in her handbag. Everyone laughed at such a clear demonstration of the power of Elvis's charisma.

Elvis: "Never ceases to amaze me, baby—I tell you!"

Bantering bandmates repeated their current catchphrase, "My boy, my boy." Everyone laughed again.

Elvis: "What is it now, man? My nose running or what?"

He patted down the sweat on his face with a tissue.

Elvis: "I'll go white in a minute! It being the time of year that it is, I'd like to do my favorite one of all the Christmas songs I've recorded—"

The room erupted again, this time with girls screaming, as Elvis launched into "Santa Claus Is Back in Town." It was an impromptu addition; a number rehearsed but dropped from the *Comeback Special*. In the scene, resplendent in his famous black leather outfit, Elvis sat on the "boxing ring" stage with his guitar. He forgot the words in the verses. Nobody cared. When Elvis mentioned Father Christmas arriving in a big black Cadillac, those girls screamed again, as if they were swooping down on a roller coaster. His performance is wonderfully loose. Screams came again when he segued into "Blue Christmas." His bandmates egged him on, saying, "Play it dirty, play it dirty!" Elvis had them in the palm of his hand. Who knew that Christmas could be sexy?

To understand the full story of "Santa Claus Is Back in Town," its writers need to be considered. When Jerry Leiber and Mike Stoller visited New York in 1957, they saw Miles Davis and Thelonious Monk. The chain-smoking Jewish beatniks loved jazz. They also happened to have a passion for R&B and a desire to emulate and extend the genre. Elvis was a fan of Leiber and Stoller's music before he recorded any of it. His publisher, Jean Aberbach, recognized that the pair's quirky, theatrical style of R&B would be ideal for expanding the Hill & Range catalog and perhaps for supplying material to Elvis. Aberbach courted Leiber and Stoller by praising "Black Denim Trousers and Motorcycle Boots" (their parody of László Benedek's 1953 feature, *The Wild One*), and he arranged for Columbia's Mitch Miller to record a version sung by Édith Piaf.[40] Both Elvis and the songwriters appeared for the first time in Jean Aberbach's daybook *on the same date*: 9 August 1955.[41] When the New York label Atlantic bought out Leiber and Stoller's Spark Records and signed them to an independent production deal, they shared their publishing with Progressive Music, a company that Atlantic and Hill & Range owned jointly. Jean and Julian Aberbach, in effect, procured publishing revenue from Leiber and Stoller two months before they secured their deal with Presley. Ironically, it was without the Aberbachs' prompting, however, that Elvis first connected with the pair—he decided to record their song "Hound Dog."

Like much of Elvis's movie material, "Santa Claus Is Back in Town" was actually made to order. Leiber and Stoller wrote it on the spot during a Hollywood studio session for him in September 1957. After Elvis struggled with some bland Yuletide fare, the pair was asked to write something more in his style. They came up with an earthy ditty called "Christmas Blues." Elvis took only seven takes to perfect Leiber and Stoller's offering, and they renamed the number "Santa Claus Is Back in Town." The distinctly low-key 1943 Bing Crosby hit, "I'll Be Home for Christmas," was next on the list at his September 1957 Radio Recorders session. The two songs could hardly have been more different.

With its smoldering sensuality, "Santa Claus Is Back in Town" was an absolute gift. Indeed, Leiber and Stoller's little firecracker was a natural choice to lead off *Elvis' Christmas Album*.[42] The studio version starts with the Jordanaires politely repeating the mantra "Christmas," like some throwback to the big-band era. Soon they are blown away, however, by DJ Fontana's famous bump-and-grind drumming, over which Elvis lets a sassy, spiky, and almost hysterical vocal performance just slide.[43] He's all over the place, in a good way, swaggering through to the jazzy piano solo with one of his raunchiest, most strutting deliveries. Elvis sounds almost criminal on the number. It might be Christmas, but nobody else—especially nobody white—could have gotten away with half as much.

88. "Whole Lotta Shakin' Goin' On" (from *A Hundred Years from Now: Essential Elvis Volume 4*, 1996)

Putting a focus only on Elvis makes it harder to remember that he lived through such turbulent times. When he recorded "Whole Lotta Shakin' Goin' On," his country was at war with Vietnam. About a year earlier, the 1960s dream ended in terror when Hells Angels murdered a drug-crazed reveler at the Altamont Speedway Free Festival. A few months afterward, the National Guard shot dead four protesting college students in Ohio. On the same day as Elvis's Nashville session, Nixon requested an extra thousand FBI agents be stationed on campuses across the country. A whole lotta shakin' *was* goin' on in society. Its effects were inevitably reshaping popular music. America's finest singer was, from one perspective, reflecting the tensions of a nation struggling with its growing contradictions.

"Whole Lotta Shakin' Goin' On" was written in the same year Elvis got his break at Sun. It was copyrighted as a collaboration between Curly Williams and Roy Hall (as Sunny David). In his teenage years, Hall backed Uncle Dave Macon. With its showstopping opening, the song got its first release early in 1955 from the Okeh label artist Big Maybelle. Her take made for a gutsy, big-band R&B version, contrasting her all-attitude vocal with a relatively straight backing. As the song's co-writer, Hall made his own version a few months later with help from Hank "Sugarfoot" Garland on guitar. "Whole Lotta Shakin' Goin' On" was rapidly adopted across a range of different genres.[44] The versatile black artist Jimmy Breedlove, meanwhile, offered a version that was even more spirited, with a rip-roaring sax solo. At the end of the 1950s—and, ironically, straight out of Compton—white faux country pickers the Ozark Jubilee Boys performed the song on the KT-TV show *Town Hall Party*. Wearing rather crisp ten-gallon hats, they pursued Williams and Hall's composition in a style that verged on cabaret swing. It was the April 1957 version from Sun Records, however, that really defined the song.

Coming on like some unhinged hurdy-gurdy man, Jerry Lee Lewis was unique in his ability to provide fun and threat in equal measure. His relentless rockabilly piano pounding made "Whole Lotta Shakin' Goin' On" sound—despite a breakdown where it starts to lose its way—like it was set aboard a spinning waltzer in a tacky traveling fair. Listening to the Killer's version of "Whole Lotta Shakin' Goin' On" leaves anyone exhausted, in the best sense. As music writer Steve Sullivan eloquently put it, Sun 267 was "overflowing with unadulterated desire and Southern-fried good humour."[45] Jerry Lee's volatile personality inevitably helped to promote the record. On *The Steve Allen Show*, he kicked his piano stool clean across the stage while performing it. It was no wonder that other rockabillies wanted a piece of the action. With his own characteristic, quietly muscular take, Carl Perkins offered it on a covers LP soon afterward. The "Queen of Rockabilly," Wanda Jackson, threw down a version so mean that it virtually answered her back.

Elvis recorded "Whole Lotta Shakin' Goin' On" more than a decade after the rock 'n' roll boom. The artist was at RCA's Nashville facility in September 1970 on a mission to add material to what became the *Elvis*

Country album. His hot little recording contained quite deep vocal tones that made Elvis sound a few years older than he was. One of the things that he borrowed from Jerry Lee's conflagration was the fade toward the end that heralded a mammoth finale. He was familiar with the delights of a fade-out-then-in ending, of course, from "Suspicious Minds." Ernst Jørgensen said that Elvis "barrelled through 'Shakin' in one take—it was almost manic, but still a fascinating performance, and a great addition to the country album."[46] On the recordings that have exposed pre-song banter from that session, Elvis certainly does sound uncharacteristically sharp with his producer and fellow musicians. James Burton did not make the session; it was down to Muscle Shoals player Eddie Hinton to add his input.[47] At one point, Elvis said, "Felton—I'm going back to LA. Tonight. 12.30," before reminding players, in no uncertain terms, that they were his employees and needed to earn their keep.[48] Since the session actually finished at 1 a.m., evidently he had reason to feel impatient.

Later, Elvis returned to "Whole Lotta Shakin' Goin' On" in concert. Though he played it at other times, he seemed most into the song during his 1971 and 1973 Las Vegas summer seasons. The televised version he delivered for his January 1973 *Aloha* concert, which began with "Long Tall Sally," was on fire, almost as if Elvis had been given a unique permit to channel Jerry Lee and liberate the high-octane madness of "Whole Lotta Shakin' Goin' On" in his own unique way. The song deserves merit in any Elvis 100 for the way it reflects the flow of an artist whose words break up into scat and express the spirit of the music that grips him. Elvis's studio version finishes with a string of "mo-mam-mah-ma-whoa-ahs," "huh-ah-hah-ha-huhs," and even a few "ka-ka-ching-bom-booms"! The staccato result is a little reminiscent of the Trashmen's crazy and abrasive 1963 West Coast number "Surfin' Bird." It is as if he is throwing verbal karate moves to match the unhinged demands of music that is not just fast paced but running away with itself.

87. "(You're the) Devil in Disguise" (from *Elvis' Gold Records Volume 4*, 1968)

TV host Hy Gardner confronted a young Elvis Presley back in July 1956, saying, "I've got a couple of questions here I'd like to sort of clear up. One of 'em—and it's sort of a silly one to me—is what about the rumor that you once shot your mother?" Elvis laughed and replied, "Well, I think that one takes the cake. I mean, that's about the funniest one I've ever heard."[49] Of course Elvis never shot Gladys. He loved her. Nevertheless, the myth frames rock 'n' roll as an act of symbolic violence: an outburst that attempts to break the bonds of parental stricture. By the late 1950s, however, Private Presley was stationed in Germany and there was a full-on backlash against the menace of rock 'n' roll. Out went the "no goods," the dirty hicks, and low-down hoodlums. In came an army of television-friendly, clean-cut white boys: innocent and romantic teen angels from Ricky Nelson to Fabian. They were prepackaged pop singers who modeled themselves more on Pat Boone than on Gene Vincent. Parents felt relieved. Their daughters felt safe enough to swoon without reservation. Magazines like *Mirabelle* and *Valentine* churned out comic-strip dramas about these young male pop stars.

When he came back from the army, Elvis rode the tide. He was destined for a life in Hollywood, acting in movies that—despite the odd fistfight—featured sanitized banter, exotic locations, and songs to children.[50] Yet Elvis was not a perfect, plastic boyfriend. He could never have become Bing Crosby; he was always too raw, too multifaceted. Presley was no predator, but he always had an edge: feral sideburns and a quick temper. His mother was safe, but more than one TV set took an impulsive bullet. Bing Crosby never used household items for target practice. To use the parlance of Elvis's movie roles: Just as innocent characters like Deke Rivers and Toby Kwimper had a vicious streak lurking in them, so not far from the surface of the singer's polite, off-stage personality was a razor-sharp Vince Everett or Danny Fisher. One explanation for Elvis's edge, suggested by his public image, was that he was always in conflict. After Gladys passed away, movie costar Dolores Hart said, "Elvis is a young man with an enormous capacity to love . . . but I don't think he has found his happiness. I think he is terribly lonely."[51] In retrospect, Hart's words seem prophetic. Any woman who wanted to get emotionally close had her work cut out. From that perspective, his sex-symbol status and constant romantic liaisons are explicable as forms of personal defense. Whatever Elvis's "real" identity, *the trouble with girls* was a constant part of his *public image*. It also reflected the concerns of his time.[52]

In the middle of May 1963, when Elvis recorded "(You're the) Devil in Disguise" during the first leg of a two-day session in RCA's Nashville Studio B, *Dr. No* topped the U.S. box office. James Bond, that most arrested of heroes, rarely committed to his own female partners. The spying playboy might have revealed his distrust for female agents by using lyrics from Elvis's number. It deserves a place in any top 100 because, almost without a doubt, "(You're the) Devil in Disguise" is the record that portrays Elvis Presley at his most delightfully suspicious of the opposite sex. Tracks like "Baby Let's Play House" and "Hound Dog" affectionately pour scorn on a female target. "(You're the) Devil in Disguise" virtually attempts to exorcize her.

The tune came from some of Elvis's 1960s New York–based supporters: a writing trio named Bill Giant, Florence Kaye, and Bernie Baum. From the astounding "Power of My Love" to those flimsy but strangely memorable numbers like "Beach Shack," "Queenie Wahine's Papaya," and worse, Giant, Baum, and Kaye contributed a wealth of songs, mostly to Elvis's movie soundtrack output. They were the short-order chefs of their era: put under pressure, often for a matter of days, by the Colonel's publishing team, to create movie numbers.

One day during a team writing session in Florence Kaye's Manhattan apartment, her fourteen-year-old daughter Karen had dolled herself up because she had a crush on a boy who was one year older. Bernie Baum commented that she was "such an angel."[53] Without missing a beat, her mother corrected: "She's a devil sometimes, a Devil in Disguise."[54] They both looked at each other and knew that they had the beginnings of a song. Elvis loved what they created. When he recorded "(You're the) Devil in Disguise," he really exploited the number's dramatic changes of tempo. He chose it as a single, and RCA rush released the record.

As soon as John Lennon heard "(You're the) Devil in Disguise" in June 1963 on the British TV show *Jukebox Jury*, he trashed the new single. Fellow panelist Katie Boyle asked, "If he did sound like Bing Crosby, would it be bad?" Lennon replied, "Well, for Elvis . . . yes."[55] John Lennon also slated every other single on the show but was at least trying to defend Elvis's rock 'n' roll incarnation:

> Well, you know, I used to go mad on Elvis, like all the groups, but not now. I don't like this. And I hate songs with "walk" and "talk" in it— you know, those lyrics. "She walks, she talks." I don't like that. And I don't like the double beat: doom-cha doom-cha, that bit. It's awful. [pause] Poor ol' Elvis.[56]

Contradicting Lennon's verdict, fans loved "(You're the) Devil in Disguise." It went top five on the *Billboard* Hot 100 in America and briefly dominated the UK singles chart. Giant, Kaye, and Baum's song gave rise to an early 1960s performance that was gloriously rambunctious. Though it sounds a little dated now, "(You're the) Devil in Disguise" still sparkles.

86. "Amazing Grace" (from *He Touched Me*, 1972)

> It may have something to do with the feeling a soloist gets when he or she is singing with a well-rehearsed group providing harmonic support. It's like leaning against a wall of sound, and it's an incredibly comforting sensation for the performer to feel. You don't get that sense of feeling all alone on stage; instead, the backup of sorts wraps around you and gives you the confidence to really lose yourself in the music, to forget about yourself and focus on the act of communicating the message of the song to the audience.[57]

When considering Elvis's vast catalog, it is easy to forget his performance of the phenomenally popular "Amazing Grace."[58] Partway through February 1973, in a year marked already by the immense success of the *Aloha from Hawaii* concert broadcast and some trouble in Vegas (a bout of the flu and a security incident at one show), Elvis was holding court in his Hilton hotel suite. "Mama Cass" Elliot, of the Mamas & Papas, was one of his many guests. When she asked him why he continually sang gospel numbers backed by quartet singers, he asked if she had ever tried. Feeling a little sheepish, she decided to sing "Amazing Grace" as she knew the words. Joe Moscheo of the Imperials immediately began playing the piano. Others fell in behind. Moscheo recalled that afterward Cass was visibly moved and hugged everyone. She experienced what Elvis already knew.

The lyrics of "Amazing Grace" date back to 1773. John Newton, a curate who had settled in Buckinghamshire, England, enlisted the services of poet William Cowper to illustrate his New Year's Day sermon. By the end of the decade, Newton and Cowper had published "Amazing Grace" as a hymn. Its progress was boosted in the early years of the next century by a Christian revival known as the Second Great Awakening. Before he found God, Newton had been a young rebel and slave trader. The themes of his famous folk hymn—that the Almighty offers forgiveness and redemption even to the lowest of sinners—suggest that he may have had some guilt about his youth. Ironically, however, "Amazing Grace" became known as the archetypal African American spiritual. Popular in both the nineteenth and early twentieth century, versions of the hymn were performed using "lining out" and other folk practices.[59] All sorts of renditions have been recorded over the years.[60]

One of the early recordings of "Amazing Grace" was offered in 1926 by the Wisdom Sisters. Released on Columbia Records, their version was full of folksy harmony, like a country hymn almost in the style of the Carter Family (who delivered their own take in 1952). Fiddlin' John Carson also released a lively, twee version on Okeh in 1930 called "At the Cross," complete with female backing. Blind Willie McTell offered a bluesy, spoken-word rendition a decade later. Apollo Records put out a vibrant, a cappella take by the Dixie Hummingbirds in 1946. The Fairfield Four released their rendition in a similar vein two years later. From the 1940s onward, Mahalia Jackson's rousing performances began to further connect the song, in the public consciousness, with its roots in suffering, conviction, and moral integrity. "Amazing Grace" was adopted again in the 1960s, in part to reflect the strife expressed in the growing momentum of the struggle for civil rights.

Robert Matthew-Walker had a colorful career in the British music industry and wrote two books on Elvis. In the first, he speculated that folk protest singer Judy Collins's version of "Amazing Grace," which had twice been popular in the few months before Elvis visited the studio, encouraged his overuse of female backing singers.[61] Elvis may have had reasons to include his sisters that were not obvious to Matthew-Walker. "Amazing Grace" was sandwiched in the session between songs written by Ewan MacColl and Gordon Lightfoot—a point that arguably indicates that Elvis was addressing the gospel classic in a folk mode. David Briggs supplied the melody line accompaniment for this March 1971 Nashville recording, his style resembling the work he did on Elvis's hit "Love Letters." According to the music historian Gordon Minto, speaking about "Amazing Grace":

> Elvis' bluesy version of it though departed from the usual treatment and, as usual, he seemed to prefer his vocal to be buried in the mix, his voice beautifully blended with the vocal groups for much of the time, though now and again his distinctive vocal style prevailed, of course.[62]

Amid the array of different versions of "Amazing Grace" reflecting the turmoil of the late 1960s era, Elvis's sounds like a bid for peace and calm.

85. "(Marie's the Name) His Latest Flame" (from *Elvis' Golden Records Volume 3*, 1963)

Hill & Range's publishing system has been painted as something that blocked Elvis's creative success, but the company had also made it in his financial interest to record material that they owned. He therefore used Hill & Range as a kind of first stop for available material. One reason that Elvis did so much Hill & Range music is that they would finance quality demos by their own songwriters, in effect both reducing the writers' financial risks and dominating the stream of new music reaching the singer. At the end of January 1956, the Aberbachs' nephew, Freddy Bienstock, was brought in to liaise with Elvis. He was a similar age to the star and comparatively in tune with the tastes of the new generation. Bienstock had a crucial role as a kind of preselector for Elvis's recording material. When it came to picking songs, as Bienstock said, Elvis "knew exactly what he wanted to do."[63] "(Marie's the Name) His Latest Flame" is not one of Elvis's greatest-ever recordings, but it is a classic and it deserves a place in any Elvis 100.[64] One of the great things about the song is that it swings.

Doc Pomus and Mort Shuman had already been asked by Bienstock to provide material for Elvis. RCA wanted a song that was strong enough to release as a single. Bienstock's new recruits—who were raised in Brooklyn's Jewish community and had already proven their talents next to the best of the Brill Building songwriters—also came in with "Little Sister," which formed the other side of the single taken from the session. Earlier that summer, they had recorded a version of "(Marie's the Name) His Latest Flame" with heartthrob Del Shannon. As Elvis's Nashville studio team set to work in RCA's Studio B, during the early hours of a quiet Monday morning in June 1961, they really licked the song into shape, keeping the Bo Diddley beat but updating different aspects of the arrangement and instrumentation. Elvis even put a late-night call through to Shuman to ask how he had got the piano sound on his demo.

Listen to Elvis's version of "(Marie's the Name) His Latest Flame" alongside Del Shannon's and the differences leap out. Shannon's version is comparatively dated, like a poor rehearsal or after-image, while the

Presley take sounds classic. The Bo Diddley beat backing, which the RCA musicians really make swing, is not so much shuffling on Shannon's take as staggering—his chorus majors on a kind of hurdy-gurdy, almost theremin-like organ. Shannon's way of bringing the song to life is to pour histrionic vocals over the top. In comparison, Elvis's take is more refined yet more exciting. His vocals are golden and almost ethereal—in that smooth Presley style. The whole thing has just a whiff of the Neapolitan majesty of "It's Now or Never"—a song that had been recorded by many of the same musicians just over a year earlier.

"(Marie's the Name) His Latest Flame" came out as the flip side of "Little Sister" and was one of only a handful of Elvis songs to feature a woman's name. [65] The single did well in its own right, topping the charts in the United Kingdom and going top five in Elvis's native country. Despite such commercial success, "(Marie's the Name) His Latest Flame" took a while to appear on any album, and then it was included only on compilations. As a part of Elvis's signature catalog, it evidently crossed over and recruited new members to his ever-expanding following. [66] Yet the song seemed to fall out of favor with its singer in later years. He never, for instance, sang it fully in concert. [67] "(Marie's the Name) His Latest Flame" provided opportunity neither to express much vocal color nor get people dancing. It also came between the filming of *Blue Hawaii* and *Follow That Dream*, in effect marking the beginning of a creative lull in Presley's film career. Nevertheless, the shifts and changes Elvis made to "(Marie's the Name) His Latest Flame" as a song provide a textbook example of how far he and his musicians could go with the material they adapted in the studio.

84. "Stuck on You" (from *Elvis' Golden Records Volume 3*, 1963)

Frank Sinatra: "He's here in person."

Nancy Sinatra [swoons]: "I may pass out."

Comedian Joey Bishop [snaps]: "Where the heck are his sideburns??"

Sammy Davis Jr. [sings]: "Well, I'll be a *hound dog!*"

In the 1950s, Frank Sinatra dismissed rock 'n' roll as "the martial music of every side-burned delinquent on the face of the earth." [68] Emerging from the world of "delinquent" music, when Elvis performed on Timex's *Frank Sinatra Show* in Miami's Fontainebleau Hotel, he turned the tables on his host. At the show's start, he strode out on stage in full army uniform to join Sinatra and sing a verse of Ol' Blue Eyes' hit, "It's Nice to Go Trav'ling." In that early part of the show, he was a little gauche and unsure of himself. Nevertheless, he got paid handsomely: $125,000 for just ten minutes on stage.[69] For that time, he managed to famously cover Sinatra's "Witchcraft" while Frank tipped his hat in exchange to "Love Me Tender."[70] Less remembered, but more interesting, was Elvis's consequent performance—after a segment promoting Timex watches—of his new single "Fame and Fortune" and its flip side, another new number called "Stuck on You." After being given the floor to promote "Fame and Fortune," Elvis had a matter of minutes to convince the youth of America that *the rock would not stop*. By the time he got to "Stuck on You," his mood had changed. Like the robust Timex watches sold earlier on the show, "Elvis the Pelvis" proved he was able to just *keep on ticking*.

On Frank Sinatra's show, "Stuck on You" united the old and new aspects of Elvis's image, proving Private Presley had not completely eclipsed the Memphis Flash.[71] To welcome his client back from the relative oblivion of Bad Nauheim, the Colonel invited three hundred fan club members along for the show. Every time their hero moved, they screamed on cue. Boosted to fever pitch by such fan support, the young singer magnetically snapped his fingers, clapped his hands, rolled his shoulders, and scissored his legs, creating a performance so sharp and on point that his audience completely lost it. Forget stagecraft. This was rock 'n' roll tai chi, pure and simple. It was a truly electric performance. Elvis was present before the youth of America yet again. Ernst Jørgensen said of the Colonel and record label:

> What they were aiming for [at that point] were the hardcore Elvis fans as RCA imagined them, now a little older and ready to make the transition from the sexy Elvis of the '50s image to a new figure, more mature but still a rocker.[72]

The U.S. army may have shorn Elvis of his sideburns. Ol' Blue Eyes might have restricted Presley's kinetic body in an awkward and formal tux. But the singer's spontaneous and self-consciously cheeky grin transcended his showbiz corsetry. His performance more than suggested that he was alive and kicking; to borrow a phrase from Jack Kerouac,

Elvis's jet-black quiff resembled "holy flowers floating in the air."[73] At least until *GI Blues* modified his image a few months later, Presley had proved to his fans that he was ready to jump right in, raise pulse rates, and bomp his way to rock 'n' roll glory.

"Stuck on You" was, in part, created by Aaron Harold Schroeder. Emerging, like Mort Shuman, from Brooklyn's Jewish community, Schroeder was a competent pianist, even though he played by ear. Working from his office in New York's Irving Berlin building in the aftermath of World War II, he created material for Rosemary Clooney and others. Schroeder became an incredibly prolific writer, well known for his ability to tailor material to specific sections of the popular music audience. By the mid-1950s, he had started working for Hill & Range. Even before "Stuck on You," which was a co-write with John Leslie McFarland, his own catalog included songs recorded by Frank Sinatra, Perry Como, and Nat King Cole.[74] Eddy Arnold told him that Elvis was "going to burn up the world."[75] When Schroeder heard a tape of the new singer, he concluded, "I thought he was great. I couldn't understand a word he was singing but his sound was terrific."[76]

According to Gordon Stoker of the Jordanaires, Elvis paid relatively little attention when he tackled "Stuck on You." He completed the song at his first post-army recording session in just three takes. Freddy Bienstock and others pushed for "Stuck on You" to be released as a single. It did well, topping the *Billboard* Hot 100. Although the Colonel's standard strategy of shipping gargantuan quantities of records on a sale-or-return basis did not fail, the total of copies that made their way back to the label's warehouse was embarrassing. When Elvis had the chance to include it on his concert set list a year later, he never actually did. Despite its mixed fortunes, however, Elvis's phrasing on "Stuck on You" is evidence of what makes it great. Although Floyd Cramer's introductory piano vamp—regularly punctuated by the Jordanaires—soon sounds overly familiar, Elvis's vocals offer a gentle sprinkling of magic. They start off capering, confident, and pedestrian, but when he shakes down that line about the "grizzly bear," he does a performative back flip, then repeatedly goes wild. As the consummate popular music stylist, with "Stuck on You," Elvis shows that he can inflect his lyrics and pull out different meanings like rabbits from a hat. His secret is he can modulate what he delivers. He can quietly creep back into the framework of his song, as if to tell listeners that his outburst never actually happened.

In August 1975, as a bittersweet coda to the shenanigans of the Timex show era, exhaustion knocked Elvis Presley flat out. Just three days into his two-week summer festival engagement in Las Vegas, he returned to Memphis and checked into the Baptist Memorial Hospital. Elvis was in a bad medical state. He was beginning to fall apart. Sinatra got in contact.[77] It is both surprising and utterly tragic that the New Jersey singer, who was born two decades *before* his Memphis friend (and made his biggest splash with the bobby-soxers in the period *before* rock 'n' roll), would survive Elvis by more than twenty years.

After "Stuck on You" was recorded—as well as creating lyrics to the monumental "It's Now or Never" around the same time—Aaron Schroeder went on to do great things: co-writing Bobby Vee's "Rubber Ball" and bringing Burt Bacharach's epic "24 Hours from Tulsa" to Gene Pitney.[78] As if that was not enough to get him knighted for services to popular culture, Schroeder rounded out the decade by providing a theme tune for the famous children's cartoon *Scooby-Doo*.

83. "Little Egypt" (from *The Complete '68 Comeback Special*, 2008)

Toward the middle of the 1960s, Elvis's film career was in full swing, with studios churning out shallow, relatively lackluster pictures. One of the stand-out moments in this treadmill of musicals came when he sang "Little Egypt" in the 1964 Paramount film *Roustabout*. By this point, he was mainly working for MGM with interludes at other studios. *Roustabout* came after two MGM projects: the relative low of *Kissin' Cousins* and high of *Viva Las Vegas*. After completing the film, Elvis made two more MGM movies within a year (*Girl Happy* and *Harum Scarum*), with the Allied Artists picture *Tickle Me* sandwiched in between.

Air force officer, waiter, carnie, nightclub singer, rodeo rider, kidnapped film star—the list of the occupations of his characters in these pictures is enough to hint at their two-dimensional quality.

The story of "Little Egypt" begins with the exotic lady who inspired its title. At the World's Columbian Exposition of 1893, down on the midway in Chicago, there was a captivating dancer. She went by the names of "Fatima" and "Little Egypt." When she shook her hips to the mesmeric rhythm of snake-charmer music, Little Egypt supposedly gave Mark Twain a heart attack, and her legend was born. Seven decades later, on screen at least, Elvis occupied Twain's role. In *Roustabout*, as if practicing for his *Comeback*, he wore a masculine black leather jacket. Like Marlon Brando in *The Wild One*, he also rode a motorbike, albeit one with modern design, which marked him out as Charlie Rogers, a character willing to embrace change. Once he joined Harry Carver's carnival spectacular, Elvis appeared on stage as an ordinary youth in a jacket and jeans. In this play within a play, he acts as a cipher of male desire: a wandering spectator entranced by thoughts of a girly show. To lure him in, the barker makes a sales pitch, bringing on the lithe and agile Little Egypt (played by Wilda Taylor): He says, "Direct from the banks of the River Nile, we've brought you the favorite of the pharaohs. . . . That's enough, honey. Don't give 'em too much." As Elvis gets closer, the barker snaps, "You there, young man. Step right up and get yourself a ticket. You've just bought yourself a trip to paradise!" Once the floor-show opens, a hesitant Elvis turns around to face the audience and starts to sing. He sheepishly confesses that he bought a ticket and sat down in the first row. The intense red of his jacket speaks of his desire, but somehow he still seems innocent. He moves relatively little—for a Presley performance, at least. As he sings of his encounter with the dancing girls, he looks rather coy. Maybe he was right to feel just a bit out of place. After all, he is singing a cheap but ear-catching novelty number about a guy who fell for a faux exotic belly dancer. Backstage, when the number finishes, Elvis asks Carver whether the audience was trying to say something with such great applause. He is reminded that they would do the same for performing seals.

So much for the movies, but what about real life? Leiber and Stoller's "Little Egypt" was one of Elvis Presley's quirkiest and most memorable film-score performances. When he entered the studio, innocent pop dominated the charts: "I Want to Hold Your Hand" and "She Loves You" by the Beatles competed for the top slot of the *Billboard* Hot 100. Credits for the *Roustabout* session material read like a who's who of Elvis's Hill & Range core writers: other songs were by Joy Byers, Ben Weisman, Sid Tepper, Roy Bennett, Fred Wise, and regulars Giant, Baum, and Kaye. Most *Roustabout* contributions, however, were relatively unmemorable. "Little Egypt" had been written when Leiber and Stoller focused on their pet project the Coasters. The black doo-wop group's funny, spirited R&B version came out in 1961. Another record that capitalized on the success of the single's sound was Joe Tex's 1962 Dial Records dance craze number "The Peck." Elvis kept that disc in his singles collection.[79] It was no surprise he began the session with "Little Egypt"; two years earlier, he recorded another Leiber and Stoller number popularized by the Coasters as a movie theme tune—the powerhouse duo's "Girls! Girls! Girls!"

Elvis Presley's 1960s Hollywood recording sessions benefited from the cream of Los Angeles's session musicians, the Wrecking Crew. Billy Strange and Barney Kessel were among the players who participated on the Monday night session on 2 March 1964 at Radio Recorders. Both of those members had worked with the singer on previous, early-1960s film-score material. Kessel was just over a decade older than Elvis. The jazz-influenced guitarist was well known, both for his knowledge of chords and for the wealth of artists he had worked with in the 1950s, including Billie Holiday. Other great players also graced the studio that day. As Piers Beagley noted:

> There was some cool interaction between Elvis and the Jordanaires in the studio and some fine drumming from Hal Blaine and Buddy Harman. Elvis's growl on "Little Egypt came out strutting" in the first twenty seconds showed more enthusiasm than at any point in the whole of the previous *Kissin' Cousins* session.[80]

Indeed, the studio version of "Little Egypt" had a complex genesis. On the first night of the session, fifteen takes were recorded. At the end of the next day's studio visit, the band recorded six more takes, slightly slower this time and with less punchy percussion. An acceptable version came from the last take of the first night. For the movie soundtrack, some of the final take from the second night was spliced into the middle and overdubs added. Four years later, Elvis revisited "Little Egypt" when the *Comeback* presented a singer who asserted that he was fully adult with a firm grip on his music.

In early 1968, Elvis was known for his celluloid performances. To reflect the Hollywood side of Elvis's career, director Steve Binder wanted several production numbers in the *Comeback*. Wedged between the more visceral "Guitar Man" and "Trouble" as a part of a medley, what makes the *Comeback* version of "Little Egypt" a cut above its inspiration is the rawness and complete certainty of Elvis's delivery. Placed, for the first time in years, in an approximation of his 1957 gold lamé jacket, the singer could at last express his sensuality shorn of any saucy postcard feel. Finally, he takes listeners on a musical journey that is so tight, it's vertiginous. The result is not exactly what one might expect with the permissive society in ascendance; not simply "adult" in the sleazy sense of the word. Instead, it is charged with a strange kind of sincerity—a kind so full, in fact, that it smolders. At these heady heights, what comes through is that the material is almost irrelevant to how great Elvis can be. He takes his audience to a place where he is in control and makes it clear that he won't be pushed around. The NBC *Comeback Special* never fails to excite because it offers a grown man, on his center, standing in the fullness of his power. Nothing else matters. Almost a century after the World's Columbian Exposition, the tables have therefore turned: A special male is now the one with the power to cause female spectators to risk coronary seizures. It was little wonder that Elvis insisted when the album of the NBC show was in preproduction that the level was raised on "Little Egypt."[81]

82. "The Lord's Prayer" (from *A Hundred Years from Now: Essential Elvis, Volume 4,* 1996)

The great thing about the "The Lord's Prayer" is, of course, that almost everyone born into Judeo-Christian culture already knows it. The liturgy appeared in the gospels of both St. Matthew and St. Luke. One source even lists the song's author as Jesus.[82] "The Lord's Prayer" acted as a stylistic base for Elvis. He knew that audiences were familiar with it, so the question became not what *could* be done, but what *he*—and he alone—could do. In 1960, Elvis home-recorded an informal version while staying in Hollywood. He also performed the prayer in the summer of 1970 during live rehearsals for the magnificent MGM feature documentary *That's the Way It Is*.[83] During the same rehearsals, as if to avoid accusations of favoritism, Elvis also tried "Hava Nagila." The most interesting version of "The Lord's Prayer" was from a 16 May 1971 Nashville session and can be found on the fourth installment of RCA's CD series *The Essential Elvis* called *A Hundred Years from Now*. That year, Elvis had been exploring folk in the studio; the session in question was set up to give his label some Christmas material. His athletic stab at "The Lord's Prayer" was captured when he was fooling around between takes. While the musicians were working out their "Steamroller Blues"–like arrangement of "I'll Be Home on Christmas Day," Elvis began departing from the playlist. His ad hoc performance began with a stretch of the vocal cords in combination with some piano fill.[84] It might seem, then, like an odd choice for the top 100. After all, this version of "The Lord's Prayer" was a spontaneous moment rather than a finished number.

"The Lord's Prayer" has a heritage in recorded music that stretches back to the form's earliest years. A decade after the release of his vaudeville classic "Ta-ra-ra Boom-de-ey," in 1902 Len Spencer delivered a somewhat pious, spoken-word version on an Edison phonograph cylinder. Columbia offered a disc of his recitation in 1911. A musical take was arranged by Albert Hay Malotte in 1935. Many artists have recorded "The Lord's Prayer" since then. In September 1937, a black vocal group called the Heavenly Gospel Singers released a version on Bluebird that began all slow and low, as if setting a model for bass singers everywhere. It bubbled into a syncopated a cappella performance with some striking lead vocal moments that resembled field hollers. Sarah Vaughn's rendition, released by Musicraft a decade later, was crooned blissfully and could not have been more different. RCA introduced the 45rpm single as a format in 1949 and capitalized with two further recordings.

Elvis may have been influenced by the rich Jewish baritone Robert Merrill, who sang for New York's Metropolitan Opera. Merrill released a powerful take of "The Lord's Prayer" on RCA Victor's Red Seal label as the B-side to his "Ole Man River." Perry Como contributed a version in the same year, backed with "Ave Maria." Sounding rather like Bing Crosby, he sang in unison with a supporting choir during the song's immense choral climax. Como rerecorded "The Lord's Prayer" in 1954, this time with a cleaner, crisper sound and harder-edged vocal that was veering toward Sinatra in style. When Mario Lanza acted in the MGM army comedy, *Because You're Mine*, in 1952, he performed the song in a similar way to Como. Unlike Elvis, when they belted that final "Amen" that lifted the song to its climax, Merrill, Como, and Lanza all kept their pitch well within bounds.

At the start of the 1950s—renamed as "Our Father," except by the Orioles who used the original title—the song also was claimed by a range of black gospel groups, including the Five Blind Boys of Mississippi on Peacock, the Sensational Nightingales on Decca, and the Harmonizing Four on Gotham Records. Just as these versions were coming out, it is possible that Elvis participated in collective performances of the song when he visited East Trigg Baptist Church. It was also the turn of black female singers Myrtle Jackson, Mahalia Jackson, and Dinah Washington to put their stamp on the standard. Mahalia was a key performer, pioneering the integration of black and white live audiences. Her version of the song was first released on her second EP for Apollo in 1954. Four years later, she closed the Newport Jazz Festival with a rendition that was assertive yet wonderfully eloquent and rousing. Elvis had a deep respect for Mahalia. He met her backstage in 1969 on the set of his last fictional feature, *Change of Habit*.

Elvis Presley's outtake of "The Lord's Prayer" does not sound quite like any of the mainstream performances that came before it. The early words in his Nashville version sound vulnerable, golden, and lingering. Soon he ramps it up and swings low in gospel style. As he attacks the song, to borrow a phrase from the Russian film director Andrei Tarkovsky, Elvis is "sculpting in time," leaping between the jungle bars of meter with unique prowess.[85] Given the lack of backing and instrumentation, his version is notably more fluid and free than Perry Como's and, at the climax, far surpasses it. Like the character challenged to achieve a high diving feat in 1963's *Fun in Acapulco*, he dares to go one better than Como and pushes his voice extra high at the song's peak. At that moment of climax, Elvis soars like an opera singer, leaping into an astounding, embarrassingly stratospheric "for-eeeever!" He then breaks off, almost without catching a breath, and coyly chuckles, "You didn't think I could do it, did you?" Immediately, Elvis gets back into the song and pushes for the finish line with an extended "Ahhhh-mennn! Whooooo!" It floors even the prepared listener.

On "The Lord's Prayer," Elvis not only sings; he ascends. The singer was just thirty-six when he nailed the famous recitation. Kathy Westmoreland, his classically trained soprano support, once observed that her employer—as a self-schooled performer—would try things that those who had professional training did not dare.[86] One of the surprising things about "The Lord's Prayer" is how little critical commentary there is about this rendition. On the Nashville 1971 version, Elvis jokes about his role as an icon, then shows exactly why he deserves it. He bares himself in a way that leaves everyone astounded . . . and this was only a throwaway?!

Absolutely flawless.

81. "Dixieland Rock" (from *King Creole*, 1958)

> If Elvis wasn't with us, or if he was asleep, we would always listen to a
> disc jockey named Moonglow McMartin in New Orleans; [his radio
> show] came on at midnight on WWL at the Roosevelt Hotel. And he
> played jazz all night long. And we could pick it up all the way out in
> Arizona and everywhere, late night.[87]

Scotty Moore recalled of the Sun-era tours that he, Bill Black, and DJ
Fontana—not Elvis—would listen to jazz on the radio. One thing that
their singer was remembered for was his ability to incorporate different
genres of popular music, from country and blues to folk and classical,
into his style. With honorable exceptions such as "City by Night," however, jazz was the genre with which Elvis was least engaged. In *Jailhouse
Rock*, when his character—the construction worker Vince Everett—is
asked to evaluate the longevity of atonality in jazz, as he walks out the
door, replacing insecurity with defiance, he snorts, "Lady, I don't know
what the hell you're talking about." Nobody should mistake Elvis for the
film characters he played, but such portrayals deliberately positioned him
as someone more feral than those who cultivated refined, intellectual,
middle-class taste. The real Elvis used his intuition and intelligence in
other ways. Despite, in effect, being a genius scat singer, he generally
kept away from jazz and therefore avoided associating with a genre that
framed black genius partially through estimations of the white intelligent-
sia. It was perhaps inevitable, then, that when Elvis came close to jazz,
his music was informed by the exuberant New Orleans style. New Orleans jazz tends to combine a bluesy form, complete with all of its earthy
connotations, with the full range of musical accompaniment.

During the recording of the *Jailhouse Rock* soundtrack, Leiber and
Stoller pitched the idea to the Aberbachs of Elia Kazan adapting Nelson
Algren's *A Walk on the Wild Side* as a musical with Hill & Range orga-
nizing the soundtrack.[88] Their offer would have been tempting. Kazan
was a big name at that point, one who personified America's tradition of
socially responsible, quality drama. After working in theater and on
Broadway, he had founded the Actors Studio and directed two of the most
significant pictures of the decade. His left-leaning brand of realist fiction
managed to bring a new sense of quality to mainstream cinema and capture the youth market. *On the Waterfront* featured a smoldering Marlon
Brando. *East of Eden* exposed the world to the incomparable James Dean.

For reasons that were perhaps psychological as much as they were financial, however, the Colonel resented an outside party "interfering" with
Elvis's career.[89] By 1958, Parker was no longer granting Leiber and
Stoller full access to his client in person, despite accepting some of their
new songs. Needless to say, Elvis never worked with Kazan, though the
director's friend Clifford Odets scripted the uneven *Wild in the Country.*With fewer Leiber and Stoller contributions, Hill & Range house writers had to fill the shortfall for Elvis's next feature project, *King Creole*.
"Dixieland Rock" was a co-write between Aaron Schroeder and Beverly
Ross.[90] It was recorded in January 1958 at Radio Recorders in Hollywood
for the *King Creole* soundtrack.[91] The previous day had been very successful, with Claude Demetrius's "Hard Headed Woman," the Ben Weisman and Fred Wise co-write "Crawfish," and two great Leiber and Stoller
numbers—the film's title track and "Trouble"—already in the bag.[92] Elvis was in top form.

Despite its almost avant-garde introduction, "Dixieland Rock" is a
cabaret number that contains a rollicking, New Orleans–style performance. It still sounds incredible. The introduction remains so odd and
modern; just like the listeners fooled by Orson Welles's *War of the
Worlds* radio broadcast back in 1938, patrons actually in the club might
have thought that aliens had landed. The initial horn blasts and hand claps
seem completely out of place, and their anticipative role is only revealed
when "Dixieland Rock" reaches its chorus. At that point, the number
indicates so little about where it is going that listeners might almost
expect it to turn into "All Shook Up." When Elvis broaches the first
verse, he's so mean, he almost raps. Ernst Jørgensen has described a
certain toughness and aggressiveness in the sound of some of Elvis's
early RCA rock 'n' roll.[93] The singer's vocals on "Dixieland Rock" extend his thesis. They are pointed, almost as if Elvis wanted to bring a
sense of rockabilly sharpness to the number. As "Dixieland Rock" reaches its staggering climax, a nifty, walking trombone line cuts in, then a
familiar, accompanying trumpet slides to bring the song back—kicking
and screaming—to a more recognizable approximation of conventional
New Orleans jazz. Two slightly different versions of "Dixieland Rock"
came out, one on the *King Creole* EP, the other on its soundtrack LP. The
song was never symphonic, but it remains a stellar performance and is
still a true showstopper.[94]

80. "My Way" (from *Aloha from Hawaii via Satellite*, 1973)

One of the strange things about "My Way" is that it is basically an assertion of ego, as if saying, "I may have seemed arrogant and upset a few people, but there we are: I fulfilled my destiny. I was a true individual." It is the ultimate ode to integrity, autonomy, and individuality.

"My Way" started life in a different language, as a fraught 1968 love song called "Comme d'habitude" ("As Usual"). Its main writer was the underestimated French talent Claude "Cloco" François. Working with his compatriots Jacques Revaux (on the music) and Gilles Thibaut (on the lyrics), François crafted a song that was tender, stirring, and finally epic.[95] In his own country, François also had great success as an artist. He wrote the first version of another 1970s Elvis classic, "My Boy."

Sensing the drama of François' "Comme d'habitude," David Bowie rewrote the lyrics as "Even a Fool Learns to Love." The song inspired his surreal and poetic 1971 anthem "Life on Mars." It was the Canadian American song master Paul Anka, however, who defined a classic when he wrote new English lyrics for "Comme d'habitude." He created the blueprint for Frank Sinatra's 1969 benchmark version.

Anka had been making records for as long as Presley. In 1958, he contributed Buddy Holly's "It Doesn't Matter Anymore." He was definitely known to Elvis: The late 1950s Paramount singles "(All of a Sudden) My Heart Sings" and "Put Your Head on My Shoulder" were in the star's personal collection.[96] Sinatra recorded Anka's rendering of "My Way" for Reprise, his own special Warner Brothers subsidiary label.[97] The single took up residence in the charts—nowhere more so than the United Kingdom—and sold more than a million copies, affirming Ol' Blue Eyes as the consummate entertainer. Part of that success was down to Anka. When he adapted "My Way" for Sinatra, he deliberately wrote lyrics that would suit the singer's heavyweight, "Chairman of the Board" persona.

Elvis first sang "My Way" in RCA's Nashville facility during a studio visit in June 1971—despite Anka, apparently, suggesting it did not suit his image. Given its popular association with Frank Sinatra, "My Way" seemed an odd choice for the singer's catalog; the opportunity to make such a dramatic song his own nevertheless proved irresistible. Both Sinatra's and Elvis's takes on "My Way" are accomplished, but where Sinatra's version is mannered and world-weary, Elvis's flows discreetly, offering music that is majestic, mature, and genuinely sublime.

When Elvis debuted "My Way" live at the start of his 1972 summer engagement in Las Vegas, he began the song a little unsure of himself and almost pious. The studio take was not his most memorable version. *Aloha from Hawaii* included a rousing live performance that made a much greater mark. In the global telecast, what Elvis pursued, much more so than Frank Sinatra, was an arrangement that contrasted the song's gentle, haunting early verses with a finale that was absolutely epic. The end of Elvis's version was so towering that it left audiences positively stunned at his musical achievement.

The version of "My Way" that Elvis performed at Rapid City, in June 1977, was judged even better by music critic Robert Matthew-Walker than the one offered during *Aloha*. As Elvis's drummer Ronnie Tutt later claimed, though, such shows featured Elvis at his poorest in terms of health. His performance was nevertheless stronger and more focused than, say, the one he offered in College Park, Maryland, late in 1974. It was the Omaha version of "My Way" that RCA released as a single. Backed by the patriotic "America the Beautiful"—which, in the middle of the decade, was sung in concert to mark the nation's bicentennial—"My Way" was the singer's first posthumous single. The RCA release went higher than Sinatra's, just missing the top twenty of the *Billboard* Hot 100, and in time sold more than a million copies. With its lines about facing the final curtain, the song seemed strangely resonant and appropriate. In one sense, "My Way" became a kind of artistic riposte to the sensationalist bodyguard book *Elvis, What Happened?*[98] After all, Elvis Presley was not only a unique individual. At the center of a legend that was far bigger than any mortal being, he had become *an icon of individuality*.

79. "A Big Hunk o' Love" (from *Worldwide 50 Gold Award Hits Volume I*, 1970)

"A Big Hunk o' Love" is a frantic love letter from Elvis to the generation that supported him. According to music writer Ace Collins, the song was "the closing of a chapter": Elvis's last truly rocking number one single for many years.[99] Collins also noted, "In truth, it might have been six years too early. The Rolling Stones would have loved this kind of song in

1966."[100] No wonder, then, that the recent live rockabilly cover versions, like Jim Jones's 2009 interpretation, sound both the most hysterical and the most appropriate.

Casual listeners associate "A Big Hunk o' Love" with Elvis's urgent *Aloha* satellite performance from 1973, but the song was first performed much earlier in his career. When Elvis hit Nashville in June 1958, pressure from RCA was mounting to create something interesting. Fans accustomed to rock 'n' roll needed a number compelling enough to keep them on the edge of their seats. The previous session produced nothing suitable. He tried again at exactly the same time when Pat Boone's relatively pedestrian "Love Letters in the Sand" dominated America's singles chart. Elvis's Nashville studio visit—his last before departing for Germany—was also his first recording session without the other Blue Moon Boys (Scotty Moore and Bill Black).[101] He was still on familiar ground, however, drawing on the services of a songwriter who had been feeding him material ever since the move to RCA Records.

Aaron Schroeder's successes had already included "I Was the One" (the second track on the "Heartbreak Hotel" EP) and "Don't Leave Me Now." He also co-wrote *Loving You*'s jaunty "Got a Lot o' Livin' to Do!" with Ben Weisman. "A Big Hunk o' Love" was another Schroeder co-write, this time with Sid Wyche (a.k.a. Sid Jaxon).[102]

Elvis's version of "A Big Hunk o' Love" was so exciting it almost came apart at the seams. The song's dynamic backing combines Floyd Cramer's tumbling, histrionic piano fills with some excellent and funky burbling by the Jordanaires.[103] Elvis arrives in the mix like someone wading into a brawl. His wonderfully rangy vocals are pitched somewhere between his British admirer Cliff Richard, whose debut single "Move It" stormed the UK charts the previous summer, and his raucous Decca contemporary Wanda Jackson.[104] He revisited "A Big Hunk o' Love" for his stage shows after 1971. Various concert versions can be heard on material recorded for both the documentary *Elvis on Tour* and, of course, the *Aloha* broadcast.

Ultimately, Schroeder and Wyche's concoction was complete flim-flam. As the song's protagonist, Elvis turns any expression of his own lust so far into parody that it disappears. What's left is the popular memory of Elvis Presley as a 1970s superhero in a jumpsuit; someone who was a "big hunk of love" in his own right. Yet the song's original intention was for the boy from Memphis who'd delivered songs like "Hound Dog" to say to fans, "Starting army duty hasn't changed me none. I'm still here and I can still rip this up."

78. "I Got a Woman / Amen" (from *Elvis Recorded Live on Stage in Memphis*, 1974)

Sometimes it is possible to forget how different Elvis was when he first walked on stage. During his days as a Sun artist, he wore clothes that almost looked like an explosion in a paint factory. Despite being a "folk fireball" success, he had yet to embrace the genteel modes of behavior required by Hollywood and national television. As his group lurched their way through their short, upbeat sets in various local venues, Elvis was known to belch and accidentally break strings on his guitar. Playing Houston's Eagles' Hall in March 1955 he quipped:

> I'd like to do a little song right here that I hope you people like. This one's called, "Little Darling, You Broke My Heart When You Went Away (But I'll Break Your Jaw When You Come Back)." Did you ever hear that one? I'd like to do this little song here; it's called "I Got a Woman, Way Over Town."[105]

He then launched into Ray Charles's "I Got a Woman," a cover that was at once funky, impassioned, and just a little bit sinister.

The idea of any stage performer joking about misogynist violence is, thankfully, a world away from today. Yet it's worth noting that female audiences knew Elvis was only *playing a game* when he conjured with such dark forces: In spite of the off-key jibe, he immediately got female audience members screaming with excitement.

Covering Ray Charles's hit was Elvis's way to connect with the hipper folk in his live audiences, kids who were listening to R&B. On one level, "I Got a Woman" appears to come from the viewpoint of a drifter who boasts about accepting sexual favors and financial handouts from a woman who understands that her place is at home.[106] Rather than simply being a song about female entrapment, however, "I Got a Woman" can also be read as a lover's eulogy to his redeeming angel.

The Wild One came out less than eighteen months before Elvis's 1955 Houston show. Maybe the singer was casting himself as Johnny Strabler, errant leader of the Black Rebels Motorcycle Club. Fitting the deviant stereotype of the biker in László Benedek's sensational exploitation feature, Strabler is falsely accused of abducting a policeman's daughter. In reality, though, he is a heart breaker, not a jaw breaker.

Perhaps because it so captivated his early audiences, "I Got a Woman" was used by Elvis Presley as a talisman. The well-known Ray Charles number has the peculiar distinction of being performed on Elvis's first national TV appearance in 1956, superb return to form in Las Vegas in 1969, and final concert in Indianapolis, 1977. It was also the first song he recorded for RCA, leading off the same January 1956 session that produced his debut single "Heartbreak Hotel." By that point, "I Got a Woman" was already a very familiar part of Elvis's catalog. He added it to his live set a matter of weeks after the December 1954 release of Ray Charles's Atlantic Records version and recorded it early in 1955.[107]

Any account of "I Got a Woman" should start *before* Ray Charles, with Bob King. The black gospel songwriter grew up in Philadelphia with Howard Carroll, who went on to play guitar with the swinging, mellifluous Dixie Hummingbirds. As teens, the two played music together at local churches and house parties. Inspired by Blind Boy Fuller (a secular, ragtime blues guitar picker from North Carolina with his own, intricate style), King went on to create gospel quartet music with an R&B undertow. In the same year that Elvis started at Sun, Duke Records released "It Must Be Jesus" sung by the Southern Tones, with the songwriter credited as lead vocalist.[108] The group's performance just glowed. Their passionate take stood out immediately because it so effortlessly managed to combine a circular, bluesy structure; soaring R&B vocal; and repeated, sung gospel vamp. After hearing it on the radio, Ray Charles set to work reformulating "It Must Be Jesus" in a way that owed less to the gospel tradition.[109] He had already graduated to Atlantic from his apprenticeship on Swing Time Records and delivered a range of covers for the label in styles that ranged from ballads to frantic boogie-woogie and jump blues.

Attuned to the R&B element in the Southern Tones single, Ray Charles immediately reworked King's song as "I Got a Woman." It was one of Charles's first compositions. In December 1954, he scored an R&B hit with his Atlantic single. Charles's soul version combined vocal acrobatics with a jazzy, urbane sax solo. When Elvis toured the southern states, he started performing the song on stage almost immediately. One of the first times he tried it was in Lubbock, Texas, early in 1955. He cut it almost as quickly, at the beginning of his fifth session as a professional recording artist for Sun, the same one in which "Trying to Get to You" was captured on tape. By that point the Blue Moon Boys had expanded to accommodate DJ Fontana, and "I Got a Woman" is recognizable as one of their numbers. Elvis's low-key vocal sounds surprisingly spectral: impassioned but also a little absent. Scotty's innovative, close-weave country picking and the familiar tick-a-tick rockabilly percussion keep the song rolling. The whole thing resembles an upbeat cousin of another of the session's gems: "Baby Let's Play House."

When Elvis changed up a gear and signed to RCA, he had access to "I Got a Woman" as part of Progressive Music, the catalog co-owned by his publishers, the Aberbachs. [110] Just over two weeks after his first Nashville session, he went on *Stage Show*, the Dorsey Brothers' weekly television spectacular broadcast from CBS Studio 50 in New York City. For his national TV debut, Elvis chose familiar material. He started with "Shake, Rattle and Roll / Flip, Flop and Fly" and then launched into "I Got a Woman." When Elvis entered any new performing environment in the 1950s, he needed to win over his listeners afresh. Despite charging into "I Got a Woman," initially, he struggled to prime the dynamo. The energy he put out was nothing like what he got back. All that, of course, was almost immediately about to change, but, at first, the song did not evoke the same explosive response that it had with Southern fans. Upon encountering this unknown, rockabilly rarity, New York audiences were confused about how to express the excitement they felt. After beginning a bit hesitant, even absent, he came into his own during the course of his performance and got lost in the moment, shaking his quiff and cutting up with the boys. Following an initial smattering of applause, the crowd broke into whoops, whistles, and even screams. Elvis then included the same provocative, half-time ending that had teased them on tour; again it was greeted with a relatively polite response.

Undaunted by the early television performance, RCA released a single version of "I Got a Woman" that summer, backing it with pianist Don Robertson's "I'm Counting on You." The disc was eclipsed in sales by both Charles's original and "Blue Suede Shoes." "I Got a Woman" had a riotous welcome, however, when Elvis played it live about a month later, clearing the way for "Don't Be Cruel" during the evening show of his homecoming visit to the Mississippi-Alabama Fair and Dairy Show. By the time that Elvis played an impassioned "I Got a Woman" near the start of his March 1961 benefit show in Pearl Harbor, the familiar

"Welllll . . ." started to emerge, and the audience screamed on the first verse.

Elvis resuscitated "I Got a Woman" to start a dressing-room rehearsal preparing for the NBC *Comeback Special* in Burbank. Ernst Jørgensen has also suggested that he finished a take of "Twenty Days and Twenty Nights" with it, starting his Nashville session in June 1970.[111]

With its comforting familiarity and proven way of teasing audiences, the song became Elvis's in-concert mascot during the 1970s. It was included in recordings associated with both rehearsals for *That's the Way It Is* and the *Elvis on Tour* documentary. The live version of "I Got a Woman" could change form at its master's will, starting as an extended vamp, transforming into something more coherent, pausing briefly for effect, roaring back to life, shaking all over, then revving up again for the ultimate, slow-paced cabaret finale. Both in Vegas and beyond, it became a regular fixture, often after "See See Rider" flashed past the audience to open the show.[112] "I Got a Woman" was both the first "proper" number in each set and, in a sense, also an afterthought, as it melded so naturally into the musical flow.

The now-familiar "Amen" has a story that is just fascinating as "I Got a Woman." Elvis started using it as a live coda in September 1970. Before that, his ending had been more traditional, repeating the chorus lyrics for a showstopping finale. "Amen" got its start much earlier with a certain professional gospel act that began just before World War II. Featuring a trademark, independent male lead, the Wings over Jordan Choir entertained troops, broadcast regularly for CBS radio, and was even invited to the White House. Compared to what came later, the choir's version of "Amen" was slow and full. It was released by RCA Victor at the end of 1948. The song received further attention when King Records in Cincinnati released a version in 1953. Reverend J. B. Crocker and Edna Gallmon Cooke had, meanwhile, circulated their own versions. "Amen" came into its own, however, when it was used in Ralph Nelson's heartwarming 1963 morality tale, *Lilies of the Field*. Sidney Poitier played a laborer who helped a sisterhood of nuns as he traveled across the Arizona desert. At the film's climax, backed by an enthusiastic chorus of European sisters, Poitier sings a version of the song arranged by the renowned spirituals expert Jester Hairston.

Two years later, the Impressions appropriated "Amen" and gave it a marching beat, creating a Christmas song that featured new lyrics. Curtis

Mayfield offered a wonderfully lilting performance.[113] It is hard to say
which version inspired Elvis, but another possibility is that he heard soul
singer Otis Redding's recording.[114] When Otis died in a plane crash in
1967 at the tender age of twenty-six, Elvis sent his widow a heartfelt
telegram of condolence. Redding extended his version of "Amen" by
interspersing sections of the gospel standard "This Little Light of Mine";
it is possible that Elvis borrowed the same idea for his "I Got a Woman"
medley. He switched church references, too, briefly adding a snatch of
"Ave Maria" instead of "Amen" for a few shows during his August 1970
Las Vegas engagement.

One of the best available versions of "I Got a Woman" can be heard
on *Elvis Recorded Live on Stage in Memphis*, the 1974 live album that
captured his show at the Mid-South Coliseum. Before the song starts, one
woman screams out. A confident Elvis quips in reply, "Honey, you have
got bad laryngitis! I mean, [squawks] 'Elvis, turn it up!'" He adds,
"Welllll,—I said that, didn't I, about an hour ago?—, well, well, welll,
well, well, well well welllll . . . " Elvis continues, "She's louder than I
am, and I've got the microphone!" Finally, he launches into a nice,
smooth, fully accomplished rendition. Everything that made his 1970s
music so exciting is right there in the mix. He slams on the brakes so hard
that "Amen" starts almost *before* "I Got a Woman" is finished. The whole
extravaganza ends with JD's famous bass note ("Go get it, JD!"), followed by the traditional chorus-repeat finale. As the crowd continues to
scream, Elvis says, "Honey, I'll turn around as much as I can without
getting dizzy and falling off the stage." He's no longer Marlon Brando,
circa 1953. He's Elvis Presley, a colossal figure in popular music.

77. "Rubberneckin'" (from *From Nashville to Memphis: The Essential '60s Masters*, 1993)

Not to be confused with the song that matches its opening lyric—Joy
Byers's relatively nondescript "Stop, Look and Listen" (which was a
Ricky Nelson cover)—Ben Weisman's 1969 number was integrated as
part of a groovy, multicultural jam session in the urban clinic of Dr. John
Carpenter for Elvis's last fictional feature, the underappreciated misfire
Change of Habit. Weisman's wife, Bunny Warren, helped him out a bit
with its songwriting, so she got a credit. The real magic started, however,
in January 1969, when Elvis cut loose just after tackling "Gentle on My

Mind" in American Sound Studio, during the same session that produced "In the Ghetto." Robert Matthew-Walker described "Rubberneckin'" as urgent, fun, zappy, and infectious. And it is.[115] The guitar work was almost as sharp and frantic as "King Creole."

Drawing shrewdly on Chips Moman's impressive roster of house musicians, "Rubberneckin'" is a respectful show tune with a propulsive tambourine and hand-clap beat—one of those numbers that was uniquely Memphis soul in its essence. Although "Rubberneckin'" was only a B-side, and sounds a little dated now, the cut remains more memorable than several others from those sessions. Perhaps that was because Elvis slaved to perfect "In the Ghetto" while "Rubberneckin'" was done in two takes. He never took it too seriously and consequently had no trouble finding his mojo.

Despite its wavering reputation, "Rubberneckin'" still had legs well after its singer left the building. Paul Oakenfold's surprisingly good 2003 remix came riding on the coattails of JXL's "A Little Less Conversation" and it shows: Oakenfold adds canned drums, amps up the funk, and supercharges the pace. As if to showcase the song's capacity to accommodate more creativity, King Junior released a seven-track "tribute" in 2010. There are myriad unofficial mixes still doing the rounds online. Pity, then, that because "Rubberneckin'" was so associated with its feature film—and not *From Elvis in Memphis*—it is rarely mentioned anywhere near a discussion of the American Sound material. This recording's solid bass work, a spectacular horn section, and bright female backing vocals all demonstrate the competence of a team who created music so neatly orchestrated that Elvis, in effect, reproduced that general sound on stage. Ironically, however, he only performed the song once in concert. His midnight Las Vegas performance on 26 August 1969 got off to a false start and did not seem to smoothly come together. Even a cut-dead ending failed to improve on the studio take. It was as if those Memphis Boys could adapt a song in ways that were hard to replicate.

76. "Tutti Frutti" (from *Elvis Presley*, 1956)

If I'd have been a rock critic (which in fact I became for a while), I might have asked what Little Richard's screams meant in "Tutti Frutti," his most famous song and one of the great happy assaults of the rock 'n' roll revolution in the mid-1950s. One answer might be that the

screams are one of many cues—along with Richard's piled-high pom-
padour, his rough lyrics, the sandpaper in his gospel vocal style, and
his way of almost eating the piano alive while he played—that told us
rock 'n' roll really *was* a revolution.[116]

In his book on the pleasure of popular music, Arved Ashby summed up
the impact of "Tutti Frutti." After noting the song was based on the same
chord progression as the Andrews Sisters' famous 1941 hit "Boogie
Woogie Bugle Boy," he said it could not have been more different. Ashby
added that the less slick and less sophisticated number represented "an
eruption of something black and primal, aimed at the heart of white
America. . . . It's no coincidence that the civil rights movement rose up at
the same time."[117] Ashby's position is part of a critical consensus that
locates "Tutti Frutti" as the first "real" rock 'n' roll record. It's not that
there were no precursors, but rather that they had less impact. Hank
Williams's gleeful "Move It on Over" was new-fangled country; "Rocket
'88'" never escaped the R&B category; "That's All Right" sold well in
particular territories. "Tutti Frutti" brought new energy to the heart of the
mainstream at a time when the United States was just about ready. One
might go further, too. Rather than being the "big bang," like Elvis, or
more accurately his first Sun and RCA recordings, had been, "Tutti Frutti" represents something more like the "alpha and omega": a perfectly
realized, popular example of rock 'n' roll, something that both formed the
template and was never significantly bettered.

Little Richard's rock 'n' roll classic was, of course, like its original
performer, one giant exclamation mark. The exuberant singer was
snapped up by Art Rupe's record label, Specialty. Robert "Bumps"
Blackwell helped shape Richard's act on behalf of the label. It was the
avuncular Blackwell who produced the New Orleans session that Little
Richard recorded in the middle of September 1955. Bumps contacted
Dorothy LaBostrie, asking her to help with a live number that he knew
was so blue it would never get exposed on radio. LaBostrie altered the
lyrics of "Tutti Frutti," helping Richard to make it into the mainstream by
changing his line about "good booty." The Specialty single entered *Billboard*'s R&B chart by the end of November. Early the next year it was
held just off the top slot due to a mighty run by the Platters' "Great
Pretender." Late in January 1956, *Cashbox* magazine still had "Tutti Frutti" as its *Sure Shot* disc of the week: a record that dealers across the nation
knew was selling in quantity.

In the early 1950s, the pop records market was highly lucrative. The R&B market was about a tenth the size; tiny and regional in comparison. Rock 'n' roll, at best, almost doubled the sales of pop, creating a new, winning formula. After "Tutti Frutti" appeared, acts in the rock 'n' roll bracket began covering it from all directions. One early take came from a veteran swing-band leader on MGM Records. Art Mooney first topped the charts just under a decade earlier with "I'm Looking over a Four Leaf Clover." For his version of "Tutti Frutti," Mooney used "Ocie" Smith as lead vocalist.[118] Born three years before Elvis, Ocie was a capable African American singer. Though he went on to have a number two hit in 1968 for Columbia with "Little Green Apples," the MGM version of "Tutti Frutti" failed to come close to Little Richard's success.[119] Pat Boone's staid version on Dot Records was a more significant contender. Boone's cover went gold, not because it had any of the vitality expressed in Richard's original but because white radio stations found it acceptable. It was boosted even further by Boone's 1957 television show. Elvis had a copy of the Dot single in his own record collection.[120]

When he toured with the song, Little Richard outwitted his imitators. He instructed drummer Charles Connor to beef up the percussion. For Richard's original recording, the studio drummer Earl Palmer played with a single backbeat. Connor made the bass drum much heavier; in effect, he gave "Tutti Frutti" a prototypical disco beat. Those who merely copied the recorded version couldn't keep up. Richard also answered back by going up tempo and recording "Long Tall Sally." Once he'd finished it in the studio, he turned to Bumps and said, "Let's see Pat Boone get his mouth together to do *this* song."[121] Ironically, although "Long Tall Sally" sold half a million copies by March for Richard and boosted sales of his "Tutti Frutti" up to the million mark, Pat Boone repeated his previous trick with a bland cover that sold more than a million.

In a sense, "Tutti Frutti" came too soon. The world was not quite ready for Little Richard. Bumps Blackwell recalled his surprise on encountering the exuberant singer: "His hair was processed a foot high over his head. His shirt was so loud it looked as though he had drunk raspberry juice, cherryade, malt, and greens, and then thrown up all over himself."[122] It is hardly surprising that until rock 'n' roll was a known commodity, television studios refused to book a performer who was both African American and outrageously camp.[123] Little Richard's live performances and recordings were incendiary. National audiences never got a full look at him until the end of 1956, however, when he appeared on celluloid. Richard missed out on the soundtrack for Pandro Berman's 1955 social issue picture, *Blackboard Jungle*, and Sam Katzman's 1956 teen exploitation flick, *Rock around the Clock*. The latter's sequel, *Don't Knock the Rock*, at last featured Richard's own performance of "Tutti Frutti." Hollywood veteran Frank Tashlin's energetic *The Girl Can't Help It* contained more of his songs, including the title track. Several months before these cinematic releases, it was Elvis Presley who performed "Tutti Frutti" for national television audiences. On an episode of the Dorsey Brothers' *Stage Show* from 4 February 1956—his second-ever guest slot—Elvis launched into "Baby Let's Play House" and "Tutti Frutti." "Heartbreak Hotel" had been released just over a week before, but Elvis sought instead to cover a song he had sung on *Louisiana Hayride* seven weeks earlier. [124]

The Tuesday before his *Stage Show* appearance, in the middle of a three-day New York session in which storming covers of songs by Carl Perkins and Lloyd Price were also captured, Elvis recorded a version of "Tutti Frutti." It was the Memphis singer himself who suggested including Little Richard's number; he thought the material offered by Steve Sholes and Hill & Range was largely below par. [125] All the ingredients are there: DJ Fontana's drumming is wonderfully on point; Scotty hangs back, then struts in the solo; and Elvis careers through the middle. RCA's mistake was recording a gospel R&B number in a kind of jumped-up, proto-rock style. Where Little Richard had been insanely raucous and raw, Elvis is slicker but, for all that, still self-consciously frantic. Unfortunately, however, Shorty Long's playing—if there at all—cannot be heard in comparison to the pounding, jive-inducing centerpiece piano vamp that sets Little Richard's performance on fire. Had history been different and "Tutti Frutti" come out during the Sun years, Elvis's studio cover might have been sharper. For him, "Tutti Frutti" was primarily a live number.

On the day of Elvis's first Dorsey Brothers' performance, Little Richard's single was nudging *Cashbox*'s top twenty. At that moment, "Heartbreak Hotel" was less known. Television viewers had already begun to understand Elvis's style. Choosing a fast, R&B crossover number that pop fans could recognize allowed him to work the audience with unrivaled intensity. After a dynamic version of "Baby Let's Play House," Elvis straightened up, saying, "Thank you, ladies and gentlemen. And now a little song that really tells a story. It really makes lots of sense." Sedately clearing his throat, he added, "And it goes a little something like this." Scotty is visible on the footage, eagerly looking over Elvis's right shoulder, ready to take up any cue. Suddenly, the singer launches in. No number ahead of "Tutti Frutti" on the *Cashbox* chart—including Bill Haley's "See You Later Alligator"—could have lent itself to such a fast country thrill ride. It was no wonder that Elvis's trio returned to it on a later *Stage Show* appearance. He kept the song in his live set for weeks and then revisited it in August. By that point, Pat Boone's cover was riding high, so RCA released Elvis's version as the B-side to "Blue Suede Shoes." With just one exception, after that summer, Elvis's interest in "Tutti Frutti" was all over. [126]

At the end of June 1974, when he was playing Kansas City, Missouri, in customary style, Elvis greeted his audience by joking around. He had taken to introducing himself as other people. On that day he said, "Good evening, ladies and gentlemen. My name is Little Richard. It's a pleasure to be here." [127] Despite emerging on television singing "Tutti Frutti," Elvis Presley had, ironically, ignored the number for many years. Little Richard's cinematic appearances had so indelibly associated *him* with the song that Elvis had abandoned the territory by 1957. Notwithstanding his own special versatility, it was as if Elvis Presley had admitted this was one performance he could not better.

75. "Little Sister" (from *Elvis' Golden Records, Volume 3*, 1963)

What people know about Elvis is that he never—except for briefly touching down at Prestwick Airport in Scotland on his way home from the army—came to the United Kingdom, despite plenty of fan support. In April 2008, London theater impresario Bill Kenwright caused a stir when he announced that his friend, the dazzling song-and-dance man Tommy Steele, had accompanied Elvis on a secret day trip around London. Had Elvis popped across to England back in 1958 during his tour of duty? Steele said he had been sworn to secrecy, in effect corroborating Kenwright's story. Memphis Mafia member Lamar Fike flatly denied Kenwright's claim, saying that *he* had visited London instead. Fike added, "On the Paris trip they did get to meet some Brits . . . a troupe of English dancing girls from a Paris nightclub they went to, who spent an evening with the guys in El's hotel suite playing Scrabble and discussing Parisian architecture."[128] Did these dancing girls really discuss Parisian architecture when they met the world's biggest male sex symbol?[129] Like the young ladies' honor, Elvis's mooted trip to London remains shrouded in mystery. What is known is that Lamar Fike and Freddy Bienstock definitely went to England in 1959, scouting out songwriting talent.[130]

Doc Pomus began his career as a blues performer but later realized that his future lay in songwriting. When he teamed up with Mort Shuman, the pair found they worked well together; the former mostly writing lyrics while Shuman added melody. They became a powerhouse team, almost on a par with their mentors and role models Leiber and Stoller. At one time they had eight hits on the national charts. Elvis rapidly came to the duo's attention when he emerged in the mid-1950s. Pomus intuitively understood Presley's style. He said, "It was the first time that I had ever seen a white singer who didn't sound like he was imitating a black singer but sounded like he was doing it the way a black singer would do it."[131] To give emphasis, he added, "He sounded completely natural."[132] Shuman also recalled, "I loved what Elvis was doing back in the early days because he seemed so anti-establishment and I was anti-everything."[133] The two were both thrilled to work with Elvis Presley, since, as Pomus put it, "He was an original. . . . He always put something in the song that maybe you never heard. . . . He always put himself in them and he was always the song plus."[134]

After three different versions of their song "Teenager in Love" rode into Britain's top thirty chart in the summer of 1959, Pomus and Shuman visited the country. Jack Good courted the pair and asked them to help with a television show devoted to their music. With encouragement from publishers the Aberbachs, they landed in London on 28 September. As a successful producer, Good already had a reputation for pop television with the BBC series *Six-Five Special* and ITV successor *Oh Boy!* He wanted his new ITV show *Boy Meets Girls* to promote Pomus and Shuman's compositions. His special, which went out less than a month later, featured the talents of Marty Wilde and the Vernons Girls. The Brooklyn-based pair's meeting with Hill & Range was also productive: Fike passed a demo of "A Mess of Blues" along to Elvis, who recorded the song within days of his return from Germany.

Despite claims that Elvis "died" when he went in the army, 1960 was a year of monumental highs. There was the Sinatra special, *Elvis Is Back!*, "It's Now or Never," (arguably) the film *GI Blues*, and *His Hand in Mine*.

In comparison, the first half of 1961 was dogged by a choice of material that seemed mediocre in both musical and commercial terms. Things changed with the success of *Blue Hawaii* and its soundtrack later in the year. In the summer, Elvis recorded several songs by Pomus and Shuman. The pair wrote "Little Sister" in the Hotel Roosevelt, across the street from Hollywood's most famous movie house, Grauman's Chinese Theatre. Bobby Vee and Bobby Darin both rejected the song. Then Elvis's publishers contacted the duo looking for material, and it was recorded toward the end of June. *Wild in the Country* was released days before the session. Elvis never made it to the film's Memphis premiere. The two-day studio engagement was relaxed because RCA only wanted two sides for a single. Three of the other four songs they recorded in Studio B were Pomus and Shuman compositions. Elvis completely reimagined "Little Sister" when he recorded it. The version that Shuman had written was much faster and had a different arrangement. Scotty added acoustic accompaniment. Using a Fender Jazz Master to achieve a funky sound, Hank "Sugarfoot" Garland, meanwhile, took the lead.

Garland got his nickname after he wrote and played guitar as a youth on Red Foley's 1950 Decca recording "Sugarfoot Rag." Around that time he was credited on several Decca, then Dot, releases. A decade later, though, Duane Eddy was king of the guitar instrumental. By including an excerpt of his recent hit "Shazam" in its introduction, "Little Sister" gives a nod to his sassy style.

Engineer Bill Porter said they'd recorded a classic and he was right. The song took only four takes to perfect—though, just in case, seven more were captured in the studio.

Backed with "(Marie's the Name) His Latest Flame," "Little Sister" topped the charts in the United Kingdom and reached number five in the United States. Recently reviewing the single, Jake Otnes called it a "two-headed monster," adding, "'Little Sister' was one of the harder rocking cuts he made in the early '60s, but gone were the days of reckless abandon. . . . This record is sleeker, punchier, and more groove-based than the early rock 'n' rollers."[135] Perhaps because of its bite, Elvis also added "Little Sister" to some of his live shows, especially around 1972 and 1977. Very occasionally, he cut it together with the Beatles' "Get Back," as if to add even more punch.[136] Pomus and Shuman, meanwhile, went on to contribute "Viva Las Vegas" to Elvis's career.[137]

74. "Run On" (from *How Great Thou Art*, 1967)

In the 1950s and 1960s, many popular artists recorded Christmas albums. From *Perry Como Sings Merry Christmas Music* in 1956 to *The Dean Martin Christmas Album* a decade later, the titles were self-explanatory. Fewer attempts were made by any stars to release Easter records. If it were not for the deep faith that inspired him to find the soul of the Christian message inside each song, Elvis's occasional offerings in this category might have seemed like decidedly secular cash-ins. He desperately wanted to convert the masses. What he created was Christian music as silky smooth as it was sincere. Working in the style of groups like the Swan Silvertones, he was, in a sense, a true son of the gospel quartet tradition: a spectacular performer who demonstrated the shape of his faith by combining sacred music with show business sophistication.

Late in May 1966, Elvis worked in the studio on one of his best-loved gospel albums, *How Great Thou Art*. Robert Matthew-Walker described "Run On," the first song recorded, as "not particularly memorable."[138] It's likely, however, that he intended the judgment primarily in a comparative sense: The song was recorded at the same session as the truly astounding "How Great Thou Art." Nevertheless, "Run On" is worthy of its own attention. The popular hymn had already been recorded by other groups. In the mid-1930s, tenor Bill Landford became a member of the Golden Gate Quartet: four African American signers who adopted the jubilee style and had great success. Just before the quartet signed to Columbia Records' subsidiary Okeh, Landford left in 1939 to form the Southern Sons. Five years later, he joined the Selah Jubilee Singers. By the end of the 1940s, Landford led his own Columbia Records' gospel outfit called the Landfordaires. One of the songs they released was an old folk tune that went under the name of "Run On for a Long Time," "Run On," or sometimes "God's Gonna Cut You Down."

The Landfordaires 1943 version of "Run On" was jaunty and breezy and sounded almost like Canned Heat.[139] Four years later, Landford's former group, the Golden Gate Quartet, also released their own brisk version for Columbia Records. It was probably this version that inspired Elvis.[140] In the same year that Presley was taking the world by storm as a new RCA signing, Odetta Holmes—already an emergent voice of the civil rights movement—also released a voice-only version on her first solo album for the folk label Tradition Records, *Odetta Sings Ballads and*

Blues. Holmes's rendition is stark, as one might expect, but all the way through to its righteous ending, there are urgent and unpredictable moments.

Elvis was credited with the particular arrangement of his version of "Run On." One of the motivations for sacred music was that Hill & Range could give traditional tunes new lyrics and then claim songwriting revenue. Felton Jarvis, who had just joined Elvis's team in Nashville as his next RCA house producer, even encouraged the band to swing during later takes. Although comparatively sedate, the resulting musical backing had minor percussive and rhythmic echoes of "Viva Las Vegas," the show tune committed to tape three years earlier in Radio Recorders. Encouraged by the way the Imperials had taken over so seamlessly from the Jordanaires, for "Run On," Elvis was in top form. His voice effortlessly tap-danced its way through the cautionary gospel tale, suggesting a singer who was gently giddy, inadvertently shifting from staid sermon to pure cabaret.

73. "Working on the Building" (from *His Hand in Mine*, 1960)

Early in March 1960, Elvis left Germany, Priscilla, and what *Life* magazine called "hordes of palpitating Fräuleins" when his army tour of duty came to its end.[141] Two weeks before Norman Taurog's romcom *GI Blues* hit cinemas across America, the fans received another treat, when, in November, RCA released Elvis's first gospel album, *His Hand in Mine*. Side two was rounded out with a short but spirited rendition of Winifred Hoyle and Lillian Bowles's "Working on the Building."[142] Its biblical origins lay in the New Testament verse: "According to the grace of God which is given unto me, as a wise master builder, I have laid the foundation, and another buildeth thereon."[143] Quite how such inspiration was adapted for the gospel lexicon is open to question. "Working on the Building" is based on the long-running practice of singing in the round. It has a wonderful, lilting feel. One version became a regular hymn in Holiness (Pentecostal) churches.

BB King said he borrowed the song from church and added it to his repertoire when he worked the streets in 1959. On the Crown LP *BB King Sings Spirituals*, he delivered a storming blues gospel interpretation, complete with a hand-clap intro and funky organ backing. Elvis's Nashville recording was something else. Observing the singer's ambition to join a gospel quartet, Ernst Jørgensen noted, "As the song progressed Elvis seemed to relish stepping from the solo spot to become part of the group performance, as he had so desperately wanted to do back in 1953."[144] Instrumental backing on the Presley version still sounds distinctly *farmyard*, like some sprightly country ditty. When Elvis comes in, he puts the track right back on course; arriving quietly, confidently, and smoothly—like some wonderfully smoky jazz man—saturating the number with his silky, understated vocals. As a spirited backing singer, he gives the song lift, then rises to the occasion, adding to the growing chorus of voices and instruments.

Gordon Stoker claimed that he reminded Elvis of "Working on the Building" at the sessions for *His Hand in Mine*. Stoker joined the Jordanaires in 1949, the same year as the group secured its place on the *Grand Ole Opry*. Capitol's standard 10-inch shellac pressing of "Working on the Building" became a hit the following year. Though a little slower than Presley's later take, this 1950 version was swinging, rousing, and alive with the group's love of harmony. Not long after, Brother Joe May, the dynamic African American "Thunderbolt of the Midwest" who was born just over forty miles east of Memphis in a little town called Macon, Tennessee, recorded a new version with the Sallie Martin Singers. May's fabulous a cappella R&B performance of "Working on the Building" came out on Art Rupe's Los Angeles label, Specialty Records.[145] During his gospel renditions, the "Thunderbolt" brimmed with what Cornel West calls *black prophetic fire*.[146] His magnificent, compelling vocals were on par with the gospel sermons of Aretha Franklin's father, the Reverend C. L. Franklin. Indeed, "Thunderbolt" approached the screaming intensity of Archie Brownlee, the highly charismatic leader of the Five Blind Boys of Mississippi. Elvis may well have known about Brother Joe May's version because the beginnings of both their takes shared a certain understatement. There were, however, much earlier interpretations of "Working on the Building" and those likely played a bigger role in his 1960 arrangement. To decipher the mystery of the Presley rendition, it is necessary to travel back before the 1950s.

Discussing "Working on the Building," the encyclopedia writer Adam Victor speculated, "Elvis likely first heard this song at his mother's knee—her favourite group the Blackwood Brothers recorded it when Elvis was just two."[147] The claim, however, is hard to substantiate. It seems more solid that Elvis had more than one Blackwood Brothers' RCA Victor record in his collection, including their 1954 single "His Hand in Mine."[148] The Tuskegee Quartet has been mooted as recording an early rendition of "Working on the Building." Firm evidence shows that in 1934 the Carter Family released a similar version of the song in typical, old-time country style. It repeated the title and chorus lyrics but was called "I'm Working on a Building." The song was a prototype and unique too in many ways.[149] In the summer of 1936, the Heavenly Gospel Singers pursued what was perhaps the first, clear spiritual take of "Working on the Building" for release on Bluebird Records. Several black gospel groups then claimed Hoyle and Bowles's song in the 1940s. It was recorded by the Five Blind Boys of Mississippi for Coleman Records, the Swan Silvertones for King, the Soul Stirrers on Aladdin, and the Soul Comforters for De Luxe. These versions evidently inspired Elvis's delivery. He drew together the snappy style of black gospel singing with a fresh, country backing. Though Stoker *reminded* Elvis Presley of "Working on the Building" in 1960, it appears likely that the singer was already keen.

72. "Don't Cry Daddy" (from *Worldwide 50 Gold Award Hits*, 1970)

On 9 June 1972, to mark Elvis's three-day run of concerts at Madison Square Garden, the Colonel staged a press conference. America was several years into its messy and protracted war with Vietnam. A few years earlier, Priscilla's father had entered the theater of operations, and Elvis gave him a Colt pistol for self-defense.[150] Due to an accident, Jerry Schilling narrowly missed being called up. He said he would have gone, not happily, but because he felt that he had no choice. Others around Elvis were directly against the war. Bass player Jerry Scheff, for instance, played at peace events. He attended three antiwar rallies, including one at Century Plaza Hotel in Los Angeles where things turned violent. The Madison Square Garden press conference started well, with one admirer shouting, "I love you" and Elvis responding, "Thank you, dear. I love you too."[151] Soon, however, the star encountered a tricky question on a military theme.

Hoping for a topical quote, one Madison Square Garden journalist asked, "Mr. Presley, as you've mentioned your time in the service, what is your opinion of war protesters, and would you today refuse to be drafted?"[152] The Swedish Elvis enthusiast Bruno Tillander has since claimed that his hero supported the Vietnam War. Tillander's main evidence seemed to be that Presley liked John Wayne in the 1968 action film *The Green Berets*.[153] What Elvis actually replied was, "Honey, I'd just sooner keep my own personal views about that to myself 'cause I'm just an entertainer and I'd rather not say."[154] The answer was in itself political. It can be taken to mean that either he did not want to speak at all, or, as a musician, he wanted his actions to speak for him. Anyone who wanted Elvis to be Bob Dylan might have taken that as a failure of nerve. There are, however, other perspectives. One is that songs like "If I Can Dream" indicate Elvis longed for an end to armed conflict, but he was in effect hamstrung. After all, he had fulfilled his army service with a sense of patriotism and duty. Being a peacetime soldier was part of his public image; his films had shown him in uniform. He had served his country in Germany, helped fund a memorial for the USS *Arizona*, and visited Richard Nixon looking for a Federal Bureau of Narcotics badge. It might have seemed a bit hypocritical now to start blaming the government. Another perspective is that Elvis constantly refused to draw lines. Instead, he pursued a kind of inclusivity in which entertainment could encompass both those who were for and those who were against the conflict, and which also—by offering hope and unity—could start to heal the trauma of a divided nation.

Someone who took a protest-orientated stance to the violence in society was the songwriter Mac Davis. He wrote a number called "The Politician" as a direct attack on the Nixon administration. A few months after Elvis's Madison Square Garden dates, Lou Rawls released an atmospheric soul version as the B-side to his MGM single "Walk On In." "Don't Cry Daddy" reflected another of Mac Davis's humanitarian stirrings. Like many other Americans in the late 1960s, Davis was distraught over the images of carnage that were beamed in nightly news bulletins from Vietnam through his domestic cathode ray tube. His young son saw that he was evidently upset one night. To console him, Mac's boy said a reassuring phrase that eventually became the song title. Davis appreciated his son's gesture and realized that his words could be set to music, reformulated in a melodrama centered on the heartbreak of a departed mother. Elvis loved "Don't Cry Daddy" when Davis played it to him, saying that it made him think of his own mother, Gladys. When Chips Moman requested country material, the songwriter sealed the deal by sending it over.[155] With the help of house arrangers Glen Spreen and Mike Leech, Elvis recorded the song at American Sound in January 1969. RCA released the single the following winter. "Don't Cry Daddy" hit a nerve. It never actually reveals why the boy's mother has gone; the song could, in effect, be a widower's lament. Rapidly escalating divorce rates, however, helped give Mac's number its charge. Elvis's new single lodged itself inside the top ten and sold more than a million copies. With pleading lyrics expressed from the perspective of an innocent child, Davis's song ruthlessly tugs at the heartstrings.

When Elvis sung otherwise maudlin ballads, they could transcend their excesses of sentimentality and become statements so simple that they were genuine again. Such was the case with "Don't Cry Daddy." Especially as his daughter, Lisa Marie, presented her own digital duet version at the Mid-South Coliseum in 1997, it is tempting to read the song as a reflection of Elvis Presley's divorce. However, "Don't Cry Daddy" was recorded nearly three years before he separated and Elvis never exploited the association. Though "Don't Cry Daddy" appeared in his early 1970 live set, with the exception of a dinner show on 13 August, it was dropped thereafter.

A true *fleur du mal* from a turbulent era.

71. "Faded Love" (from *Elvis Country (I'm 10,000 Years Old)*, 1971)

"Faded Love" was a signature song for Bob Wills and the Texas Playboys, who released it as a single on MGM in 1950, scoring a top ten hit on *Billboard*'s country chart. By that point, Wills was in his mid-fifties. In a recording career that stretched back more than fifteen years, he released a string of singles with the Texas Playboys for Vocalion, Okeh, and Columbia. Wills's particular blend of music combined elements of pop, jazz, blues, and comedy within the sphere of country. His group entertained live audiences before the end of World War II with a special, up-tempo fiddle style called Western Swing.[156] After the war, Wills scored several country number ones, including "Sugar Moon" and "New Spanish Two Step." "Faded Love" was a family affair; Wills co-wrote it with his father, John. His brother Billy provided the lyrics. The melody was taken from Benjamin Hanby's mid-nineteenth-century tune "Darling Nelly Gray." Hanby was musically talented—a white abolitionist who came up with the number to dramatize the plight of a runaway slave in Kentucky whose beloved had been taken to Georgia while he toiled in the fields. By the advent of recording, the song was already a staple; artists across a range of genres soon recorded it. The Romanian-born Jewish opera soprano Alma Gluck offered a mannered yet strangely celestial version released in 1917 on Victor's Victrola imprint. Twenty years later, joined by the Mills Brothers, Louis Armstrong recorded a relaxed, jazzy, nostalgic interpretation and his label Decca released it. The effortlessly smooth artist prefaced his solo by saying, "Now, boys, what do you think of this?"

By rewriting "Darling Nelly Gray" as "Faded Love," Wills created a sentimental and comparatively "private" offering: an old-time country singer's wonderfully wistful, introspective monologue. Rounding it out with sweet, rustic fiddle, he turned a socially conscious narrative song into a country-style lament. Compared to Elvis's interpretation, the approach was genteel. Covers that came later included a performance by the golden-voiced Dottie West, who presented it in 1968 as a down-tempo, traditional country number for RCA. Conway Twitty, who was also an MGM artist like Wills, recorded a jaunty, nearly alpine version the next year, completely ignoring the point of Wills's original.

Elvis reinvented "Faded Love" as a punchy, flamboyant, rock cabaret tune. He left his mark on the song during a five-night bout in the studio that took place early in June 1970. The mammoth session began with "Twenty Days and Twenty Nights" and ended with "Patch It Up." Much of the material became part of *That's the Way It Is*, *Love Letters from Elvis*, or *Elvis Country*. "Faded Love" was edited down and appeared on the latter LP. Elvis hardly ever performed it in a live setting. When he did, the enchanting "Can't Help Falling in Love" usually preceded it.

The first live version of "Faded Love" available comes from a Las Vegas dinner show, one day after Valentine's Day in 1973, performed just before Elvis sang "I'm So Lonesome I Could Cry" for the last time on stage. Unfortunately, the star had the flu at the time and was working against his doctor's advice. The results were less than premium. A better take came together three months later when he played the Sahara in Lake Tahoe. [157] After that, Elvis hardly played the song at all.

Where Wills's "Faded Love" is plaintive and introspective, Elvis's version—as if overcompensating for the heartbreaking loss of his departed lover—is brimming with bravura. An urgent kernel of emotion breaks to the surface when his voice starts yearning with desperation partway through. "Faded Love" is far from being Elvis's best tune, but it still showcases his ability to express emotions in ways that were simultaneously more personal, modern, flexible, and sincere than the heavily genre-marked stylings of traditional country music.

70. "Viva Las Vegas" (from *Viva Las Vegas*, 2007)

It's easy to pretend that Elvis's career was simply a matter of new plateaus of triumph. Though he often gave more than his all, there were inevitably both peaks and troughs—moments of great achievement, times of indifference, phases of desperation and despair. Contrary to popular belief, Elvis had a mixed time on the UK singles chart. His 1956 debut, "Heartbreak Hotel," took seven weeks to near the top slot, held off by Pat Boone's sedate "I'll Be Home." "Hound Dog" fared marginally better, taking six weeks to reach the same place and lingering there for three weeks rather than two, this time held off by Frankie Laine's dramatic "A Woman in Love." "All Shook Up" hit the top after three weeks and stayed there for six. It was Elvis's eleventh UK release and his first number one single. He managed it again with "Jailhouse Rock" late in January 1958, but that was ten records later. From November 1960 to July 1963, Elvis hit a purple patch, scoring ten number ones in thirteen releases.

The picture on the other side of the Atlantic was not so different. Doc Pomus and Mort Shuman's famous movie title track "Viva Las Vegas" was recorded in Hollywood during the summer of 1963. When RCA released it in March 1964, however, Elvis's previous two releases had failed to make the U.S. top ten. Backed with Ray Charles's "What'd I Say," "Viva Las Vegas" only just broke the top twenty. Part of the issue was that Elvis had been forced to inadvertently compete with himself. Two years earlier, "Suspicion" was released in the United States on side two of Elvis's *Pot Luck* LP. An upcoming singer called Terry Stafford cut a cover version that was picked up by Crusader Records. It stormed the *Billboard* Hot 100. To capitalize, RCA rush-released Elvis's take as a single backed with "Kiss Me Quick." "Viva Las Vegas" was promoted only twelve days later, initially as a scout record offered before the release of its movie. The single had to work its magic in isolation, without any visual accompaniment to fix it in the minds of listeners. What was worse, RCA also released an EP called *Viva Las Vegas* featuring other tracks from the movie but without the title song actually included. In the event, the new single's famous A-side failed to score as high as its B-side: "What'd I Say" beat "Viva Las Vegas" but failed to make the top twenty of *Billboard*'s Hot 100.

Albert Hand, who led the Official Elvis Presley Fan Club of Great Britain back then, lamented in its publication *Elvis Monthly*:

> Brothers and sisters . . . I've got news for you. After the "Viva Las Vegas" tragedy, lo and behold I make another prophecy. The subsequent release, "Kissin' Cousins," will suffer the same horrible fate that I think "Las Vegas" is a-going to get. Oblivion.[158]

Sensing the first stirrings of the British Invasion up ahead, Hand worried that Elvis's musical style was starting to sound comparatively obsolete. In a sense he was right. Bolting ahead of "Viva Las Vegas" in the UK charts were the Swinging Blue Jeans, the Dave Clark Five, the Hollies, and, mightiest of all, the dreaded Beatles. Elvis struggled on the UK charts after that, hitting the top slot only twice more in his lifetime: "Crying in the Chapel" in 1965 and "The Wonder of You" in 1970.

Part of the problem with "Viva Las Vegas" was that some considered it hard to dance to or sing along with; lightweight, chart fodder without much soul. Nevertheless, not all *Elvis Monthly* readers shared Albert Hand's view. A letter published in the same issue implied he was betraying his hero and noted that "Viva Las Vegas" had received rave reviews in *Record Mirror*, *Disc*, the *New Musical Express*, and British daily newspapers. Nevertheless, according to Lamar Fike, "Elvis didn't think it was a great song at the time."[159] Over the years, however, many entries in the Presley catalog have been recategorized. According to music writer Dylan Jones, "Viva Las Vegas" was "unintentionally ironic."[160] It told audiences what they already knew about the fast pace of the desert resort, but "as the city itself becomes more preposterous, so the song becomes more authentic."[161] "Viva Las Vegas" has therefore graduated from "medium cool" to "cult classic."

With its frenetic, Latin, urban beat, the title track for Elvis's glittering movie still seems as fizzy and vivacious as Ann-Margret when she played Rusty Martin on screen. In the monumental three-volume *Ultimate Elvis* anthology, Erik Lorentzen and his co-writers complain that the Colonel never allowed *Viva Las Vegas* a soundtrack LP, and that the film took so long in post-production that it was partially eclipsed by the British Invasion (though it trumped *A Hard Day's Night* at the U.S. box office). Of the recording, they also note, "Take one was extraordinary for having such a different arrangement from the final release. Sounding like an acoustic, 'unplugged' version, with a Spanish guitar influence, it was quite different from the well-known record release version."[162] They have it about right; with backing almost like "Gentle on My Mind," take one sounds like it was recorded one late evening around the campfire in some forgotten Western. The second take is more characteristically frenetic, as Elvis was when he sold the song in the film itself. It appears that, despite his triumphant return to Las Vegas in 1969, however, Presley never played more than a snatch of "Viva Las Vegas" live in the city.[163] What did happen, though, was that RCA rereleased the track on a four-disc LP compilation, *Worldwide 50 Gold Hits, Vol. 1*. While it contained one or two curios, including "Kissin' Cousins"—and at least one excerpt from the historic, spoken-word *Elvis Sales* EP—the bulk of the box set was solid gold. It offered an essential compendium of 1950s and 1960s hits, placing "Viva Las Vegas" back where it belonged, as a gem in Presley's "signature" catalog.

69. "Wearin' That Loved On Look" (from *From Elvis in Memphis*, 1969)

Elvis Presley left behind a multifaceted music catalog. On the surface are the tasty morsels that absolutely everyone knows: songs like "Always on My Mind" and "Love Me Tender." Just below that are about another thirty "signature" songs—things like "The Wonder of You" and "Surrender." Yet Elvis honed so many more jewels. "Wearin' That Loved On Look" was the third song he recorded at American Sound Studio on his first visit in January 1969. In many ways, it was an American Sound classic. From its dramatic intro to frisky fade, the song effortlessly integrated several strands of American music, including rock, soul, and a touch of funk and gospel. There were some cheeky "shoop shoops" too—vocalizations already associated, of course, with female performers. Betty Everett, for instance, topped the charts with "The Shoop Shoop Song (It's in His Kiss)" back in 1964—a girl group classic if ever there was one.

The conduit for "Wearing That Loved On Look" was a member of Elvis's own retinue, the Memphis Mafia. When the singer entered Chips

Moman's American Sound Studio early in 1969, Lamar Fike brought some songs to his attention that included "Kentucky Rain" and the wonderfully feisty "Wearin' That Loved On Look." Dallas Frazier and A. L. "Doodle" Owens penned the number. Frazier, who was just thirty years old, had established his reputation as a country artist on Capitol Records a little earlier with the quirky and dramatic "Elvira."[164] When Ken Sharp asked him about "Wearin' That Loved On Look," he positioned it as an R&B number, saying, "I played a trumpet as a kid and I had a flair for the blues. I loved the old rhythm and blues like Big Joe Turner with 'Shake, Rattle and Roll,' those old classics."[165]

Elvis struggled with a throat infection when he recorded Frazier and Owens's tale of female infidelity. On take three, he blew the introduction and laughed it off, ad-libbing the chorus of his 1968 single "A Little Less Conversation" before starting again. By take twelve, he said, "If we get one good [take] on the first part, we'd better keep it."[166] He need not have worried. "Wearin' That Loved On Look" is near perfect, a glorious combination of contributions that came together in the moment: Frazier's off-edge lyrics, Chips Moman's production, Bobby Emmons's astute organ work, Reggie Young's funky guitar, the wonderful gospel breakdown. Elvis's intense vocals really hold the song together. In the introduction, he sounds so raw and infuriated; it's almost like he lassoes his errant lover. He never lets up, laying into his lines with an urgent ferocity every step of the way. Dallas Frazier once explained, "I really liked Elvis' version of 'Wearin' That Loved On Look.' He hooked it, he really did. . . . Elvis had that magic spark. He didn't have to drum it up. It was in him."[167] It is amazing, then, that "Wearin' That Loved On Look" is not better known outside of fan circles.

68. "Good Rockin' Tonight" (from *A Date with Elvis*, 1959)

Elvis, when he played his guitar standing up, he'd just come up on the balls of his feet, and with the big breeches back then—big pants leg—when he'd do that and playing, well the things would start shaking. That's what the little girls started [enjoying]; they thought he was doing that on purpose. When he came off stage he said, "What did I do? What's going on?" Me and Bill started laughing. "Well," we said, "when you started shaking your legs they started screaming." He said,

"I wasn't doing anything on purpose," which was true, but he was a fast learner.[168]

"Good Rockin' Tonight" deserves a central place in the canon because—more so than "That's All Right"—this rockabilly classic introduced Elvis Presley to the world. Scotty Moore had fun recalling an innocent moment from the summer of 1954 when Elvis played two shows in a day at Memphis's four-thousand-capacity version of the Hollywood Bowl, the Overton Park Shell. During the afternoon set, Presley only sung ballads and did not fully win the crowd over. In the evening, he played his local hit and more up-tempo numbers, shaking his leg in time to the music.[169] Two years later, the singer recalled, "I was scared stiff. And it was my first big appearance in front of an audience."[170] At that point, Elvis's leg shaking was a way to disarm anxiety arising from his emergent position as a star. Although he grew confident as a tease in his stage role, his slight nervousness worked as an element that positively informed his sexual chemistry. When he returned to the Overton Park Shell in 1955 for Bob Neal's eighth annual Country Music Jamboree, however, the song he used to prompt a wild audience response was "Good Rockin' Tonight." Country singer Webb Pierce, who was on the same bill, knew he had been trumped. All he could say was "Sonofabitch!"[171] The number showed that Elvis could be sexy and dangerous, edgy and fun, all at once. As Peter Carlin said, Elvis "not only looked like a sexed-up riot, but sounded like one too."[172]

Years before Elvis's Sun release, Roy Brown, an ex-boxer from New Orleans, established himself as a successful R&B artist. His music took a special form: jump blues infused by gospel swing. Brown recalled:

> Cecil Gant was at the Dew Drop Inn and Wynonie Harris was appearing at Foster's Rainbow Room. . . . He was flamboyant, he was a good looking guy, very brash. He was good and he knew it. He just took charge, I liked the style. Anyway, when I was in New Orleans I had one suit and there was no bottom in my shoes, I had cardboard. I didn't even have a bus fare to the club. So I wrote "Good Rockin' Tonight" on a piece of brown paper bag, something you might buy at the grocery store, you put onions in, and I wrote out "Good Rockin' Tonight" on this brown paper sack and I took it to Wynonie Harris.[173]

Wynonie Harris was, despite his rather country-sounding name, a magnificently slick R&B singer. When he saw Brown coming, he asked the amateur to stop bothering him before he had even heard the composition. Brown got over the rejection and started performing his own song to scout label attention. On the strength of it, he was picked up by De Luxe Records. When the single took off in 1947, Harris took note and decided that he would cover "Good Rockin' Tonight." The next year his jazzy and very swinging version became a much bigger R&B hit than Brown's release.

One of Brown's first follow-up releases was called "Mighty, Mighty Man."[174] De Luxe put it out in 1948 as a shellac pressing. The label lost its legal foundation after Syd Nathan gained a controlling stake. Brown was eventually transferred to Nathan's talent roster at King Records. In January 1953, a King Records single called "Hurry Hurry Baby" was credited to "Roy Brown and his Mighty-Mighty Men." In mid-September of the following year, when the Blue Moon Boys recorded "Good Rockin' Tonight" down on Union Avenue, Elvis included the "Mighty Man" phrase. Sam Phillips chose "Good Rockin' Tonight" as an R&B-style A-side for the group's second single which was released on 25 September.

Talking about his faster music, Elvis said to one journalist in 1956:

> The colored folks been singing it and playing it just like I'm doing now, man, for more years than I know. They played it like that in their shanties and in their juke joints and nobody paid it no mind 'til I goosed it up. I got it from them.[175]

This chimed with Brown's own view. After he found out that his song had been covered by a white boy, Brown later recalled: "Elvis was singing this song with a hillbilly band but he never did sell because he hadn't become Elvis as yet, you know."[176] For *Blues Unlimited* magazine, in 1977, Brown expanded his thesis:

> What really happened, when these guys got on television, and do all these dances they had copied us from guys like the Drifters, the Little Richards but we had never gotten the chance to perform before the white kids and they thought all these guys, the Elvis Presleys, were original with that stuff. They weren't original. We'd been doing that stuff for years.[177]

Regarding segregation and prejudice in the media, Brown had it about right. He also had a rough time fighting for his rights and royalties in the early 1950s. However, there was a key difference between the R&B versions of "Good Rockin' Tonight" and Elvis's take. As *Billboard* explained in its Spotlight review, Elvis's style was "both country and R&B," and it could "appeal to pop."[178] What Sun 210 delivered, then, was a young country singer who was much more confidently rocking—cheekier and perhaps more carnally knowing—than he had ever been on his first single. Elvis was charting the form of rockabilly, defining exactly what it could mean. New dimensions could be heard in his impassioned live version of Brown's song captured when the Blue Moon Boys played at the Eagles' Hall in Houston on 19 March 1955. The Hillbilly Cat got so swept away by his performance that he added an extra "We're gonna rock!" right at the end, as if to drive the song home. A sexy, truck-driving space alien had just hit America, and its name was Elvis Presley.

67. "Shake, Rattle and Roll" (from *For LP Fans Only*, 1959)

On the Dorsey Brothers' show, 28 January 1956, Bill Randle first offered a testimony on camera before Elvis's first appearance on national television. Looking genteel, rather formal, and slightly awkward in his suit and tie, the Cleveland DJ announced:

> We'd like this time to introduce you to a young fellow who, like many performers—Johnnie Ray among them—come out of nowhere to be, overnight, very big stars. This young fellow we saw while making a movie short. We think tonight that he's going to make television history for you. We'd like you to meet him now: Elvis Presley. And here he is!

Randle's claim about making "television history" was correct. Clad in a signature Lansky Brothers' jacket, black shirt, and contrasting tie, Elvis came out swinging.[179] He launched into a medley that started with "Shake, Rattle and Roll" and transformed into "Flip, Flop and Fly." The RCA star understood that listeners would know the tunes and recognize them as an invitation to just cut up, party, and have a good time. His performance was good. To begin with, Elvis could not quite feel the warmth of the crowd and seemed a little hesitant. When he cut loose during the instrumental break, the studio audience was not yet sure if screaming was sanctioned. It greeted him instead with intense applause. Nevertheless, Elvis was as animated by the music as a leaf on the breeze. His quiff was bobbing, his eyes darting, and his upper lip curling. The words that he sang seem to explode with attitude. As he went to cut up a second time, Bill and Scotty started hollering like they might have done in a honky-tonk, trying to scare up a more intense reaction. This time enthusiastic applause carried on *throughout* the break. The group segued seamlessly into "Flip, Flop and Fly." Viewers might have been forgiven for believing it was the same song with different lyrics. By the end, Elvis had given so much that he nearly collapsed. In the subsequent television performances, the taboo against screaming disappeared, and things got even more daring. "Shake, Rattle and Roll" deserves a prominent place in any Elvis collection, then, because it was the song that he chose to perform in order to introduce himself to the nation.

The story of the barnstorming rock 'n' roll masterpiece starts with Jesse Stone. Born in 1901, Stone had made his way to Harlem by the mid-1930s and become a big-band leader. He joined Atlantic a decade later and spent years on the payroll as a contracted songwriter, arranger, and producer. The maestro proved his worth in the pop market, arranging "Sh-Boom" by the Chords and writing "Money Honey" for the Drifters. Early in 1954, Atlantic's dynamic president, Ahmet Ertegun, asked Stone to come up with material for veteran R&B singer Big Joe Turner. Ertegun knew that both men had similar roots: both were from Kansas, both were inspired by the blues, and both had played at the Apollo. Under the name of Charles Calhoun, Stone created "Shake, Rattle and Roll." The title seemed to conjoin all the illicit pleasures of Saturday night: gambling (shaking the dice), sex (the rattle of loose joints: rocking and rolling), and music (dance, percussion). Stone's lyrics, meanwhile, tied the recent, carefree, and communal spirit of jump blues back into the Delta tradition. Turner's recorded version appeared in April and rapidly became a template for crossover music. Underwritten by a frantic series of boogie-woogie-style piano triplets, his driving vocals were accompanied by hand claps and a slick, roaring sax—played by Sam "The Man" Taylor—which created a big, dance-band sound. In June, Decca released a more angular version by Bill Haley's group, featuring repeated sax patterns and a tick-a-tick, country, slap-bass beat. The result was a very determined party anthem: a version both more muscular and more dynamic than Turner's, with the Comets shouting, "Go!" at regular intervals during the break.

"Shake, Rattle and Roll" crept into Elvis's live set late in 1954, and he debuted the song on *Louisiana Hayride* on 18 December. He played it again on KDAV in Lubbock, Texas, and WJOI in Florence, Alabama, early in the new year and then again on *Hayride* in March and April.[180] In May, he performed it at the Municipal Auditorium in Orlando. The next year, he paired "Shake, Rattle and Roll" with another Stone-penned, Big Joe Turner Atlantic release called "Flip, Flop and Fly" on the Dorsey Brothers' *Stage Show*. Early in 1955 and 1956, he also performed Stone's "Money Honey" quite regularly. Further Joe Turner numbers such as "Corrine, Corrina" were on Elvis's radar.[181]

Like "I Got a Woman," "Shake, Rattle and Roll" was part of the catalog held by Progressive Music, a company that Hill & Range co-owned with Atlantic Records. Once Elvis had secured his connection to Hill & Range in November 1955, it was in everyone's financial interests to use the song. An RCA single version of "Shake, Rattle and Roll" was released the following September. Compared to both Turner's and Haley's recordings, Elvis's version was more explosive, guitar-driven, and rockabilly oriented. Even down to Scotty's roundabout guitar motifs, its sound was an update of Sun numbers like "Good Rockin' Tonight." What is really captivating is the ostentatious unfolding of Elvis's vocals. He swoops into the music with tongue firmly in cheek, flashes across the meter, and struts all over the place; just mugging and quivering to the beat. Once he has established his role, he collapses back into the joyous racket, still a little deranged. A rock 'n' roll master at work.

66. "Lawdy Miss Clawdy" (from *The Complete '68 Comeback Special*, 2008)

> Presley has a solid sense of tempo, in traditional two-beat country style. His guitar playing is loud, powerful, uncomplicated. . . . Presley's gift is not, and never was, musical ability. What he's selling, with astonishing flair, is a solid-gold public personality. . . . To put it another way, the product is magnetism, sex.[182]

Reviewing the *Comeback* soundtrack for the audiophile magazine *High Fidelity*, Morgan Ames wrote an article titled, "Presley: The Product Is Sex." Ames was not entirely off the mark with his comments; he suggests, for instance, that Elvis moves "like a panther."[183] Nevertheless, his recognition of Elvis's eroticism is couched in a kind of reductive framework. Ames's writing is part of a bigger picture. After the rock 'n' roll singers seduced ordinary Americans with their dance music beats, they were accused of evoking dangerous and primitive forces. One handbill from the Citizens Council of New Orleans claimed: "The screaming, idiotic words, and savage music of these records are undermining the morals of our white youth in *America*."[184]

Historically, racist codes have always positioned African Americans as more animal and primitive than whites. When white rock 'n' rollers branched out, they were framed as civilized *on the surface* but smoldering underneath. Elvis's music became a byword for simple, instinct-driven, animal directness. Often, the press contrasted him with cerebral complexity or sophistication. Commenting in August 1969 on what he called Elvis's "comeback bid," for example, a *Time* journalist said, "Teenagers seem to be tiring of bloodless electronic experimentation and intellectualism, and may be ready to discover for themselves the simplistic, hard-driving, Big Beat."[185] Such claims are highly reductive since they use stark binary oppositions to guide readers. They suppose it is a case of body, *rather than* mind, selling sex appeal *rather than* making music—at least music of any artistic worth. The problem with such interpretations is that they rather miss the mark. As soon as he could, Charlie Hodge corrected them by saying, "First of all, people should know that Elvis was a very intelligent man. He knew where he was going and he knew how much he had to learn."[186]

Like Elvis's other obsession—karate—his music *combined* philosophy and action, awareness and reflex, craft and feel. To put it another way, in aural terms, Elvis's music is sexy because it is replete with emotions that are nuanced, convoluted, and multilayered, hinting at forces that are sensual *and* almost sinister. In his performance, he was not just some cute, one-dimensional country boy. He was deliciously adult: tender *and* angry, vulnerable *and* defiant, deferential (like a mother's boy), and ferocious (like a panther) . . . *all at once*. The reduction of Elvis's image to cornball moments and cowpoke lines has more to do with American biases in the 1950s and 1960s than anything that Elvis actually did. What he offered was not simple but tumultuous. His music was presented as magnetic appeal rather than intellectual puzzle, but it was complex, nevertheless—as compellingly complex, and fascinating, as the play of sexuality in human communication. As music journalist

Julie Burns, talking about Elvis's singing, so eloquently put it, "A world of emotion lies in every phrase."[187]

"Lawdy Miss Clawdy" deserves its place in any Elvis top 100 for its undertow of raw feeling. Its story began with the formation of the independent R&B label Specialty Records. Impressed by the music of Fats Domino, Specialty's founder Art Rupe took a field trip to New Orleans to scout for talent. Lloyd Price passed Rupe's audition and went on to establish "Lawdy Miss Clawdy" as a staple. Price's original, released on Specialty 428, was big and ballsy. The single was released back in the days when the Presleys lived in Lauderdale Courts. Elvis kept a copy in his collection, then added material from Price's later catalog.[188] "Lawdy Miss Clawdy" had a distinct style that created a new recipe for crossover hits. Fats Domino played piano on the 1952 cut. What made it work beyond, say, the similarly blustering Domino number "The Fat Man" was the appealing, bittersweet tone of its narration.

Elvis's first attempt at recording "Lawdy Miss Clawdy" *in the studio* occurred one Friday morning in February 1956. It happened during the same set of New York sessions that produced "Blue Suede Shoes" and the other cuts that made his eponymous debut studio LP. On an episode of the *Classic Albums* television series devoted to the record, Ernst Jørgensen said that the New York recordings were audibly different from Elvis's Memphis and Nashville material and expressed a harder, more aggressive sound. However, "Lawdy Miss Clawdy" was not included, at first, on Elvis's debut LP; the track made it onto the album's reissue in 1999.

Back in the 1950s, albums were, due to their general sales potential, usually seen as an afterthought to singles. RCA released "Lawdy Miss Clawdy" on 45rpm as the flip side of "Shake, Rattle and Roll." It wasn't until Elvis was away in the army, in 1959, that his label offered the track on a compilation of Sun and 1956 RCA material, appropriately called *For LP Fans Only*.

While an instrumental jam of "Lawdy Miss Clawdy" was featured in Elvis's last fictional picture, *Change of Habit*, and the song was also performed at live shows—notably in August 1971—the 1968 NBC *Comeback Special* contained one of its most electric performances. For that unique production, the director Steve Binder attempted to summon up and explore the wild side of Presley's image.

The iconic black leather outfit came about when both Bill Belew and Binder were inspired by a photo of Elvis's early hero, Marlon Brando, in *The Wild One*.[189] It was cut using a denim pattern from a jean jacket. A new archetype was born. Beyond its nod to Elvis's Hollywood career, the *Comeback Special* was designed as a revivalist meeting that would bring Elvis's past into the present. Scotty and DJ Fontana were flown in especially for the purpose.[190] Filmed on the informal, "boxing ring" stage, their encounter remains mesmeric. As they jam together, Scotty gives a cue and Elvis tears into "Lawdy Miss Clawdy" with a raw assault of mixed emotion. His performance is so intense that it almost—in the best way—scratches the ears. Vocal cords that, so far, have proved their owner's mastery with smooth singing are pushed to the point of fraying at the edges. As Greil Marcus noticed, when Elvis lurches into the number, what he experiences is a feeling that is both joshing and liberated.[191] At one point, as the musicians jam together, it's possible to hear Charlie Hodge getting carried away with laughter, as if bobbing in the fray of a heady, almost oceanic moment. In his underrated 2004 pocket volume *The Rough Guide to Elvis*, Paul Simpson describes "Lawdy Miss Clawdy" as "Elvis's answer to Jack Kerouac's *On the Road*."[192] Taking on this old staple in the *Comeback*, what the singer delivers is lusty, passionate, and commanding, yet also desperate, angry, and sad. He conjures with immense powers.

65. "A Little Less Conversation" (from *ELVIS: 30 #1 Hits*, 2002)

In 1957, if the takings of the three most successful films on release in America—*The Bridge over the River Kwai*, *Peyton Place*, and *Island in the Sun*—were averaged, they made five times as much as *Jailhouse Rock*. A decade later, the top three films—*The Jungle Book*, *Guess Who's Coming to Dinner*, and *You Only Live Twice*—on average took more than *forty* times the profits of Elvis's biggest movie of the year, *Double Trouble*. As 1960s youth culture began to reflect a society that was turbulent and political, Elvis's film output generally went in the opposite direction. It seemed to degenerate. Pictures like *Harum Scarum* catered primarily to children and die-hard fans. Audiences of young adults wanted something more interesting and sophisticated for their ticket spend.

As movie audiences deserted Elvis, the quality of songs available to him went down. His publishers held competitions for writers to come up with numbers based on the title of each new movie. Small teams worked to craft songs that would fit particular scenes. Many of their compositions were never actually used. Frequently, the unpicked material was too specialized to be offered elsewhere. As fewer fans bought Elvis soundtrack albums, rewards on offer to Elvis's successful songwriters got smaller. Hill & Range's pool of writers no longer saw the financial returns they had in the past. As the best songwriting talent moved on to fresh pastures, the caliber of Elvis's film material began to waver. By 1967, the quality of songs available to record as film-score material had dwindled significantly. Recording a session for the *Double Trouble* soundtrack, the singer was livid: "You mean it's come to this? Those damn fools got me singing 'Old MacDonald' on the back of a truck with a bunch of animals. Man, it's a joke and the joke's on me."[193] The Colonel's team finally had to shift some ground and look for new talent. One writer who came to the fore was Mac Davis.

Back in 1954, when the Memphis Flash played a makeshift stage in Lubbock at the Hub Motor Company, Mac Davis—who was only a high school student at the time—was in the audience. He was so inspired by the show that when he got home, he wrote his first song. Finding his way in the music world, Davis later left for Atlanta where he formed a frat party band called the Sots. He also started work for the promotions team of Vee-Jay Records. The youngster signed a songwriting contract with Bill Lowery; his skill evidently lay in fusing pop with elements of contemporary country and soul. After Kenny Rogers recorded one of his compositions, Davis started working with Liberty Records. The label moved him to Hollywood, where he managed Liberty's publishing arm, Metric Music. A local contract writer then introduced him to Billy Strange. The talented studio guitarist was four years older than Elvis and already among the cream of West Coast musicians. He worked with Phil Spector in 1962 and had become part of the Wrecking Crew, a very busy team who had acquired a national reputation in the industry as the elite of California's session musicians. Strange played guitar on "Viva Las Vegas" and had also scored a hit in the interim arranging Lee Hazlewood's "These Boots Were Made for Walking" for Nancy Sinatra. Billy Strange also formed a publishing company with Ms. Sinatra called BnB Music.

Mac Davis received a call asking him if anyone at Metric might have suitable material for Elvis's next movie, *Live a Little, Love a Little*. He met Strange in a Hollywood coffee shop and offered him "A Little Less

Conversation." It seemed like a good general fit. The song was originally written with Aretha Franklin in mind as its ideal performer. Elvis recorded it in March 1968, in a style that was faster and less funky than Davis had originally intended.[194] Colonel Parker and the MGM executives insisted on a change of verse lyrics; originally, Davis's song had been about nagging a neglectful partner into showing some respect, but it did not fit the theme of the movie. RCA released the song that September as the B-side to "Almost in Love." With the profile-boosting NBC *Comeback Special* yet to air, more interesting social and political sounds were competing for the ears of a new generation: songs like "People Got to Be Free" by the Rascals. At least in part, the world had dismissed Elvis Presley as the face of forgettable Hollywood entertainment; his single charted but never climbed anywhere near the top forty.

In conjunction with a Nike commercial, JXL remixed the *Comeback* version in 2002 and scored a UK number one smash.[195] It's easy to see why. The JXL version of "A Little Less Conversation" felt refreshingly snappy and contemporary without losing any of its star's vocal clarity. It was proof that Elvis had been spectacularly on point in the first place.

64. "Fever" (from *Aloha from Hawaii via Satellite*, 1973)

Looking back over his 1950s press coverage, those who do not know any better might misguidedly surmise that Elvis was styled as a feminine or effeminate performer. Nothing could be further from the truth. Although he was young, on numbers like "Lonesome Cowboy," his voice was powerfully masculine. His demeanor was more manly than Johnnie Ray and Neil Sedaka, competing pop sensations who came immediately before and after. So why the confusion? He may have been misidentified because "Elvis the Pelvis" knew how to tease on stage with his movements; he was willing to submit to objectification by the audience. There was no clear vocabulary at the time to describe any guy who did that. On "Fever," where Peggy Lee had sung in the final verse about "chicks" being born to make guys hot under the collar, Elvis turned the lyric around. He talked about "cats" (hip males) being born to get *women* excited.[196]

The story of "Fever" starts, in part, with the black entertainer Eddie Cooley. Born five years before Elvis and raised in Atlanta, Cooley had moved to New York by the mid-1950s. Together with his backing trio the

Dimples, he scored a smash on Royal Roost Records with "Priscilla," a jaunty but comparatively pedestrian pop sing-along with a raunchy sax solo. Under the pen name of John Davenport, Cooley collaborated with Otis Blackwell to write a new song recorded by the R&B artist Little Willie John, called "Fever." Syd Nathan's King Records released John's rendition and it became a hit. The record still sounds assertive, extravagant, and jazzy, if comparatively staid. John remains carefully on meter, leaving a result that keeps to time and still has its charms but never gets very explosive. Peggy Lee's 1958 version, meanwhile—with its sly double bass, syncopated clicks, smoky vocals with plenty of reverb, and subtly bumpy percussion—took "Fever" to another level of sophistication.

Lee was an extraordinary entertainer in her own right. Since the early 1940s, the famous platinum blonde notched up some great achievements as both a singer and songwriter, including the chart toppers "Somebody Else Is Taking My Place" and "Mañana (Is Soon Enough for Me)." In the 1950s, she transferred from Capitol Records to Decca, and back again. As well as being nominated for an Academy Award for playing an alcoholic blues singer in Jack Webb's unique 1955 crime musical *Pete Kelly's Blues*, she wrote and performed songs for Disney's phenomenal *Lady and the Tramp*.

In Lee's capable hands, "Fever" became private and sensual. Her delivery was almost breathy, speaking the lines discreetly, as if between two lovers. It was hardly surprising that Lee's career lasted for another thirty years and "Fever" became her signature song. In its very slyness, the song was powerfully erotic; a history lesson about the timelessness of human sensuality. Peggy Lee made "Fever" assume its full role as a fable, a moment of self-disclosure, and a shimmering expression of lust. Her slow motion, *film noir*–style delivery is so delightfully slinky that it almost crawls on its belly.

After Lee's extraordinary performance of "Fever" climbed the charts in 1958, it set the benchmark. Audiences who heard later covers of the song were able to predict exactly how they would end; what counted was how the singer would get there.

Elvis recorded "Fever" at a session in RCA's Studio B in Nashville, just over a week after singing for ABC on the Frank Sinatra show in Miami. The surprisingly subdued April 1960 version came from the same studio visit that produced "It's Now or Never" and "Are You Lonesome

Tonight?" Elvis drew on Lee's pared-down, syncopated arrangement but very subtly changed it: shortening the introduction, as was typical; removing an instrumental break; and almost imperceptibly slowing down the tempo.

The drummer DJ Fontana joined Elvis's band late in 1954 after they first met on the *Louisiana Hayride*. In the studio and on tour, including this session, Fontana spontaneously accented his bandleader's timing, later claiming that he learned his craft backing local burlesque dancers. [197]

From 1972 onward, "Fever" became one of Elvis's favorite toys, unleashed on live audiences with devastating effect. The version in *Aloha from Hawaii* is deliberately slowed down, offering the feel of a big cat pacing; the same energy that animated his performances on the *Comeback Special*. Elvis was at the height of his masculine powers, resplendent in his own sexual confidence and evidently enjoying the whole experience of teasing women who scream in his audience. As if to mark his journey from young star to virile icon, his voice was gently epic, less breathy and mature than his 1960 studio version. The drumrolls still hit like shrapnel, and he still makes full use of the space in the verses for his characteristically acrobatic phrasing.

Over the years, "Fever" proved its worth for Elvis as a resilient, signature number. Even the live version that he stumbled his way through at College Park on 28 September 1974—one of his worst shows ever—remains fascinating as a systematic deconstruction of the song's different elements. During another live rendering, from his closing Vegas show in September 1973, Elvis quipped, "Myrna Smith and JD Sumner, had a very mad affair; when their wives and husbands caught them, you saw nothing but teeth and hair." [198] A different version can be heard on the recent success, *Elvis and the Royal Philharmonic*, produced by Don Reedman and Nick Patrick for Sony's subsidiary label, Legacy Recordings. Unfortunately, relatively speaking, this virtual duet with the swinging Great American Songbook singer Michael Bublé fails to gel. Though the Philharmonic does its job very well, the whole thing sounds too full. A less-cluttered version appears on another recent reboot. Larry Jordan of VoiceMasters managed to create a new take for H&H Records in 2015 that was both punchy and orchestral. His update, on *Elvis: The New Recordings*, avoids the failings of the Bublé duet.

63. "If You Love Me (Let Me Know)" (from *Moody Blue*, 1977)

Elvis often repurposed hit songs written by male writers that exposed the emotional turmoil of female artists. Other songs in this category, like the operatically painful "Hurt," expressed a kind of vulnerability and depth that was uncharacteristic of male artists of the era. In comparison to "Hurt," however, "If You Love Me (Let Me Know)" was already a unisex song. An impressive aspect about this truly timeless number is that it seems so familiar, yet only became part of his repertoire as late as 1974.

The story of "If You Love Me (Let Me Know)" begins with its writer John Rostill, an innovative bass player who was born in the English city of Birmingham during World War II. After the rock 'n' roll boom hit, he backed visiting artists like the Everly Brothers. Working as a hired hand, Rostill became one of the busiest bass players in the region. His abilities did not go unnoticed; he joined the Shadows after the departure of Brian "Licorice" Locking in 1964. The newcomer's smooth and syncopated bass helped the group mature in style. He then became part of Tom Jones's line-up. Rostill also wrote songs throughout his career as a working musician. Olivia Newton-John, meanwhile, was born in Britain but raised in Australia. Newton-John was engaged to Rostill's Shadows bandmate, Bruce Welch. Those around the female singer, including her manager Peter Gormley, were big fans of American country music. They thought Newton-John's voice was suited to that style. MCA released her cover of John Denver's "Take Me Home Country Roads" in the United States. The single failed to chart. When the label's vice president of A&R, Artie Mogull—the man who signed Dylan—noticed that country stations were playing it in the Southeast, he pushed for a country-style pop record. In November 1973, Newton-John released Rostill's flowing country pop tune "Let Me Be There," produced by Welch and the Australian music veteran John Farrar.[199] With its uplifting key change, the song was released twice in the United Kingdom without much commercial interest. Due to differences in radio formatting, America consistently proved more receptive to Newton-John's music. "Let Me Be There" climbed the country charts and crossed over into the pop market.

A month after her song "Long Live Love" came runner-up to ABBA's glorious "Waterloo" at the April 1974 Eurovision Song Contest, Newton-John had a top five, follow-up hit across the pond with another Rostill composition: "If You Love Me (Let Me Know)." The appealing blonde soon found herself on NBC's *Dean Martin Show*. When she won a Country Music Association award for Female Vocalist of the Year, more traditional artists like George Jones and Tammy Wynette were up in arms. Controversy over whether Newton-John's music deserved to be categorized as country or pop caused purists to create the Association for Country Entertainers. Nevertheless, Rostill's compositions received awards for Broadcast Music Inc.'s Most Performed Country Song of the Year, both in 1974 for "Let Me Be There" and in 1975 for "If You Love Me (Let Me Know)." The two rapidly became staples, covered by artists from Slim Whitman to Tina Turner. Elvis immediately included both in his concert sets. A lack of later studio visits meant that live takes formed the basis of his vinyl output.

After Elvis featured "If You Love Me (Let Me Know)" in some late January 1974 Vegas shows, it became a firm favorite. Two generations of Presley aficionados now descended on his arena-filling concerts. He started making more room for family-friendly numbers that could add variety and go alongside old standards like "Fever." As Elvis experimented with numbers like "Big Boss Man," his live concert list was shaken up that year. The version of "If You Love Me (Let Me Know)" on *Moody Blue* was recorded on tour in Kalamazoo, 26 April 1977.[200] By then, Elvis usually performed it between the beguiling "Love Me" and world-weary "You Gave Me a Mountain."

One reason that "If You Love Me (Let Me Know)" established itself as such a favorite before joining any compilations or box sets was that it also appeared on the posthumous double album from the CBS television documentary, *Elvis in Concert*. While the song was not featured on the TV special itself, the album went top five after its release in October 1977. The chart success was not surprising. "If You Love Me (Let Me Know)" effortlessly merges the communal feel of quartet gospel singing with the accessibility of easy listening pop. It was a prime opportunity for a collective sing-along—a sonic walk in the park.

62. "Way Down" (from *Moody Blue*, 1977)

"Way Down" is well known as the last single that Elvis released while he was alive. He recorded it in Graceland in October 1976. Its genre template was established when the country songwriter Layng Martine Jr. wrote a precursor hit called "Rub It In." Although that song's chord changes sounded a bit like Joe South's "Walk a Mile in My Shoes," "Rub It In" was a flirty, smug little number; its title referred to the application of suntan lotion. Billy "Crash" Craddock gave ABC Records a huge hit with his cover of the song in 1974.[201] What mattered was the generous feel. Craddock's version was *knowing* music for good ole boys. "Rub It In" was lighthearted; easy listening, sure, but also sassy—ideal for those who wore their Stetsons perfectly pressed while they crisscrossed the continent by air. For a contemporary country market transformed by Southern rock, it seemed tailor-made.[202]

Another genre-blending number that Martine wrote was "Way Down." It was, in effect, an easy listening, country soul tribute to rock 'n' roll that leaned slightly toward disco. Martine explained in interview:

> I often write songs in Elvis's style because that's what's in my blood. I didn't write especially for him, I just wrote it because I felt it. I love excitement-oriented songs—"Hound Dog" and "Whole Lotta Shakin' Goin' On" were powerful early influences of mine. And then of course the whole boy, girl sexuality thing seems like what rock 'n' roll is all about. I guess I was hoping "Way Down" had some of that.[203]

On the day he wrote it, Martine debuted the song to his publisher, Ray Stevens. They recorded a demo immediately with Stevens singing the low bass part. "Way Down" was filed under Ray Stevens Music. Although the song was offered to various artists without success, Martine strongly believed in it.[204]

Elvis's producer Felton Jarvis had an association with the Nashville publisher Bob Beckham. He used Beckham's company, Combine Music, as a way to scout material from outside the Hill & Range stable. Beckham was expecting a late afternoon visit from Jarvis. The RCA producer wanted to know if there was any material that would be suitable for Elvis. One of the songs Martine put forward was "Way Down." A week later Ray Stevens got a call from Jarvis saying they wanted to do the song.

Elvis recorded "Way Down" at the end of October 1976.[205] He addressed it near the start of a two-day session that captured only three other numbers: "It's Easy for You," "Pledging My Love," and "He'll Have to Go." These songs were mature but not in the same way as the jaded, contemporary singer-songwriter folk that Elvis pursued earlier in the decade. In comparison to Martine's number, they were relatively downbeat and shared a broad kind of retro, easy listening, country feel. "Way

Down" was gentle but faster and more energetic in comparison. When Jarvis mixed the song at Creative Workshop, he invited Martine to come along. Walking back to his car after the session, the tunesmith recalled: "I couldn't help thinking of all those nights I'd spent loading trucks for Roadway as a Teamster, wondering if I was just dreaming to think I could ever be a professional songwriter, were so worth it."[206] He was over the moon.

When Martine was in Rhode Island the following summer, a promoter called him to say, "I just got the advance numbers from *Billboard*, and your song goes to number one [on the Hot Country chart] next week."[207] Three days later, news came that Elvis had died. In other words, "Way Down" did not reach the top of the hit parade *because* its singer passed on. On *Billboard*'s Hot Country chart at least, it was already heading for glory.

61. "Blue Moon of Kentucky" (from *A Date with Elvis*, 1959)

The story of "Blue Moon of Kentucky" starts with Bill Monroe. At the end of the 1930s, the legendary Kentucky-born bluegrass player emerged from his roots in the string-band tradition to win a regular slot on Nashville's *Grand Ole Opry* radio show. He was known for his virtuosity on the mandolin and other stringed instruments. It was the addition, six years later, of banjo picker Earl Scruggs and guitarist Lester Flat to his band the Bluegrass Boys that gave Monroe his trademark style. Among the songs they recorded for Columbia was a lighthearted ballad called "Blue Moon of Kentucky." With its genteel fiddling, clip-clopperty percussion (though no drums, of course), and plaintive vocals, Monroe's "old-time" version of the song is calculatedly quaint. The bluegrass pioneer nevertheless achieved some uncannily high notes at the end as he veered toward an unhinged semi-yodel.

Once Sam Phillips found the energy he wanted from the musical interaction of Elvis, Scotty, and Bill on "That's All Right," he needed a B-side for the single. Although "That's All Right" has become seen as a kind of Rosetta Stone of rock 'n' roll, it was this flip side that supercharged country music and effectively modernized the genre. Where the A-side of Elvis's first single reconstructed gutbucket blues as light country, the Sun version of "Blue Moon of Kentucky" reversed the miracle equation. Bill

Black set the ball rolling by goofing around on his double bass and singing part of Monroe's number in a daft falsetto style.

Creating a sound that was, in effect, superlative rockabilly, the new cover of "Blue Moon of Kentucky" mixed country instrumentation with an exciting whiff of jump blues. Compared to Monroe's original, the Blue Moon Boys' approach was breezy, assertive, and histrionic, all at the same time. The other take from the day sounded smoother, plainer, and more like Monroe's version in comparison, with Sam Phillips emerging afterward from his recording booth in the back room to enthuse, "That's fine, man. Hell, that's different—that's a pop song there, near 'bout." He was spot on—that particular take changed Monroe's number into pop, while the rockabilly cut took it straight by the scruff of the neck. The Sun trio sounds positively alive. It is almost as if the first disc has been ripped from the player so fast that the needle has scratched across it and another inserted in its place. Right from the get-go, Monroe's novelty genre record is replaced, in effect, by a rave. In comparison with Bill Monroe's yowling country rendition, Elvis, Scotty, and Bill come across as if they are *there*, right in the moment, desperate to have a ball. Not only does the backing bounce along at a much faster tempo, the singer bobs and twists his way through the number like a streaker in a riot. His approach is mannered here and impassioned there; he uses his voice as if he were a Broadway showman finding his way across a crowded fiddling contest. More than six decades since its first recording, "Blue Moon of Kentucky" remains a performance that won't just simply be heard. Instead, Elvis's version demands that listeners *keep up*.

"That's All Right" worked well with forward-thinking radio stations. In contrast, "Blue Moon of Kentucky" helped Elvis, Scotty, and Bill find much wider airplay with what was, in effect, an especially "hot" country folk record. By the middle of August, the trio's debut single sold around twenty thousand copies and made the top three of *Billboard*'s Memphis Country and Western chart. "Blue Moon of Kentucky" became the Blue Moon Boys' anthem as they played a weekly slot on the widely syndicated *Louisiana Hayride* and motored across the South on a string of dates. Its success opened up the live music scene.

Dressing like an eccentric hipster, calling on the rowdy electricity of the blues, shaking out nervous excitement, and teasing local audiences wherever he went, Elvis—although he was a little gauche at first—soon found his feet. His nickname, "The Hillbilly Cat," exactly caught the way he was transforming the country genre for a new era. After hearing "Blue Moon of Kentucky," a young Bob Dylan started listening to him.[208] Bill Monroe also rerecorded his own song in the Presley style, proving that even "old timers" are never too old to rock 'n' roll.

60. "Green, Green Grass of Home" (from *Today*, 1975)

"Haven't you bothered me enough, you big banana head?" That was how gangster's moll Marilyn Monroe greeted an unwelcomed policeman in John Huston's 1950 noir *The Asphalt Jungle*. In the final scene, fugitive jewel thief Dix—played by the imposing figure of Sterling Hayden— makes it to the Hickorywood horse-farm field and lies down, nursing a fatal gunshot wound. The moment inspired Curly Putman Jr. to write "Green, Green Grass of Home." Putman saw a TV rerun of the movie in the mid-1960s; his song came together by the end of the evening. It was adopted as a standard, covered by Johnny Darrell, the blond *Opry* veteran and TV star Porter Wagoner, and Tom Jones. The latter transformed Putman's staple from a prison breakout fantasy dressed in country style to a power ballad, a vehicle that captured the widespread feeling that "home" is timeless compared to the hectic pace of modern life. Putman, meanwhile, went on to write "D-I-V-O-R-C-E" for Tammy Wynette.

Red West initially alerted Elvis to the Putman composition, only to be told that it was too country for the Presley catalog. A year later, on 29 October 1966, during one of his many drives back from Hollywood to Memphis, Elvis, then in Arkansas, heard his friend George Klein playing Jones's version on WHBQ. He asked one of his entourage to call Klein over and over that day, requesting further airplay. By the time he recorded his own version of the classic for RCA in March 1975, the grass was no longer so green at home. America had been marred by the Watergate scandal, possible impeachment, and resignation of President Nixon. Elvis was jaded in the wake of his divorce. Since December 1973, he had recorded nothing in the studio. Yet, the South, his home, had come into its own. So there, in Studio C, somewhere between delivering the quietly monumental "Fairytale" and a cheerful, single-take version of "I Can Help," he addressed "Green, Green Grass of Home" with what Peter Guralnick called "real feeling."[209] No wonder, then, that the cut was selected as the closing number for the 1975 LP *Today*.

Of course, even while it is rousing, "Green, Green Grass of Home" is a gently introspective song. It explores the ongoing, fond, and perhaps fraught relationship we all have to youth and childhood, being in the bosom of the family, and the blissful innocence of first love. "Green, Green Grass of Home" takes its resonance from the tension between our instinct that home is a haven and the knowledge that *we can never go home again*. As life moves on, our earliest refuge is inevitably left behind. Over a bed of tambourine beats and jazzy, gospel piano, Tom Jones's carefully enunciated vocal shifted from initial restraint to a soaring attack. Elvis began his version like a gospel song but almost immediately found his confidence and began to soar, supported by some gently haunting female backing. The spoken-word section wasn't played for contrast, as it had been in Porter Wagoner's rendition. Instead, it was performed more stylishly, as if to emphasize that it was only a story. To the untrained ear, alongside Tony Joe White's "Polk Salad Annie," "Green, Green Grass of Home" is one of Elvis's least altered covers and has even been dismissed by some critics as tepid and innocuous. It shows, however, that even a minimally reworked adaption can easily become Elvis's property. Though Jones's version is more famous, Elvis's cover is still recognizably *his own*. "Green, Green Grass of Home" is pure country, a style that would have been unthinkable, even to Elvis himself, just a decade earlier.

59. "Joshua Fit the Battle" (from *His Hand in Mine*, 1960)

Discussing *His Hand in Mine* in their book *Elvis Day by Day*, Peter Guralnick and Ernst Jørgensen noted it would fulfill "Elvis' long-standing ambition to make a full album that will stand as a tribute to his faith, serve as a memorial to his mother, and express his love for the music that first motivated him and which he will always love most."[210] What is interesting about their claim is that, with the exception of three 1961 performances of "Swing Down Sweet Chariot," the material from this album was not performed on stage again in the rest of Elvis's career.[211] Neither during the *Comeback*, nor in all those years when he was backed by JD Sumner and the Stamps, did he sing songs again like "Joshua Fit the Battle." The hymn deserves its place in any top 100 because of the verve with which he performed it. In the liner notes for the 2009 box set *I Believe: Gospel Masters*, talking about Elvis's awe-inspiring memory for lyrics, Jordanaire Gordon Stoker recalled, "He had the ability to hear any song and record it immediately without using a lyric sheet. 'Joshua Fit the Battle' was another one of those songs he didn't know when we decided to record it."[212] Stoker continued, "After rehearsing it a few times, he was ready to roll tape. He recorded 'Joshua' by memory. Listen to it; those words are not easy."[213]

Listed under various similar titles, "Joshua Fit the Battle" can be traced back into the mid-nineteenth century. When Elvis tackled the old spiritual at the Nashville session for *His Hand in Mine* on 30 October 1960, at least twenty different versions had already been released. Jimmie Rodgers's single on Roulette Records the previous March might have nudged him. Not to be confused with the "Singing Brakeman" of the same name, who found fame decades earlier with a country blues yodel, *this* Rodgers released music for twenty years, singing on a range of folk and pop records from the late 1950s. His gently swinging rendition of "Joshua Fit the Battle" had the same attack as Presley's, talking about men of Gideon and men of Saul. The song's roots go back further, however.

A few years before Victor joined with RCA, the label put out a version of "Joshua Fit the Battle" sung by Paul Robeson. Intelligent, well educated, and highly successful, Robeson epitomized the "new negro."[214] He established a musical partnership with the African American pianist Lawrence Brown. The pair first met in London. In 1925, they sang together in Greenwich Village for the theater director Jimmy Light. It was a positive experience. Robeson and Brown decided to form a working partnership: Brown toured with Robeson, accompanied him on piano, and arranged the songs. Their interplay is showcased on Robeson's 1926 version of "Joshua Fit the Battle." In this Victor rendition, Robeson's deep, commanding voice booms over scuttling piano accompaniment, supported by vocal backing in the round. Robeson also released a heavily labored version of "Sometimes I Feel Like a Motherless Child," the number picked for an instrumental segment of Elvis's NBC *Comeback Special*.[215]

As well as Paul Robeson, the Jordanaires had also had a crack at "Joshua Fit the Battle." Like "(There'll Be) Peace in the Valley (For Me)," "I'm Gonna Walk Dem Golden Stairs," and "Run On," it was already part of the group's pre-1956 back catalog: Decca released the quartet's typically wholesome version as a single in 1950 and again in 1952. One of the most startling subsequent performances came from Mahalia Jackson, the powerful singer who dominated the 1950s gospel scene with her soulful interpretations of various standards. Columbia offered her version on the 1958 EP *You'll Never Walk Alone*.[216] The most likely candidate for Elvis's "Joshua Fit the Battle" template, however, remains the Golden Gate Quartet. Its conduit to the singer was his favorite assistant, Charlie Hodge.

Hodge sang in the Foggy River Boys and backed Red Foley on his ABC TV show *Ozark Jubilee*. He first met Elvis backstage at the Ellis Auditorium in 1955. After Presley was conscripted, Hodge reconnected with him in 1958 on a train that took both to Fort Chaffee. Hodge soon became Elvis's friend and sidekick. While Private Presley was stationed in Bad Nauheim, Hodge brought him a Golden Gate Quartet record. Elvis researcher Mike Eder has suggested it was *That Golden Chariot*, which was released on the Columbia's budget label Harmony in 1957.[217] There is some support for the idea; the album in question also contained "Swing Down, Chariot," and "I Will Be Home Again"—a song that Elvis and Charlie sang together while in Germany. The Golden Gate Quartet's version of "Joshua Fit the Battle" was recorded in the summer of 1946 and Columbia released it several times in subsequent years. By jacking up the beginning of certain lines, the gospel quartet's interpretation injected a note of surprise into an otherwise staid tune. Elvis further exploited the concept, almost evoking the same kind of manic self-consciousness that he exhibited during moments in other songs like "Don't Be Cruel" and "Run On." The result is a performance that seems both joyously righteous and *accusatory*, in the best possible sense of the term.

58. "Got a Lot o' Livin' to Do!" (from *Loving You*, 1957)

In what remains perhaps the closest he got to a fictional biopic, *Loving You*, Elvis was transformed, as Deke Rivers, from a manual laborer to a singing sensation. Paramount needed a fast, rocking number for the picture. What is amazing about Presley's performance of "Got a Lot o' Livin' to Do!" is the way it joins the concerns of gospel and rock 'n' roll so seamlessly. At one point in Hal Kanter's 1957 film, as a denim-clad rocker, Deke leads an all-age, mostly female audience through a song that seems based on recognizing communality by virtue of its hand-clapping rhythm. Just as "Got a Lot o' Livin' to Do!" gets going, however, its singer pulls out his most incendiary stage moves. He leaps into the audience, ending the whole thing with his trademark bump-and-grind poses. Two older ladies, who seemed unconvinced at the start, are now beside themselves. In that sense, Elvis's film performance of "Got a Lot o' Livin' to Do!" fulfills the song's promise as a giant *double entendre*.

Born at the start of the 1920s, Ben Weisman had, in his youth, trained as a concert pianist at the Juilliard School of Music. After playing in an Air Force band during the war years, he joined New York's songwriting community. Weisman worked in various nightclubs as a professional pianist and accompanied famous singers like Eddie Fisher. Gradually, his career as a songwriter began to take shape. In 1949, Dean Martin recorded one of Weisman's compositions. In the next decade, a fruitful encounter with the famous Columbia A&R man, Mitch Miller, resulted in song placements with Doris Day and other stars.

Weisman had been on the Hill & Range team since 1950 and got along so well with Jean Aberbach that they even went on double dates.[218] Once the Aberbach brothers started working with Elvis in a publishing capacity, they called upon the pianist's ample talents. Weisman's initial mission, in February 1956, was simply to study Elvis's performance on *Stage Show*. At first, the songwriter came up with a slow, doo-woppy ballad, "First in Line," which Elvis recorded for his eponymous second studio album. It was the start of a productive association, with the "Mad Professor" writing many of Elvis's movie songs over the years.

Ben Weisman usually wrote with Fred Wise and Kay Twomey. On this occasion, he was paired with Aaron Schroeder. Elvis recorded their song "Got a Lot o' Livin' to Do!" in January 1957 at a session in Radio Recorders. Weisman visited the studio that day. He found Elvis playing some blues on guitar. The writer recalled, "Without saying anything, I sat down next to him and started to play piano along with him, just jamming away. When he was done, he asked who I was and I told him that I co-wrote 'Got a Lot o' Livin' to Do!'"[219]

Once Elvis discovered Weisman's identity, he got inspired and decided to record "Got a Lot o' Livin' to Do!" on the spot. The songwriter remembered, "There was a lot of energy and excitement in the studio that day. And it was recorded very fast."[220] A week after that album cut was committed to tape, two further versions were recorded, both on the Paramount sound stage. All three were used in various places during the film; the finale version was not actually released on record until two decades after Elvis's passing.

"Got a Lot o' Livin' to Do!" was a hedonistic manifesto for the new generation, one that said life is there to be lived to its fullest. It was also an appropriately ambiguous combination of lovingly declared monogamy and a downright come-on. From that place, Elvis could both mesmerize girls who adored him and also please his own parents, who were given roles as extras, sat in the live audience on set, and appeared on screen. *Loving You*, after all, is about nothing if it is not about transition and compromise. Elvis begins as a country boy and manual laborer, then finds himself celebrated as a modern entertainer: a ranch hand, home, not on the range, but on the sound stage.

57. "You Gave Me a Mountain" (from *Aloha from Hawaii via Satellite*, 1973)

> Sometimes I feel that I carry with me ghosts; ghosts of many different artists. . . . Artists that I knew, artists that I started out with who aren't around anymore, artists that I heard as a little boy on the radio, who I carry with me. And I bring them out of my magical musical box and there they are in the room for a while.[221]

When Don McLean introduced his live performance of "You Gave Me a Mountain," he explained to the audience, "I carry with me ghosts . . . of many different artists."[222] He added, "So I want to do a beautiful Marty Robbins song. These men—Marty Robbins and Roy Orbison—sang almost in some cases a kind of light opera that's unheard of today, but somehow they created this."[223] McLean further clarified his perspective, "They heard these marvelous operatic chord changes and [had] the great vocal range that was required to sing these songs. It makes them very challenging as well as very beautiful."[224]

A real tearjerker, "You Gave Me a Mountain" is an epic vision of human suffering. Its narrator describes a life so traumatic, one wonders how he has managed to keep going: He is guilty about the accident that killed his mother as she gave birth to him, blamed by his father for taking away the light of his life, abandoned by his wife, and, finally, deprived of his only child. By the end of the song, he is not just crestfallen. He is existentially marooned.

The writer of "You Gave Me a Mountain," Marty Robbins, was a decade older than Elvis, but he emerged as a country artist around the same time. The pair's first encounter came late in 1954 when they both played the *Grand Ole Opry*. They also shared the bill on a tour of the South that summer. Robbins covered "That's All Right" but kept his output broadly in the country genre for the period that followed. For several years, he was a regular on the *Opry*. The country star envisioned "You Gave Me a Mountain" as a cowboy song. Though he struggled to keep pitch in the chorus, Robbins's performance demonstrated how his music lent itself to the intense portrayal of personal anguish. From then on, "You Gave Me a Mountain" rapidly became a country staple.

Especially in their verses, the early versions of "You Gave Me a Mountain" recorded by male singers sounded like a Johnny Cash tribute contest. Frankie Laine made the song an easy listening hit in 1969. By that point, Laine was already a trouper with a strong track record of hits behind him. His pedigree was impressive and included "Mule Train," "I Believe," and "Up Above My Head." Both Robbins and Laine pursued the first verses of "You Gave Me a Mountain" in appropriately straight fashion, but in Laine's take, the backing is smoother and more orchestral. Laine's voice is more ponderous and sincere; he almost turns the song into a spoken-word monologue. When he gets to the chorus, sometimes he seems to waver, as if avoiding the challenge of an operatic delivery, then adds a few more syllables as a trade-off. One of the other people to record the song in 1969 was Johnny Bush. His version seems determined to unite various strands of country music. Bush delivers some rictal Johnny Cash vocals in the verses, then—backed by steel guitar and, finally, more folky strings—he yodels his way to freedom in the chorus. Carl Vaughn's 1969 Monument Records version took the song back to the early 1960s with a female choral backing reminiscent of hits like "Johnny Remember Me." The tragedy of Vaughn's predicament is highlighted by a beautiful, weeping angel soprano, in much the same way Elvis would use Millie Kirkham and Kathy Westmoreland.

"You Gave Me a Mountain" was also adapted, again in 1969, by a female country singer called Margie Singleton. With a voice that expresss undercurrents of immense hurt and aggravation, even as it assumes cold objectivity, she utters rather than croons the verses. Singleton's interpretation tugs on the heartstrings all the more since it describes horrors that can uniquely befall a woman. The tragic heroine is someone who has learned to be dependent all her life but is then deprived of the means to do so and forced to live alone. Even her faith is shaken. In Singleton's capable hands, "You Gave Me a Mountain" is devastating—a heartbreaking depiction of life's cruelty, one that is especially impactful because it never becomes maudlin.

Elvis said that he heard Frankie Laine's rendition of "You Gave Me a Mountain" and just loved the song. He started including "You Gave Me a Mountain" in his concerts from 1972 onward and performed it on the *Aloha* global telecast. At a Las Vegas show in September 1974, Elvis felt moved to separate this song from his personal life, saying, "I've been singing that song for a long time, and a lot of people kind of got it associated with me because they think it's a personal need. . . . I just love the song and it has nothing to do with me personally, or with my ex-wife, Priscilla."[225] As one commentator noted, however, "It's almost like he has to convince himself."[226] "You Gave Me a Mountain" stayed in Elvis's live set right through to 1977. After Elvis took charge of Robbins's number, it became smooth and twinkling—a lush show tune and opportunity to display vocal power. After one of his magnificent *Aloha* performances, the singer was visited backstage by Jack Lord, a dynamic actor who played Detective Captain Steve McGarrett in the CBS series *Hawaii Five-O*. According to Charlie Hodge, Lord exclaimed, "That was some of the most dramatic music that I have ever heard!" Elvis responded by saying, "Get that man a chair, Charlie; we don't want to lose him!"[227]

56. "Blue Christmas" (from *Elvis' Christmas Album*, 1957)

The story of "Blue Christmas" begins with Jay Johnson, a man who supplied scripts and advertising jingles to local radio but dreamed of making much larger ripples in the world of popular music. When Johnson commuted from his home in Connecticut to New York in the late 1940s, he would think up new ideas. As the rain lashed his 1939 Mercury, water got in through a hole in the roof. Johnson was forced to drive with an umbrella up for protection. On the second leg of his journey, speeding along in a commuter train in a state of drenched melancholy, he started contemplating how Christmas is sadder, for many of us, than we might think. He dreamed up an outline of the song. After his friend Billy Hayes tidied it up, they recruited Choice Music to organize its publishing and promotion. The distinct title color and associated emotional tone made Johnson and Hayes's song a real contrast to Irving Berlin's "White

Christmas," which had been recorded by Bing Crosby and was released twice in the 1940s. "Blue Christmas" was almost an answer record.

Country singer Doye O'Dell's previous output was characterized by novelty singles like the Odeon Electric release, "Shut Up and Drink Your Beer," a record so inebriated, it sounded like Hank Williams gone oom-pah. With its gentle walking beat, good ol' country strings, shimmering Hawaiian steel guitar, and Bing Crosby–style vocals, O'Dell's 1948 original of "Blue Christmas" still sounds nicely "old time," as if it comes straight off the range. Ernest Tubb's 1949 country and western cover exchanged nostalgia for something more contemporary: strong, masculine—but insistently "down-home"—vocals and playful piano fills. It proved very popular on the jukebox market.[228] The same year, big band leader Russ Morgan released a harmonized version on Decca that was more festive; it featured bell chimes and vocal backing in full Bing Crosby style. Easy listening maestro Hugo Winterhalter held the song even closer to its seasonal promise with his own version. After studying violin at the New England Conservatory of Music, the talented Winterhalter had, among other things, been a sideman for Count Basie, arranged studio sessions for Dinah Shore, and worked as musical director at MGM.

Adopting a very similar style to Morgan on "Blue Christmas," Winterhalter created something that was festive, sedate, and very traditional—almost barbershop in places.[229] It started with a melody based on a Christmas carol, "The First Noel." The master arranger moved to RCA Victor in 1950 and released a string of popular instrumentals, which he described as bringing symphonic quality and appeal to pop music. He also oversaw various recording sessions and arranged scores for label mates the likes of Perry Como and Eddie Fisher. Less than a year after Elvis covered "Blue Christmas," Winterhalter said to a reporter at *The Milwaukee Sentinel* that he was optimistic about the future of rock 'n' roll. He also praised his more dynamic label mate, describing Presley as "the most fantastic thing that has ever happened in our business, barring none, and that includes Bing Crosby."[230] Winterhalter added that the young singer "introduced a style, a sound, and appealed to the public. In other words, he has individuality and that's the secret of any great artist."[231] Elvis's version of "Blue Christmas" absolutely reflected as much. Winterhalter's take was in the singer's record collection, too.[232]

On the first leg of a three-day session at the Radio Recorders in Hollywood, Elvis completely reconfigured Johnson and Hayes's song in September 1957 as a more upbeat number, performing it straight after Leiber and Stoller's sparky "Treat Me Nice."

Inaugurating what became known as "the Nashville sound," Ferlin Husky's smooth interpretation of Western Swing maestro Eugene "Smokey" Rogers's rueful ballad "Gone" topped the country charts at the same time. The Jordanaires backed Husky on the recording and were accompanied by the angel voice of Tennessee-born Millie Kirkham.[233] Looking for a similar sound for his new ballad "Don't," Elvis invited Kirkham to the session so she could offer her beguiling, trademark soprano.

Kirkham was pregnant with her daughter Shelley at the time but flew in from Nashville. When she arrived the previous day, Elvis said, "Someone, please get this woman a chair."[234] She soon proved her worth. While the open-throated Jordanaires maintained their traditional harmonizing, Millie Kirkham came in with a provocative, gently aroused backing, offering the curvy "whoo-ooh-ooh" inflection as she accompanied Elvis on "Blue Christmas." As Ernst Jørgensen noted, she worried that her "wordless soprano obligato" might sound ridiculous, but the results were excellent.[235] He also observed that Scotty Moore's guitar was used in the same way as on the urgent "One Night."[236] Elvis, meanwhile, sang in the style that he adopted partway through "I Was the One": adding extra syllables to some of the words. Finding a hint of the Neapolitan assertiveness that he would later use on "It's Now or Never," the singer parlayed his material into something with more bravado than the original. His endearing stammer returned, however, when he repeated the first word of Johnson and Hayes's song's title. The newly energized Presley version of "Blue Christmas" was a sonic bridge between the staid, old world of the 1940s and the new generation's increasingly liberated attitudes. Modern times had arrived.

Just over a month after its studio recording, "Blue Christmas" appeared on *Elvis' Christmas Album*. The song also found its way onto the festive 1957 EP *Elvis Sings Christmas Songs*, which included the raunchy "Santa Claus Is Back in Town."

In 1964, RCA put "Blue Christmas" out as a single, backing it with "Wooden Heart."[237] The timing of its sale, ironically, clashed with the release of a new single and album version of the song by the Beach Boys. Their very different take featured a conservative, twinkling, orchestral backing and vocals from Brian Wilson that were excruciatingly drawn out, hinting at drug intoxication and mental decline. RCA also created a 1976 compilation album called *Blue Christmas* that featured some of the same content as *Elvis' Christmas Album* alongside other songs like "Mama Liked the Roses." The most arresting version of "Blue Christmas," however, was recorded when Elvis again gestured toward seasonal tidings; he revisited the song in his NBC *Comeback Special*, sitting in the "boxing ring" stage and playing guitar while his bandmates added percussive interest. Not least because his fans were so behind him, the result remains compelling.[238] According to Greil Marcus: "A woman in the audience cries as he plays 'Blue Christmas'—as Hodge shouts, 'Play it dirty, play it dirty!' But Elvis is already playing it dirty, reaching as if under the guitar for tones that can't be advertised."[239]

55. "Let Yourself Go" (from *Speedway*, 1968)

At a time when women were becoming more socially and romantically assertive, Elvis was marketed to them as a tender ladies' man.[240] It is important to realize, though, that there were, from Gladys Presley and Marion Keisker onward, female powers behind the throne. Not only did Presley's managers and agents put him forward as an appealing "U.S. Male" on albums like 1959's *A Date with Elvis*, and not only did he choose material made popular by women—"Fever" being a good example—Elvis also interpreted emotional worlds scripted for him by female songwriters such as Mae Boren Axton and Florence Kaye. Joy Byers was one such writer. In the 1960s, her husband, Bob Johnson, ran Columbia's Nashville division and produced some of the company's biggest albums. In turn, she cowrote "What's a Matter Baby (Is It Hurting You)" for Timi Yuro and delivered several classic Elvis numbers including "It Hurts Me."[241] Her composition "Let Yourself Go" was recorded in June 1967 at MGM studios in Culver City and used on the *Speedway* soundtrack.

Amid the flotsam of the two-day MGM session—which included "Five Sleepy Heads"—"Let Yourself Go" stood out as a contender: the sort of song in which Elvis actually believed. The gulf between his rocking material and usual film fare was registered by the critic Robert Matthew-Walker, who observed that in his own estimation, "'He's Your Uncle Not Your Dad' is not worthy of Presley. 'Let Yourself Go,' however, a mean blues-type song, is a good number by most standards, and is enhanced by Presley's performance, full of raunchy passion."[242]

From its subtle hand-clap intro, Byers's song just builds. Boots Randolph's repeated sax blast accents its serious, big beat, shuffle drumming. Piano player Larry Muhoberac's counterpoint is smooth, playful, jazzy, and intricate. When Elvis arrives, he comes on all manly and Southern, but he is also wonderfully sinuous. This is superbly smoky soul, a sound that would not have been out of place a year and a half later at the American Sound sessions. Ironically, when "Let Yourself Go" was released in May 1968, the song was relegated to the B-side of the super-mellow "Your Time Hasn't Come Yet Baby"—a tune that ended with a nod to Mendelssohn's "Wedding March."

In the midst of the civil rights era, soul funk was the music with its finger most on the social pulse. Weeks after the Culver City session, Atlantic released *The Sound of Wilson Pickett*, an album featuring the awesome "Mojo Mama"—a song that came complete with backing singers issuing injunctions to "let your baby go."[243] It was reworked the following September by Edwin Starr as his even sharper Tamla Motown classic, "25 Miles"—a number so pointed and percussive it could have bust down doors. Those two were records of glitter and grit.

Between the releases by Pickett and Starr, Elvis came back in *Speedway*, which saw him singing "Let Yourself Go" in a trendy go-go club that featured car seats as booths. Clad in a startling red jacket with white stripes, he'd seduced three mesmerized girls before the song even reached its bridge.

After soul songs like "Mojo Mama" in the *Comeback Special*, Elvis looked to "Let Yourself Go" as a way to get back his mojo. While *Speedway* had seen him sing soul to a white audience, the *Comeback* responded directly to the turmoil of civil rights struggle, locating Elvis much more squarely in relation to racial issues. According to Steve Binder:

> I'd just come from this amazing controversy with Petula [Clark] and [Harry] Belafonte, so I was a little shell shocked at the time. When I put the Elvis Presley special together I had a black choreographer [Claude Thompson], I had a Puerto Rican choreographer [Jaime Rogers, who played one of the Sharks in the film version of *West Side Story*], I had The Blossoms on camera accompanying Elvis throughout most of the special [the trio was African American], and the entire core of musicians, extras, dancers, were totally integrated among all races. And not one comment was made in terms of race on the entire production. I found that really significant, that everybody accepted them as

colourless and was blinded to any kind of controversy over prejudice or anything. Everybody just said, "Great."[244]

"Let Yourself Go" was recorded again at Western Recorders in Burbank on 20 June 1968 for the *Comeback*.

Epic, adult, and widescreen in its ambitions, the beefed-up *Comeback* version of "Let Yourself Go" sounded almost violent in its execution, with Elvis's raw and desperate vocals every match for the gargantuan, aggressive horns and percussion that dominated the mix. A big, sweaty, dusty monster of a take towered over the Culver City version and perfectly captured the tumultuous social and political strife of its era in dissonant musical form. This new version of "Let Yourself Go" was unfailingly magnificent in its vision. The storm before the calm of "If I Can Dream."

A barely restrained encounter with chaos.

54. "Got My Mojo Working" (from *A Hundred Years from Now: Essential Elvis Volume 4*, 1996)

> I was studying to be an electrician and one day I was driving my truck, and I had a lunch break, and I went into a little record shop and I made a record for a guy, a little demonstration record. Well, the guy put the record out in Memphis. *Memphus* . . . *Memphus*! That's my home-town. You gotta be loose when you say it. Where you from, boy? *Memphus*! If I get any looser, I'll fall apart.[245]

When Elvis sang "Got My Mojo Working" in 1970, the social and musical universe in which he worked had changed dramatically since his early days in Memphis. Early in August 1969, during one of his first shows at the International Hotel in Las Vegas, he reminded the live audience about his past. His joshing was partly a reflection of his own nerves on the day, but it was also a way to tell a sophisticated cabaret audience that he had also come a long way himself and could look back with a sense of distance on his past. When asked about his old Sun records at the Houston Astrodome the next year, he said, "They sound funny, boy!" He added:

> They got a lot of echo on 'em, man, I'll tell you. That's what I mean, I think the overall sound has improved today. There's probably more

gimmicks, but I think the engineers have improved, and I think that the
techniques have improved the overall recording.[246]

Of course, he was speaking in a time after the moon landing. Life had
changed radically since the 1950s, both inside and outside music studios.
As multi-tracking advanced, the number of recording tracks available for
separate instruments on magnetic tape consoles in studios had revolution-
ized recording. With further advances in instrumentation and playing
style, new effects pedals and associated sound devices, cleaner audio
technologies, and other developments, the world of recorded music had
changed radically. Separate instrument recording (often at different
times), overdubbing, and splicing between different takes of each track
had become routine practice. Contemporary material sounded less
"warm," but crisper, lighter, and more dynamic than it could ever have
done before. Navigating this shifting framework of studio practice, Elvis
retained his knack of finding the heart of compositions and, at best, liber-
ating the emotional energy that they contained.

Any informative account of "Got My Mojo Working" should start
with the dashing Preston Foster, a one-time wrestler whose show business
career took him first to Broadway in the late 1920s, then Hollywood by
the early 1930s. The multitalented Foster was part of a successful vocal
trio and sang basso parts in opera. He also starred in more than 120
feature films, including Phil Karlson's famous 1952 noir, *Kansas City
Confidential*. Beyond all that, Foster was the unlikely writer of "Got My
Mojo Working," a song seized by the upcoming R&B singer Ann Cole at
the height of the rock 'n' roll era. Signed to New York's Baton Records,
Cole had already made her name with "In the Chapel."

Ann Cole and the Suburbans' version of "Got My Mojo Working"
came out on Baton Records in 1957. Her recording took the form of
showy, jazzy R&B with an impressive vocal and sax solo. Cole toured the
South with Muddy Waters, the father of Chicago blues. He was so impressed when she sang the song live that he decided to record his own
interpretation. Chess released Muddy's arrangement. In a musical sense
at least, he absolutely owned the song.[247] With its call and response
structure and prominent blues harp accompaniment, Muddy's "Got My
Mojo Working" was rowdy and gritty. It was also heavyweight—
astounding in retrospect, grounded in Muddy's characteristically rich,
deep, manly vocals. The trademark sound of "Got My Mojo Working"

came roaring out of the blues tradition, with Muddy Waters's version not the first but certainly the most definitive.

More than a decade after Cole and Waters had battled it out on their respective independent labels, Elvis tackled "Got My Mojo Working" on the spur of the moment during a studio session in June 1970. At the start of the second of a four-day spell in RCA's Studio B, in order to change the pace after completing the epic "Bridge over Troubled Water," Elvis addressed "Got My Mojo Working." As the assembled musicians tore into it, everyone was swept away. Jerry Carrigan's drumming is outstanding from the start. All others present match his level of intensity. Though Elvis loses the words at one point, as Muddy had perhaps more deliberately done, he draws upon everything within himself to maintain the song's spirit. Urging James Burton to add a blinding guitar solo, he nudges, "Play it, James, play it!" As the studio jam continues, Elvis segues into and then out of the lyrics of another song called "Keep Your Hands Off."[248] He finishes by burning up with the same raw, soul excitement that he had found during the *Comeback Special*. As "Got My Mojo Working" coasts to its spectacular conclusion, he sounds puffed out and chuckles at his own success, saying, "Let's go a little bit!" In comparison, the version he recorded for a rehearsal of the MGM feature documentary *That's the Way It Is* had the same vocal spontaneity but was a product of several iterations. Both a horn section and the Sweet Inspirations accented the song, moving into call and response at one point like Muddy had done. The result remained excellent but was somehow more encumbered than the Nashville studio jam.

Muddy still cannot be bettered for the earthy feel he brought to the number, but Elvis's version is more streamlined and aerodynamic, shooting forward in a way that still leaves the listener standing.

"Got My Mojo Working" is a charismatic song about losing one's charisma—a number that went gutbucket and never came back.

53. "Milky White Way" (from *His Hand in Mine*, 1960)

There was always a haunting quality about Elvis as a celebrity; he was both there and not there, always present and somewhere else. His ghostly vocal style reflected exactly that quality. It was as if his energy was magical or spiritual, rousing one minute and ebbing the next. Perhaps Elvis's *strangest* ever piece of music was recorded at home in February

1966: a gospel quartet–type rendition of Beethoven's "Moonlight Sonata." Accompanied by piano, the piece is performed without words, with Elvis continuously intoning as the composition's mood rises and falls. "Moonlight Sonata" was finally released in 2007 on the FTD compilation *In a Private Moment*. It is recognizably Elvis, but at the same time the spookiest thing he ever recorded. Perhaps the most *cosmic* song he sang was Shirl Milete's "Life," even though it now sounds dated, shapeless, but nevertheless inspiring in its ambition. The most *celestial* number recorded by Elvis, however, by far, is "Milky White Way." Committed to tape at the end of October 1960, at the same Nashville session that produced other tracks for *His Hand in Mind*, the gospel standard deserves its place in this top 100 for showcasing Elvis at his smoothest and most ethereal.

Elvis's voice is pitch perfect on "Milky White Way," in the best style of the gospel tradition. It effortlessly blends and harmonizes with others around it. Beyond the evident backing of the Jordanaires, two of the secret ingredients that help to define the song are an unobtrusive but subtly jazzy piano and Millie Kirkham's very gentle intonations. The whole thing is performed so perfectly that Elvis sounds like he is already in heaven and dancing on a cloud of joy.

Black gospel group the Trumpeteers had a breakfast show on the CBS network toward the end of the 1940s. "Milky White Way" was the show's theme tune and became a top ten R&B hit for them when it was released in 1947 through the Aladdin Records subsidiary Score.[249] Elvis had the record in his collection.[250] The group's lead singer, Joseph Armstrong, had been in the Golden Gate Quartet. Armstrong's vocal gives the song an earthy, deliberate feel, making it near a folk or blues number. The outfit's harmonizing, meanwhile, clearly aligns "Milky White Way" with gospel. Little Richard created a wonderful and typically showy, bombastic version on Top Records in 1950 as the B-side of one of his pre-Specialty releases "I've Just Come from the Fountain."[251] Several other versions came out around this period. Perhaps the most crucial was "Mr. Country Music" Red Foley's 1950 Decca rendition because it was backed by the Jordanaires and the ending was the same as Elvis's.

Compared to its predecessors, the Elvis Presley version of "Milky White Way" is unblemished. Its flawlessly pitched, clear tones achieve a perfect state of harmony. What is truly astounding, though, is the unself-conscious way that Elvis sings the lyric line about meeting his mother in heaven. The singer was only in his mid-twenties at that point. His own mother, Gladys Presley, passed away just over two years earlier. To believers, "Milky White Way" demonstrates that heaven is a place of immortal love where no family need ever part and members are bathed in the blissful radiance of an endless moment.

Immaculate.

52. "See See Rider" (from *On Stage*, 1970)

He said, "Come on back stage and watch me go on." . . . We're back stage in the wings, and that band starts that "2000" thing. Boom! And now the women are screaming. The emotion just got like it was nuts. And they were starting to fix him up a little bit, make sure his hair was right. So I backed away a little bit, about ten feet. They're getting him ready, and he's looking over at me, saying, "Boy, are you all right?" It was the first time I saw him from about twelve feet away, in the shadows, with the band playing that "2000" and the girls screaming, and I said, "Holy Criminy! *That's* ELVIS PRESLEY!"[252]

One of the things that made Elvis special was his intuitive grasp of how to constantly refurbish songs to give his audiences the thrill of their lives. He knew what music was about and used it to truly raise the human spirit. At his concerts, "Also Sprach Zarathustra" brought audience anticipation to fever pitch. Bill Medley of the Righteous Brothers never quite understood the commotion about Elvis until he saw him prepare to go on stage. As the first song to come after the instrumental opening, "See See Rider" brought Elvis into focus every time it was broached. Like the first kiss from a great date, the number detonated hormones. Elvis's up-tempo rock 'n' roll opener accompanied the spectacle of his first appearance on stage. It cued an urgent moment where immense anticipation and fantastic reality came together. It let fans know Elvis was audibly in the building. A drumroll signaled that they were in the presence of a man with genuine charisma. "See See Rider" usually ended with Elvis posing carefully, thrusting out his acoustic guitar, as if crowned champion of his own domain.

Sometimes listed as "CC Rider," the old blues tune dated back to the early years of the twentieth century and may have referred, in the title, to either a preacher or sexually liberated character. Song historian David

Neale noted that Big Bill Broonzy recorded and claimed credit for the tune as early as the 1920s, but Ma Rainey, Leadbelly, and a range of other musicians also covered it.[253] Wee Bea Booze and Chuck Willis had hits with different versions in 1942 and 1957 respectively. Jerry Lee Lewis and LaVern Baker also tried their hands. In the 1960s, the staple was taken up by white performers who sang folk blues. Janis Joplin delivered a straight version of it in her early set lists. The Animals also released a raw, ballsy, Doors-like (but, of course, pre-Doors) version in 1966. One of the sources of inspiration for Elvis's version—at least in terms of its supersharp delivery—may have been Joe Tex's punchy 1967 soul version, which comes across like Jackie Wilson tackling a remix of "Mustang Sally."[254]

Elvis never actually performed "See See Rider" before February 1970; it was not part of his 1950s repertoire. Its inclusion in his set represented an accommodation of music history on his part. To borrow Le Corbusier's famous phrase about housing, each of Elvis's song staples was "a machine for living in": fashioned and refashioned to suit new situations.[255] Once the Memphis Flash took hold of "See See Rider," he performed it at breakneck speed.

Most sources claim Elvis's rock 'n' roll tunes got "thrown away" in his 1970s live show—performed because the audience wanted them but discarded as quickly as possible in the set. There is, however, a different argument to be made. In part due to their urgent pace, which came from their R&B heritage, Elvis's 1950s rock 'n' roll numbers were always known as "hot" records.[256] In comparison to previous versions, their beats per minute seemed raised, marking the energetic excitement of the moment in which Elvis appeared. By the 1970s, "See See Rider" was jetfueled, adapted for modern speed, and repurposed as the set piece that began Elvis's concerts. As he came back to the song, over and over, his vocals began to pick up polish and loose a little verve; Elvis knew he was home. The song functioned as a kind of in-concert litmus test. Every time the audience heard Elvis singing it, they could begin to assess the sound and to feel his particular mood.

51. "Steamroller Blues" (from *Aloha from Hawaii via Satellite*, 1973)

It was a little known R&B group from Detroit called the Masqueraders that took James Taylor's "Steamroller Blues" in a serious, funky direction. The members moved from Detroit to Memphis, hoping Chips Moman and Tommy Cogbill might sprinkle some commercial magic on their output. They were in luck. The pair helped the Masqueraders release eight singles on various labels. Mike Leech, the arranger who shaped "Don't Cry Daddy," helped to oversee the recording of their sassy version of Taylor's blues song. The Amy Records subsidiary Bell released it in 1970, simply titled as "Steamroller." After his own highly productive visit to American Sound, Elvis kept an eye on what was coming out of the Memphis hit factory. The Masqueraders single did inspire Elvis, but more in terms of general style and guitar solo than his own vocals.[257]

Once Elvis signed with RCA and hit the big time, his choice of material was carefully guided. The Colonel, Steve Sholes, the Aberbachs, William Morris Agency, and the likes of Hal Wallis all had an interest in protecting and maintaining a highly lucrative asset. Any outsiders trying to entice Elvis into unsolicited creative partnerships were consequently rebuffed. Elvis's return to concert performance in July 1969 was a significant turning point, however. The singer had always been contractually committed to his RCA release schedule. If he became reluctant to enter the studio, his annual quota of recorded material could now be made up from live releases. When Elvis went in his own musical direction, to an extent the Colonel, and the Aberbachs, would have to live with it. "Steamroller Blues" crept into his live set during his August 1972 Las Vegas engagement. Sandwiched between "You Gave Me a Mountain" and "My Way," it was both performed at the January 1973 *Aloha* shows and released as a top ten single.

The song had an intriguing pedigree. James Taylor's original, knowing version was an exercise in hipster savvy:

> We played this eight month-long gig at a place called the Night Owl Café, down in Greenwich Village, in New York. It used to be in MacDougal and Third, but it might have moved since then—I don't know—but anyhow, at that time there were a lot of so-called blues groups in New York City, you know, and they were making a lot of noise. They weren't very good; they were mostly white kids in from

the suburbs, with electric guitars and amplifiers that the parents had bought them for Christmas and birthdays, and stuff. Their idea of soul was volume; they just cranked it up, you know. They were singing all these heavy songs, like "I'm a Man" or "I'm a Jackhammer" or "I'm a Steam Ship" or whatever; "I'm the Queen Mary" or "A Ton of Bricks." We weren't to be left out of all this, so I wrote this next song, which is the heaviest blues I know, ladies and gentlemen, called "I'm a Steamroller."[258]

Taylor placed the song on his 1970 album, *Sweet Baby James*. "Steamroller Blues" suggested the racial authenticity of the blues was a mirage. In his later performances, Taylor pulled the stops out and played it hard, so listeners could never be sure if he was a blues parodist or blues master. The irony of this unassuming approach was that, even within the same moment, he could start by giving the audience a laugh at the arrogance of silly white kids who thought they could just pitch up and play the blues. Then—usually toward the end of his rendition—he would reach into the song and find its authentic soul. In the middle, Taylor would sometimes josh, "Pick it, James. Get on it, man. Mmm mmm mmm, my my my. Look at those magic fingers just boogie up and down them silver frets. I don't know nothing about the blues."[259]

Elvis's version of "Steamroller Blues," which is comparatively heavy from the start, assertively sweeps aside Taylor's ambiguous, ironic style. The song's performance is knowing, but in a completely different way to Taylor. There is no question about whether *this* performer has the requisite mojo. Elvis's humor is different in focus, making "Steamroller Blues" no longer a parody of arrogant whiteness, but instead an exciting exploration of an icon's virility—a song focused on *Elvis's* own aura and how it informs his uniquely potent, masculine, seductive power.

On the *Aloha* broadcast version of "Steamroller Blues," a weary Elvis initially seems more visually than vocally committed to his song. The band carries the mix until he pulls it out of the bag, after James Burton's pink paisley guitar solo. Elvis continually rolls with the music, getting under its skin. The result is both slick and monumental. Unfortunately, the Royal Philharmonic's Southern gothic slides—which took their cue from the keyboard fills—on the 2015 revamp have largely cluttered the original arrangement. However, many of Elvis's live versions are superb.

50. "Don't" (from *50,000,000 Elvis Fans Can't Be Wrong*, 1959)

"Don't" deserves its place in any top 100 Elvis numbers because of its remarkable tenderness. Leiber and Stoller's intoxicatingly earnest ballad was commissioned by Elvis himself during the *Jailhouse Rock* sessions. It was inspired when the songwriters discovered that he liked the existing generation of crooners. According to Ernst Jørgensen, "Elvis sang it as if it were his last stab at becoming another Dean Martin, or Bill Kenny, or Roy Hamilton."[260] Other writers have suggested the song's feel reflects singers like Mel Tormé or Tony Bennett.[261]

In his musical output, Elvis explored romantic fun and intimacy right from the start. His first Sun single featured parents who moaned that the male protagonist was "fooling with" a girl. Its sequel proclaimed the news that "everybody's rocking tonight." Talking about "A Big Hunk o' Love" from 1958, music writer Ace Collins noted that the protagonist was "asking for much more than dinner and a movie. Would radio stations play a song that featured a message so overtly sexual?"[262]

Leiber and Stoller's ballad "Don't" seems to be one of the first places where a new, directly sensual Elvis comes into play—a man whose expressions of desire continued that year with "One Night" and exploded in 1960 with "It's Now or Never." This Elvis is direct and impassioned, not hiding behind any metaphors or comic patter. In some senses, he is a phantom here. Of course, it was a tactic, one more persona for him to project alongside the sexual showman of "Trouble" from 1958 or "Fever" from 1960. Elvis rounded out the ways in which he could communicate with, and about, desire here—not least, of course, by being its willing object. He often used the ballad—a traditional musical form—to more directly express the urgency of desire implicit in rock 'n' roll.

One of the interesting things about "Don't" was the way it allowed Elvis to move roles and reflect the anxieties of a time when growing female independence was counterbalanced by softer forms of masculinity, and all parties were confused about how far they could go. "Don't" starts off in sedate mode. At first the listener does not know that Elvis is describing the stance of his female lover. His "don'ts" are in theory interpretable as his own. However, as the song unfolds, we find that he is wounded and chiding her for her reluctance. "Don't" is innocent but also intimate—adult in a way that nods to a previous era (aided by the Jordanaires) and beautifully hints at the fire Elvis would later find in songs like "It's Now or Never."

If "Don't" seems a little dated and slow on the surface, its lack of pretence is utterly palpable and makes it sound as if it should frame the most intimate moment in some classic romantic movie.

RCA was concerned that "Don't" might cause controversy, since it sounded like a bid to coax a lover into sex, but the single release—where the song was backed with "I Beg of You"—proved uneventful. Elvis had already rounded out his image by that point and contradicted the early assumptions that he was just some Humes High hoodlum. The singer of "Don't" sounds so convincing in his emotional tone that his pledges of love and loyalty are beyond doubt.

Even though it took place in September, the idea of the Radio Recorders session in which Elvis recorded "Don't" was to find new material for a Christmas album. When he addressed the song, he had already committed his own versions of Irving Berlin's "White Christmas" and "Silent Night" to tape in the studio. Those classics set a beautifully languid tone for this last number. Leiber and Stoller rarely wrote ballads, but here they came up trumps.

Compare "Don't" to the other songs in its class and the advantages are obvious. "Love Me"—also written by the duo—is similar, in comparison, but its protagonist is fronting. Country crooner Don Gibson's "I Can't Stop Loving You"—which Elvis added to his repertoire more than a decade after "Don't" was released—had already been handled eloquently by Ray Charles. Compared to "Don't," such songs find their soul through more recognizable displays of vocal finesse.

Elvis maintained an interest in "Don't," even coming back to it during the marathon of songs he practiced in the summer 1970 Vegas rehearsal sessions that were captured on *That's the Way It Is*. After tuning up, he finds the thread alongside a simple piano backing and gradually explores the song, as if for the first time. Unlike his 1950s incarnation, however, by then he had a slightly cheeky sense of distance from it, something that surfaces just occasionally in the performance.

Right from its breathy introduction, the song is made from silk.

49. "Guitar Man" (from *The Complete '68 Comeback Special,* 2008)

> I hooked up that electric gut string, tuned the B-string up a whole tone, and I toned the low E-string down a whole tone, so I could bar straight across, and as soon as we hit the intro, you could see Elvis' eyes light up. He knew we had it.[263]

Most remembered as the autobiographical vignette that graced intermediate moments of the 1968 NBC *Comeback Special,* "Guitar Man" should have a place in any hot 100 simply because it's the nearest Elvis came to a spoken-word rap. Its story belongs to songwriter Jerry Reed. After being picked by the Atlanta-based country music entrepreneur Bill Lowery, the fair-haired country singer found his feet as a musician at the end of the 1950s on the down-home side of rockabilly. In the next decade, Reed graduated from Lowery's National Recording Corporation to Capitol Records. Chet Atkins produced his version of "Guitar Man," a take that early in 1967 narrowly missed the top fifty. Toward the end of the summer, Elvis was driving down southern California's Ventura Freeway. He heard Reed's song on the radio and realized it reflected the experiences of many around him.

Elvis and Jerry were both about the same age. They liked each other's style. The association had benefits for both. Jerry released an Elvis tribute song and eventually recorded a whole covers LP. Elvis's association with Reed, meanwhile, marked the beginning of him seeing light at the end of his own 1960s career tunnel. Along with performers like Glen Campbell, both Elvis and Jerry catalyzed the process of "Southernization" that made things from below the Mason-Dixon line become cool in mainstream 1970s America. As Jerry Reed had it, much later, "We were two poor white boys that just got lucky."[264]

Early in September 1967, a two-night recording session was arranged in Nashville to find bonus songs to fill up the *Clambake* soundtrack LP. The singer took a chance and recorded material that he liked. Elvis's studio production team contacted Jerry Reed to help get the sound right on his cover of the song.[265] When Reed arrived at the session, by all accounts looking rather informal, he got straight down to business. With its distinct intro and style, the song began to gel after five takes, though the band completed twelve altogether.[266] As the musicians jammed, Elvis began to finish the song in the style of Ray Charles's "What'd I Say."[267]

Unfortunately, the excitement turned a little sour when Freddy Bienstock requested that Reed hand over his publishing rights. The maverick guitarist walked out.

RCA released "Guitar Man" as a single at the start of 1968, complete with a country-picking introduction. Elvis's voice was an arresting combination of firm, restrained, yet still swinging. Although "Guitar Man" failed to enter the top forty, RCA responded by rapidly releasing another Reed/Vector Music composition, "U.S. Male." That charted more strongly, especially in the United Kingdom, where it went top twenty. By that point, early in 1968, Elvis had begun to turn away from the distraction of his Circle G ranch and set his sights on reclaiming the peak of his music career.[268]

On the version of "Guitar Man" from the *1968 Comeback Special*, Elvis really went for broke. He busted clean through the reshaped showtune version with vocals that were among his rawest and most desperate. The last verse still sounds completely reckless and overdriven, with Elvis frantically pursuing the music, finally roping it down as he gives his last breath. The result is astounding. Spontaneous combustion in action. As music critic Robert Matthew-Walker explained, it was "a tremendous performance full of dark surging qualities from Presley; and the orchestra, helped by squealing high trumpets, is fabulous."[269] No wonder that Reed said of his Memphis friend, "He was just a whirlwind that came through in our lifetime."[270]

48. "It's Now or Never" (from *Elvis Is Back!*, 1960)

It is now safe to say that the sales of Presley records have passed that coveted one billion milestone and possibly may even have done so about five years ago. That places him several hundred million ahead of anyone else.[271]

At the end of 2015, Michael Jackson was credited as the world's biggest-selling solo artist, with more than one hundred million in global sales for his *Thriller* album and more than a billion for all units. Not to be outdone, with help from Sony-BMG, the Elvis writer Nick Keene launched a detailed investigation. Keene found that RCA quoted a *Washington Post* story from 1982 that said Elvis Presley's records had already topped one billion in sales. He added, "It is no easy task trying to establish whether or not his sales have actually exceeded one billion copies."[272] One thing we can say more decisively, however, is that "It's Now or Never" added no small amount to the total. With upward of twenty million in single sales by 2006, it remains one of Elvis's top-selling recordings.[273] According to music writer Julie Burns, Neapolitan music represents an "often forgotten X factor ingredient" in Elvis's music.[274] Along with "Surrender," "It's Now or Never" allowed the singer to dramatically express assertive and passionate masculinity in his early 1960s catalog.

The history of "It's Now or Never" begins with Eduardo di Capua and poet Giovanni Capurro, who respectively wrote the music and words for the late nineteenth-century Neapolitan classic "'O sole mio" ("My Sunshine"). Various versions were recorded throughout the twentieth century. Two that almost certainly influenced Elvis's interpretation were Enrico Caruso's Spanish-style 1916 rendition with the Victrola orchestra, plus Mario Lanza's commanding 1950 take for RCA Victor. Their operatic styles emphasized the song's gently breaking damn of high emotion. Paul Simpson claims that Caruso's version was a favorite of Gladys Presley and Elvis's interpretation was a tribute to Lanza.[275] Indeed, in 1972, Elvis said, "I had records by Mario Lanza when I was seventeen, eighteen years old. I would listen to the Metropolitan Opera."[276] By his own dating, that would place his listening in 1952 or 1953, not long after Lanza's recording appeared. It was another urbane orchestral version from the same time, however, that finally piqued Elvis's interest. In November 1949, the capable crooner Tony Martin—who had recently married the dancer Cyd Charisse—released "There's No Tomorrow" on RCA Victor, and it proved a hit, lingering on the chart for six months.[277] Elvis heard Martin's version while stationed in Germany and decided that he wanted to record it. The FTD collector's release *In a Private Moment* contains a home taping in which, accompanied by just a piano, he fearlessly tackled the ballad.

Freddy Bienstock realized that "There's No Tomorrow" was based on a song so old it was in the public domain, so he immediately seconded the capable and available duo Aaron Schroeder and Wally Gold to write new lyrics.[278] When Gold raised the issue of Martin's existing set of lyrics, Bienstock replied, "Oh yes, Elvis knows that lyric. He just doesn't think it's hip enough. It's not him."[279] Schroeder and Gold completed the job in about twenty minutes. After Elvis's tour of duty, the former songwriters' other number, "Stuck on You," was the safe choice for a single, so he recorded it straight away in the first 1960 Nashville session. It was in the second visit that Elvis tackled "It's Now or Never," after "Fever" and "Like a Baby." Schroeder was in the studio; Elvis said to him immediately beforehand, "I'm sorry, Aaron. I don't know if I can do this song justice."[280] The performer need not have feared his task. He completed the Neapolitan ballad in four takes. In fact, after one or two false starts, take one was pretty decent, though the vocals were slightly hesitant and the end, comparatively speaking, lacking in boldness. Elvis hit the second take harder and dropped back with more confidence, as if finding his Latin soul. Again, the timing of the ending did not quite come together. After more false starts, the third take rang true and was suitably trembling, but backing instruments occasionally lacked force and the ending seemed rushed.[281] The fourth take, however, was absolutely spine tingling; it became the one used, spliced with take two. Elvis's voice was perfect on that fourth take—assertive, tender, haunting, golden—and his ending never lost its power. The singer cared so much that when his label altered the recording's compression between the acetate and test pressing stages of its production, he was quick to complain about the sound quality.

RCA released "It's Now or Never" as a single backed with "A Mess of Blues," a strategy that indicated the label was hedging its bet on such a young entertainer and offering a light aria as a hit. In effect, the company gave radio stations a chance to flip the single. Nevertheless, "It's Now or Never" proved a phenomenal hit, entering the charts just above the top forty in mid-July 1960, then rising to the top within a week. It gave the world a sneak peek at a different side of an iconic performer. As one UK fan wrote in the *1964 Elvis Special*: "The disc showed us a new Elvis, an Elvis to astound all critics. The power in his voice was unbelievable at first. This is Elvis? That was the whole crux of the matter, this was Elvis!"[282]

One of the many immediate benefits of "It's Now or Never" was that it redeemed the bearded African American music maestro Barry White from a life of crime.[283] White heard the song while he was serving time in jail. In response, he chose a different path and embraced a career in music, pleasing a vast female audience for several decades with his soothing and sensual blend of soul and funk. By 1970, White was, ironically, contracted to the publishing company Aaron Schroeder Music. The two wrote songs together.

Elvis performed "It's Now or Never" live as soon as he could—at his 1961 Ellis Auditorium shows and USS *Arizona* charity benefit, about a year after recording it. The song was periodically revived for his 1970s concerts, becoming a regular set piece in the final years. For a counterpoint, Elvis would often get Sherrill Nielsen to sing "'O sole mio" beforehand. In December 1976, he quipped, "Sherrill Nielsen is going to do the Italian version and I'm going to do the ancient Hindu version."[284] At the 1972 New York press conference, Elvis said that "It's Now or Never" was his personal favorite.[285] Audiences always appreciated the song, however vintage it was. Those enthusiastic fan responses were justified; "It's Now or Never" remains impeccable. It warrants a place in anyone's top 100, not just because it is an Elvis signature song—one that few pretenders have attempted since—but more specifically because, as much if not more so than "Hurt," it offers the greatest example.

After a Vegas rendition in September 1974, he said: "I couldn't have a better audience if I'd stood outside and paid everybody twenty dollars to come in here. You are out of sight!"[286]

47. "Trouble" (from *The Complete '68 Comeback Special*, 2008)

Picture the scene from *King Creole*: Elvis Presley plays Danny Fisher, who works as a busboy clearing up glasses in gangster Maxie Field's club, The Blue Shade. When Fields strolls in with his moll, Ronnie, Danny grabs her by the arm and says, "Well, hello there!" She replies awkwardly, "Could I get by please?" Fields restrains Danny and asks, "Who is this guy, Ron?" Ronnie shoots back, "The king of Yugoslavia! How should I know?" Under pressure to explain himself, Danny says, "We met in Paris last year; the king of France introduced us." As Maxie sits down with Ronnie at their table, he forces her to confess, saying, "Don't lie to me. I'll break every finger you've got!" Under duress, Ronnie explains, "I heard him sing a song, that's all. He sang here once for your big-shot friends. I told him he had a nice voice. That's all." Having challenged the biggest shot in town by getting overly familiar with his woman, Danny is backed into a corner. Evil Maxie now holds all the cards. To show that the lady is not lying, he gets Danny to sing. Even the emcee's introduction is humiliating: he asks the audience to listen to "Caruso, the busboy!" The only response possible is a snarl of defiance. It takes the form of a song. As he cuts loose, the busboy's quiff and hips seem to float in the air. He gets into a quivering, finger-clicking frenzy.

"Trouble" deserves its place in any Elvis 100 because it stylizes his role as the ultimate juvenile delinquent. The song's inspiration goes way back. Perhaps it starts with the atmospheric snake-charming tune "Kradoutja," an Arabic folk delight that was reformulated as "The Streets of Cairo" in the late nineteenth century. A vaudeville performer named James Thornton was inspired to add lyrics. Soon a popular expression— to dance the "hoochie coohie"—came into existence, referring to the motions practiced when belly dancer's hips took on a life of their own. In the 1929 Mickey Mouse cartoon, *The Karnival Kid*, a talented monkey plays "The Streets of Cairo" as a one-man band, while a scruffy tom cat with a top hat and fat belly advertises the tent of Minnie the Shimmy Dancer. The cat ushers visitors to "see the hoochie coochie dance." He is, of course, a *hoochie coochie man.* "Hoochie coochie" was not only associated with the public eroticism of belly dancing; it was also connected to the illicit thrill of women's desire. "Hoochie coochie man" became a vague term for any male powerful enough to control women as a stud or pimp, exploiting their bodies for his own benefit. Drawing on that particular theme, Muddy Waters's tenth hit, "Hoochie Coochie Man," replaced the Orient, musically, with the Delta. In Waters's world, the "hoochie coochie" man is mythical. His record was seen as the missing link because it arrived between blues and rock 'n' roll, just as the latter boom was beginning, and could be performed in both genres. Delightfully macho, blustering, and circular, the stop-start riff structure of Waters's swinging 1954 Chess Records number is arguably also proto-funk. The "stop time" riff had been reused already in Elmer Bernstein's theme for Otto Preminger's 1956 Frank Sinatra picture, *The Man with the Golden Arm.* After "Trouble," Brook Benton used the riff in his song "Kiddio," then Leiber and Stoller further recycled it. The two were partly in the business of creating unofficial adaptations and answer records—inspired updates, as it were, based on classic blues. They drew on both Bo Diddley's "I'm a Man" and Muddy's "Mannish Boy" to create "I'm a Woman." Capitol released Peggy Lee's recording of the knowing, sassy number in 1962. Vee-Jay put out a version by Christine Kittrell in the same year.

Elvis addressed "Trouble" in a January 1958 Hollywood studio visit that was scheduled to record music for *King Creole.* That whole session was both swinging and wonderfully polished. "Trouble" came between the equally dynamic "Hard Headed Woman" and showy doo-wop of "New Orleans," songs in which Elvis's voice again neared the bawling style he perfected in "Jailhouse Rock." After that, "King Creole" and "Crawfish" rounded out the first day of the session.

Enveloped in the off-kilter sound of New Orleans jazz, "Trouble" is just about as punk as young Elvis gets. In the verses, he seems cool, surly, self-justifying, as if playing the role of an escaped slave or recalcitrant outlaw. All hell breaks loose, in contrast, when he lifts the lid on the song in the chorus and talks about his family heritage. A more familiar vocal style appears there; his voice is smooth, soaring, elastic, desperate, electric, and expressive. What is interesting about the song, however, is that this second, effusive persona is both interrupted and complemented by the beleaguered speaker of the verses; he says "yeah, yeah" in the first chorus, then finishes off the drama by adding a knowing and funny "yeah" in agreement at the end. The whole thing is a playlet; a one-man dialogue.

The potent "Hoochie Coochie Man" was already a figure of legend in Muddy Waters's blues number, making "Trouble," in effect, a parody of a parody of masculinity. What Elvis does with the song is turn it into an expression of entrapment and escape that is riotous, rousing, and funny at the same time. Film reviewer Eric Braun observed, "This is a prime example of singing with acting—Elvis expresses sheer contempt with every timbre of his voice and expression."[287] "Trouble" secured Elvis's image as a young upstart who was simmering and angry; both a lover *and* a fighter. Its moment is innately symbolic. The boy has charmed an older woman, has been forced to defend her honor, and can only respond to the challenge from a high-status older male by singing. No wonder that "Trouble" became a signature for Elvis, the song that he used to kick-start the *Comeback Special*. That snatch of "Trouble" at the start of the show raised the ghost of Danny Fisher—this time bursting with adult rage— and united him (through set design) with criminal Vince Everett from *Jailhouse Rock*. Elvis was, of course—with the help of director Steve Binder—using those two characters to speak about the potency of his image as a superstar. The instantly iconic *Comeback* opener remains absolutely hypnotic.

"Trouble" was not one of Elvis's favorite songs in concert, but he frequently performed it in his summer 1973 Las Vegas shows, placing it early on the set list. By that point, his famous voice was a bit too mature and full, his commitment was a bit wavering, and the arrangement a tad poor, failing to make the song work as well as before. He inspired a vast range of other artists and left an avalanche in his wake: tributes, tryouts, transformations, and transgressions. Suzi Quatro's 1974 cover version might sound like a bad impression, but her plucky attempt to strut like "The Man" is really in the song's tradition. One of the most unusual covers has to be by Amanda Lear. In 2014, the decadent 1970s disco diva offered a whole album of Presley covers that sounded like an Elvis-themed Berlin cabaret. It was appropriately called *My Happiness*. The album had been a long time coming. At the height of fame, in 1975, Lear released a French-language version "Trouble" ("La Bagarre") as a single, backed, rather appropriately, by "Lethal Leading Lady." Needless to say, Elvis's original was much better. The Memphis singer may never have quite predicted where his musical legacy would travel and how big his phenomenon would become.

46. "Let It Be Me" (from *On Stage*, 1970)

"Let It Be Me" has its place in any Elvis countdown because it expresses the innate generosity of his music. Cast your mind back, if you can, to early 1970. Simon and Garfunkel's "Bridge over Troubled Water" was on top of the U.S. charts and BJ Thomas's "Raindrops Keep Falling on My Head" not far behind. In the United Kingdom, Edison Lighthouse led singles sales with "Love Grows (Where My Rosemary Goes)." Canned Heat's "Let's Work Together" and Peter, Paul and Mary's "Leavin' on a Jet Plane" took second and third place. Problems existed out there in society and people were looking for something soothing in the world of popular music. At his midnight show in Las Vegas, on Tuesday, 17 February, Elvis had just finished singing his latest single, Eddie Rabbitt and Dick Heard's "Kentucky Rain." With a note of humbleness in his voice, he announced, "There's a beautiful song that came out a few years ago. It's not my song, but I'd like to sing it for you anyway." His modesty was, perhaps, because he knew that another of the song's singers, Sonny Bono, was in the audience. Sonny & Cher released a version five years earlier on their Atlantic LP *Look at Us*.

The story of "Let It Be Me" actually began in France, where the Paris Olympia cabaret super crooner Gilbert Bécaud—sometimes known as

"Mr. 100,000 Volts"—had a 1955 hit on the La Voix de Son Maître (HMV) label with the beautiful and poignant "Je t'appartiens" ("I Belong to You"). Bécaud wrote the music. His associate Pierre Delanoë—who composed "What Now My Love" six years later—added the words.[288] Together, they created a rousing gem of a song. The Everly Brothers were not the first to sing it with English lyrics, but their 1960 version, "Let It Be Me," scored a *Billboard* top ten and became the benchmark for others to follow. Chet Atkins and Andy Williams were among those who did.

The Everly Brothers' version of "Let It Be Me" begins with bright, sweet strings before showcasing their earnest and sentimental vocals. It ends with Don and Phil luxuriating in the ring of their own voices. The next important version, which peaked even higher, was offered in 1964 by African Americans Jerry "The Iceman" Butler and Betty Everett on Vee-Jay Records. Butler and Everett both had excellent reputations at the time. The former had sung in the same church as Curtis Mayfield. Before Mayfield stepped out of the shadows, Butler sang lead vocals for the Impressions. Betty Everett, meanwhile, had just released "The Shoop Shoop Song (It's in His Kiss)" for the label. Butler and Everett's duet was more epic and heroic than the Everlys' version. There were, of course, further takes of "Let It Be Me." Before they teamed up with Elvis, the Sweet Inspirations had some success after Atlantic's executive vice president, Jerry Wexler, made them featured performers in 1967. The group's soulful approach emerged from its gospel foundation. Sounding a little like the Supremes, the female singers released a funky, angelic version. Bobbie Gentry and Glen Campbell also had a 1969 hit with "Let It Be Me." Their gentle and measured country interpretation owed much to the Everlys' rendition. It was, as likely as not, from the Butler-Everett duet version, though, that Elvis drew his inspiration.[289]

In 1968, Jerry Butler released "Only the Strong Survive," a song that he had also co-written. Elvis delivered a fairly straight cover of it, complete with spoken-word introduction for his session at American the next year. Another year on, and he performed "Let It Be Me" in his Vegas show. Where the Everlys settled for an intro of a few strummed guitar chords, Butler and Everett's take started with an orchestral flourish. Elvis used that arrangement when he covered "Let It Be Me" in concert. While it might sound like the most "white bread" of easy listening ballads, Elvis's cover is an indication that he did not give up on black music. He often placed "Let It Be Me" after "Kentucky Rain," as if offering a clue to the song's pedigree and making the American Sound connection clear.[290] Unfortunately, though, Elvis Presley only sang the song during his February 1970 engagement. One of the best performances appears on the consistently excellent *On Stage* album. The introduction seems both generous and gentle. Elvis's voice is powerful, restrained, and quietly yearning. As he sings about making love, the female soprano lifts. It is clear that the moment has arrived. The rest of the song cruises in a way that is as relaxed as a Sunday afternoon drive.

45. "Let Me Be There" (from *Elvis Recorded Live on Stage in Memphis*, 1974)

There is something to be said for the *unhip* Elvis Presley; not the hillbilly cat of the Sun sessions, or the black leather panther of the *Comeback*, but the mass entertainer who crooned ballads that sounded bland on first hearing. Some of his easy listening material is better than expected. One example is "Love Letters." The ballad was originally recorded by Elvis in 1966 but revamped at the start of the next decade for an album called *Love Letters from Elvis*. In a sense, it was riding a trend. The success of contemporary singer-songwriters had influenced acts working in various genres, from rock to country. As established genres *softened up*, easy listening charts accommodated the sea change. Crossover acts like John Denver found broad audiences. As an accessible fusion of pop, country, and gospel style, John Rostill's "Let Me Be There" was typical of this vogue for pleasant music. The song deserves its place in any countdown because it showed that Elvis did not need vocal acrobatics or heavy lifting to assume his role as leader. It is a sing-along number, par excellence.

In the Stax sessions that rounded off 1973, some of the songs had been outstanding. The next year was the first, outside of his army duty, that Elvis did not record new material. Relatively speaking, his interest in being a *studio* recording artist appeared to diminish and he focused on his live set. RCA had already released four albums of live material. In March 1974, Elvis returned to his hometown for his first concerts there in well over a decade. The album *Elvis Recorded on Stage in Memphis* captured his atmospheric final show at the Mid-South Coliseum. Fans had their purple tickets ripped at the door. They walked in, sat down, and enjoyed the experience of Elvis singing a wide range of songs, including some medleys. After the monumental "An American Trilogy," he tackled a number that had entered into his set less than two months before.

Olivia Newton-John's single version of "Let Me Be There" just missed the U.S. *Billboard* top five and fared even better in the easy listening market. Starting off with a soft and innocent female voice standing stark in the arrangement, then building toward a stronger, sassier, gospel-style climax, her version of "Let Me Be There" has a contemporary, "Western" feel. In comparison, Elvis's take begins with a classic, easy, country guitar riff, but soon emerges as a full-on, Vegas-style showstopper. Placed on an album that showed Graceland on the front, it featured JD Sumner bringing up the rear as part of a magnificent, driven marathon of a performance.[291] When "Let Me Be There" finishes, the title is repeated, as if nobody can quite get enough. Once it ends, it starts up again from out of nowhere.

Compared to Newton-John's breezy rendering, Elvis's cover of "Let Me Be There" is a tour de force. The joy of communality reigns supreme. It was hardly surprising that both Newton-John and Presley went on to record another Rostill classic, "If You Love Me (Let Me Know)," which was very much a sister record. For Elvis, both were laid down as live rather than studio recordings, though in 1977 "If You Love Me (Let Me Know)" was overdubbed in Nashville.

Elvis's Memphis performance of "Let Me Be There" was so cherished that he kept it in his live set on a fairly regular basis until early 1976. The 20 March 1974 Mid-South Coliseum recording was even dusted off to round out the first side of what became his last will and testament, the LP *Moody Blue*. Elvis's live takes of "Let Me Be There" differ in their tempo and tone, with some sounding rushed. One of the better performances was captured when he played the Dallas Memorial Auditorium in June 1975. In this wonderfully uplifting take, Elvis leans into the chorus, yelling "Yeah!" as if he is performing an eviction. The result is positively volcanic: a moment so enthralling that those involved only become aware of exactly where they are once it is over.

44. "Power of My Love" (from *From Elvis in Memphis*, 1969)

It was a cool Saturday in Memphis, two years to the day, in fact, since the controversial scientist and "Godfather of the bomb" J. Robert Oppenheimer died in New Jersey. The "atomic-powered singer," however, was still on top form. He delivered a majestic, gentle version of Neil Diamond's "And the Grass Won't Pay No Mind," as payment for taking up a time slot that was already earmarked for Diamond's recording session. When the musicians came back for the evening, they tried a new number by Giant, Baum, and Kaye. "Power of My Love" ranks in any Elvis compilation for the simple reason that it showcases him at his most masculine, adult, and sensual. Elvis had also begun to explore a sense of sexual defiance as early as "Good Rockin' Tonight." He had already sung with a commanding voice on studio cuts like "Lonesome Cowboy" and "It's Now or Never." What is unique about "Power of My Love," however, is the way that it effortlessly bridges between the raw urgency of the *Comeback Special* and virile confidence of his early 1970s shows. In fact, with support from his female backing singers and the Memphis horn section, Elvis absolutely sizzles. As critic Robert Matthew-Walker said, correctly:

> Solid and raunchy, Presley's performance is irresistible: full of sly innuendoes and *double-entendres.* There are few singers who can manage this, yet it stems from the Presley of 1954 / 1955. It is explosive, breathy and rich, with an extraordinary ending.[292]

"Power of My Love" was supplied during the second, marathon bout at American Sound in Memphis.[293] By that point, on the *Comeback*, Elvis had already reigned triumphant in black leather; his performance style embraced both vocal urgency and sexual directness.

"Power of My Love" owes much to its writers. New York native Florence Kaye was almost a generation older than Elvis. Kaye was drawn to the Brill Building, where she met her two younger, male co-writers: the classically trained Bernie Baum in 1950 and his friend Harvey Zimmerman (known as "Bill Giant") a few years later. Kaye majored on the lyrics and Baum, the harmonies. Giant recorded the demos and concentrated on vocal inflections. The first song that Elvis recorded by the trio, in the summer of 1961, was "Sound Advice." The *Follow That Dream* number was dropped from its soundtrack LP for being too weak and surfaced four years later on the leftovers compilation album, *Elvis for Everyone!*[294] Giant, Baum, and Kaye continued to supply material, mostly made for Hollywood, over the next few years, including the quirky, rapid-fire "Beach Shack" and "(You're the) Devil in Disguise." With "Power of My Love," however, the trio struck gold. It was not simply nonsense that Presley could convincingly sing; by the time he tackled the number, it was *a vehicle for who he could be.*

What a song like "Power of My Love" affirmed in Elvis's profile was a certain macho gravitas. Florence Kaye explained, "When we wrote it we wanted to write the ultimate song. It was very sensual and provocative."[295]

"Power of My Love" is uniquely *heavy.* One of the changes allowed by multi-tracking was that Elvis could record a guide vocal for the players, then come back later to complete the music. On different takes, the singer can be heard suffering slight traces of the cold that bugged him earlier that year. He sings a few snatches of different songs. The vocal for "Power of My Love" actually includes harmony overdubs by Elvis on it. His different attempts reflected constant commitment on his part. Only in the released version, however, does his performance have quite enough controlled force to take the matter successfully in hand. Marked by undertones of barely repressed anger, his growling voice is righteous, uncompromising, and finally conquering. When he sang "Burning Love" for the *Aloha* telecast, Elvis was so sure-footed in his role as a sex symbol that he no longer had to try, and he could relax into the ritual of it all. "Power of My Love," however, showcases him at his most potent. The recording reveals a man who is extraordinarily strong, unflinching, and relentless in his eroticism.

Knockout.

43. "Johnny B. Goode" (from *From Memphis to Vegas/From Vegas to Memphis,* 1969)

Rock 'n' roll was a popular, commercial style that brought America's social factions together in a way that was more sustained than any modern music had previously. At the time, fans of all races enjoyed black artists like Chuck Berry and Little Richard for the exuberance they brought to the party. When it came to discussing Elvis, one of the charges frequently made was that Chuck Berry was the musician who truly deserved the title King of Rock 'n' Roll. In some senses, the argument seems churlish. Why compare? Elvis was charismatic and versatile; Chuck was focused. The notion of a stolen crown is based upon the idea that America was so racially biased that it forgot a black genius and instead lauded a white performer. If that is so, the fault lies with America, not Elvis. Even so, the real picture is more complex. Elvis's energetic rockabilly was part of an ongoing dialogue. It bust the door down for many black artists to find white audiences in the following years. Indeed, in what was his first encounter with Berry's music, Elvis added "Maybellene" to his repertoire within weeks of its July 1955, Chess Records release.

Like Elvis, Chuck Berry was set in a genius mold. Take "Johnny B. Goode"—a song that borrowed its opening riff from Louis Jordan's 1946 number "Ain't That Just Like a Woman (They'll Do It Every Time)" and showcased what Berry could do. Jordan and his Tympany Five stormed the postwar jukebox market with their Decca singles. "Ain't That Just Like a Woman (They'll Do It Every Time)" combined a jazzy, understated jump blues foundation with a piano boogie-woogie melody and some knowing vocals. Its introduction was carefree, sly, and fly, reminiscent of the relative tranquility of an afternoon's fishing. Chuck, in contrast, stuck it straight to the audience. When Berry made the introduction his own, he changed its energy, charging it up to sound like something more apt for jiving, hot-rod racing, or having a riot. His style was rampant, restless, and comparatively aggressive. No wonder that Chuck and his swinging twelve-bar blues had some claim on the kingdom. What Berry never quite achieved, however, was versatility. When he hit big, he stayed more or less with the formula of rock 'n' roll. In the summer of 1969, he was still rehashing his semiautobiographical 1958 hit, now called "Concerto in B. Goode," as a monster blues jam. Nothing wrong with that, in theory: If it ain't broke, don't fix it. The list of artists who have covered "Johnny B. Goode" reads like its own rock 'n' roll roll call.

Given the ubiquity of "Johnny B. Goode," it is interesting that Elvis first chose to cover it toward the end of August 1969 during his opening engagement in Las Vegas. It was as if he was finding and showing his own unique voice through a piece of pop culture that everyone would recognize. By amping the tension right up, Elvis created rocket-fueled rock 'n' roll, a number for the interstellar age. He knew that the drama of the record came from the singer trying to keep on top of it. As the other musicians struggle to keep pace, his vocals flash past like a tiger is at his rear. He would address the tune again, many, many times, both live and in studio jams. The 1973 *Aloha* version, for instance, is more measured than those early Vegas takes. It pans out as an instrumental spectacular, with Elvis sounding more like a spectator, pointing the audience to moments in the chorus where James Burton jumps hoops with his guitar. Burton, in fact, developed a stage routine in which he played the entire song with the guitar behind his head, something that can be seen during the show taped for the CBS television special *Elvis in Concert* in Omaha, 19 June 1977.

Alongside the work of Beethoven, Berry's original of "Johnny B. Goode" ended up on NASA's *Voyager 1* mission, which launched less than a month after Elvis died. The song was celebrated as a monumental reflection of human achievement. Relatively speaking, however, Chuck Berry's take on genre differed from Elvis's. Chuck was comparatively narrow in his musical focus. Elvis Presley, on the other hand, became an icon by embracing America's musical melting pot and finding a playful, expressive voice that transcended any one fad or moment. As a live tune, "Johnny B. Goode" became a country-rock boogie in Elvis's hands: rapid, rollicking, and, at best, elevated to supercharged cabaret.

42. "One Night" (from *The Complete '68 Comeback Special*, 2008)

"One Night" deserves its place in any Elvis countdown because it shows the focus that the artist could find in even the simplest of music. The song's story began with one-time Imperial Records A&R man Dave Bartholomew. While Dave was experienced in expressing himself with brass instruments, his co-writer and fellow New Orleans music veteran Earl King played guitar. Their songs together included several recorded by the local live music veteran Overton Amos Lemons. On account of his wide grin and evident dental problems, Lemons was better known as Smiley Lewis. He released several classic Bartholomew-King compositions but never had as much success as those who covered him, including Elvis and Fats Domino.

Smiley Lewis's 1956 R&B version of "One Night of Sin" is slow and measured. His phrasing dawdles in places, though he hits his mark by the end of the number. In comparison, Elvis's remake is explosive—frantic and swashbuckling; hooking its lines like ducks at a fair. Like some of his other rock 'n' roll classics (notably "Jailhouse Rock" and "Trouble"), the desperate phrasing may have owed something to performers like Emmett Miller, who were themselves early shapers of the swinging blues style. Elvis originally sang "One Night" at the Paramount Scoring Stage in January 1957 on the same day he did "(Let Me Be Your) Teddy Bear."

The dirty connotations of the song's title spooked RCA so much that the song was recut at Radio Recorders with milder lyrics the following month. It is plausibly, after all, the confession of a sorry but satisfied fellow whose "helping hand" gave him the elbow after finding he was unfaithful.

Rather than bury "One Night" on the *Loving You* soundtrack LP, RCA put it on hold and released it as a single late the following year, backed with "I Got Stung." At the time, the number was second only to "Jailhouse Rock" in sales. It became part of Elvis's stage act and was included in the set list for his 1961 Pearl Harbor show. Immediately immersed in a chaotic deluge of screams from his audience, Elvis completely tears the place up, despite a relatively languid live performance.[296] When he launches enthusiastically into the song during the stage set on *That's the Way It Is*, the sly, cabaret backing is no match for his slightly desperate vocals. His best performance of "One Night," however, hands down, is in the NBC *Comeback Special*.

Smiley Lewis's number was an ideal way to convey the central message of the black leather segment from the NBC show: Elvis was back, supremely confident, unrepressed, and ready to supercharge his early material to prove it. After looking for his guitar strap, Presley lambasts the flimsiness of Jimmy Webb's "MacArthur Park." Casting aside any such preconceptions, he opts instead for the scorching immediacy of rock 'n' roll. Once the song begins, the merest of his cut-ups orchestrate screams from the studio audience. Suddenly, everyone is on for the ride. In the *Comeback*, Elvis is a rocker at the height of his powers. Rivers of sweat run down his chest. His legs no longer shake; they pump. The use of his guitar is as much percussive as it is rhythmic. Elvis is, all at once, powerful, charismatic, burning up, funny, and shockingly committed. With one foot on a shabby blue studio chair, he plays "music that any musicians can tell you anyone can make and almost no one can."[297] When he jokes that someone has pulled the plug on his guitar, the relief is audible. Then he starts up again and finishes with an intensity that demands only screams in response. At that moment, everyone, including Elvis, has to recover from what had been spent. Music critic Robert Matthew-Walker reported, "'One Night' is another classic: a slow rocker, Presley's voice takes on a 'constricted' quality, which forces its way through the music."[298]

Simply put, "One Night" is *among the best* of a whole spate of magnetic *'68 Special* performances.

41. "And I Love You So" (from *Today*, 1975)

It does us no good to dwell too much on Elvis's worst moments, but what they at least indicate is that for more than twenty years he had a vast audience in the palm of his hand. On 19 June 1977, he played Omaha. CBS cameras were there to capture the singer. He was not just portly. At times, during those last shows, Elvis seemed almost half awake, stumbling through a haze of medication. His enslavement to prescription pills left his face so bloated that it became like a mask. Elvis's final predicament teaches us nothing if not to have compassion for addicts. Even with music on his side, his spirit appeared to waver. On a few occasions, between songs, he was at his lowest ebb. For one or two brief moments, Elvis Presley, the King of Rock 'n' Roll, was simply someone *out there* on stage, tragically alone—a man who just *happened to be* in front of an audience. Such rare moments show that Elvis was human and mortal. His aura was immense but so fragile and transient that it could easily be extinguished. By revealing there was nothing inevitable about what he achieved, even those worst moments show the full nature of his talent. Before he offered a surprisingly passable performance of "And I Love You So," he slurred, "The next song is a song we did in an alblum. An 'alblum'? S'called, 'And I Love You So.'"

As with a few other pearls in the Presley catalog, "And I Love You So" is a case of genius meeting genius; its writer was the uniquely gifted Don McLean. Encouraged by Pete Seeger, McLean became a leading light of the folk singer-songwriter boom. He recorded "And I Love You So" in the summer of 1969, and it was released the next spring, both as a single and on his first album, *Tapestry*. McLean's version is as brightly bittersweet, searching and devastating, as might be expected. The single was reissued a year later, after his record company, Mediarts, was swallowed up by United Artists. With the tremendous interest in McLean's subsequent songs "American Pie" and "Vincent," "And I Love You So" took on a life of its own. Shirley Bassey found an operatic depth in its sadness when she powered her way through a 1972 version that was as beautiful and belting as its singer. Perry Como also made it his swan song, releasing a gently paternal take in 1973 when he was over sixty.

Elvis recorded his version of "And I Love You So" in March 1975. It entered his live repertoire around the same time and stayed until the summer of 1977. One of the reasons McLean's ballad worked for him was its theme. The song tugs hard on the heartstrings, not just because it expresses the fragility of life—it also shows the way that human beings cling to each other in its wake.

This is Elvis the insomniac, the loner, the depressive. A man who loved to watch Max Ophüls's 1948 weepy *Letter from an Unknown Woman* and hear gloomy recitations by Charles Boyer.[299] A man for whom love was intense, but so utterly fleeting. A soul whose whole life had been shaped by the loss of those who were nearest to him. He was the same man who said to Red West in October 1976, "I felt terribly alone."[300] Elvis was not only the life and soul of the rock 'n' roll party but also a profoundly lonely man. He lived in a solitude orchestrated around the presence of other people. In that sense, more than the theatrics of, say, "Hurt," "And I Love You So" provides a window on the inner life of the King in a way that is consistent with what else is known about him. It's no wonder that he could be heard in the studio saying to girlfriend Sheila Ryan, "Step up here, Sheila. Let me sing to you, baby."[301] It's also indicative that Ryan, a *Playboy* cover girl, moved on from Elvis to marry James Caan within less than a year.

"And I Love You So" is Elvis being the Phantom of the Opera being Elvis.[302] To borrow from Leroux's dark novel, the song "seemed to me at first one long, awful, magnificent sob. But, little by little, it expressed every emotion, every suffering of which mankind is capable."[303] After the ballad's benign start, Elvis begins to audibly grasp the nature of its gloom. Millie Kirkham's delightfully piercing soprano motif perfectly conveys the emotional pain of McLean's heartbreaking composition. This is Elvis as a lonely specter quietly trying to make human contact. Even in his melancholy, however, his yearnings remain infectious. Indeed, the worth of this masterpiece needs no explanation. It deserves its place in any countdown because of its power to reflect the deepest tragedies of the human spirit.

"And I Love You So" is a mature record, presenting Elvis at his most existentially broken. Perhaps only Don McLean could have written it, and only Elvis Presley could have so fearlessly embraced its emotional challenge.

Who among us, except the most soulless, could not in response shed a tear?

40. "Help Me Make It Through the Night" (from *Elvis Now*, 1972)

Religion. Existentialism. Metaphysics. These were not only topics on Elvis Presley's reading list. They were the scholarly interests of professor of philosophy Frederick Sontag, who taught for more than half a century at Pomona College in California. One of Sontag's most able and famous pupils was Kris Kristofferson. Like Elvis, he was a strange combination of "rugged sports" player, deep thinker, and hopeless romantic. Kristofferson began writing songs while he studied English literature as a Rhodes Scholar at Oxford University. He had a fascination for the mystic poetry of William Blake and the country songs of Hank Williams. After a spell in the army, Kristofferson spent the second half of the 1960s in Nashville as a songwriter. His debut album, *Kristofferson*, was a combination of mature country sound and themes appropriate to the counterculture. Within a year, tracks from it were covered by artists as different as Johnny Cash and Janis Joplin.

Elvis recorded "Help Me Make It Through the Night" in May 1971. Efforts were inevitably made to strike a publishing deal before or, worse, after he made any recording. Nevertheless, at this point in his career, the singer was probably more free than he had ever been to record material from beyond the Hill & Range stable. Kristofferson was a hot property. His publishers were not interested in a deal.

Except for early in 1972 and the following summer, Elvis sang "Help Me Make It Through the Night" infrequently in the live arena. Ernst Jørgensen reported that the tape recorder was actually turned off during the former period, as the Colonel's camp was still sore about the publishing issue.[304]

What made "Help Me Make It Through the Night" contemporary was its compromised perspective on romantic relationships. Half a decade earlier, the Beach Boys dared to dream of sharing a bed in "Wouldn't It Be Nice." Then, in "Let's Spend the Night Together," the Stones made it a demand. By 1970, the utopianism expressed in Woodstock had already given way to Altamont. Country folk singers were changing to keep pace, finding new material that rejected youthful idealism in favor of a pragmatic approach to relationships. Stephen Stills's "Love the One You're With" was one example, and Kris Kristofferson's "Help Me Make It Through the Night" was another. As fellow country singer Bobby Bare said, "Before 'Help Me Make It Through the Night,' one would be hard pressed to figure out what a honky-tonk angel did when you got her out of the honky-tonk."[305] The record is, however, hardly graphic. Its points are morally challenging, but they are made through implication. The intimacy sought by the singer is really about avoiding isolation. If no lover materializes, then a "friend" who can offer close company as a favor is acceptable. Given the social expectations placed on the female sex, it is hardly surprising that the song was even more controversial when sung by a woman. Beginning with a peculiarly moribund sexual invitation, the country singer Dottie West, who was Kristofferson's first choice, later sang her own jaded and mature version. "Help Me Make It Through the Night" deserves its stripes because it showcases the moral and emotional weight that Elvis could bring to his 1970s repertoire. His choice of such material showed that he was maturing as a person.

Kristofferson's original of "Help Me Make It Through the Night" sounds surly and macho compared to Elvis's version; the song's bittersweet theme emerges, for him, through the difference between its vocals and carefree country backing. In contrast, Elvis's interpretation does not start so much as unfurl. David Briggs's flowing piano is accompanied by one of the softest first verses that Elvis had ever accomplished. As the song rolls on, the tone of his voice suggests restrained power with an appealing undertow of desperation. Propelled by the slightest nudge from the Imperials, the whole thing bobs along like a boat on the waves.

Not satisfied with one Kristofferson classic, Elvis was also interested in covering "Sunday Morning Coming Down," a song about the sadness of waking up lonesome with a hangover, first commandeered by Johnny Cash. In the event, within a year of "Help Me Make It Through the Night," he recorded another, less maudlin and more sentimental number: "For the Good Times."[306] From 1974 onward, Elvis also addressed himself in concert to Kristofferson's "Why Me Lord?" in part to showcase JD Sumner's unfeasibly low bass tone. Kristofferson, meanwhile, went on to play a role in 1976 that should, by rights, have gone to Elvis. He starred opposite Barbra Streisand as John Norman Howard in *A Star Is Born*.

39. "Bossa Nova Baby" (from *Fun in Acapulco*, 1963)

Cut for an otherwise lackluster movie soundtrack, Leiber and Stoller's "Bossa Nova Baby" deserves its role in Elvis's canon because it demonstrates that even flimflam can be good. "Bossa Nova Baby" was in keeping with the faux exotic theme that proved so popular during the vacation package boom that hit when Americans discovered affordable air travel. Released as a single backed with "Witchcraft," "Bossa Nova Baby" was a promotion for Elvis's sixth Paramount picture. The film studio even designed numbered promotional "passports" and proudly announced they were "Your Passport to 'Fun in Acapulco.'" Leiber and Stoller's daft tune had nothing to do with Bossa Nova or Acapulco, and nobody could quite dance or sing along to it, but the number took off all the same. Perhaps it was the way that its lyrics needed a machine gun to deliver them or Elvis's hip-swiveling performance. It might sound a little dated now, but "Bossa Nova Baby" still comes with a bite.

Leiber and Stoller initially gave "Bossa Nova Baby" to the Clovers, an African American doo-wop outfit who stormed the R&B charts in 1951 when "Don't You Know I Love You" came out through Atlantic. Another hit from the group's first year—"Fool, Fool, Fool"—was covered by Elvis when he played live on *Louisiana Hayride* on 20 November 1954. He added their song "Little Mama" to his live repertoire by March of the following year; it was the B-side to the Clovers' February 1954 Atlantic single "Lovey Dovey." He may also have had the group's Atlantic single "Blue Velvet" in his collection.[307]

By the end of the 1950s, Leiber and Stoller aided the Clovers' ongoing success by offering them the delightfully quirky "Love Potion No. 9"; Billy Mitchell sang lead on what became a top thirty hit for United Artists Records in 1959. It was one of only a couple of records to break his group out of the R&B category. When "Bossa Nova Baby" was released, Roosevelt "Tippie" Hubbard had replaced Mitchell; the single was credited to "Tippie and the Clovers."[308] It christened Leiber and Stoller's own label, Tiger Records. With a capering samba shuffle and groovy Farfisa hook, the Clovers' version formed a clear template for Elvis's more produced interpretation. Alan Lorber is probably to thank: He was a song shaper who arranged and conducted the Clovers' energetic yet understated version.[309]

When Elvis recorded "Bossa Nova Baby" in Hollywood, teen angel Bobby Vee's "The Night Has a Thousand Eyes" was in the top five, indicating the innocent flavor of the times. Freddy Bienstock brought Leiber and Stoller's breezy song forward. "Bossa Nova Baby" was recorded at the start of the session, and the energy shows. The performance features a modern, delightfully spiky organ riff. To reflect the Mexican theme of Elvis's thirteenth Hollywood feature, it also showcases some mariachi-style magic during the break. The vocals are on point too. "Bossa Nova Baby" is still one of Elvis's "grooviest" records, in the best, and worst, sense of the term.

Magnificent.

38. "Promised Land" (from *Promised Land*, 1975)

With its continuous, desperate dash by bus, train, and then airplane, Elvis's masterful evocation of Chuck Berry's "Promised Land" deserves its place in any 100 countdown for reflecting the way he could stay on top of whatever lyric line was thrown at him. The song's story starts not with Chuck Berry, but with J. A. Roff, who captured an American folk classic in his 1882 sheet music for "The Great Rock Island Route." Just over twenty years later, the tune was reworked as "Wabash Cannonball," an earnest, down-home ditty that soon became a ringing country staple. The Carter Family and Roy Acuff, among many others, included it in their repertoire.

The list of artists who covered "Wabash Cannonball" before 1977 reads like a rolodex of Elvis's country associates. It includes Eddy Arnold, Ernest Tubb, Wanda Jackson, Chet Atkins, the Louvin Brothers, Billy Strange, Hank Snow, and Boots Randolph. Johnny Cash produced a characteristically stoic version on his 1966 CBS album *Happiness Is You*. He sounded, as ever, like the brother of John Wayne singing country. Jerry Reed also included a take on his 1968 RCA showcase, *Nashville Underground*. Elvis, meanwhile, intended to perform the song, rehearsing it late in July 1969 and on 14 August 1974 in preparation for his Las Vegas shows.

The many different sung and recorded versions of "Wabash Cannonball" differ significantly in their lyrics. What they share is a propulsive style and innocent take on the theme of railroad travel. Ironically, Berry's 1964 revamp was written from inside prison. Three weeks after a fourteen-year-old hat-check girl called Janice Escalanti was sacked at his St. Louis nightclub, she complained about his behavior. He was arrested on Christmas Eve in 1959 and charged under the Mann Act with transporting a minor across state lines for "immoral purposes." As a successful black performer associated with the rock 'n' roll boom, and with an arrest record dating back to 1944, Berry stood little chance, especially as he was up before an entirely white jury. His rather circumspect testimony was of little help. When a witness explained that Berry and Ms. Escalanti—who was of Apache descent—shared a hotel room with one bed, Judge George H. Moore intervened: "Is that hotel patronized by the white? Is it patronized by white people?"[310] As the case closed, Moore refused to set any bail and framed Berry as a sexual predator:

> I would not turn this man loose to go out and prey on a lot of ignorant Indian girls and colored girls, and white girls, if any. I would not have that on my soul. That man would be out committing offences while his case is on appeal, if this court is any judge. I have never sentenced a more vicious character than that kind, I don't believe.[311]

In the end, Berry lost a retrial and spent nearly two years behind bars in Indiana, Kansas, and Missouri. Within a few months of his release late in 1963, he recorded "Promised Land" at Chess Records in Chicago. It was something Berry had been cooking up during the time he served his sentence. He had trouble acquiring the materials that would help him realize his inspiration. Chuck Berry later said: "The penal institutions then were not so generous as to offer a map of any kind, for fear of providing a route for escape."[312]

The best part of a decade after Berry wrote "Promised Land," *Shaft*'s cinematic release launched a five-year spell of blaxploitation cinema. Stax had been the studio where Isaac Hayes had recorded *Shaft*'s theme tune. Elvis reconnected to black culture through his *Superfly* clothing. He recorded his own version of "Promised Land" during one of his famous sessions at the studio. According to insiders, the singer had been addressing himself to various Chuck Berry numbers in previous months. This was the only one captured on his 15 December 1973 visit. The most obvious difference to Berry's original was that Elvis removed the second verse of the song. On the first run-through, rhythm guitarist Johnny Christopher fluffed the introduction. The band continued for at least five more takes. Elvis's cover of "Promised Land" only approached the top forty, but its intricate lyric line far surpassed Berry's traditional material.

Elvis would return to "Promised Land" live in Vegas and at a handful of other venues, particularly in summer 1974 and spring 1975. Though James Burton's guitar was unfailingly sharp on these concert versions, the inclusion of thundering horns and other elements meant that the studio takes are slightly fresher. Rehearsing for his Vegas dates, his comment went straight to the point: "Boy, that's a movin' mother."[313]

37. "Don't Be Cruel" (from *Elvis*, 1956)

Pop scholar Richard Middleton once said that in Elvis's music, "rational control is heard as being threatened by hints of ecstasy, physical and spiritual, and therefore by a touch of the irrational."[314] Perhaps he was talking about "Don't Be Cruel." Scratch the surface of this innocent pop song and its vocals hint at other things. The writers, Otis Blackwell and Winfield Scott, had a special arrangement with Elvis's publishers Hill & Range: The company had first refusal on their compositions. If songs were not taken up, the writers could shop them elsewhere. Blackwell's R&B compositions and business acumen were not the only things working in his favor: His voice was surprisingly similar to Elvis's and he sang on his own demos. Elvis was so keen to perfect his performance of "Don't Be Cruel" that he recorded more than two dozen takes in the studio. When RCA released the single in the summer of 1956, Blackwell's gem was backed with Leiber and Stoller's "Hound Dog"—a dynamite pairing. The two sides competed with each other, and together they reigned supreme on the charts.

"Don't Be Cruel" is still special because Elvis makes a plea for fidelity in a performance that is at once both lighthearted and swelteringly erotic. Two instances are particularly demonstrative. The first came when, on 6 January 1957, Elvis was shot from the waist up on the *Ed Sullivan Show*. The attempt to constrain the Memphis upstart and pin him like a butterfly failed utterly. In full battle mode, he brings a commanding combination of surliness and sensuality to the performance. Even as they support him, the Jordanaires, in their smart jackets, look more like sports commentators than musicians. In contrast, Elvis wears a glittering waistcoat. At first, it is as if he is just doing a job. He is so off-edge he won't even look at the camera. As those who watch in the studio just melt, he gets more committed. His quiff bounces, his lip curls, and an occasional smile of recognition to the audience brings the music home. He is young. He is hot. And his voice absolutely shimmers. Toward the end of the song, when he murmurs—even though he is simultaneously expressing a thrill and mocking it—girls in the audience automatically surrender their screams. Track forward just over a decade, and a leather-clad Elvis revisits the song on the *Comeback*, this time envisioning it as a driving, confident show tune. What's amazing, as with many of Elvis's other performances, is his command of tempo. It is as if the song is delivered not so much in a hurry but *ahead of time*, so that the ending falls out neatly, like the coda to a moment of controlled mayhem.

36. "Memories" (from *The Complete '68 Comeback Special*, 2008)

"Memories" represents one of the best examples of Elvis exposing his soft and gentle side. One way to understand its value is to go back to late June 1968 when he performed on the NBC *Comeback Special*. At the very time when American youth had become a political force, Elvis spent several years in Hollywood making family movies. The show's director, Steve Binder, wanted to test the star's commitment to contemporary music in the run-up to the taping. Both Binder and the show's music director, Billy Goldenberg, admired the music of Jimmy Webb. In 1967, Webb scored multiple Grammy Awards for his unforgettably cinematic Glen Campbell number "By the Time I Get to Phoenix" and the rather breezy "Up, Up and Away." The next year, actor Richard Harris released a version of Webb's dramatic, convoluted "MacArthur Park."

In order to test whether Elvis wanted to be relevant to contemporary music or saw himself as a throwback, Binder suggested that he sing his own version of "MacArthur Park" for the *Special*.[315] Initially, Elvis seemed positive about the idea. When he was asked about the song in a press conference the next year, he said, "I think it's a great song. If Richard Harris hadn't recorded it, and they had given it to me, I would have done it."[316] However, the performance based on Binder's suggestion never fully came to pass. There was, of course, the issue of publishing. For all its extended, grandiloquent style and chart-topping success, "MacArthur Park" also seemed indulgent—its lyrics were inconsequential and relatively cryptic. When Elvis had sung roundabout lyrics in earlier years—in numbers like "Hound Dog"—they usually expressed some form of sexual innuendo and were part of a game with his live audience. By 1968, wordplay that once belonged to rock 'n' roll had been taken over by art rock. Elvis now preferred direct words and direct emotions. Nodding to Binder, in the middle of one of the informal segments of the *Comeback*, he did, however, offer a few lines to skit "MacArthur Park," as if to mock its false sincerity.[317]

In some moments of the *Special*, Elvis's performance was genuinely tender. Like "If I Can Dream," the Mac Davis and Billy Strange ballad "Memories" was custom written for the show. Although the live version that he performed was still overdubbed in the studio, "Memories" was—unlike some other songs in the *Special*—shown in its entirety. The song has not always been appreciated by commentators; one said, "It was precisely this kind of momentum-killer that Binder had battled with Parker to leave out of the show, but even Elvis was a sucker for Hallmark card sentiment."[318] Such claims, however, misrecognize both the *Comeback* and the place of such songs in Elvis's catalog. Binder was building a show that aimed to highlight *all* previous aspects of Elvis career, from rock 'n' roll to post-army movies and ballads. What "Memories" offered above was "MacArthur Park" was romance without abstraction, and it was less an enemy of the rocker-in-black-leather image than its counterpart.

In February 1969, two months after the NBC show aired, "Memories" became a single but peaked at only number 35.[319] Nevertheless, Elvis frequently performed it during his first season in Las Vegas in 1969. It became the closing theme for his later feature documentaries, Robert Abel and Pierre Adidge's *Elvis on Tour* from 1972 and Andrew Solt and Malcolm Leo's posthumous 1981 feature, *This Is Elvis*. One of the interesting things about the number was the way that Elvis and others around him ignored its limited success as a single in order to place it as a classic in his catalog—a case of short-term commercialism overridden in the name of good taste.[320] Crucially, in 1968 Elvis sang "Memories" in his black leather outfit. The song's magic, therefore, was that it could be used to effortlessly unite the "butch god" and "teddy bear" sides of his celebrity image.

35. "You've Lost That Lovin' Feelin'" (from *That's the Way It Is*, 1970)

Bill Medley and his singing partner Bobby "The Blond Bomber" Hatfield met in Long Beach. Under the name the Paramours, they started performing as a duo in 1962. Soon they released records as the Righteous Brothers. The name arose when some marines in the audience wisecracked about their similarity to black vocal harmony groups. Phil Spector picked them up for his Philles label in 1964 and asked Brill Building husband-and-wife team Barry Mann and Cynthia Weil to write something of sufficient stature to do justice to his new act. Mann had already had success in his own right as an artist who supplied charismatic vocals for the novelty hit "Who Put the Bomp (In the Bomp, Bomp, Bomp)." As a couple, he and Weil notched up several more hits together including a Leiber and Stoller co-write, the Drifters' "On Broadway."

"You've Lost That Lovin' Feelin'" was not an immediate fit for the Righteous Brothers. According to Medley, "At first, when Barry and Phil played it, I thought the song sounded perfect for the Everly Brothers, not us. I love the Everly Brothers, but Bobby and I were about soul."[321] If Mann and Weil's talents were to serve Hatfield and Medley, some adjustments would have to be made. Spector lowered the key of the demo and slowed down its pace. The result was phenomenal. Right from the time that Medley's gently, smoky, almost gloomy voice ushers in the first verse through to the majestic chorus, Spector's interpretation of "You've Lost That Lovin' Feelin'" remains timeless: a recognizably cinematic, Wall of Sound production.[322] It was overdubbed thirteen times—fleshed out by the elite of Los Angeles's studio musicians (the Wrecking Crew, including female bassist Carol Kaye) and augmented by support from both Cher and from the Blossoms (the trio that later worked with Elvis on the *Comeback*). "You've Lost That Lovin' Feelin'" was so big that the duo virtually became a house act on the ABC show *Shindig*. Mann and Weil went on to write "We Gotta Get out of This Place," which the Animals made a hit. Spector, meanwhile, signed Ike and Tina Turner. After the Righteous Brothers split toward the end of the decade, Bill Medley recorded in Memphis with Chips Moman, befriended Elvis, and visited Graceland.

Elvis tackled "You've Lost That Lovin' Feelin'" in concert from 1970 to 1972, then early in 1974. Where Spector goes straight for Medley's low bass tones as an opener, Elvis's version builds upon a brooding, instrumental introduction. When his vocals hit, they are clearer and deeper than the Righteous Brothers' rendition. By turns, he sounds outraged, carefree, heartbroken, down with the band, nonchalant, powerful, and wounded. After the line about getting down on his knees to revive his waning lover, only Elvis can add, with insane seriousness, "If this suit wasn't too tight!" Where Spector opts for a reprise ending, effectively starting the record up again, Elvis slams on the brakes and delivers a kind of doo-wop, gospel refrain, before his band explodes in a showstopping wall of sound. The feel is quite different from Spector's version: more punchy and less panoramic.

"You've Lost That Lovin' Feelin'" formed the centerpiece of Elvis's set on *That's the Way It Is*. He is first seen exploring the song at a rehearsal on 7 August 1970. During the live set on the same documentary, after completing a respectable version of "Patch It Up," the spotlight goes down. Elvis stands with his back to the audience. He announces the introduction of "You've Lost That Lovin' Feelin'," then amps up the drama by turning around for the first chorus. Though he struggles at times, it's a committed performance. "You've Lost That Lovin' Feelin'" was one of the first songs in the set to demonstrate how powerful and mature Elvis Presley could be as a vocalist. As Priscilla Presley recalled, once Elvis found his feet, that loving feeling was still there:

> His voice had strengthened, his range had widened, his soul had deepened. Doing "You've Lost That Lovin' Feelin'," he saw he still had something that, before those spectacular Vegas shows, he thought he had lost—the ability to move a live audience to tears. [323]

Occasionally, in 1971, Elvis decided to take things in a goofy direction by turning around in a gorilla mask. [324] He also presented the song at Madison Square Garden, pulling out a solid performance despite a shaky start, during the 10 June 1972 evening show. [325] In the orchestral reboot that Sony Music/RCA released in 2015, the style has changed again, paring the song down to Elvis's vocal with some female backing, while the Royal Philharmonic offers a more regal and serene canvas.

34. "Tryin' to Get to You" (from *Elvis Presley*, 1956)

One of the secrets of catchy pop songs is that they can be sung to romantic partners but can also be interpreted as personal love letters to fans. In turn, music fans participate by singing them back to their stars. Such songs are often about longing and desire. Elvis Presley pursued his quest to become a professional musician with quiet determination. He sang at school and on WELO in Tupelo. As a teen growing up in Memphis, he tried out for a kind of junior gospel quartet called the Songfellows.[326] On 15 May 1954, he auditioned for Eddie Bond's band at the Hi-Hat Club.[327] When that didn't work out, he secured a recording session at Sun on account of his ability to sing ballads. After his first Sun record was out, he still bombed at the *Grand Ole Opry*. In April and May 1956, he received a lukewarm response at the New Frontier Hotel in Las Vegas, despite "Heartbreak Hotel" storming the charts. Elvis never stopped on his quest to serve his audience. In the process he achieved the American dream.

"Tryin' to Get to You" was written by the African American songwriter Rose McCoy and her writing partner, Charlie Singleton. Born in Arkansas, McCoy traveled to New York. Together with Singleton, she set up shop in a booth at Beefsteak Charlie's, a happening joint near the Brill Building where budding songwriters would offer their creations to publishers by playing on the spot. McCoy and Singleton made quite a team and hit their stride in 1957, contributing "One More Time" to Ruth Brown's repertoire. McCoy also provided "I Think It's Gonna Work Out Fine" for Ike and Tina Turner. The songwriting pair's composition "Tryin' to Get to You" was recorded in 1954 by a Washington, D.C.–based R&B band called the Eagles for release as a single on Mercury Records.[328] It was Elvis's first but not last engagement with material by the African American writers.[329]

The Sun single version of "Tryin' to Get to You" deserves glory because it delivers a rookie Elvis at his most urgent, earnest, polite, and sincere. He recorded the track early in 1955.[330] After this abortive first attempt, he secured a more adequate take that summer, on 21 July. Elvis had the Eagles' release in his collection.[331] He evidently took note of the singer's almost yodeling vocals. Elvis's voice is every bit as showy but even more flexible and performative, with a production sound that makes his recording more crisp, bright, and celestial. It is as if 1950s masculinity has turned a corner and shifted from prioritizing the role of swashbuckler to celebrating the teen angel. This may be because Elvis took a tip from the softer sounds of white college vocal groups like the Hilltoppers; the first syllable of his record resembles the group's 1952 debut, "Trying," a little, albeit more, up tempo.

Sam Phillips reckoned on "Tryin' to Get to You" being Elvis's final Sun single, but, thanks to Colonel Parker, his charge signed to RCA before that could happen. Set against Elvis's emergent reputation for rock 'n' roll, a Sun release would have been intriguing: friendly to country stations but also contradictory. The studio's warm and intimate production space helps to give the track its folksy feel. Scotty Moore's gently cantering guitar patterns nicely complement Elvis's innocent yet urgent vocals. The result is not simply a collaboration. It is a triumph that lets listeners know that the singer is available to them. No wonder, then, that Elvis sang further versions of the mesmeric song, both in the NBC *Comeback Special* and right the way through to his final tour in 1977. He was just as keen to emotionally touch fans as they were to touch him.

33. "Love Me Tender" (from *Elvis' Golden Records*, 1958)

"Love Me Tender" is a gem that deserves its place in any countdown. In its music-box simplicity, Elvis's performance of this ballad showed he could express the innocence of a child in the midst of adult romance. More than many other songs, however, "Love Me Tender" reflected, in its story, the compromises of Elvis's career. David Weisbart, who worked with Twentieth Century Fox, had recently produced a movie that Elvis respected: James Dean's torrid and compelling drama *Rebel Without a Cause*. After signing with Hal Wallis at Paramount, Elvis's contract allowed him to work with other studios once per year if the right opportunity arose. Weisbart provided such a project: a rural, historical drama called *The Reno Brothers*. Its director, Robert D. Webb, came into his own that decade, making intimate Westerns with small casts. He had just directed a young Robert Wagner in *White Feather*. Elvis was invited to take up the part that would have gone to Wagner in the new movie. It was a supporting role, which meant that he would function as an ensemble player. By working with a cast of Hollywood professionals, Elvis would get a special opportunity to learn on the job and hone his acting skills. The Colonel, however, had other ideas. He saw movies as promotional vehicles for Elvis's music.

The Colonel understood the commercial, not creative, value of movie appearances. In the 1960s, he asked Brian Stone and Charlie Greene as Sonny & Cher's managers how much their act was paid per night. He then suggested that they make it six times bigger, adding, "And have the kids do a movie. Do it fast and do it cheap. Nothing artsy-crafty."[332] At first, at least, this strategy, when applied to Elvis, meant that RCA and the Aberbachs were happy too. Screen performances would almost certainly increase records sales on an exponential basis and lead to television appearances that could generate lucrative streams of synchronization royalties. Hollywood studio executives, meanwhile, saw the pulling power of Elvis and his music as a way to enhance their picture's box-office potential. That Elvis would die in the movie, in his role as young Clint Reno, only added to the publicity.

What *The Reno Brothers* lacked was music. Although the picture was a drama, not a musical, Hill & Range scrambled to cut a deal and four songs were added. Lionel Newman was the film's music director. He started out playing accompaniment for Mae West on the vaudeville circuit, then succeeded in Hollywood with the help of his brother Alfred, who led the music department at Twentieth Century Fox in the 1940s and 1950s. Lionel already had a reputation for his work with Marilyn Monroe. For *The Reno Brothers*, vocal arranger Ken Darby was chief among his staff. Darby was already a multitalented and accomplished studio music supervisor. He was known for a string of features, from *The Wizard of Oz* to *The King and I*. Darby was asked to craft Elvis's musical numbers so that they would fit smoothly into the plot of the film. The deal was that he would adapt a tune in the public domain for the picture and give Elvis half the rights.

The lyrics for "Love Me Tender" were developed by Ken Darby but credited to his wife, Vera Matson, and to Elvis. The song's creation was complex. It was common practice by the 1950s to find songwriting revenue by rewriting folk tunes. The ballad's heritage went back to the Civil War standard "Aura Lee," which was claimed by George Poulton and William Fosdick in the 1860s. Darby reworked the lyrics and, most likely for business reasons, credited them to his wife. Elvis got his songwriter's credit as a sweetener. That said, when Darby was interviewed about the songwriting process, he said Elvis possessed an instinctual sense of certainty when picking music that suited his particular style. Presley supposedly chose between several different adaptations of the tune. Darby also claimed that his wife wrote "a few stanzas" of the song's lyrics.[333] Whether he was explaining what actually happened, or simply justifying the credit split, his claims suggested that creative process was shared between the different parties.

One of the next issues that occurred in relation to the song was that Darby needed talented musicians to perform on its recording. Elvis's existing backing band was auditioned, but because nobody told them that an old-time country sound was required, Scotty, Bill, and DJ played in a rock 'n' roll style. As a result, they never got the job and were suspicious that the Colonel might have had a hand in the process. Elvis told them that there would be other film opportunities. Eventually they complained about their mistreatment and talked to newspapers to let fans know about what happened. After that, they were taken back on a per diem basis—a business relationship that put the musicians at arm's length with Elvis. Darby assembled a raft of other talent to play on "Love Me Tender." One of the most notable players was the stringed instrument expert Vito Mumolo, whose guitar playing had recently been used on Marilyn's film *Bus Stop*. Darby's new number was recorded on 24 August 1956 at the premier Fox soundstage. Elvis recorded two versions of the song. The single version was captured toward the end of the month. At the start of October, he returned to produce a different take for the end credits of his first Hollywood feature.

Previously, Elvis was not known for singing ballads. Sam Phillips had only released up-tempo, rockabilly material on the Sun label. Apart from "Heartbreak Hotel," Elvis was best known on RCA for his electrifying rock 'n' roll. "Love Me Tender" introduced his gentle side, something that would shift his image well beyond Southern rockabilly, endearing him to the parents, conservatives, and romantics in mainstream America. Colonel Parker got himself credited as technical adviser on the film. "Love Me Tender" was a flagship number. For Elvis, it would indicate a change of direction, rounding out his public image.

What rather disappointed Elvis himself was not just that he was now singing the movie's theme tune but also that he had to perform more Darby numbers: "Poor Boy," "Let Me," and "We're Gonna Move." While the last of these was passable, the other two were somewhat limited. Any reluctance that Elvis expressed was overruled when it was pointed out that he was contracted to sing four numbers. The plan was never any different. In fact, Elvis's original Paramount screen test featured him lip-synching to "Blue Suede Shoes." His hope of becoming known as the new James Dean was slipping, though for a while a productive compromise was reached: *Jailhouse Rock* and *King Creole* were two of his most exciting films because they got the balance right.

The Colonel's plan to generate cross-promotion worked. For less than two months' labor, Elvis got a lot from the project. Webb's film was renamed *Love Me Tender* to capitalize on the primacy of Elvis's performance. The singer's role was extended beyond the bit part that Robert Wagner rejected. When the movie was released, publicity interest focused almost entirely on Presley and his performance, pushing actors like Richard Egan and Debra Paget into the background. Despite critics pursuing elitist, anti-Southern viewpoints in their reviews of the movie, Elvis got a musical opportunity to diversify his public image and begin his Hollywood career. For the Colonel, the film's lesson was evident: Audiences already understood the singer as a star musician, and Presley could not be taken afresh as an actor. Existing stardom already formed a kind of genre expectation.

As a song, "Love Me Tender" really caught public interest. On Ed Sullivan's *Toast of the Town*, with the help of Elvis's performances on 9 September and 28 October 1956—the first of which featured the song— "Love Me Tender" shipped more than half a million copies. It was the first single to go gold before release and, when it appeared, spent a month on the top slot. Two-and-a-half-million singles were sold by Christmas, firmly establishing "Love Me Tender" as a Presley signature song. Frank Sinatra even ghosted a swinging tribute version on his famous 1960 special.

For more than a decade, the cross-promotion model came to dominate Elvis Presley's career. He performed songs that sold movies. Movies advertised vinyl records that in turn created royalties and sales figures. Mass commercial success formed the foundation of the singer's stardom. Sales figures helped to promote Elvis to new audiences and the cycle started again. It was a money machine that created revenue streams for the Hollywood studios, for Hill & Range, for RCA, for the Colonel, and ultimately for Elvis. When the scripts and songs were sizzling, it worked. The problem, as Elvis articulated it, was that after a while he was not being stretched as either a musician or as an actor.

On the last day of shooting *Roustabout* in 1964, the *Las Vegas Desert News and Telegram* ran a story featuring part of an interview with Elvis

Presley's movie supervisor. Hal Wallis explained that Presley pictures financed quality dramas like *Becket*, a historical character study of Thomas Becket, which starred the acting heavyweights Richard Burton and John Gielgud. When he found out, a disappointed Elvis approached the Hollywood producer and said, "Mr. Wallis, when do I get to do my *Becket?*"[334] The situation bothered him. On the *Comeback Special*, when Elvis returned to "Love Me Tender," he quipped, "You have made my life a wreck."

32. "In the Ghetto" (from *From Elvis in Memphis*, 1969)

In an era where international travel was beginning to confront Americans with their responsibility as global citizens, Elvis straddled the mainstream of society and held together the center ground. It was a musical balancing act. In the second half of the 1950s, he had emerged from regional roots as a country music fireball to set alight the youth of America. Next he attempted to tamp down parental backlash by joining the army and re-branding himself as a family entertainer. As Greil Marcus put it, the singer had the "nerve" to inadvertently cross color lines in music. It would not be true to say, however, that Elvis *entirely* retreated. In the same year he made *GI Blues*, for example, he also appeared in *Flaming Star* as a Native American "half-breed." The film had a plot that directly involved race; it implied that once Elvis became "safe," he could act as a symbol of the melting pot. While his Southern, working-class identity marked him out as someone different and moderately "exotic," many of the 1960s features also presented him as an innocent, young romantic partner: a would-be father figure acceptable to teens, to conservative parents, and, eventually, to children. His music sounded different, too; it diversified across a wider range of genres and, at least in that sense, resembled the output of an easy listening maestro, as he drew upon a variety of songs and remodeled them in his own style. Of course, such a strategy made no sense from the perspective of 1960s rock, where artists like Bob Dylan, the Beatles, and the Stones drew lines and protested in ways that reflected a generation gap. Instead Elvis offered *something for everyone* by bringing all people together.

In order to occupy a constantly expanding center ground, Elvis needed songs with themes that would unite people. "In the Ghetto" had a universal message. At a press conference marking the start of his return to Las

Vegas, he was asked in the summer of 1969 whether, by recording "In the Ghetto," he was changing his image. Elvis responded, "No—'Ghetto' was such a great song, I just couldn't pass it up after I heard it."[335] On one level the reply was simple; "In the Ghetto" *is* a great song, but there is more to say. There were always two sides to Elvis Presley: tough and tender, revolutionary and conservative. He told the FBI that he thought J. Edgar Hoover was the greatest living American. Yet he also quietly supported civil rights and poured every ounce of his being into what was one of the most compassionate message songs of its era.

Ghettoes had been an issue in American society for a long time. By the late 1960s, they had been a problem for nearly twenty years. The 1961 film *West Side Story*, for example, dramatized the issue in a stylized way. It was the continuous rise of the civil rights movement that bought about a shift in society sufficient to be reflected in the music industry. Toward the end of the 1960s, socially conscious songwriters like Curtis Mayfield were well established. As the civil rights struggle came to the fore of public consciousness, a new spate of ghetto songs suddenly appeared. This flurry made direct, if sentimental, reference to inner-city poverty. After the Beatles started discussing revolution in their work, artists from James Brown and the Jive Five to the Staple Singers, Joan Baez, and Delaney & Bonnie all had records out with songs featuring "ghetto" in the title. Warren Lee, for example, released "Born in the Ghetto" on Wand Records late in 1968. His single did not sound the same as Elvis's number, but it explored a similar theme.

The writing of "In the Ghetto" has an interesting story. News footage of ghettoes in U.S. cities reminded Mac Davis of Smitty, a black friend that he knew in his childhood back in Texas. He recalled:

> My dad had a warehouse in the area where they lived. After we would play together, we would often take Smitty home. Basically, their home was on a dirt street lined with houses that had broken windows, leaking roofs, and peeling paint. The area was called Queen City. I always wanted to know why did this little black kid have to live where he did, and why he couldn't live in the nice part of town, like I did.[336]

Fooling around after he'd been taught a guitar lick by his friend Freddy Weller—who played with Paul Revere & the Raiders—Davis developed a song around the theme of racism and social injustice. "Dying is a metaphor," he explained, "for being born into failure. Being born into a situation where you have no hope."[337]

"In the Ghetto"'s initial subtitle, "The Vicious Circle," referred to anthropologist Oscar Lewis's "culture of poverty" argument. At the University of Illinois, Professor Lewis analyzed the social effects of poverty from the 1950s. His 1966 book, *La Vida: A Puerto Rican Family in the Culture of Poverty*, brought the idea into focus. Lewis suggested that poor folk were not to blame for their plight. Instead they were held back by social expectations and forced to adapt to their own marginal living conditions. In making these adaptations to ongoing poverty, they had taken up some bad habits. The idea fitted in with liberal civil rights doctrine.

Chips Moman asked Billy Strange for some country material. The issue was that Chips's request for "country" was a bit vague. By the end of the 1960s, the genre had expanded to include a wide variety of styles. Billy tapped Mac Davis. Together they sent in a tape with seventeen songs on it. One of the first numbers on the tape was "In the Ghetto." Davis and Strange offered the song to Bill Medley of the Righteous Brothers, who rejected it because he thought he had already sung enough protest material.[338] Mac sent the song to Elvis and also played it live in the studio control room so that Chips could understand its feel. When Elvis first heard "In the Ghetto," he told Davis, "That's a smash."[339]

In the 1950s, Elvis had articulated social concerns *through* music, but, so far, it was not his style to sing protest songs—with all the easy moralism and line-drawing they could entail. His 1968 NBC *Comeback Special* nevertheless showed that he could make universal statements that offered hope in a turbulent time. Although friends advised Elvis not to record "In the Ghetto," he knew it would work.[340] He liked the song but was hesitant, as Parker had already warned him off message songs. He slept on it. Chips started thinking *he* could instead record a version with a black soul singer—perhaps Joe Simon or Roosevelt "Rosie" Grier—but Elvis committed himself to the number. Reggie Young simply reproduced Mac's guitar style on the final cut.[341] "In the Ghetto" was recorded as part of Elvis's American Sound sessions in January 1969. Ironically, the singer had to cross a color line just to record it. American Sound was in a part of town that was run-down and had a predominantly black population; in effect, Elvis was singing "In the Ghetto" in the ghetto.

On duty at his Houston Astrodome press conference, when asked about "In the Ghetto" in February 1970, Elvis said, "I wouldn't like to do all that type of stuff. In other words, I wouldn't like for everything to be a [political] message 'cause I think there's still entertainment to be considered."[342] He was, however, right about the song's impact. As the scout single for *From Elvis in Memphis*, "In the Ghetto" quickly sold more than a million copies and made the top five. This was not simply a case of a famous singer exploiting liberal white guilt for his own profit; Elvis was warned off recording such a political song by both Colonel Parker and RCA. According to Priscilla Presley, "The Colonel was against it. He thought it was risky and identified Elvis too closely with black America. He came close to talking Elvis out of releasing it."[343] The performance was, for Ernst Jørgensen, "another step forward" in Elvis's "development as a serious contemporary artist . . . an inner-city morality tale that pointed the finger at social (and, by extension, racial) injustices."[344]

After Elvis had a hit, the song became a staple, with covers appearing in short order from Dolly Parton and Candi Staton. Gene West powered his way through a gritty soul version. Mac produced a similar, heartfelt 1970 cover of the song by Solomon Burke on Bell Records. Sammy Davis offered a funky, forthright spoken-word version the same year. A few months later, Rip 'n' Lan even released a reggae cover. Continuing the family tradition, Lisa Marie Presley augmented the song in 2007 to create a duet with her late father, releasing the result as a download to help victims of Hurricane Katrina.[345]

Like Ralph McTell's devastating "Streets of London"—which was also recorded in 1969 but did not become a hit for another four years— "In the Ghetto" asked listeners to think again about the plight of the urban poor.

Despite making some shallow movies during the late 1960s, Elvis also explored human interconnectedness as part of his spiritual quest. He might have had in mind the bible passage from Matthew 25, verse 40: "Whatever you did for one of the least of these brothers and sisters of mine, you did for me." It is clear, at least, that Elvis Presley wished to help the "least of these" in American life by publicizing the nature of their plight, even telling friends that he felt a "calling" to sing "In the Ghetto."[346]

When Elvis performs the song, his embellishments are minimal. He sings serenely—like a detached observer looking down on the drama, an eagle in flight. He coolly describes what he can see—*until* he brings listeners up short, pouring full passion into asking if people are "too blind" to recognize what is before them. As if to emphasize the point, the song also changes tempo, slowing down and swooping low to finish its chorus. Elvis's transparent, emotive performance still arouses empathy, quietly insisting—through the subtle force of sheer emotion—that on this planet, addressing poverty remains a moral priority.

Along with his rock 'n' roll reputation and the *Comeback*, sales of the "In the Ghetto" single formed another point of contact that allowed Elvis to win over live audiences in Las Vegas. In *The New Yorker*, Ellen Willis dismissed the song as "weak on beat and strong on slush."[347] Nevertheless, even she succumbed to Elvis's charms when she saw him performing it, saying later in the same 1969 live review, "When he did 'In The Ghetto,' his emotion was so honest it transformed the song; for the first time, I saw it as representing a white Southern boy's feeling for black music, with all that that implied."[348]

31. "Can't Help Falling in Love" (from *Aloha from Hawaii via Satellite*, 1973)

> High society blue bloods are dancing it in New York's most fashionable hotels . . . and here is the first great movie about this new sensation of the now and the 1960s![349]

The trailer for Paramount's feature *Hey, Let's Twist* said it all. Greg Garrison's exploitation movie capitalized on the fashionable Twist craze. Using the power of cinema, it promoted Joey Dee and the Starliters' "Peppermint Twist–Part 1"—an innocuous but energetic little number that, ironically, held Elvis Presley's more majestic "Can't Help Falling in Love" off the top of the singles chart. The victory was only temporary; Elvis's song is far more remembered. It emerged when Hugo Peretti, George David Weiss, and Luigi Creatore put new lyrics to Giovanni Martin's eighteenth-century classic "Plaisir d'amour." The songwriters developed their tune at the behest of Hill & Range. The Aberbachs explained that Elvis needed a song with a European flavor to enliven a section of *Blue Hawaii* in which he returns from Europe with a music box for his girlfriend's grandmother. Presley pursued "Can't Help Falling in Love" at Radio Recorders in March 1961, claiming to fellow musicians that he was singing for the girl he had left behind in Germany, Priscilla Beaulieu. When "Can't Help Falling in Love" became a single that November, it sold more than a million in the United States. That was despite Steve Sholes actually forbidding Luigi Creatore from doing any promotion; RCA pushed the snappy but lightweight "Rock-A-Hula Baby" as the A-side. Nevertheless, radio DJs spontaneously turned over the record and started championing the ballad.

"Can't Help Falling in Love" became Elvis's signature song, a true romantic classic that he trusted in concert, time and again, and featured on all his most famous 1970s live recordings. It has been estimated that he sang the song more than seven hundred times. He performed it at his benefit show for the USS *Arizona* Memorial Fund in March 1961 and made it the theme of his Las Vegas wedding in May 1967. When he returned to Peretti, Weiss, and Creatore's number for the NBC *Comeback Special*, he combined a humble vocal with a more expansive, symphonic arrangement. Elvis closed his set with the song when he went on to conquer Las Vegas in 1969. By the time he did the *Aloha from Hawaii* telecast in 1973, "Can't Help Falling in Love" had become supremely majestic, a lap of honor. It was even featured as the last song of what became his final concert on 26 June 1977 at the Indianapolis Market Square Arena.

It is hardly surprising that "Can't Help Falling in Love" has been covered by a wide range of artists—not just Perry Como and Andy Williams. Bob Dylan's version is absurdly meandering and gruff. Awards for worst and best covers, though, should go to UB40 and Lick the Tins respectively, the former for their overfamiliarity and the latter for their sublime Celtic innocence. Surely, that is what is so great about this song and about Elvis's version: when reaching down for love, even in the most jaded world, sometimes innocent emotion can be found.

30. "Mystery Train" (from *For LP Fans Only*, 1959)

Writing an entry for "Mystery Train" in his book, *The Elvis Encyclopedia*, Adam Victor noted, "Bizarrely, the song was used during the war in Iraq as a soundtrack to an amateur video of Iraqi contractors shooting at civilians."[350] This usage may not be quite as bizarre as Victor suggested. After all, with its existential, almost gothic theme, "Mystery Train" expresses the capricious cruelty that can be an unwelcome part of life itself. Its history begins with the spectral "Worried Man Blues," a 1930 country blues number sung by the Carter Family and kept alive, in various forms, by artists as diverse as Woody Guthrie and Devo.[351] In the Carter Family's characteristic and powerfully repetitive, rustic folk version, the focus is squarely on life's woes: criminal judgment, enslavement, and loss. One verse describes a train "sixteen coaches long" that takes away all hope of a better life, reflected in the shape of a disappearing female partner. With its runaway train vamp, Junior Parker's "Mystery Train" extended the same concern. Its story was set in a darkly churning world of chaos, loss, and heartbreak. Parker's smooth, often carefree vocal veered between Southern blues and a more uptown soul style. The 1953 number may have been one of the records that inspired Elvis to stay focused on the Memphis Recording Service; Sun 192 was released between the young truck driver's first and second visits to the studio on 706 Union Avenue. He finally tackled "Mystery Train" on 21 July 1955 during his sixth and penultimate professional session for Sun. Sam Phillips co-owned copyright in the song as he had released Junior Parker's 1953 version. According to Phillips, "It's a big thing to put a loved one on a train; maybe they'll never come back."[352]

"Mystery Train" demonstrates some of the debt paid by rockabilly to its black influences. Though Elvis's vocal owed relatively little to Junior Parker, Scotty Moore's style was formed in the tradition of the Blue Flames guitarist, Pat Hare.[353] Moore was always modest about his own skills: "I just stole from every guitar player that I could over the years."[354] Not only was "Mystery Train" an amalgamation of Parker's original with another of his Sun singles, "Love My Baby," but Parker's other Sun Record, "Feelin' Good," was also a precursor to Scotty's style.

In his recent book on Sam Phillips, Peter Guralnick suggested that the uncanny producer aimed to capture the "perfect imperfection" of Memphis music in his recordings.[355] "Mystery Train" has an unforced quality reflected in Elvis's spontaneous whoop of joy and slight chuckle at the end of his performance.[356] What is also interesting about Elvis's version, however, is the way it transforms "Mystery Train" from a subtle bluesy potboiler to a swashbuckling rockabilly classic—one that is existentially dark *and* gently riotous. Of course, the song is a cult record. When it was released as the B-side to disc 223, "I Forgot to Remember to Forget," the Sun single went top ten on *Billboard*'s Country & Western chart. It should endure in any Elvis fan's catalog, however, because of its emotional depth. After all, the song is about loss, a subject that Elvis, above many others, seemed destined to explore in his music. Indeed, "Mystery

Train" sounds as if three young men from Memphis are having a party in the shadow of monumental deprivation; strangely exuberant in the face, not only of relationship breakup but also of shared grief, perhaps only known best to singers of the blues. Doc Pomus, who eventually co-wrote several Elvis classics, recalled the impact of "Mystery Train" by saying:

> I was still a singer and I was working in the club one night and on the jukebox we played "Mystery Train." That was the first record I ever heard of Elvis and it really knocked me out and nobody knew anything about him. The next thing I know he did this Dorsey Brothers show and I thought he was unbelievable.[357]

In August 1969, Elvis would turn to "Mystery Train" in his live set, naturally merging it with "Tiger Man." What is interesting about this hybrid version—an example of which can be seen at the start of *That's the Way It Is*—is how its vamp became Elvis's excuse for charismatic displays of holy roller–type shaking that overwhelmed his more excitable female fans.

As colored lights flash like fireworks across a dark sky, he rocks like a man in combat, in full command of the spectacle.

29. "Big Boss Man" (from *The Complete '68 Comeback Special*, 2008)

The story of "Big Boss Man" belongs to blues man Mathis James "Jimmy" Reed. Not to be confused with the Atlanta country guitarist Jerry Reed, Jimmy was an African American R&B interpreter whose smooth rhythms neatly matched his avuncular singing voice. At about the same time as Elvis, Reed emerged on the national stage with a string of bluesy R&B hits for Vee-Jay that would last half a decade. He could play harmonica and guitar at the same time. He also knew a hit when he heard one, even if he did not write it. "Big Boss Man" was developed by Reed's manager, Al Smith, and Luther Dixon.[358] Reed observed that Smith was right for the role of manager because "he ain't no big liquor drinker like me."[359] Dixon, meanwhile, was a staff writer for Vee-Jay who moved on to Scepter Records in New York where he composed and produced records for groups like the Shirelles. Reed made his cover of their song a hit in 1961. His version sounds both magnificent and leery, like a tanked-up moment from some after-hours honky-tonk. Its hard-driven beat is countered by the singer's characteristically sly, languid, slurred vocal performance.

In September 1967, Elvis visited RCA's Studio B in Nashville for a turning-point session where he would record the music of a different Mr. Reed. The blond country singer Jerry Reed played strings in the studio on his own unique composition, "Guitar Man." When it came to the next choice, Elvis may have wanted to try Jimmy Reed's "Baby What You Want Me to Do," but instead he approached "Big Boss Man." Jerry stayed on, lending his ornate picking style to the party. The song takes off, aided by Boots Randolph's assertive sax playing, which forms the backbone of the initial mix. It begins with an elaborate guitar introduction, is further picked up by the vocals, and is patterned as a shuffle or twist. As "Big Boss Man" starts to swing, Charlie McCoy's harp accompaniment becomes delightfully unraveled and exploratory. Elvis, meanwhile, delivers a performance that is characterized, at best, by a kind of barely disguised indignation. Despite his obvious commitment, he is keen to experiment. As he exaggerates the emotional valence of each line, at times the result sounds overly mugging. On take two, Elvis says "I-I-I-I" and "call-ha-ho-ho-all," ending with some "Pa Pa Oom Mow Mow"–type surf scat, for example.[360] In this rare instance, his vocal acrobatics come off as tomfoolery.

The single version of Elvis's "Big Boss Man" just managed to break the *Billboard* top forty. In *The Village Voice*, Robert Christgau said, in September 1969, that Elvis had shown signs of changing. For the past eighteen months, he "was not content to drift into million dollar oblivion." Citing "Big Boss Man," Christgau continued, "His singles suddenly became much funkier."[361]

Preparing for the *Comeback Special*, Elvis recorded another, swinging version of "Big Boss Man" at Western Recorders for use in the medley part of the show and accompanying album. This time, the track hit its stride in an intriguing medley created for the "Blue Bird" segment.[362] After the fleeting, sly glory of "Nothingville"—a song about hometown disillusion and, in a sense, curiosity—a spoken-word interlude evokes a traditional carnie sideshow. It includes a reference to the dancer Little Egypt: "Folks, step right up. The biggest and the greatest show on the Midway. . . . She walks, she talks, she crawls on her belly like a reptile." The implication is that Little Egypt is exploited as both labor and spectacle; something that may reflect upon the lot of both women and working musicians. Suddenly, retribution looms in the shape of "Big Boss Man." Tipping his hat to its accusatory theme, Garth Cartwright of *The Guardian* called Reed's song a "class-conscious shuffle."[363]

In the *Comeback*, the spark of unjust treatment almost kindles a riot; for this strictly no-nonsense medley version of the song, Elvis is at the helm of a steaming, gleaming, up-tempo Vegas juggernaut. This time, his righteous indignation is charged with just a little threat; the result is both aggressive and spellbinding. As the adrenaline-soaked music switches gear, having just rectified labor exploitation, in true superhero style, Elvis urges—no, demands—his lover to "Let Yourself Go."[364] As his slick medley rides the changes, the whole thing is without question one of the most accomplished moments in Elvis's entire catalog.[365]

Fearless, focused, and ferocious.

28. "Burning Love" (from *ELVIS: 30 #1 Hits*, 2002)

Hollywood columnist Hedda Hopper once said, "I am convinced that when the history of the jet age is written, Elvis Presley will go down as its king of entertainment."[366] One of the interesting things about Elvis's image is the way that it so effortlessly unites America's folksy past with the cutting edge of modernity. Elvis might have begun as a poor country boy, but his material obsessions place him firmly at the forefront of the 1970s. He owned a Convair 880 jet aircraft and loved the latest cars. Before almost anyone else, he also embraced finer advances: gadgets like digital watches, microwave ovens, remote control TV, and video recording. It was almost like he was a kind of astronaut, plunging gleefully into a technological world, humanizing it along the way. When he died, he was even planning to wear a laser suit in concert.[367] In March 2008, NASA sent Space Shuttle *Endeavour* on mission STS-123 to the International Space Station. A wake-up heard by astronauts on the mission was the song "Burning Love."

Any account of "Burning Love" should start with Dennis Linde, a singer-songwriter who was eight years younger than Elvis. Linde spent his early adulthood in St. Louis, Missouri, driving a dry-cleaning delivery truck and playing with the Starlighters. After speeding fines caught up with him, Linde focused his attention on songwriting and moved to Nashville in the 1960s.

Music industry entrepreneur Fred Foster had success with two companies he set up back in 1958: a record label called Monument (which was
home to Roy Orbison) and a publishing house called Combine Music.
Foster hired Bob Beckham to run Combine. Kris Kristofferson was on its
books. Linde was contracted to the company as a writer. He soon proved
his worth, supplying a hit to Roy Drusky, the Perry Como of country
music. The Texan-born songsmith also signed a solo recording contract
with Mercury and released the LP *Linde Manor*. Bergen White arranged
the material and Billy Swan produced the album. Although Linde had a
reputation for being relatively reclusive, he was clearly in the orbit of
some of the musicians in Nashville connected to Elvis.

Linde's composition "Burning Love" was initially placed with the
Muscle Shoals soul stirrer, Arthur Alexander, who cut it with Tommy
Cogbill at American Sound for Warner Brothers. Alexander's vocal is
light and breezy—a bit like Sam & Dave—but the song's backing got full
horn treatment. By that point, in August 1971, the studio was reaching the
end of its run; its staff decamped to Nashville not long after. Red West,
George Klein, and Marty Lacker all had strong connections of different
sorts with American Sound. After he had hits there, Elvis was willing to
lend a careful ear to its output. Felton Jarvis introduced the number to the
singer; he recorded it in Hollywood. What distinguished that visit to
Studio C was that Elvis drafted in John Wilkinson, Glen D. Hardin, and
Ronnie Tutt from his 1970s concert band. During the three-day March
1972 sessions, Elvis also sang two regretful ballads, "Separate Ways" and
"Always on My Mind." Those songs were indications of his mental state.
His marriage was heading into a phase of terminal decline. In the end,
Jarvis, Joe Esposito, Red West, Charlie Hodge, and Jerry Schilling *all*
had to persuade Elvis to try the up-tempo number. Where "Separate
Ways" took twenty-five takes, "Burning Love" was finished in six.[368] At
the end of the month, Presley also included the song in the live rehearsal
filmed for *Elvis on Tour*. "Burning Love" became an occasional part of
his repertoire soon after.[369] The next year, he went global with it on the
famous *Aloha* concert telecast.[370]

In Elvis's catalog, "Burning Love" sits uneasily, in some ways, as a
marker of descent between the showstopping power of "Suspicious
Minds" and slightly hokey and childish parody pop of "I Can Help." And
yet, and yet . . . this comfortingly familiar music towers over most movie
soundtrack output.

Elvis's ability to transcend basic material by adding vocal inflection to it is still incredible.

27. "Saved" (from *The Complete '68 Comeback Special*, 2008)

In 1957, Elvis was on a roll with songs he was recording by Jerry Leiber and Mike Stoller. He even called the writers his "good luck charms."[371] Unfortunately, those claiming to protect the singer poisoned the relationship. When Elvis requested a tailor-made ballad, the pair had already weathered a tense encounter with Freddy Bienstock. Upon writing "Don't," an enthusiastic Mike Stoller handed it directly to Elvis and just assumed Presley's camp would require half the publishing. The Colonel and Aberbachs saw any direct form of contact as contradicting protocol. Following the triumphs of *Jailhouse Rock*, the songwriting duo was called into the studio and asked to create a Christmas song. They came up with "Santa Claus Is Back in Town" on the spot, in just fifteen minutes. Colonel Parker guffawed, "What took you so long?"[372] Not long after, the pair was called to Jean Aberbach's house on Hollywood Boulevard. When they got there, Aberbach explained, "The Colonel wants to manage you."[373] Jerry and Mike were taken aback. They asked if it was a joke and explained that they were unmanageable. Aberbach quickly produced a blank contract with only a signature line, adding, "The Colonel said we can fill it in later, but basically it's a matter of mutual trust."[374] It was a joke with all the charm of a mafia calling card. After that, the duo contributed further movie songs, but never again did they try getting close to Elvis.

By the late 1960s, it had been years since the Colonel's Machiavellian machinations had caused Leiber and Stoller to retreat. Elvis, however, had not lost his passion for their music. The songwriters were unsure whether their material would be used for the *Comeback*. Living in hope, Mike Stoller's wife threw a viewing party, inviting around thirty people over and plugging in several TV sets around their living room. Decades later, Stoller recalled with delight, "I had no idea Elvis would perform 'Saved.'"[375]

The first person to have a chart hit with Leiber and Stoller's "Saved" was Atlantic artist Delores LaVern Baker, a wonderfully gutsy African American singer who started her career in Chicago as "Little Miss Sharecropper" and was best known for her sedate yet rousing ballad "I Cried a

Tear." When Baker's punchy and righteous version of "Saved" was released in 1961, it grazed the top twenty of the national R&B chart.[376] Elvis was aware of Baker from her first hit on Atlantic Records, "Tweedlee Dee." Two months after its November 1954 release, he started to perform it in his own set.[377] Later, he added two less energetic Atlantic singles from Baker to his record collection: "Still" (backed with "I Can't Love You Enough") from 1956 and "No Love So True" (backed with "Must I Cry Again") from 1962.[378] Elvis may have considered "Saved" as early as June 1966, when he prepared soundtrack material for the *Double Trouble* sessions.[379] Freddy Bienstock—who sought out Brill Building material when working for his cousins the Aberbachs at Hill & Range—also suggested "Saved" for John Rich's second Presley feature, *Easy Come, Easy Go.*

In the *Comeback*, "Saved" was used to broadly connect the supremely collected "Where Could I Go But to the Lord" to the full force majesty of "Up Above My Head."[380] It was during this "in between" section that Elvis seemed to pull out the stops and really ramp up the energy. He adopted Baker's template when he recorded the song, taking her styling even further: raising the tempo, emphasizing female support, delivering even more snappy and desperate phrasing, dropping out the backing for greater effect, and launching at the climax with a peculiar but appropriate laughing scat. It is as if some kind of crazy spirit has taken over Elvis's body, and he is "speaking in tongues." He seems only able to utter some kind of stylized laughter.[381] After "Saved" was recorded in Burbank one Saturday night in June 1968, take six of the song had the end of take five spliced to it for the final cut. Noticing a "new, desperate roughness" in the singer's voice, Ernst Jørgensen wrote that Elvis, with help from the Blossoms on backing vocals, "obliterated the songwriters' irony with the sheer passion of his performance."[382] Jørgensen added, "In his hands it was a pure gospel rave-up."[383] He was right. With this exuberant, uptempo, happy-clappy style workout of a number, Leiber and Stoller perfectly parodied the evangelical practice of testifying. If R&B emerged out of gospel, under supervision from these two unique, Brill Building–era R&B songwriters, it also went straight back. With "Saved," they reformulated the excitement of a Pentecostal service within the format of throwaway rock 'n' roll.

26. "(You're So Square) Baby I Don't Care" (from *The Other Sides—Elvis Worldwide Gold Award Hits Vol. 2*, 1971)

Right from the menacing bass that propelled its introduction, Leiber and Stoller's cheeky and magnificent "(You're So Square) Baby I Don't Care" showcased the rock 'n' roll incarnation of Elvis at his most carefree. A month before the singer recorded "(You're So Square) Baby I Don't Care," Gord Atkinson of CFRA Radio in Ottawa asked him whether his singing style was country, pop, or a combination of the two. Elvis replied, "I guess I kind of like 'em both—more rock 'n' roll than anything else. Rock 'n' roll is actually, you see, what put me over."[384] "(You're So Square) Baby I Don't Care" had its origins in a songwriting session that Leiber and Stoller undertook ahead of his third film, MGM's *Jailhouse Rock*.

Jailhouse Rock was the ultimate rock 'n' roll movie. It presents a coming-of-age story in which a macho young buck has to reconsider his maverick ways. The stubborn and surly Vince Everett is a total rebel: someone who can only undergo ethical transformation after his wild impulses are fully unleashed. Playing such a character, Elvis was at his most punk: busting up instruments, sneering his words, leading riots, smashing faces, and tasting the whip for his sins. By contrast, the women in the film, particularly the forgiving Peggy, are never nearly as dangerous. These female players quietly gain status precisely because they stay safe and play by inside rules. In comparison to the animalistic and primitive Vince, the women in *Jailhouse Rock* really are *so square*. When he comes on too hard, he quips, "That ain't tactics, honey. It's just the beast in me."

When Leiber and Stoller had been a little tardy in creating material, Jean Aberbach stopped by their New York hotel room one day at lunchtime and said, "Well, boys, where are my songs?"[385] He promptly pushed a large sofa across the entrance door, dozed off, and awoke at 6 p.m. to find that the chain-smoking duo had completed their duties. In the event, several of their songs were picked for the soundtrack, including the title tune, plus "Treat Me Nice" and "I Want to Be Free." Consequently, the songwriters visited studio sessions in Hollywood at Elvis's request and began to informally oversee his music production. Coming from the same generation as Elvis, they found common ground with his perfectionist work ethic, deep love of R&B, and knowledge of obscure recordings.

Elvis addressed "(You're So Square) Baby I Don't Care" at Radio Recorders on 3 May 1957. At that point, "All Shook Up" was at number one. Presley was already a confident, global musician: an accomplished professional who had already used studios more than twenty-five times in his career. When Bill Black, who had just bought an electric bass, struggled and then gave up trying to reproduce the line that opened the song, Elvis seized his Fender and jammed out the introduction with Jerry Leiber singing a scratch vocal.[386] He overdubbed his voice track at the start of the afternoon session; the following Wednesday he tried again on the MGM Sound Stage. In total, as was fairly normal at that point, they managed fifteen additional takes in the studio and overdubbed the vocal several more times.

What is so unique about "(You're So Square) Baby I Don't Care" is its wonderful sense of anticipation. One of Leiber and Stoller's trademarks was to begin with a bass riff as a kind of launch-pad introduction for songs (consider, for example, "King Creole"). The repetitive, angular bass introduction of "(You're So Square) Baby I Don't Care" hits with a force so thrilling that it may just have inspired Eddie Cochran and Jerry Capehart's riotously delinquent "C'mon Everybody," which was released the next year.[387] The song's recorded version was neatly paced, with a vocal that sounds a little tinny now. It is in his film performance, however, that Elvis really excels. At the on-screen pool party, the young singer raises his arms in the air as if coming alive and ushering in the music. Once he feels it inside him, he transforms the beginnings of a shaking frenzy into the ultra-hip, finger-snapping dance steps of a real cool cat. With the help of a Mike Stoller piano fill—one that sounds distinctly like Floyd Cramer—the first verse really swings. It is terminated by Vince's supersharp cut-up, offering a glimmer of Elvis's commanding stagecraft. As the song progresses, his arms jerk loosely about his sides and legs judder like a marionette. Clad in knitwear but with his collar turned up, the well-groomed young rocker transfixes a man-hungry audience of female bathers. When the instrumental break begins, he shakes down, then steps aside to highlight the band, and finally cuts up. Suddenly, Elvis is the smoothest rocker in the world, looking great and in full control of his music. The number ends with a crash that sounds like DJ Fontana's drum kit has just toppled over. Vince exclaims, "Hah!" as if to show everyone that the party has finally come to the boil. As he leaves the stage, the libidinous energy that fueled his electric performance is free to dissipate into a smattering of polite applause. A bathing beauty fawns, "Gee, Vince, when you sing it's really Gonesville." The fact that he shakes her hand and replies, "All for you, honey," indicates that he might have begun to settle down a bit. In that sense, "(You're So Square) Baby I Don't Care" is the ultimate song about acceptance. The women don't need to shun their social conformity or adopt "bad girl" poses to match Vince. They are fine just the way they are.

25. "Baby What You Want Me to Do" (from *The Complete '68 Comeback Special*, 2008)

> When Elvis relaxes into the first of five dives into Jimmy Reed's "Baby What You Want Me to Do"—the deep well of the sessions, where every few minutes Elvis returns for a more open rhythm, a harder beat, a knowledge that cannot be put into words—it's as if the song itself is a train to ride. . . . He dives into "Baby What You Want Me to Do" for a fourth time and suddenly he is Casey Jones, holding down the train whistle until it is the only sound in the world. The music rises, slams down, rises again, as if a whole new language has been discovered—as if, this night, it has to be made to say everything, because it never will be spoken again.[388]

Greil Marcus captures the moment perfectly. In the 1950s, through music, Elvis—as the Moses of rock 'n' roll—led innocent young Americans into a new territory beyond the barren realm of sexual repression. After a glut of family-friendly movies, he struggled to overcome his own wilderness years and to embrace the freedom of his youth, this time in a more adult way. By the late 1960s, rock music brought the blues back into vogue. Elvis used the prevailing back-to-basics ethos to revitalize his career in the *Comeback Special*. The compositions of Jimmy Reed were some of the vehicles that he chose to help.[389] Reed's "Baby What You Want Me to Do" was the perfect matrix from which fun could emerge. The sequence was supposed to resemble the spontaneity of a dressing-room party. Enthusiastic versions that Elvis recorded as he sat down with friends showcase a confident, cheeky, slightly nonchalant performer who gets so caught up in the musical flow that he whoops, "Yeah, Baby!" and forgets to wipe the sweat off his face. There is one good reason for including "Baby What You Want Me to Do" in an Elvis top 100—it shows that the singer could sure work up a jam.

Featuring his wife, Mary, on backing (some credit her as an agent in the song's composition), Reed's languid, shuffling, late 1959 version of "Baby What You Want Me to Do" places his cautious vocals and fine harmonica solo above a simple, memorable blues structure—chords E, A, and B7—played in self-accompanying style. Reed avoids the official title lyrics and instead sings, "Why you wanna let go," which was his original name for the song. Not least since "Baby What You Want Me to Do" had been embraced widely as a live music staple, Jimmy Reed was already highly celebrated.[390] Elvis not only recorded "Baby What You Want Me to Do," the previous year he also released Reed's "Big Boss Man" as a single, and he reached for it again on the *Comeback*. His enthusiasm for Reed's style also extended to reformulating the accompaniment for a version of Smiley Lewis's "One Night" on the show, a song that originally featured a standard backbeat shuffle in much the same style as Fats Domino's "Blueberry Hill."

One record that springs to mind upon a closer listen to the *Comeback* version of "Baby What You Want Me to Do" is a 1956 instrumental that Elvis had in his personal record collection: Bill Doggett's swinging "Honky Tonk Part I."[391] This mesmeric number presents a bass line so laid-back, it calls to mind some hipster walking the town's coolest hound dog on a lazy Sunday afternoon. "Honky Tonk Part I" was a huge R&B smash when it was released as King Records' single 4950 in 1956. Elvis even collected Doggett's sassy sax follow-up, "Hammer Head."[392] Coming after "Honky Tonk Part I," in its vamp, Elvis's "Baby What You Want Me to Do" gave a nod to Doggett's distinct style.[393] Most of those who covered Reed's number—including Fontella Bass and Bobby McClure, whose January 1965 Checker single Elvis had in his collection, and Little Richard, who offered his slow, soulful cover in 1966—emphasized its mesmeric, lilting tones.[394] In the *Comeback*, however, Elvis returned to the root of "Baby What You Want Me to Do," its most likely inspiration. Hardly anybody seemed to recognize the connection.

24. "Hurt" (from *From Elvis Presley Boulevard, Memphis, Tennessee,* 1976)

One of the interesting things about Elvis was the way he found so much inspiration in songs previously performed by women. Numbers like "Hound Dog" and "Fever" allowed him to tease and play with fans by using his image as a male sex object, but there is also a special case to be made for him as a unique torch singer. Sometimes it seemed as if only women had previously expressed the intensity of raw emotion that he conveyed. Unusual for a man, he shared a depth of tenderness with women and the kind of emotional courageousness that allowed such deep expression. Nowhere more is this the case than with "Hurt." Peter Guralnick described Elvis's version as "opening with a bellow almost resembling a Tarzan yell."[395] The phrase seems oddly appropriate, not only because the song was recorded in the Jungle Room at Graceland but also because of the power and maturity of Elvis's forty-one-year-old voice. Ernst Jørgensen describes "Hurt" as "a performance of spellbinding ambition and sincerity . . . probably the most convincing recording of Elvis's twilight career."[396] It deserves its place in any countdown because it reflects Elvis Presley at his most blisteringly operatic.

"Hurt" was written by Jimmie Crane and Al Jacobs before Presley broke in the mid-1950s. One of Elvis's biggest African American heroes, the R&B balladeer Roy Hamilton, cut an early version in 1954. When both singers recorded at American Sound Studio on 22 January 1969, Elvis arrived early to listen to his hero perform; he loved Hamilton's style so much. Hamilton's "Hurt" was a rueful yet powerful interpretation delivered in a style akin to Nat King Cole. When Epic Records released it in 1954, the trade magazine *Cashbox* tipped the singer for the big time. Elvis was evidently on close terms with Hamilton's rendition, and he had it in his personal collection.[397] Various other singers also attempted the song. Bobby Vinton reinvented it in 1973 in a way that drew on its 1950s roots, but offered a gentle, sing-along, country ballad. The young, blonde country singer Connie Cato released a similar but more syrupy version on Capitol Records when she turned twenty in 1975. However, one of the most famous interpretations of the song was recorded by Timi Yuro.

Despite her exotic name, Yuro was Italian American, not Japanese.[398] Clyde Otis, who was fresh from launching Dinah Washington as a crossover artist, produced her debut session for Liberty Records.[399] She gazed into the same well of romantic melancholy that made girl groups like the Chantels create some of the most engaging performances of the era. Yuro augmented her achingly sad version of "Hurt" with a powerful spoken-word section. The result grazed the top five of the *Billboard* Hot 100 in 1961.

Elvis's rendition of "Hurt" sounded similar to Yuro's. Decades after Enrico Caruso's demise, it was also as if Elvis had imagined the famous tenor was back, but now pursuing the sentimental style of those 1950s ballads. The February 1976 Graceland sessions produced some of the saddest music of Elvis's career. It seemed as if he was at his most existentially stuck; the end was nigh. "Hurt" was recorded in several takes between Dennis Linde's tragic "For the Heart" and the timelessly arresting "Danny Boy." Those two rather solemn numbers suggest that day's tone might have been a bit maudlin. Yet on the 1996 Whitehaven record, *Elvis Amongst Friends*, an X-rated studio version of "Hurt" can also be heard, with Elvis swearing as a way to josh his father, who was present at the session. The contrast suggests a man of many moods and colors.

While some critics have challenged Elvis's bombastic delivery of "Hurt," they miss the point. From the spring of 1976 to the summer of 1977, "Hurt" joined Elvis Presley's live set as a key number. On stage, the song became a way for him, as the consummate entertainer, to show fans what he could *do* with his voice. He used the 1950s sentimental ballad form as a reason to do some heavy lifting. And all the while there is a Memphis boy saying, "Listen to this—wow! What pipes I've been given!"

One of the things that separates genius from ordinary performance is not just a capacity to play with form, but an ability to intuitively transcend it and find humanity in the most unlikely places. In the midst of his own vocal feats, in the torrential flow of his own authoritative, macho bravura, Elvis went so far as to touch the soul of a truly remarkable song.

He was not just "hurt." He was mortally wounded.

23. "All Shook Up" (from *Elvis' Golden Records*, 1958)

When Hy Gardner asked Elvis in July 1956 if he shook and quaked as an involuntary response to the hysteria of his audience, the singer replied, "Involuntary? Well, I'm aware of everything I do, at all times. But, it's the way I feel."[400] In other words, rock 'n' roll was not some kind of savage reflex, nor was it about abstract self-consciousness. It came about through *acuity*: thought and action united in the moment, so to speak. The difference between Presley and, say, Jerry Lee Lewis was that Elvis was funny and not at all threatening when he played the role of the "white primitive." He obeyed God and country, loved his mother, and would never cross the line. Nevertheless, in its mythology, rock 'n' roll was *shaking all over*. The electric shocks were always ambiguous. Whether innocent or knowing, musical or sexual, nervous or out of control, those frenzied spasms associated with the music made it what it was. "All Shook Up" deserves a place on any Elvis playlist since, more than any other song, it captures the innocent thrill of his shaking.

The story of "All Shook Up" starts at the end of 1955, when an unassuming Brooklyn-born R&B songwriter, Otis Blackwell, loitered in the snow in front of the Brill Building, hoping to sell his tunes. Three years earlier, he landed a contract with RCA after winning amateur night at the Apollo in Harlem. The hopeful piano player had already dropped his career as an artist. He wanted to specialize in songwriting. Arranger Leroy Kirkland introduced Blackwell to the team at Shalimar Music publishers. One employee, Al Stanton, knew Paul Cates, who could liaise with Hill & Range. Blackwell played seven songs. "Don't Be Cruel" was snapped up by Stanton to offer to Elvis.

It is hard to understand, now, just how amazingly popular Elvis was back in the late 1950s. In the two calendar years after signing to RCA—a time when, to both the public and to record companies, singles mattered way more than albums—he topped the *Billboard* national singles charts in total for about *half* the time. The Memphis Flash notched up a string of eight smash 45rpm discs, including the monumental double-sided "Don't Be Cruel" backed with "Hound Dog," which dominated the top slot for nearly three months. After the success of "Don't Be Cruel," Blackwell was asked to write more material. One fellow at Shalimar came in with a bottle of Pepsi and quipped, "Why don't you write a song called 'All Shook Up'?"[401] Taking him at his word, Blackwell had the number down within two days. In what became an ironic turn of events, the first person to record it was David Alexander Hess, the multitalented son of an opera singer.

Right up until he branched into film work in the 1970s and became an actor best known for his infamous role in Wes Craven's 1972 horror bloodbath, *Last House on the Left*, David Hess dedicated himself to a career in the music industry. Eventually, he became head of A&R at Mercury for a while. Back in the 1950s, under the name of David Hill, he wrote material for Shalimar and performed some of it in his own right. Accompanied by Ray Ellis and his orchestra, his version of Otis Black-well's "All Shook Up" was released early in 1957. When Dick Clark asked Hess what he thought of Elvis's cover on *American Bandstand*, he said that he preferred it and thus helped to knock his own version back into obscurity. Hess regarded his Aladdin Records release as "a bubble gum piece of crap."[402] He was more interested in being a blues singer at the time. As a songwriter, Hess later contributed "Come Along" for the *Frankie and Johnny* soundtrack. Another of his songs, "I Got Stung," which was a co-write with Aaron Schroeder, proved more memorable.

David Hess's version of "All Shook Up" combined jaunty, slightly countrified vocals with some frantic piano triplets, female choral re-sponses, and a roaring, snazzy sax solo. It ended with him repeating the song's title in an increasingly hysterical spiral, frantically disclosing his precarious mental state. Recorded in January 1957, Elvis's studio version is energetic yet controlled, as was his style. The vocal seems more time-less than Hess's: unusually slow and deliberate, working within distinct confines and only cutting loose during moments of emphasis.[403] Com-pare, say, "Jailhouse Rock" from that same era; it is clear that Elvis is singing in a whole different register. His voice is powerful, yet he has control whatever the form. What he retains from the Sun days, if any-thing, is a kind of subtly crafted, spontaneous innocence.

"All Shook Up" was not so much *rockabilly gone pop* as the other way round: *pop gone rockabilly*.

One plausible guess for the new interpretation might be that Elvis aimed to get away from Hess's version, not because it failed to chart, but rather because, at the end—through an all-too-easy reference to insan-ity—its style so obviously emphasized the personal turmoil denoted in the title.

Since the early 1940s, Perry Como had set the standard for the home-ly, all-round ballad singer. "All Shook Up" ironically knocked Como's safe, progressively rousing "Round and Round" off the top slot, though Elvis's next hit in 1957 was "(Let Me Be Your) Teddy Bear." Well before any army service, Presley was trying out for the role of teen angel. The chart landscape of R&B and pop was changing by early 1957. After the rock 'n' roll boom created its controversy, the music that next gained favor offered softer and more sentimental types of masculinity. Elvis's conformist side had already been expressed on "(There'll Be) Peace in the Valley (For Me)."

As a contradiction between form and style—a frolicking song about a young man going frantically to pieces—"All Shook Up" was not fully understood by the critics; one writer in *Variety* said that Elvis had descended from the category of "sensational" to being "merely terrific."[404] Audiences, however, loved the song's infectious, carefree qualities. It not only stormed the U.S. charts, in Britain "All Shook Up" became Elvis's first number one. Blackwell's number was rapidly added to his touring repertoire. He included it many times from 1969 onward, after his return to concert performance. Elvis often performed a spirited, warp-speed version of the song in his famous Las Vegas sets, opening his shows with it in January and February 1970. Among others, he also chose it as an opener for his 27 February 1970 Houston Astrodome evening show. The number stayed in his repertoire all the way through to 1977. Introducing it at one August 1969 Vegas show, he goofed, "Here we go again, man. It's like my horse has left."[405]

22. "Good Time Charlie's Got the Blues" (from *Good Times*, 1974)

Familiar to fans but almost unknown to casual listeners, "Good Time Charlie's Got the Blues" is a jewel in the Presley catalog. Upon first listen, the heartbreaking country ballad is one of those Elvis records that evokes thoughts like: "This is so mature, timeless, and amazing. Why haven't I heard it before? Why isn't it one of his greatest hits?" "Good Time Charlie's Got the Blues" was initially written in 1967 by the singer-songwriter Danny O'Keefe. Dressed casually, like a frontier trapper, O'Keefe—who was born in Spokane—combined aspects of R&B and jazz with country folk. His work came in a late 1960s country-folk tradition of singer-songwriters that included artists such as John Prine. As O'Keefe's musician friends looked for the bright lights and moved out of the region, forging ahead with their careers, his frustration at being left behind became a source of inspiration. Almost waltz-like in its construction, "Good Time Charlie's Got the Blues" expresses the lament of a disappointed, washed-up hedonist.

O'Keefe originally released his number on the independent label Jerden, the same one that put out the Kingsmen's famous "Louie Louie." In 1970, O'Keefe's manager had him sing "Good Time Charlie's Got the Blues" down the telephone to Ahmet Ertegun, who then produced O'Keefe's album for the Atlantic Records' soul music subsidiary Cotillion. When that failed to sell, the singer-songwriter met up with Arif Mardin and tried again. This time, the number was rerecorded at American Sound with the help of keyboard player Bobby Wood and rhythm guitarist Johnny Christopher. Though the pair left partway through the recording session, O'Keefe's song made *Billboard*'s top ten pop singles chart; despite the steel guitar motif, however, it failed to dent the country top forty.

In 1973, Elvis visited Stax studio in Memphis for two recording sessions. The first, in July, had been rather awkward. Isaac Hayes was virtually bumped out of the studio. Elvis insisted that Stax staff be kept to a minimum and that he would only listen to any demo recordings once they had been transferred to disc. Engineer Al Pachucki decided not to ask for any local advice, then recorded everything without EQ.[406] In December, the singer returned and it was then that he recorded "Good Time Charlie's Got the Blues."

With light snow falling outside, Elvis walked into the studio wearing a short cape, burgundy corduroy shirt, and black pants and shoes. Elegiac country ballads were the order of the day: "My Boy" and "Loving Arms" were recorded at the same session. Johnny Christopher had previously co-written Elvis's hit "Always on My Mind." Now he pulled out the O'Keefe ballad he had worked on at American Sound. Elvis asked his fellow musicians to keep everything down to earth; the spare arrangement gave "Good Time Charlie's Got the Blues" a certain poetic beauty. In nine takes, it was finished.

Other musicians, such as Glen Campbell, previously rejected "Good Time Charlie's Got the Blues" because of a lyric line that O'Keefe included referencing a codeine addiction that he developed after crashing his motorcycle. The controversial line about taking pills to "ease the pain" was simply omitted by Elvis, perhaps because he found it too close to home.

"Good Time Charlie's Got the Blues" connected Elvis Presley to his country soul roots. It reflected his tendency to pursue covers of contemporary hits and his ongoing interest in folk pop. Somehow, Elvis's vocal—although equally country—is slightly less nasal and abrasive than O'Keefe's. He sticks broadly to the original, rueful rendition, keeping the song's lingering symmetry, gentle steel guitar licks, and drip-dropping vamp. The song comes across as almost serene; a kind of gentle, introspective ode to masculine immaturity. "Good Time Charlie's Got the Blues," and songs like it, announced that Elvis had become an unhappy person: someone who, not so far beneath the mask, was suffering because he had lost the love of his life. Since Elvis's divorce had been finalized two months before the Stax session, he knew that fans would understand how much "Good Time Charlie's Got the Blues" resonated with his own unspoken regrets. When, in a rare moment, he performed it live at the Las Vegas Hilton in August 1974, he even joked about the subject. Unfortunately, however, the number never made it into Elvis's regular set list.

21. "I'll Remember You" (from *Aloha from Hawaii via Satellite*, 1973)

The wonderfully lilting "I'll Remember You" begins with a heartbreakingly understated and bittersweet instrumental introduction. This caressing number deserves its place in any top 100 because it showcases Elvis's abilities, not just as a straight ballad singer, but also as a *song selector* of the highest caliber: someone who could see into the emotional core of each piece of music. Its story begins with the writer, Kuiokalani "Kui" Lee, who was born in Shanghai, of mixed Chinese-Hawaiian descent. Lee was raised in Hawaii, where he became a celebrated entertainer and worked different clubs. According to Marty Pasetta, who directed the *Aloha* satellite telecast, "Kui Lee was a very, very good friend of Elvis's."[407] With its swaying bossa nova accompaniment and dreamy phrasing, Lee's own version of the song sounded like something Andy Williams might have cooked up for his television show.[408] The enveloping ballad was covered by the better-known, also Chinese-Hawaiian, singer Don Ho. His entertaining cabaret live sets led to an album on Reprise Records in 1965, titled, *Hawaiian Heart Beat . . . The Vocal Romance of The Don Ho Show!* For the third track, the charismatic entertainer included "I'll Remember You."

When Elvis began thinking of recording Lee's song in the spring of 1966, he had an association with Hawaii that went back almost a decade. He managed to record it at a Nashville session that summer, the same one in which he also delivered a yuletide single ("If Every Day Was Like Christmas"). Elvis's interpretation built upon Don Ho's vocal style and subdued instrumental backing. It started with a gentle, frilly, Spanish guitar introduction and ended with a continuous wash of angelic voices supplied by Millie Kirkham, June Page, and Dolores Egan.[409] Red West first laid down scratch vocals. His employer stayed back at the hotel, saying he had a cold. When Elvis arrived, he carried the song off with his usual flair. Compared to the later concert versions, Elvis's voice seems sharper and more reverberating. At the end of that year, unfortunately, Lee died after a battle with cancer of the lymph glands. Columbia released a posthumous compilation, *The Extraordinary Kui Lee*. The Hawaiian singer had not even reached his mid-thirties.

"I'll Remember You" was featured periodically in sets between 1972 and the early summer of 1976. Elvis included the song at an afternoon show at his Madison Square Garden engagement on 10 June 1972. The vocals are soft and subdued, gently commanding and yet haunting, rising to a more anxious pitch. They sound slightly more Latin toward the end of the New York performance. The most famous version, however, was produced for the *Aloha* concert, which raised money for the Kui Lee Cancer Fund. "I'll Remember You" has a dramatic ending there, much in the Don Ho style. Toward the end, Elvis offers a cheeky smile before fixing his eyes on the middle distance. He finishes the song looking gently swept away.

What is interesting about "I'll Remember You" is that while it seems to reflect thoughts of a sentimental lover lamenting the end of a relationship, the depth that it offers, ultimately, is spiritual. It is a love song that opens out onto profound loss, focusing not so much on the missing beloved, but rather on the pain of the singer. Compare, for instance, Bob Dylan's song of the same name, which was recorded for his 1985 album *Empire Burlesque*: Dylan frames his emotions as reflections of loyalty to the departed. Lee, in contrast, laments the growing isolation of the one left behind. The ending is gently hopeful, precisely because it offers the possibility of metaphysical reunion. Rather like the celestial gospel of "Milky White Way," it is hard not to hear "I'll Remember You" without wondering about Elvis's bond with his mother. Lee's ballad is so deeply affecting, however, because it never quite becomes maudlin; its calm emphasis is on gentleness in process, not building a monument. In Elvis's hands, "I'll Remember You" is sublime, a tender eulogy seeming to epitomize a phrase sometimes used by the hypnotist Milton Erickson: "My voice will go with you."[410]

Beyond his rock 'n' roll beginnings, Elvis was nothing if he was not a gothic singer. "I'll Remember You" therefore deserves a genre category of its own; it's Elvis singing the Hawaiian gothic.

20. "Are You Lonesome Tonight?" (from *Elvis' Golden Records, Volume 3*, 1963)

One of the places where Elvis almost certainly got the sound and style for his more sedate, early RCA material was listening to an outfit called the Hilltoppers. Despite its folksy-sounding name, the vocal group had a clean-cut, rather preppy image.[411] Members wore college beanies, sweaters, gray flannels, and white buck shoes on stage. Their act was formed when pianist Billy Vaughn recruited three students from Western Kentucky State College to record a demo for a composition called "Trying." He gave a campus security guard $10 to "borrow" the Van Meter Auditorium and captured their first performance on a reel-to-reel tape recorder. At this impromptu session, football player Bill "Greek" Ploumis helped out by lying on the floor and holding down the piano pedal with his head. Led by the debonair voice of Jimmy Sacca, the Hilltoppers effortlessly updated the gospel quartet style, creating a kind of doo-woppy, commercial pop before the shocking epiphany that was rock 'n' roll.

The Hilltoppers combined a sense of ordinariness with a gently classy, heroic sound. Before 1952 was out, the group made it onto *The Ed Sullivan Show*. In the year that Elvis cut his first demo, jukebox owners voted the Hilltoppers *Cashbox* magazine's top vocal group. During the Korean conflict, foreshadowing Elvis Presley's career, Vaughn's act also survived Jimmy Sacca's conscription by having recordings in the can, ready to cover any absence. By the time Elvis recorded "That's All Right" at Sun, the Hilltoppers had notched up more than ten hits on the *Billboard* charts.[412] They were even embraced by British fans just before the rock 'n' roll explosion. It is no surprise that Elvis had heard of the group. Rock 'n' roll, unfortunately, did not serve the Hilltoppers well: "Do the Bop," a 1956 attempt to enter the market, lacked spontaneity. Elvis retained his appreciation of Vaughn's creativity, however. When Vaughn went on to record with his own outfit, Elvis acquired a copy of his single "The Shifting Whispering Sands."[413] In 1959 he called Billy Vaughn and his orchestra "one of the finest instrumental groups that is making records today."[414]

The Hilltoppers appealed to the conservative side of the mainstream youth market when Elvis was emerging, so it is not surprising that he understood their style as an appropriate point of entry. Once he signed to RCA and could make ballads in the style he wanted, it is likely that he looked to the group, and acts like them, for inspiration in terms of vocal style, backing, and arrangement. Elvis knew their number "To Be Alone" and its sound was echoed, slightly, on his performance of "Crying in the Chapel."[415] Two other songs—the vocal group's debut "Trying" and a later update of the Inkspots' "If I Didn't Care"—seem to inform the tone of "Are You Lonesome Tonight?"

"Are You Lonesome Tonight?" dates from the mid-1920s, when two vaudevillians, Roy Turk and Lou Handman, wrote the original version. In its first year or so, the song was recorded by several artists, including Vaughan "The Original Radio Girl" De Leath (for Edison) and Charles Hart (for Harmony). De Leath's rendition verged on parlor music. Hart's was mannered. When he worked for Bourne Music, the veteran songsmith Dave Dreyer may have created the characteristic spoken-word section for use in live renditions of the song; after that it was then included on the sheet music.[416] Capitalizing on his harmless 1949 chart-topper, "Cruising down the River," a big-band leader from Ohio called Blue Barron (real name Harry Freidman) released a "sweet" version that included the monologue the following March. The relevant point of departure for any account of Elvis's cover of "Are You Lonesome Tonight?" however, is Bitsy Mott. From the mid-1950s onward, the one-time infielder for the Philadelphia Phillies accompanied Elvis as a kind of road manager. Mott got the job because he was trusted; his sister, Marie Mott Ross Sayer, became the Colonel's devoted partner back in the 1930s. She worked as a carnival assistant and knew how to cook Southern food, and the Colonel loved her.

"Are You Lonesome Tonight?" was one of Marie's favorite records. In what was probably the best creative musical steer that Parker gave Presley in their whole liaison, he suggested the song was worth a try. As he spent time in the U.S. Army, the singer expanded his vocal range and sought out new material. A version of the song could have been performed at a home-taping session in Bad Nauheim as early as April 1959. Less than a month after he returned home, and just over a week after performing on Frank Sinatra's ABC *Timex Special* in April 1960, Elvis reentered RCA Studio B in Nashville to address a number of songs that could combine his urgency, eroticism, and vocal prowess with a more family-friendly persona. Among them were "Fever," "It's Now or Never," and "Such a Night."

In the early hours of a weary Monday morning, with lights dimmed, the Presley rendition of "Are You Lonesome Tonight?" was born. It was as if Elvis was summoning up the maudlin style of the precursor songs he recorded at Sun, particularly "That's When Your Heartaches Begin."

With the Jordanaires adding their lulling refrain, Elvis's version of "Are You Lonesome Tonight?" begins gently, as a strummed, downtempo, country-style ballad. His vocals work well within their limit above this subdued arrangement. They begin crisp, sway slightly into unbalanced affectation, then alternate and flutter until they find their own ghostly sincerity.

One of the key parts of Elvis's take on "Are You Lonesome Tonight?" is its dramatic monologue. In the spring of 1950, the famous minstrel star Al Jolson—then inching toward his mid-1960s—delivered a version of the ballad for Decca that included a spoken-word section. Committed to record just a few months before Jolson's fatal heart attack, this version is as syrupy and croaky a swan song as might be expected. At one point, as if anticipating the unlucky character Frost from Ingmar Bergman's film *Sawdust and Tinsel*—which came out three years later—Jolie angrily ad-libs, "The stage is bare, and I'm standing there . . . in the part of a broken clown!" Elvis begins his own interlude in a similarly jaded manner, but the added reverb presents someone who sounds more like a betrayed teen idol. Ironically—and tragically—the powerful monologue was perhaps the nearest Elvis came to both Shakespeare and serious acting. It's well known that he couldn't keep a straight face, though, in August 1969. One Las Vegas live performance gave rise to a "laughing version" of the song that was officially released in 1980 on disc five of RCA's eight-LP compilation, *Elvis Aron Presley*. On the FTD live release from the same month, *Elvis: The Return to Vegas*, there is a version with wistful backing more akin to "Love Letters," used as the perfect segue between the lighthearted "Baby What You Want Me to Do" and subdued "Yesterday." Such sequences indicate that Elvis used songs intuitively as mood modifiers.

The trade magazines *Variety* and *Billboard* both understood "Are You Lonesome Tonight?" as a revamped oldie.[417] Based on Elvis's reputation, they predicted it would be a hit. By that point, the star's appeal was broad enough, in effect, that he could alternate between assertive showcase pieces and softer ballads. "Are You Lonesome Tonight" topped the charts between "It's Now or Never" and "Surrender." When it hogged the top slot on *Billboard*'s pop countdown for six weeks, several female artists launched answer records, with at least four titled "Yes, I'm Lonesome Tonight." In an equal but opposite version that contained a delightfully feminine monologue, Dodie Stevens explained that there had been a misunderstanding: she had never changed. Thelma Carpenter's pointed retort accused her lover of telling all his friends that she lied, when he knew it could never be true. As the 1950s turned into the 1960s, young women were finding their feet. Later versions of the song by Frank Sinatra, Pat Boone, and Doris Day catered to an older market and tactfully avoided the spoken-word section. Teenaged melodrama had breathed its last.

In 1991, two years after East German authorities announced that Berliners could cross between different sides of their long-divided city, Boris Yeltsin took over from Mikhail Gorbachev as the leader of a newly post-Communist Russian Republic. Yeltsin, who was known for his hard drinking and sentimentalism, assented to the ultimate triumph of Western culture. He was an avid fan of Elvis, and his favorite song was "Are You Lonesome Tonight?" It was as if—less than two decades after the global telecast of *Aloha from Hawaii*—Elvis Presley's music had finally brought the world together.

19. "I Washed My Hands in Muddy Water" (from *Elvis Country (I'm 10,000 Years Old)*, 1971)

As the confessional tale of a runaway robber, "I Washed My Hands in Muddy Water" absolutely swings. Any understanding of the song should begin with its writer "Cowboy Joe" Babcock. He was part of the Nashville Edition, an outfit second only to the Jordanaires for their prolific session work. In May 1963, Babcock momentarily replaced Hoyt Hawkins in the more famous quartet when they backed songs that Elvis laid down in Studio B, such as "(You're the) Devil in Disguise." Speaking about "I Washed My Hands in Muddy Water," Babcock later claimed, "I recorded it and my record didn't sell anything."[418] Nevertheless, the number was soon taken up by Columbia Records artist Stonewall Jackson, who released it in 1965. Jackson had much greater success. His effort peaked in the top ten of the country chart. The propulsive number also became a mid-1960s release for Charlie Rich, Warner Mack, and Johnny Rivers and was later covered by the Spencer Davis Group.[419] In the early 1970s, as part of the Nashville Edition, Babcock helped to overdub some of Elvis's recordings. Although the two never met in the studio, the session man added gloss to material from the same early June 1970 Nashville visit that produced versions of the bittersweet "Funny How Time Slips Away" and "Love Letters." He contributed backing vocals to "It Ain't No Big Thing (But It's Growing)," which was captured on the third evening. Toward the end of the next day's studio session, Elvis recorded Babcock's "I Washed My Hands in Muddy Water."[420]

Though Johnny Rivers produced the most funky and fluid interpretation—and a top twenty country hit—all the early versions of "I Washed My Hands in Muddy Water" sound comparatively staid. Elvis's early takes begin in the same vein. To lighten the material and add a little humor, he ends one with a cheeky scat vocal. The version that was finally used, however, raised the tempo and gave the number—which already proved it could be stretched elastically between country, funk, and gospel—a turbocharged feel, turning it into a rock 'n' roll jam of epic proportions. Right from Charlie McCoy's delightfully crisp harmonica solo, the jam comes together without needing to be forced. Backed by showy horns and Jerry Lee Lewis–like slashes of piano, Elvis offers a vocal that proves he is just having a ball. In some parts, he is in dialogue with the guitar, in others just ad-libbing with himself. It is as if he takes a novelty song about guilt and redemption, strips it down to its roots, then reenergizes it, putting a dash of that old rock 'n' roll magic straight back into the heart of country.

The "muddy water" of the song's title, of course, referenced the earthy backwash of the mighty Mississippi. Its fertile sediment was understood as a rejuvenating force in the South, a quality that made it emblematic of black slave labor. Washing hands also indicated religious redemption, alluding to baptism and the possibility of living a "clean" life. The song is an indirect advertisement for Christianity. Indeed, Charlie Rich basically performed "I Washed My Hands in Muddy Water" as a gospel number. Despite its branding as country on his genre concept album, Elvis's version can, nevertheless, be interpreted as a demonstration that Christianity can be fun because the burden of human guilt is not half as heavy as many imagine. After all, we are all sinners. What is so sneakingly majestic about Elvis's performance of "I Washed My Hands in Muddy Water" is its immediacy. His jam avoids the complex musical architecture of ballads and rock operas from its era—it never needs it as such. Pace is everything here. The jam version captures a time when the musicians seized the moment and found their spirit. Its singer is in a race to get there before the other instruments. Sucked into the flow of his own music, Elvis becomes ecstatic. Since everyone is on their game, the whole group loses its moorings and takes its playing beyond the limits of meter.

18. "Tiger Man" (from *The Complete '68 Comeback Special*, 2008)

In the 1960s, there was an Australian soldier called Barry Petersen who was nicknamed "The Tiger Man of Vietnam." Petersen led jungle campaigns against the Viet Cong, but his life was not well known until after 1977. The story has it that "The Tiger Man"—who, like Elvis, was twenty-eight in 1963—was sent under CIA orders into the mountains of South Vietnam to turn local tribes into a guerrilla task force. He must have taken on the humid hell of the Vietnam jungle in taut silence, one step at a time. And somehow that might have been a parallel life for Elvis; sent straight from secret training in Germany, ready with some swift kenpō, his razor-sharp reflexes triggered by the merest sign of trouble. It's a crazy fantasy, but in the realm of music at least, Elvis was undoubtedly the Tiger Man. Despite the millions of words in print written about him, despite all the biographers and music obsessives who have pored over the smallest details of his life and career, after sixty years of global fame, one mystery remains unsolved: Was "Tiger Man" actually his second Sun recording?

Not long before 9 p.m. on 27 June 1968—a pleasantly warm Thursday evening—while taping one of the informal segments for the NBC *Comeback Special*, Elvis reached back into his catalog. Toward the end of his set, just after "Blue Christmas," he laid into "Tiger Man," saying that it had been his second-ever record. Investigations, so far, however, have found no firm grounding or historical evidence to support his claim.[421] Not through want of trying, we will probably never know. "Tiger Man" has remained a mystery. That is not the point. The song needs no myth to affirm its propulsive energy. It is hardly surprising that from the time Elvis returned to live music right through to 1977, he continued to perform the number.

"Tiger Man" got its start a little before Elvis's first Sun session. Probably best known for his compelling 1969 comedy funk outing, "Do the Funky Chicken," Rufus Thomas had, many years earlier, been the first DJ to play Elvis on local black radio. During his tenure at WDIA, from the early 1950s to the mid-1970s, the intelligent, energetic, and avuncular Thomas was a crucial figure in Memphis music. With his cheeky, tent show charisma, he was a notable radio DJ, recording artist, networker, and, above all, comedian. Recording for Sun, Stax, Chess, and other labels, Thomas wasn't just at the center of the local music scene, he embodied it. In 1989, years after his heyday, he popped up as a shrewd local in Jim Jarmush's quirky, downbeat Memphis road movie, *Mystery Train*. Back in 1951, the African American singer teamed up with Sam Phillips to release "Bear Cat," an answer record to Big Mama Thornton's "Hound Dog." Rufus Thomas continued his Sun output with "Tiger Man," a tune written by Joe Louis Hill and Sam Phillips (as "Sam Burns"). The spirited original begins with an explosion of pounding tribal drums and a full-throated yodel. It continues with some delightfully raspy, wailing vocals, offering words that skip over a funky, fast-moving blues vamp. Thomas ends the number with an atmospheric big cat snarl and yet another yodel. The result is a rollicking, funny, carry-on-up-the-jungle record.

Elvis's version of "Tiger Man" was faster, straighter, smoother, and more throwaway than Thomas's, and brilliant, all the same. Where Rufus had shown his sophistication by skitting racist assumptions that linked provincial black folk to primitivism, the magic of Elvis's performance came from listening to a country boy playfully adopting the mantle of a primal, alpha male—and taking his fantasy so far that he basically *becomes* that character for a while. Once Elvis rediscovered "Tiger Man," in 1968, it became a regular feature of his concerts, usually appended as an exhilarating coda to "Mystery Train." The two Sun numbers complemented each other so well that it made perfect sense to keep that train rolling and run them together. A good example comes from the 25 August 1969 midnight show, selected tracks from which were released on the LP *From Memphis to Vegas*. Accelerating the energy that Elvis created with "My Babe," he lunged into "Mystery Train/Tiger Man" as a way to shake things out before the more sedate "Words." The rip-roaring Sun song couplet speeds along so fast it almost proceeds in double time. Not only is Elvis in top form, but his voice is masterfully complemented by some of James Burton's most mesmeric picking. Listeners are given just long enough to realize what "Tiger Man" is really about: the excitement of speed *and* syncopation. The song zips along before being hit by the percussive turbulence of its own jungle breaks. "Tiger Man" feels like riding the bumper cars: being on a fairground attraction that is exhilarating, exhausting, and ultimately triumphant. This time, the proverbial battle cat has bolted so far that it is no longer in earshot. Other live versions exist of "Mystery Train/Tiger Man," like those found on the 1980 vinyl set *Elvis Aron Presley* (from a Shreveport show in June 1975) and the widely acclaimed 1997 compilation *Platinum* (from a May 1977 engagement in Chicago). Elvis also jammed the raucous Sun couplet to warm up his June 1970 Nashville studio visit—a session that began with the comparatively limp "Twenty Days and Twenty Nights" but also spawned the more engaging "I've Lost You."

An interesting studio take of "Tiger Man" can be found on a five-disc bonanza of Elvis's 1970s material: the 1995 box set *Walk a Mile in My Shoes*. This particular moment came in the midst of a three-day RCA Studio C session in Hollywood aimed at providing material for the 1975 *Today* album. When they begin to jam "Tiger Man" between them, his band members weave a fabric that is far looser and more funky than any of the throwaway live versions. Elvis joins in, although he is tired. The house engineer, Rick Ruggieri, caught the moment on tape. The performance is spacious, slick and jazzy, and strangely electric, as if the song had been reformulated by Eumir Deodato and dropped off its edge. For all of that, however, the version in Elvis's second *Comeback Special* show is the most direct, a moment so compelling that its audience screamed with pure delight. At the end, it is as if the musicians can be heard wondering, "How did we get out of that one?"

17. "Baby Let's Play House" (from *A Date with Elvis*, 1959)

With its hiccoughing vocals, gently angular guitar, and bopping, tic-a-tic bass pattern, "Baby Let's Play House" deserves inclusion in any top 100 Elvis for one obvious reason—this is rockabilly at its darkest and very best. The tale of "Baby Let's Play House" starts with Cy Coben. After

Coben co-wrote "My Little Cousin," which went top twenty for Peggy Lee and Benny Goodman in 1942, his songwriting talents were in high demand.[422] Coben penned "I Wanna Play House with You." Eddy Arnold put it out in 1951 as a cheerful and timeless country and western single.[423] In his youth, the Nashville-born singer Arthur Gunter had been in a gospel quartet called the Gunter Brothers. He switched to blues in the 1950s and signed to an off-shoot of the Nashboro gospel label, Ernie Young's newly formed Excello Records. Gunter had a local hit with what was likely an answer to the Coben number: "Baby Let's Play House." With its twanging introduction and accompaniment, Gunter's own version sounded a little like Big Boy Crudup. The rendition combined a carefree vocal with jaunty backing. Excello 2047 had the same charm as a good skiffle record, but lacked both the smoothness and edge of Elvis's version—almost to the point where Gunter's vision, in the lyrics, of rather seeing his girl dead, seemed rather incongruous.

From "Tutti Frutti" to "Great Balls of Fire," evidence suggests that rock 'n' roll usually works best as a spontaneous explosion. "Baby Let's Play House" is more like an incantation. Its charismatic protagonist does not plead when his baby starts walking out the door. Instead, he summons her back with all the dark forces at his disposal. At a time when sexuality was coyly expressed in Hollywood show tunes and romantic glances, "Baby Let's Play House" positively bristled with something much more subversive. There is a sense that the "little girl" in question might not only miss her fun; the song's lyrics imply she is under threat for breaking free. Elvis tackled the song at Sun early in February 1955 and played it live on 18 February in Monroe, Louisiana, and 19 March in Houston, Texas. He also performed Coben's number later that year on *Louisiana Hayride*. The instrumentation, pace, and mood of Elvis's "Baby Let's Play House" made it light and carefree, with the singer marshalling every trick he knew: accenting high notes, changing tempo, working different inflections. The galloping pace and eccentric styling of his vocal adds up to a rangy, acrobatic, one-man attack on the principle of meter. Scotty Moore keeps up and does not simply play his solos, either; he positively talks them. Elvis eggs him on, at one point shouting, "Yeah!" The result is breathtaking. It gives just a whiff of what Elvis might have been like when playing live as he toured the South before 1956—back when he wore his clothes unfeasibly loud, like a traveling magic man.

Buddy Holly, who was inspired by Elvis, also did his own version of the song, confusingly titled "I Wanna Play House with You." His hiccoughing vocal is higher pitched, almost like a chipmunk. Of course, it's more Holly than Presley, and oddly dated for all that. In a way that it was never possible to hear in the music of the Blue Moon Boys, Holly's performance quietly suggests the birth of the British rock 'n' roll, coming across almost as fey in comparison to the Presley cut.

"Baby Let's Play House" represents everything that Elvis had to censor to become a mainstream family entertainer. It's delightfully unhinged; sensual, carefree, and sinister, as if there was something in the water back there in Tupelo that outsiders never knew about.

Still unbelievable.

16. "The Wonder of You" (from *On Stage*, 1970)

Baker Knight was a huge Elvis fan and an example of the many half-forgotten songwriters that the singer chose to celebrate when he recorded their songs. In 1956, Knight formed his own rockabilly band, appropriately called Baker Knight and the Knightmares. They had some success with the roaring "Bring My Cadillac Back." Knight's songwriting career continued for many years, riding to a series of musical trends that came and went. In 1967, for example, he released "Hallucinations," a funky slice of post-Beatles, psychedelic pop that would not have been out of place in the Monkees' catalog. Knight's monumental ballad, "The Wonder of You," is among Elvis Presley's most accessible, loving recordings. It deserves its place in any list because it shows that Elvis could infuse even easy listening material with a majestic sense of power.

Knight started composing "The Wonder of You" while he was in hospital in Alabama with an ulcer, doing some soul-searching. The songwriter came through a terrible time in which he hit rock bottom due to alcohol. He was inspired to offer "a prayer of thanks for God not giving up on me."[424] Knight earmarked "The Wonder of You" for Perry Como, but Ray Peterson overhead the song when he played it to Como's arranger, Dick Pierce. Peterson wanted to make a recording. Vince Edwards was the first person to actually cut the song. Peterson launched it in 1959 as a *Billboard* top forty hit. He became more remembered for the hauntingly earnest "Tell Laura I Love Her," which was released the next year. Peterson's interpretation of "The Wonder of You" was very much in the yearning style of a 1950s ballad. Within months, Ronnie Hilton covered the song and scored a hit in England. Hilton became better known later for his mid-1960s sing-along favorite, "A Windmill in Old Amsterdam." His version of "The Wonder of You" was like something from an old Bing Crosby movie: quaint, with cotton-wool female backing and fluttering strings. Nevertheless, he managed to pull out a spectacular ending.

Elvis's interest in "The Wonder of You" went right back to Ray Peterson's original. He asked Peterson to visit him on a movie set in 1960 and politely requested permission to cover "The Wonder of You." A decade later, in January 1970, Elvis started working with Glen D. Hardin, his new pianist. Hardin grew up in Texas and first saw the Memphis Flash play Lubbock in 1955. After Buddy Holly died, the Crickets backed good ole boy Sonny Curtis, with Hardin accompanying. Later he graduated to the house band at North Hollywood's bastion of country music, the Palomino Club. Then he got a regular slot with Delaney Bramlett and James Burton in the Shindogs, who were the backing group for ABC's mid-1960s show *Shindig*. When Hardin became Elvis's pianist, he immediately started arranging songs.

Just over a decade after Peterson's and Hilton's versions of "The Wonder of You," Baker Knight got an early morning call from Hardin saying that Elvis wanted a lyric sheet for the song. Hardin and Knight already knew each other. They worked together with the singer-turned-impresario Jimmy Bowen, who had links to Frank Sinatra's label Reprise Records.[425] Hardin concocted an appropriate arrangement and Elvis began performing the ballad in concert. No studio version was ever recorded. The live take that finished the first side of the *On Stage* album, and was released as a single, came from the 19 February 1970 Las Vegas show. Another rendition was captured that summer, again in Vegas, on 13 August 1970. In this version, released much later on *Elvis: The Lost Performances*, the singer carries "The Wonder of You" in a way that is slightly weary but commanding at the same time.[426] The Royal Philharmonic's recent revamp offered a softer backing behind this slightly more hesitant vocal.

It made good sense for Elvis to choose Knight's ballad. In his younger years, he admired the success of Perry Como as a mainstream family entertainer. He also hero-worshipped Dean Martin, an artist who came to record several of Knight's compositions. From one angle, "The Wonder of You" suggests Elvis's withdrawal from the youth market into the bland world of mushy ballads and easy listening music. That reading, however, is not quite true. Hardin's arrangement of "The Wonder of You" was crisper and more contemporary, less yearning and more generous than any of the 1950s versions. It was almost as if he set out to purge the mush but keep the song's heartfelt sincerity. The result sounds nothing less than a powerful embrace.

Backed with "Mama Liked the Roses," "The Wonder of You" was released a couple of months after Elvis first performed it as a scout single for the album *On Stage*. Knight was overjoyed when he heard that his hero had given such an endorsement. A few in Elvis's camp were less thrilled by the idea of a live single. Nevertheless, in the United States alone, sales of "The Wonder of You" almost hit the million mark. It rapidly became a top ten hit. In the United Kingdom, the record dominated the singles chart for six weeks. British fans always had a special relationship with their idol. They created the largest fan club for Elvis and received occasional personalized messages from him in return, thanking them for their support. Later, the leading British fan club took people to Las Vegas to see Elvis perform. It is no wonder, then, that when he sang the song during his 1974–1975 tours, it became a firm fan favorite, a central number in the set lists of tribute artists ever since.

In a sense, Baker Knight made a "song of praise" that worked equally well as an appreciative love song. By fully articulating its generosity of spirit, Elvis left a heartfelt love letter to his most prominent followers.

15. "King Creole" (from *King Creole*, 1958)

One of the surprising things about Elvis was the extent to which, as a young man, he could be confident, commanding, and powerful in his voice and masculinity. Sometimes he seemed well ahead of his years. The trailer for *King Creole* announced that he played a "hard loving, hard hitting Danny Fisher who sang his way up from the gutters of lusty, brawling New Orleans." The film broke new ground—it caused the *New York Times* to admit that Elvis could act. Because *King Creole* combined aspects of his existing image—juvenile delinquency, country innocence, existential struggle—it was an ideal vehicle. The film's quality was further enhanced by a wealth of good songs that emerged smoothly from its narrative. Above all others, Leiber and Stoller's title number stood out from the pack.

"King Creole" was recorded toward the end of a soundtrack session at Radio Recorders in Hollywood on 15 January 1958. Music publishing historian Bar Biszick-Lockwood notes that RCA hired Leiber and Stoller to oversee the session as independent producers, despite the Colonel already having fallen out with them.[427] Steve Sholes knew Elvis valued the duo. The Memphis singer was living on borrowed time: Initially scheduled to be inducted into the army just five days later, by that point he had achieved a deferral until the following March. After another eight days, the singer and his team returned to the same studio, this time to re-record the title track and an instrumental version ready for the film. On the new sung version, the Jordanaires emphasized the song's title in the introduction, primarily for the sake of the film.

Because *King Creole*'s director, Hollywood veteran Michael Curtiz, cared so much about the project, he came to the recording sessions. RCA was so doubtful about the new material, however, that it marked the film's theatrical release by offering two consecutive EPs rather than one LP. Both sold better than anticipated.

As a performance, the EP version of "King Creole" is a great example of the rapid interplay between Elvis and his backing group. Early takes sound nothing like this final incarnation—not so much because of Elvis's vocal but because of everything else; the horns have a different timing and Scotty's solo is a notch slower. Such disparities make the final version sound both pared-down and supercharged: bright, crisp, and unhinged from a pace that is dragging it down. Beyond its wonderfully frenetic pace, two elements of the final version of the track really make it stand out: the spontaneous feel of Scotty's flashy guitar solo and the Jordanaires' crescendo of a cabaret ending. The movie version even had sound effects at key moments.

Supremely together music.

14. "Blue Suede Shoes" (from *Elvis Presley*, 1956)

The original version is full of the fire that Elvis used in so many of his early rocking recordings. Quantities of breath-catching and hiccoughing. I love "Let's go, cats" before the instrumental break. The guitar in the background is loud and raucous—that word can be applied to instruments. Elvis's voice matches to perfection, and he really belts out these unusual words from the heart.[428]

Let's go, cats . . . Back in the mid-1960s, *Elvis Monthly* magazine ran a series of features on Elvis's most "Queer Discs." The eighth platter chosen was "Blue Suede Shoes." Its enthusiastic reviewer explained its charm. The song, of course, needs no introduction. It holds a high place in any countdown because it epitomizes the glorious, life-affirming explosion of noise so joyously detonated at Sun Record Company.

Once Elvis's career took off, Sun became a magnet for a new generation of eccentrics who infused pop—the breezy music of youth—with Southern tones: the earthy authenticity of country, swinging coolness of R&B, and, most significantly, the frantic pace of rockabilly. Partway toward Nashville, on Interstate 40, a sharecropper's son named Carl Perkins had been working up a storm with his brothers in a Jackson-based live music band. Upon hearing the B-side of Elvis Presley's debut single, Perkins decided Sun might provide a home for his style. After all, "Blue Moon of Kentucky" had been a staple in the Perkins boys' live set for five years. Sam Phillips showed interest. Perkins's first song for him, "Movie Magg," was leased to Los Angeles's Flip Records. It came out just after Elvis's "Milkcow Blues Boogie" and was a jaunty little ditty but lacked overall bite. The B-side, "Turn Around," which was a pitch-perfect, Hank Williams impression, became a regional country hit. Perkins started touring as Elvis's opening act. His next single, "Let the Jukebox Keep On Playing" continued in the Williams vein, but its B-side, "Gone, Gone, Gone," was nothing short of hopped-up hillbilly music: a real, raw, rockabilly recording. Captured in two takes and rush released at the start of 1956—after Elvis had left the Sun label—it was Perkins's next record however, that struck gold.

Backed with the swinging "Honey Don't," when Perkins's original version of "Blues Suede Shoes" spread across the country, it tore up the airwaves. The music journalist Nik Cohn was accurate about its theme: "It was important—the idea that clothes could dominate your life. . . . It was the first [song] to hint at an obsession with material objects—motorbikes, clothes and so on—that was going to become central."[429]

When Elvis first signed to RCA, both the label and publishers the Aberbachs were in a tight spot. On one hand, his career was exploding, with live tours, television slots, and other delights. On the other, he was getting too busy to find time to visit the studio. There was precious little new material available for which Hill & Range owned publishing rights. RCA was in danger of failing to capitalize on its unprecedented investment. Because the Dorsey Orchestra struggled to work out a suitable arrangement, Elvis could not promote "Heartbreak Hotel" on his first national television appearance. As music industry historian Bar Biszick-Lockwood observed, "Steve Sholes was going nuts."[430] Sholes called Sam Phillips. The Sun producer gave permission for Elvis to try Perkins's "Blue Suede Shoes" as a cover option.[431] At the end of January 1956, Elvis kicked off his second session for the label with Perkins's number. The recording was finished in ten takes.

"Blues Suede Shoes" began the third and fifth sets of Elvis's national television debut appearance for the Dorsey Brothers' weekly CBS variety program *Stage Show*. In the second of these Dorsey Brothers' performances, on 17 March, it is as if Scotty Moore is busy shoplifting and Elvis is his getaway: The singer shouts, "Rock it! Go man, go man! Go! Go!!" The Blue Moon Boys' performance from the deck of USS *Hancock* for *The Milton Berle Show* in April superbly conveys the jumpy excitement of a rockabilly house party. Despite experiencing a slight guitar malfunction, Elvis still cuts up. He puts the spotlight back on Scotty for the break.[432] Things have really hotted up by the time Moore does his solo. At the end, Bill Black goes hog wild, riding his bass like a trouper and belting it for all it is worth.

Unfortunately, tragedy struck for Perkins early in the new year. His Chrysler limousine made it more than three-quarters of the way to New York, where he was due to appear on Perry Como's television show. He stopped off to perform a 21 March gig in Norfolk, Virginia. As his car was approaching Dover, Delaware, during the early hours, its driver—a Memphis DJ called Stuart "Poor Richard" Pinkham—fell asleep at the wheel. Pinkham hit a truck and flipped the Chrysler four times, demolishing a guardrail and plunging off a bridge. The truck driver was killed instantly. Pinkham, drummer W. S. "Fluke" Holland, and Carl's brother Clayton, meanwhile, were all relatively unharmed. Carl's other brother, Jay, was thrown half out of the car window; he was in a serious condition. Perkins himself had been thrown clear of the vehicle and was now unconscious and facedown in the stream.[433] He had a broken collarbone, several lacerations, and a severe concussion. In an instant, Holland jumped up and rescued him.

Even without promotion on *The Perry Como Show*, "Blue Suede Shoes" went on to top the pop, R&B, and country charts. Despite having more hits and signing to Columbia, Perkins's career never hit the same level. Fame was getting to him, so he opted for the smaller game, later saying:

> I felt out of place when "Blue Suede Shoes" was Number One. I stood on the Steel Pier in 1956 in Atlantic City . . . and the Goodyear blimp flew over with my name in big lights. And I stood there and shook and actually cried. That should have been something that would elevate a guy to say, "Well, I've made it." But it put fear in me. [434]

In its brief moment of glory, Perkins's version of "Blue Suede Shoes" significantly outsold Elvis's RCA single. For rock 'n' roll mythologist Nik Cohn, however, Elvis gave "wholly new dimensions" to Perkins's number. [435] Not only did Presley record "Blue Suede Shoes" in 1956, he rerecorded it in 1960 as well to create a stereo take for the soundtrack of *GI Blues*. The song was played on a jukebox in that film, framed as an example of "original" rock 'n' roll, as opposed to the more recent trend for sanitized ballads.

Contrasting Perkins's original performance—which became Sun's first million-selling single—with Elvis's RCA studio versions from both 1956 and 1960 is an enlightening exercise. Their interpretations are similar in some ways, but in others worlds apart. In full control of his introduction on his original version, Perkins is a country boy rocking out. His capable style parallels the innocence of Presley's early Sun sides. Perkins's vocal delivery remains delightfully mannered; in the second verse, it is he who sounds rawer than either of Elvis's studio masters. When he brings the song back from its instrumental section, Perkins sings in a way that points out every word he says. In contrast, in his 1956 cover version, Elvis paints a vision of some delinquent driving a musical hot rod with his foot to the floor. Due, almost certainly, to the record getting sped up, his voice quivers with a fast vibrato, sounding like its excited owner is spinning plates. As the familiar rhythm comes in, Scotty and Bill play faster and swing tighter than any musician on Perkins's record. Elvis is equally frantic. He makes a pass at the lyrics and then gets mad in the chorus when it doesn't work out. Scotty's active, angular 1956 guitar solo, meanwhile, comes over like a bag of nickels escaping in all directions across a stone floor. When Elvis emerges from the break, he sulks and sparkles. The singer is unstoppable.

In the 1960 version, Elvis begins a little closer to Perkins, infusing his performance with the confidence of a big, ballsy lounge act. He almost slurs the lyrics, offering a kind of assured collectedness. He then steps back, finds a reason to have fun, and laughs at the song's narcissistic insanity. Scotty's 1960 guitar solo, meanwhile, is super slick. It hints at the extremely rich decade in popular music to come. After the break, Elvis drops a hint of his uniquely sultry charm. He sounds slightly more blue-blooded now, like an uptown swinger. Part of the reason for the smoothness may actually have been that Elvis had to concentrate on making his diction clear for the movies. He was maturing. His voice was developing. Those around him had to fall in step. Freddy Bienstock started presenting Elvis with material that was "less juvenile . . . a little bit more sophisticated" than the rock 'n' roll from his days of glory.[436] In its original form, Elvis's first studio version of "Blue Suede Shoes" was now a snapshot of times past. What a comparison between the different versions by Perkins and Presley really suggests is *not* that Elvis "died" when he went in the army, but that he could no longer, due to his own maturation, produce a sound—even in the *Comeback*—that had *exactly the same kind* of fire as his rock 'n' roll years.

13. "That's All Right" (from *For LP Fans Only*, 1959)

One summer evening in 1954, a young trucker, a dry cleaner, and a refrigerator repairman got together in a Memphis recording studio. The truck driver's twin brother, Jesse Garon, had died at birth. His father had been in prison. He had closely bonded with his mother. The studio owner's father died before he left his teens. He had been ravaged by mental illness. The others served in the Korean conflict. All their lives, they were looking for something. The first song they tried was old-time country singer Leon Payne's "I Love You Because," but their version was no better than its original release, so the musicians kept looking for inspiration.[437] It was then that they stumbled on a different kind of sound. On that July night, together in that little Memphis studio, using secondhand recording equipment, they crossed a line. They channeled something much bigger than almost anyone expected. The young singer maintained, "We just more or less landed upon it accidentally. Nobody knew what they were doin' until we had already done it."[438]

On its fiftieth anniversary in July 2004, fans made "That's All Right" the oldest record to reach number one on the U.S. singles chart. With good reason. In life, everyone faces two challenges. The first is to mature beyond the ties that bind our first relationship (that with our parents) without losing appreciation for the gift of unending love. A second challenge is to thrive, to give and find love, even in the face of emotional loss and desolation: when one feels misunderstood or to blame, when life feels like a burden, when everything meaningful is gone, when one is all alone (even in a crowd), when others are a torment, when all the world seems devoid of hope. Jean-Paul Sartre, the existentialist philosopher, expressed as much in his 1944 play *No Exit*, which contained the chilling diagnosis, "Hell is other people." As the twentieth century matured, the two challenges were expressed in art high and low, including country music and the blues.

During a break in the session, a song popped into Elvis's head, and he just started jumping around and singing it. Bill and Scotty joined in, but the tape was not rolling, so Sam asked them to do it again. In the magazine *Elvis Answers Back* from August 1956, the singer explained that fateful session:

> When I was called to make my first record, I went to the studio and they told me what they wanted me to sing and how they wanted me to sing it. Well, I tried it their way, but it didn't work out so good. So while most of 'em were sitting around resting, a couple of us just started playing around with "That's All Right," a great beat number. . . . It came off pretty good, and Mr. [Sam] Phillips, the man who owned the record company, said I should go ahead and sing all the songs my own way, the way I knew best. We tried it, and everything went a lot better. . . . When Mr. Phillips called me to make that first record, I went into the studio and started singing.[439]

Listed in several ways, as befitted the "Mama" in its chorus, "That's All Right" deserves a high position in any hot 100 for being Elvis's first professional recording, yet it is more than that. To understand its place, it seems relevant to consider what the song is not. "That's All Right" is *not* Elvis's first studio recording: He had already recorded four songs himself, tracks that were not released commercially at the time. Neither is it the world's first rock 'n' roll number—anyone who knows usually points to other records, notably the magnificent "Rocket '88'" by Jackie Brenston and his Delta Cats. "That's All Right" remains nothing less than the Rosetta Stone of late twentieth-century popular music, however. The platter changed everything in its wake because it let the world know precisely what was to come. On that first night, one of the amazing things about it was that neither of Elvis's backing musicians actually knew the song. What they created to support his vocal was, in effect, an improvisation.[440] Scotty later said, "I feel that if we'd have been there with a full band and drums and piano, then it might not have happened."[441]

"That's All Right" starts out like a lightly strummed country ditty. Elvis's delivery effortlessly implies undercurrents that are a whole lot darker and more delinquent. In the chorus, he playfully tells his mother that her warnings are her own. What "That's All Right" delivers, in equal measure, is uncommitted intimacy, parental injunction, defiance and rebellion, laughing it all off, cutting up, and starting over again. Decent white folk—at least the professional middle-class ones who dominated the record charts—just did not do or talk about such things. Black folk had more license to explore them. Elvis's song gave permission to everybody. He took the blues and reinvented it as a Tennessee teen drama. For that there was no precedent. Nicholas Ray's incendiary James Dean movie, *Rebel Without a Cause*, for example, was still over a year away.

To comprehend the magnitude of "That's All Right," listen not just to the Sun recording but also to the Gaylords' Mercury Records single, "The Little Shoemaker." It topped the *Billboard* national chart on that Monday night back in 1954. "The Little Shoemaker" was so popular at the time that the maestro Hugo Winterhalter made it to number three on the same chart with his own version. Looking back, "The Little Shoemaker" and "That's All Right" both sound innocent, but in totally different ways. The Gaylords' number is *chaste*: precocious, jaunty, and more than a little silly. It advocates exactly the sort of innocuous fun that might be shared by parents entertaining small children. "That's All Right," meanwhile, is a breezy country blues number, but its energy comes from a completely different place. Where "The Little Shoemaker" is pristine and "infantile" (in the best sense), the A-side of Elvis's first single is pointed and adolescent.

In order to fully understand "That's All Right," it is necessary to start with its writer. Arthur "Big Boy" Crudup was already a kind of "old time" or retro-artist when he recorded for RCA Victor in the 1940s. What made Crudup radically different to Elvis was that he was so clearly rooted in the idiom of the blues. With its "cow catcher" introduction, Crudup's gloriously sly, swinging version—which was recorded in September 1946 and registered the following March—offers a snappy rebuke to some ill-fated female. After an instrumental break in which the song revels in its own bliss, Crudup comes roaring back, citing mathematical logic as a cast-iron reason to let go of his woman. He had been working his way toward Oedipal themes in earlier songs, ones where being ambiguously "rocked" by his "mama" weighed in somewhere between parental affection and sexual thrill. There were traces of such concerns in the titles of both "My Mama Don't Allow Me"and "Rock Me Mama." The original single featuring "That's All Right" was backed with the musically similar "Crudup's After Hours." After RCA released "That's All Right," Crudup had another crack at his patented formula by offering the remarkably similar "I Don't Know It." To celebrate the birth of its new line, the mass-produced 45rpm single, RCA rereleased Crudup's "That's All Right" in 1949, this time on a special cerise (red orange) pressing.

In those early years, Elvis's engagement with Crudup's repertoire was considerable. He may have pursued his own version of "That's All Right" for a while; Bill Black's brother Johnny even claimed that he heard him sing it when the Presleys lived at Lauderdale Courts. [442]

When Elvis recorded "That's All Right," he shifted the tune away from Crudup's showy and funky but somewhat lackadaisical blues, toward a breezy, gently jangling, country pop number. It was reformulated, with smoothly careening vocals and some bopping, percussive bass work. In Crudup's version, the singer's womanizing lifestyle gives cause for parental concern. Elvis plays up the idea that his folks disapprove of one particular girl, as if she is a femme fatale to which he cannot quite commit. Yet it is the way that he attacks the song, as much if not more so than its lyrics, that still makes it spellbinding. Compared to Crudup, not only are Elvis's lyrics different, his new version is faster and its phrasing is smoother. And, of course, the backing is more country. Peter Guralnick explained this in detail, suggesting "That's All Right" is both a homage to Crudup and an "entirely different" song, one in which Elvis probes the emotional resonance of each line in a way that sounds "unrehearsed . . . spontaneous . . . springing right from the soul."[443] Like a horse bolting for freedom, Elvis showed that he can sing *around* the traditional timing of the beat. His excessive and performative up-tempo vocal style created a special sense of immediacy, one that aurally characterized the cover's vocal delivery.

"That's All Right" struck a chord precisely because it represented a moment when Elvis's musical fancies chimed with Sam's ongoing interest in gutbucket material. The trio mixed country and blues, and by implication "white" and "black" music, bringing together genres that were previously segregated in terms of marketing and recording, if not live performance. Sam observed, "I knew we had something that wasn't fish and wasn't fowl, but that had tremendous excitement and abandon."[444] When the trio recorded "Blue Moon of Kentucky" soon after, Scotty Moore's exclamation (that the music sounded like it had "too much Vaseline") and Elvis's retort ("You ain't just a woofin'") playfully demonstrated how aware they were of the racial implication of their sound.[445] Scotty thought the new music was exciting but warned, "Good God, they'll run us out of town when they hear it."[446] He feared the Blue Moon Boys would be hounded for showing a flagrant lack of care about the unspoken rule of musical segregation.[447] For his part, Sam claimed:

> I didn't want an imitation. I didn't want someone trying to sound like a black man. I wanted singers who instinctively had a feel for a song, who'd get that emotion across. You'd never believe the amount of prejudice we ran into early on. You'd better believe that if I've ever achieved anything then it's been to help break down some of that prejudice. And I think that rock 'n' roll music has had more favorable impact on the understanding of people of all races and all nationalities than all of what them diplomats have been doing. The young aren't so prejudiced as the old, and if I've helped stop some of that prejudice from growing up, then I think I've done something.[448]

The irony was that despite all the hullabaloo down south, "That's All Right" sold perhaps only twenty thousand original copies. Dewey Phillips at WHBQ was the first to take note of Elvis's potential. A *Billboard* reviewer also said, "Presley is a potent new chanter who can sock over a tune for either the country or the R&B markets. . . . A strong new talent."[449] With a gloss of added echo, "That's All Right" was used later as something to keep fans occupied while their hero was away in Germany. Ironically, it was not until RCA's 1959 afterthought compilation, *For LP Fans Only*, that the performance that delivered Elvis to the world got proper national distribution.

It is hardly surprising that "That's All Right" was a staple of Elvis's early live sets. He also kept it in play for his 1961 USS *Arizona* memorial show and *Comeback Special* (though it was not used in the final broadcast). Conversely, the song appeared on *That's the Way It Is* but not its

LP. Elvis sang a spirited, up-tempo version, as part of his early rehearsal scenes. For the performance that began the showroom segment, he was again beguilingly nervous, as if reliving the summer of 1954. Elvis would constantly return to "That's All Right" in his later live shows, both as a kind of historic marker, a biographic statement, and a way to find the moment.

In the wake of Elvis Presley's global popularity, "That's All Right" was covered by the Beatles and many other groups. One of the artists who became fascinated with it was Bob Dylan. His covers suggest he kept peering in, trying hard to understand what was inside the song, as he was eager to extract, or extend, its essence. It remained something of a mystery to him. As if dusting off some strange object from outer space, he returned to it more than once. The version from 1962 that appeared on Vigotone's 1993 compilation, *The Freewheelin' Bob Dylan Outtakes*, is typically zesty and features flashes of Dylan's signature harmonica theatrics. He also recorded a 1969 duet version with Johnny Cash sharing lead vocals and Carl Perkins on guitar. The aim was to capture more material for the *Nashville Skyline* LP. Their quirky performance found its home much later, however, when Spank Records released *The Dylan/Cash Sessions* in 1994.

With its uniquely understated Oedipal quality and existential crosscurrents, "That's All Right" remains a microcosm, both for Elvis Presley's own story and for the whole cultural explosion that was rock 'n' roll. If Elvis was the boy who discovered fire, then "That's All Right" was the comet that he made from it, the first tool he used to write his name in the sky.

12. "Unchained Melody" (from *Elvis Aron Presley*, 1998)

Music critic Robert Matthew-Walker once called Elvis's voice "infinitely the most important aspect of Presley as a performer."[450] That is undoubtedly true. Since everyone has a voice, it is something that helps us understand the shape of a musical gift. As Elvis's career developed, he became able on a range of other instruments, however. In his early days, he was known for strumming his guitar and accidentally breaking strings on stage. He started learning piano before he made it to Graceland. One magic evening, when he met the Beatles in 1965, he was learning electric bass. His final performance, in private at Graceland, was self-accompanied on piano. In a short tour from 27 to 31 December 1976, Elvis performed "Unchained Melody" regularly on stage, accompanied by his own piano playing. The spectacle of one man driving himself to new peaks of musical achievement rapidly became the centerpiece of each show, with only an established favorite—"Can't Help Falling in Love"—as the nightly follow-up. Elvis was evidently a proficient piano player. What "Unchained Melody" showed was that he was, in the final analysis, a superhuman singer.

Like many staples, "Unchained Melody" is a unique song. Only "White Christmas" has been a hit for more artists. The composition was crafted by Alex North and Hy Zaret.[451] North studied at the forefront of classical music in Paris with Aaron Copeland. Both composers translated elements of their education into more popular fare. Copeland became famous in 1942 for his monumental "Fanfare for the Common Man." Before the great Elia Kazan introduced him to Hollywood, North wrote for the stage in New York. His scores combined lyrical and symphonic elements with dissonance and darkness. In retrospect, they marked a high point of 1950s and 1960s American popular cinema. North wrote "Unchained Melody," together with his New York writing partner Hy Zaret, for Hall Bartlett's prison drama, *Unchained.* Todd Duncan looks weary and strangely entranced in the movie as he sings the ballad, accompanied by just one acoustic guitarist.

Popular music performers soon took up North and Zaret's masterpiece. They gave it a profile way beyond *Unchained*, to the extent that the film is relatively forgotten. Swing band arranger Les Baxter offered one of the first versions. Baxter's Capitol Records release features a long introduction with a choir repeatedly requesting to be unchained over backing from a Mantovani-style orchestra. After its singer adds somewhat bloodless vocals, the whole thing builds into a glorious, celestial finish. The African American baritone Al Hibbler delivered a different take on Decca. Less than five years earlier, Hibbler had gone solo after working with Duke Ellington. With its delightful symphonic backing, his March 1955 rendition of "Unchained Melody" was mannered and confident.

A month after Hibbler's release, June Valli maximized the drama of "Unchained Melody" and gave the song a feminine touch. Valli had achieved something that Elvis did not: she won *Arthur Godfrey's Talent Scouts* in New York. A few months before Elvis joined the label, she released a version on RCA that made the top thirty with the help of backing from Hugo Winterhalter and his orchestra. Beginning with an introduction formed of precipitous piano chords, the Bronx-born singer's interpretation included highly impassioned vocals over a "Bolero"-style backing and marching band beats. The confident baritone Don Cornell brought out a similar version to Hamilton's in May on Coral Records. His take featured a precise, crooning, swashbuckling delivery. Cornell's masterful voice sounded a tad like Al Jolson.

Various other artists soon covered "Unchained Melody," notably Liberace, Eddy Arnold, Perry Como, and Harry Belafonte. The Righteous Brothers made it their own, however, when they cracked the top five with it in 1965. The story went that Bill Medley produced less important cuts for the famous duo. He and Bobby Hatfield released music through Phil Spector's Philles label. "Unchained Melody" was first released as the B-side to "Hung on You," but the single sold more rapidly once radio DJs flipped it over. Spector then tried to take credit for the song's production.[452] The magic of the Righteous Brothers' version came less from its subdued backing than from the smooth voice of Hatfield. Hatfield added a final lyric line about needing love. It beautifully embodied the song's emotional theme and allowed him to reach high notes. The result was a record that sounded like it was bathed in gold.

One version of "Unchained Melody" that probably influenced Elvis more than any other was Roy Hamilton's take, which Epic Records released in March 1955. Bill Medley was a fellow fan of Hamilton. Speaking of Elvis, Medley said, "His favorite song was 'Unchained Melody' by Roy Hamilton, not the Righteous Brothers."[453]

With a rich, deep, powerful voice, Hamilton had been spotted in a New Jersey club and signed to Columbia two years earlier, achieving great success with "You'll Never Walk Alone."[454] His interpretation of "Unchained Melody" combined the force of a gospel-tinged voice with a cinematic orchestral string section. Hamilton's performance is bold but neatly phrased and has an operatic quality. It is like Caruso come back as an African American, singing a Disney theme tune.

Like "Bridge over Troubled Water" and "Hurt," "Unchained Melody" was, in a sense, a "feat" song for Elvis. It marked a place in each concert where he could show his exceptional vocal ability. Presley turned North and Zaret's composition into a one-man opera. He performed what had already become the ultimate example of blue-eyed soul in a way that showcased his vocal prowess and gymnastic style. His interpretation is replete with mesmerizing aural moves: making his voice sound plaintive or understated, repeating himself, changing tempo, belting, hitting highs, and holding notes. He uses them to convey a range of moods and emotional tones. In short order, his truly breathtaking performance of "Unchained Melody" expresses tenderness, pleading, hesitation, emotional pain, bravura, an almost metaphysical yearning, and, finally, a sense of deep, existential heroism. The version on Elvis's final album, *Moody Blue*, came from a show held in Ann Arbor on 24 April 1977. Six months after he died, his performance from 21 June 1977 was released by RCA in single form, backed, appropriately, with "Softly As I Leave You."

11. "Walk a Mile in My Shoes" (from *On Stage*, 1970)

Ironically, Elvis was misunderstood both by 1950s elitists who disliked delinquent music and their later opposition, the 1960s rebels who demanded public commitment to an alternative society. Elvis, meanwhile, quietly stood for equality, plain and simple. As his daughter Lisa Marie had it, "When he started out, at a time when the Ku Klux Klan was still burning crosses, people thought he was black. He couldn't have cared less."[455] By dressing black and making music that questioned racial divisions, by thematically bringing together Big Boy Crudup and Bill Monroe on the same terrain, Presley fired the first salvo. Soon, however, he went missing in action: There are plenty of indications that Elvis maintained his cross-racial empathy, yet he failed to publicly advocate the civil rights agenda. The thing is, sometimes he went undercover, working *through* the medium of music, pulling his country together, creating a larger and larger center ground. Rather like the time Elvis visited Richard Nixon, "Walk a Mile in My Shoes" suggests that he could go *deep cover* and work under the radar to pursue his secret mission.

In the 1960s, Elvis omnivorously worked through many genres and styles of music, drawing them together under his umbrella and reshaping (one might even say "branding") them in his own image. Writing to the U.S. Department of Justice's John Finlator in a mission to obtain his special-agent badge, he said, "I am an entertainer and I believe entertainers should entertain and make people happy and not try to impose his personal philosophy on anyone, through songs, television or through the guise of comedy."[456] Yet at the height of the civil rights era, Elvis was the mole at the heart of the mainstream. He kept burrowing away quietly: inviting the black comedian Red Foxx to his wedding, singing "In the Ghetto," proudly showing his black backing singers at the white-bread Houston Astrodome, befriending Muhammad Ali, wearing *Superfly* clothes, covering the Drifters, and so on.

Anyone who thinks Elvis forgot black culture after 1956 should recall the time two decades later when, to Myrna Smith of the Sweet Inspirations, he recounted *all* the dialogue from Barry Shear's extraordinary 1972 blaxploitation drama, *Across 110th Street*—a film that explicitly dealt with racial prejudice.[457] They might also take note that on tour, he allowed his black backing group to virtually raise his daughter.[458] It is also indicative of Elvis's outlook that when he played his Vegas midnight show on 21 February 1970, he ran "Walk a Mile in My Shoes" straight into "In the Ghetto," as if to emphasize their thematic connection.

Joe South, the writer of "Walk a Mile in My Shoes," recorded music for Bill Lowery's impressively titled National Recording Corporation (NRC). In that sense, he and Jerry Reed shared a similar start to their careers. Parodying the rock 'n' roll game, Sheb Wooley's crazy comedy record "Purple People Eater" topped the *Billboard* pop chart for nearly a month in the summer of 1958. Cashing in on its popularity, South made his mark early, with his NRC novelty single, "The Purple People Eater Meets the Witch Doctor." After the daft answer record became a hit in its own right, South's career took a number of turns. When Bob Dylan's producer Bob Johnson moved the sessions for his famous 1966 album *Blonde on Blonde* from New York to Nashville, he called on South to play guitar on the album. The songwriter later returned to performing. He specialized in mature country music of the kind that pointed up impasses in personal relations. Two of South's most prominent numbers were "Games People Play"—which some said was inspired by psychiatrist Eric Berne's popular ideas—and Lynn Anderson's famous "I Never Promised You a Rose Garden."

"Walk a Mile in My Shoes" was released as a single by Capitol in 1969, credited to Joe South and the Believers. It missed the *Billboard* top ten by a whisker. South's take, which is wonderful in its own right, begins with a syncopated, guitar-tapping introduction. He comes in with earnest and slightly plaintive country vocals, supported by funky guitar licks and sparkling female gospel backing. The message in South's lyrics, however, is what makes the song unique. "Walk a Mile in My Shoes" is not just a vague bid for empathy. By referencing folk who are out on reservations and in the ghetto, by calling them "people" (not resorting to generalizations based on race), by saying that suffering hardship is not of their own making (it is only by "the grace of God" that whites are not there), and by couching it all in the idiom of pure country soul, South created powerful social medicine. The point was recognized by Harry Belafonte, who, in some ways, paralleled Elvis during this period. Belafonte and Lena Horne performed a funky, instructive live version of the song for their ABC special, *Harry & Lena.*

South wasn't too pleased with what Elvis did with "Walk a Mile in My Shoes":

> I was happy he cut it, but Elvis didn't sing it with enough conviction for me. I think he could have paid more attention to the song itself rather than singing it like it was "Stardust." He wasn't as committed to the song as I would have liked. He was doing it like he was winking his eyes at some fox over here and some fox over there who was fixing to take his picture.[459]

Other interpretations are possible. The idea of Elvis being a moral philosopher may not come easy, but for Ernst Jørgensen: "Joe South's wonderful 'Walk a Mile in My Shoes' was the kind of song he must have been aching to do when he hold Steve Binder 'I'm never going to do another song I don't believe in.'"[460] At the midnight show that Elvis performed in the Las Vegas International on 11 August 1970, he started the song off with a spoken-word introduction: "You never stood in that man's shoes or saw things through his eyes. Or stood and watched with helpless hands while the heart inside you dies."[461] The "Men with Broken Hearts" monologue came from a 1955 MGM LP called *Hank Williams as Luke the Drifter.*

Perhaps the most crisp version of "Walk a Mile in My Shoes" appeared on Elvis's quietly phenomenal 1970 album, *On Stage.* Bergen White's meticulous arrangement and choice of instrumentation make that performance superb.

What happened was not so much that Elvis missed the point of "Walk a Mile in My Shoes," but instead that he delayed its action. As an undercover cipher in popular music, he was sliding something dangerous into his Las Vegas dinner-show cabaret with "Walk a Mile in My Shoes," gently addressing the conservative heart of the mainstream. His efforts were fixed upon those who wanted "just an entertainer," among them the very people *least* likely to be moved by compassionate support for social justice and equality. Hearing his cabaret performance, it wasn't impossible that they might, someday, realize the true gold of the song's message, glimmering like hidden treasure beneath tides of the sea.

10. "Hound Dog" (from *Elvis*, 1956)

In the summer of 1956, songwriter Mike Stoller spent his first big royalty check on a trip to Europe with his wife. They returned on an ill-fated ocean liner, the SS *Andrea Doria*. On foggy seas, en route between Genoa and New York, the vessel collided with the MS *Stockholm*. When Stoller finally made it back to the United States, Jerry Leiber told him the news that Elvis Presley had scored a hit with their song "Hound Dog." Recalling the moment years later with interviewer Cleothus Hardcastle, Stoller said, "I heard the record and I was disappointed. It just sounded terribly nervous, too fast—"; without skipping a beat, his songwriting partner added, "—too white."[462] Despite their estimations, "Hound Dog" topped the R&B chart, while the other side of its single, "Don't Be Cruel," dominated the national chart. The song became an Elvis staple. One website lists more than seven hundred concert performances of "Hound Dog" during Elvis's last years.[463] Perhaps his most committed performance came in the *'68 Comeback Special*, when the song was sandwiched in a medley between rapid-fire versions of "Heartbreak Hotel" and "All Shook Up." Clad in his signature Bill Belew black leather outfit, in the middle of the performance, Elvis shook his shoulders at warp speed and immediately dropped to his knees, provoking a round of squeals from surprised female spectators. Once again, he proved what a deadly weapon "Hound Dog" could be.

"Hound Dog" deserves its place in any Elvis 100 because it is pure rock 'n' roll. As late as 1960, Perry Como told the *Saturday Evening Post* that when he heard it, he felt a need to "vomit a little."[464] He also recognized a classic in the making. To really understand the song, contemplative listening is not enough. In Elvis's hands, "Hound Dog" was almost punk: a tease, a thrill, a game played with the audience, an interactive musical experience. The song's history begins with the sturdy figure of Willie Mae "Big Mama" Thornton, a stocky blues belter in the tradition of Bessie Smith with an imposing manner. She was born just under a decade before Elvis and joined the Hot Harlem Revue when barely in her teens. By her mid-twenties, Thornton was scouted by Don Robey, who had her play his Bronze Peacock Club in Texas. She later plowed the Chitlin' Circuit and, in 1952, met Johnny Otis. The black singer topped the bill of his traveling revue not long after. She became a key artist for Peacock Records.

Jerry Leiber and Mike Stoller wrote "Hound Dog" in fifteen minutes to order for Thornton. At that point, they were not yet even in their twenties. They thought of themselves as black. Stoller said that they based the song on Thornton's looks as much as her sound and used euphemisms where expletives might have made sense. He added, "We wanted her to growl it."[465] At first she refused and gazed at Leiber "like looks could kill," saying, "White boy, don't you be tellin' me how to sing the blues."[466] Thornton pursued several songs at Radio Recorders in Los Angeles that summer, including "Hound Dog." Otis was supposed to produce the session for Robey, but Leiber and Stoller took charge because they needed him on percussion; only Otis could supply the same drum sound that he managed on the demo. The number was completed in just two takes, the first just a little too smooth and syncopated. Released the next year, with Otis billed as "Kansas City Bill and His Orchestra" (on account of his binding Mercury Records contract), the single was so successful that Thornton headlined alongside Junior Parker and Johnny Ace on the Peacock Blues Consolidated Tour Package Show. Elvis had "Big Mama" Thornton's March 1953 Peacock single in his personal record collection.[467] In some ways, its B-side, "Nightmare," sounded like a prototype for "Heartbreak Hotel."

After Peacock cleaned up with Thornton's record, a spate of R&B and country variations appeared. One of the most famous of those was Sun Records number 181, "Bear Cat." Rufus Thomas's outrageous March 1953 release caused legal problems for the label after it was billed, on the single, as "The Answer to Hound Dog."

Philadelphia native Freddie Bell caught the public imagination with his cabaret swing-band sound, performing the punchy, up-tempo "Teach You to Rock" and frantic "Giddy Up a Ding Dong" on Sam Katzman's phenomenally popular 1956 rock 'n' roll exploitation feature, *Rock around the Clock. TV Teen Club* was a forerunner to *American Bandstand*; its musical director Bernie Lowe had a hand in Bell fixing his sights on "Hound Dog." Lowe formed Teen Records with the salesman

Harry Chipetz, as a subsidiary of Sound Records.[468] He encouraged Bell to revamp "Hound Dog" and make it work as a show tune. Bell's performance became a regional hit for Teen.[469]

Elvis saw Freddie Bell and the Bellboys perform their version of "Hound Dog" in Las Vegas when he visited their show at the Silver Queen Bar and Lounge in the Sands, during downtime from his relatively unsuccessful stint at the New Frontier Hotel. It was soon after this first spell in Vegas that the song became a showstopper in Elvis's set.[470] He performed it on TV that summer: shockingly on *Milton Berle* and sedately on *Steve Allen*. After being encouraged to sing "Hound Dog" to a hound dog while wearing a tuxedo, years later Elvis summarized his feelings toward Allen when he played a Vegas dinner show: "I love him for it, but I'll never forgive him!"[471]

"Hound Dog" was thrilling because it involved a kind of power game on stage: Elvis went from lambasting the audience to being controlled by his own song, communicating to enthusiastic fans not only with gyration, but with flash and tease. He would point straight at the audience, stand on the balls of his feet, and say, "You . . . " When the beat took him, he stood with knees bent and started to judder and scissor his legs in time to DJ Fontana's machine-gun drumming. Once he finished one version of the song, he struck his arm back for the band to stop, then launched into a coda in slow tempo, continuing to scissor his legs and lock his hips as he moved forward in time to the music. Finally, he knelt down, kicking each leg out immediately after every drum beat. On *The Milton Berle Show*, the camera cut to girls in the audience that were visibly bouncing up and down with excitement. The Colonel and Steve Sholes persuaded Elvis to release the song, not just use it as a novelty live number.[472] Representatives from Hill & Range, meanwhile, leaned on Leiber and Stoller to give up a portion of their royalties. In the studio, Elvis pursued thirty-one takes, with the help of Gordon Stoker on the piano.

Elvis Presley and "Big Mama" Thornton's versions of "Hound Dog" were worlds apart. Her sassy, bluesy rendition punctures the arrogance of a sly male hanger-on who pretends to be classy and interested but is, in reality, just taking advantage. In the very act of chiding him, she shows that she is more outrageously cool than he can ever be. In Elvis's hands, meanwhile, "Hound Dog" takes off like a rocket. Cheeky hand claps let the audience in on the sound. Scotty's guitar has more attitude than ever. It is not long before Fontana's military percussion knocks everyone out cold. Elvis, meanwhile, positively glows, coming straight in with a voice brimming full of glorious arrogance and utter contempt. By syncopating the lyrics right on the second line, he really shows his mettle. After he repeats his attack once again, the Jordanaires—minus Stoker's tenor—open their throats, backing one of the sassiest guitar solos in rock history.

Elvis's "Hound Dog" is light-years from blues, beyond rockabilly, meaner than pop, and purer than most rock 'n' roll. It is everything that had gone before and much, much more. At the end, the performance comes unraveled as quickly as it arrived, revealing itself to be some burlesque cabaret number. "Big Mama" Thornton was bound to respond. Despite having the highest-selling blues record in America in the spring of 1953, and number three on the *Billboard* R&B chart, she was displeased at her relative lack of royalties. When Elvis's version came along, she complained, "He's making a million, I'm making a zillion nothing, you understand?" More than once, she also claimed that Elvis refused to share a bill with her, on account of a supposedly racist attitude: "He refused, saying nothing a coloured person could do for him but shine his shoes."[473] While her grievances over royalties were genuine, the claims about racism were never matched by other accounts.[474] Ironically, Peacock rereleased her single in both 1956 and 1958, in part to cash in on the success of the Presley remake.

9. "How Great Thou Art" (from *How Great Thou Art*, 1967)

The rousing "How Great Thou Art" deserves a high place in any countdown because it is no less than a work of religious art. When Charlie Hodge and his boss were traveling by limousine in November 1970, Elvis turned to him and said that he wanted to perform the song that night for the first time on stage. Hodge was the only one who knew how to play the song on piano. He met with the other musicians and told keyboard player Glen D. Hardin, "I'll sit at the piano and play it, until you learn Elvis's phrasing on it."[475] Bandleader Joe Guercio wrote an orchestration. Without even a rehearsal, they rapidly created one of the greatest songs in the show. After three concerts, Hardin had learned to anticipate Elvis's phrasing. In recordings of those live concert versions, the song's ending is continually held up, like nobody quite wants it to finish. Elvis repeats "How great!—," as if he is mustering enough strength to fully lift an unfeasibly heavy burden. He sounds magnificent.

"How Great Thou Art" began life as "O Great God," a poem composed in the late nineteenth century by Carl Gustav Boberg, set to a
traditional Swedish melody. Within two decades it had been translated
into German and Russian. By the end of the 1940s, the song found its way
to the English-speaking world. The British missionary Stuart Keene Hine
published his own lyrics in his gospel magazine *Grace and Peace*.
George Beverly Shea had success singing on various national gospel
radio shows. He joined the Billy Graham Evangelistic Association in the
early 1950s. In the spring of 1954, Shea traveled to Europe with one of
Graham's Crusades and was given the sheet music in London by Andrew
Gray, a friend who worked for the Glasgow-based publishing house Pick-
ering and Inglis. When Graham's evangelical campaign rolled into Toronto the following summer, Shea performed the song at Maple Leaf
Gardens. He was a sensation. With support from a choir, in 1957 he
regularly raised the roof at Madison Square Garden. Many of the Crusade
performances were broadcast on Saturday evening television.[476] It was
not surprising, following Shea's great success, that other religious outfits
covered the song.

The Blackwood Brothers began their quartet in the mid-1930s. At the
height of their popularity, a decade and a half later, they moved to Memphis. Those were successful days. The group presented shows twice daily
on WMPS, ran its own record label, and frequently played the Ellis Auditorium. Elvis unsuccessfully tried out for their nephew Cecil Blackwood's vocal group, the Songfellows. He was rejected on account of an
inability to harmonize when not singing lead. After he signed to Sun, the
group offered him another audition, but it was too late then. In the meantime, the Blackwood Brothers achieved national success on CBS. Just
before Elvis recorded "That's All Right," they appeared on *Arthur Godfrey's Talent Scouts*. Elvis would drop by the quartet's monthly *All-Night
Sings* at the Ellis Auditorium. He visited a mass public funeral performance for two of the quartet's members at the Ellis Auditorium just
before "That's All Right" was recorded. When cofounder Doyle Blackwood later ran for office as a state representative of Tennessee, Elvis lent
his pink Cadillac for the downtown parade. In 1956, the Memphis Flash
joined members in an impromptu gospel sing-along backstage that may
have included "How Great Thou Art."[477] The Brothers were asked to sing
at Gladys Presley's funeral in August 1958. Ironically, James Blackwood,

accompanied by the Stamps, would eventually sing "How Great Thou Art" at Elvis's own funeral.[478]

The Blackwood Brothers produced a deep, rich, testosterone-fueled version of "How Great Thou Art" and released it on the 1960 RCA Victor LP *The Blackwood Brothers in Concert*. Four years later it also appeared on *The Best of the Blackwood Brothers*.[479] Another RCA gospel quartet called the Statesmen released a version of "How Great Thou Art" on the 1964 Camden imprint album *Songs of Faith*. The Statemen's rendition was even deeper and more pious, smoothly driving toward an intense, bright gospel ending.

Elvis recorded "How Great Thou Art" for the album of the same name. Just as his movie career was beginning to lose momentum, he was given a fresh opportunity to make another gospel LP on the back of steady sales of *His Hand in Mine*. There are two stories about how he came to record the title track. In the first, the Jordanaires suggested that they prompted him to think about the song in May 1966 when he was rehearsing material for the album. Gordon Stoker recalled Elvis saying he had not actually heard of the standard (which seems unlikely). According to Stoker, Ray Walker got out a hymn book and the Jordanaires sang it on the spot, with Neal Matthews then custom designing an arrangement.[480] Walker corroborated the story, saying that he suggested "How Great Thou Art" to Elvis after George Beverly Shea's renditions made it a favorite at Billy Graham missionary events.[481] Walker knew it could become a signature tune. The second version of events came from Charlie Hodge, who played Elvis a recording by the Sons of the Pioneers and noted that Presley was also familiar with the Statesmen's 1964 rendition.[482]

As Dave Marsh noted, the "How Great Thou Art" album was the first time that Elvis recorded with producer Felton Jarvis and his first non-soundtrack recording for more than two years.[483] This time Elvis enlisted one of his heroes. Jake Hess had been in the Statesmen from 1948, and in 1954, Elvis classed the quartet as one of his favorite acts.

Hess recorded for Benson Records from 1964 onward. He founded a new vocal group called the Imperials that toured and released a couple of albums per year. In the 1960s, West Coast contemporary Christian music took over from gospel. The Imperials accompanied a charismatic county crooner and television presenter named Jimmy Dean and had some independent success.[484] Elvis was thrilled to secure the services of Hess and his group at his May 1966 recording session for "How Great Thou Art."[485]

Released in February 1967, "How Great Thou Art" became the center-piece of Elvis's second gospel album. The song's vocal harmony obsessed him. He practiced intensely for the session, singing each different part himself to fully understand the song. He wanted a choir to record it but opted for doubling vocals from the Jordanaires, the Imperials, and two female singers. "How Great Thou Art" was finished in just four takes. According to Ernst Jørgensen, "In an extraordinary fulfilment of his vocal ambitions, he had become a kind of one-man quartet, making the song both a personal challenge and a tribute to the singing style he'd always loved."[486]

Elvis was the consummate vocal stylist. For this record, it is what he chose *not* to do that is interesting. The male singer with perhaps the most emotionally expressive voice of the twentieth century decided to perform Boberg and Hine's famous hymn *absolutely straight*, with hardly any of the usual intriguing inflections coloring his delivery. The focus is not on him anymore. His choice indicates that even an icon must step aside. Certainly, Elvis occasionally expresses slight awe and amazement, but he generally puts duty over show business, delivering a confident rendition that speaks on behalf of the whole community and points squarely to the Almighty. No wonder, then, that he won two of his three Grammy Awards for different versions of this inspiring and colossal sacred song.[487]

8. "Polk Salad Annie" (from *On Stage*, 1970)

One of the interesting things about Elvis's career was the way that sometimes he came around to doing the opposite of what he had done before. His rock 'n' roll was often contrasted to the sedateness of Patti Page's 1950 hit "Tennessee Waltz," but in 1966 Elvis did his own home taping of the song. Equally, he had been ribbed on *The Milton Berle Show*—where the host played his hick twin brother, Melvin ("Television—what the heck is that?")—and later he participated in mediocre Southsploitation features like *Follow That Dream* and *Kissin' Cousins*. In 1970, however, Elvis presented his own update of the genre by covering Tony Joe White's "Polk Salad Annie." Of course, America had changed out of all recognition by then. It was no longer quite so acceptable to dismiss the

South as backward. For younger people, the place was cool. By curating a quirky tale of Southern life, Elvis was able to delight his Vegas audiences with one of the ultimate cabaret tunes of the era. What was unusual about it was that he stuck quite close to the original version, rather than, as was customary practice, opting to reshape it.

Southerners used to pick poke weed and make "polk sallet" from its asparagus-like shoots. "Polk Salad Annie" was therefore based on a fictionalized reality. Poke weed had to be gathered by hand. It was one of the earliest of the annual crop of spring greens. From the middle of the twentieth century right through to its end, the Allen Canning Company of Siloam Springs in Arkansas paid pickers to gather a mess of it ready for preservation in tins. The main market for canned polk sallet consisted of those who fled the South during the Dust Bowl era and settled in other parts of the country. It is easy to see why Tony Joe White's number became a crowd-pleasing staple of Elvis's 1970s set. The song kept everything light and funny. It offered an unsurpassed blending of funk and gospel within a highly contemporary rock format. Hardly surprising, then, that funk soul brother Clarence Reid covered it in 1969. Tom Jones released his own take in 1970. The writer of "Polk Salad Annie" also performed a duet on television with Johnny Cash. None of those quite touched Elvis's effort for sheer Vegas glamour.

During his intro to "Polk Salad Annie" from the rehearsal section of *That's the Way It Is*, Elvis launches into a series of comedy yaps but then returns to finish a sharp cut. Director Denis Sanders emphasizes the song's dynamism with split-screen (though he also pairs the soundtrack with irrelevant shots of hotel catering activities). After rushing through "All Shook Up" during the final show, Elvis unleashes the song, evidently aware of its devastating potential. In rising moments of electric anticipation, he playfully assumes the role of an army sergeant, counting out a comedy "hup two three four." As the number reaches its climax, Sanders's camera—after showing shots of the audience transfixed—rapidly pans in and out on Elvis, emphasizing his dynamic stage moves. The singer finally jumps up and cuts the song to its close. He is rewarded by thunderous applause.

"Polk Salad Annie" allowed Elvis to display a masterful control of his band. It's not surprising that the live incarnation usually featured a funky extended bass solo from Jerry Scheff. The Californian bassist began his working life with interests in jazz and classical music. He became a

favored session player whose career scaled new heights when he produced a studio hit in 1966 for the Association. He joined Elvis's Vegas
band when it formed in 1969, taking a break from February 1973 to April
1975. Even while working with Elvis, Scheff did other things, including
bass parts for the Doors' 1971 album, *LA Woman*. He and percussionist
Ronnie Tutt also toured with Delaney & Bonnie and Friends. The Bram-
letts' band was a unique Southern blues rock ensemble. It functioned as a
training ground for many notable musicians. Even though the Vegas
shows only contained twelve to fifteen songs, Elvis probably rehearsed
more than one hundred with the band. He wanted to make sure they were
flexible enough to cope with anything that would be thrown at them.
Scheff was challenged by the demand for spontaneity. He recalled:

> The music was so intense. It was a kind of punk lounge music. I was
> playing very busy parts and to this day, I can't listen to any of the
> albums we did, because everything is so intense feeling. . . . I went
> right on stage with no rehearsals. During that first part, '69 to '73, we
> would play and it was just WHAAMM!!![488]

When Scheff rejoined Elvis in 1975, the music was slightly mellower,
and he was better prepared for it. Nevertheless, his description reveals the
way that the band was kept on its toes. Playing had to be a reflex response. Elvis was attuned the audience, and the band was attuned to
Elvis. Energetically, "Polk Salad Annie" *was* "punk lounge music": a
sister tune, in many ways, to "Suspicious Minds." Both offered exciting
vamps and both culminated in an immense release of energy, signified by
squealing horns, as Elvis cut to his musical climax. Ultimately, "Polk
Salad Annie" was therefore a song that showcased how knowing and
feral Elvis could be. For that reason, it is almost impossible to tire of
hearing his take on Tony Joe White's number. Right from those anticipa-
tory hand claps, it welcomes listeners, building excitement and inviting
them "down South" in a way that is sexy and commanding at the same
time.

Punk lounge music, indeed.

7. "Jailhouse Rock" (from *Elvis' Golden Records*, 1958)

By the spring of 1957, Elvis had already scored a number one with Leiber
and Stoller's song "Hound Dog." The pair had written the title tune for

his previous film, *Loving You*. How would they depict life inside prison, with any seriousness, for his new movie? According to music historian Ace Collins, the songwriters faced a challenge: "It seemed as though the scene was supposed to combine the feel of a tough Bogie or Cagney movie with the excitement of a Broadway show—a strange marriage."[489] They almost had to choose mirth. As Elvis investigator Paul Simpson put it, the lyrics are "at best satirical and at worst subversive."[490] "Jailhouse Rock" remains a joke in Elvis's hands, but one that is also completely serious in its delivery. As with some other Leiber and Stoller classics— notably "Saved" and "Trouble"—it is sung with a directness and intensity that by far eclipses the songwriters' original meaning. The result is a symphony.

Pop songs are always collaborations. Everything about "Jailhouse Rock" is right. Taken together, at the beginning, Scotty Moore and DJ Fontana behave like they are in the midst of a high-noon shoot-out. Scotty's awesome two-note riff really starts things off, feeling like a sudden change of perspective set to music. Scotty and DJ's intro was worked up from a 1940s swing version of "The Anvil Chorus." Fontana's percussion was apparently inspired by workers breaking rocks on a chain gang.[491] One candidate for a musical precursor was the foxtrot version of Verdi's classic, released by Glenn Miller and his orchestra in 1941 on the Bluebird label as a 78rpm 10-inch. Miller's big band is super sharp and jazzy. The probable inspiration for Fontana's famous drumming can be heard early on part II from the B-side. When "Jailhouse Rock" begins, Elvis comes in over the top, all guns blazing. He is pulled up sharp at the end of the first verse when the accompaniment momentarily drops out. In the chorus, DJ shifts to a more rhythmic, pounding pattern. Bill Black adds his comforting, walking bass figure. Mike Stoller's piano offers new color, and Elvis—who seems powerful, smooth, and slightly desperate, all at once—gets right back in the saddle. The second and third verse choruses repeat the trick, before Scotty lands one of his most subtle and convincing solos. In a sense, after that, the song restarts, with Black's electric bass and Stoller's piano becoming more adventurous.[492] "Jailhouse Rock" ends with a smooth fade-out, as if the innate drama has never quite died, just fallen from view. Collins called it "a joyful challenge . . . the hardest-driving song they had ever attempted . . . [with] an almost heavy-metal feel."[493] He was not entirely wide of the mark: Ozzy Osbourne covered "Jailhouse Rock" on a six-week tour of UK prisons in

1987. Mötley Crüe tackled it at the Moscow Peace Festival two years later. The "angry tone" Collins detected was not expressed through the heavy style of Scotty's guitar—though it was assertive—so much as the bawling intensity of Elvis's voice, which approached something like Emmett Miller on speed.

In the movie incarnation, "Jailhouse Rock" gets a show business makeover. Scotty and DJ's introduction is replaced by a big-band horn section. Various whoops plus stabs of slide trombone and saxophone accompany the proceedings. Alex Romero's phenomenal choreography sets the whole thing off to create what remains Elvis's first truly iconic performance. In the 1950s, however, it was surprising how rarely Elvis performed the song in public. By the time RCA released the number, he was doing fewer stage shows. Before he was drafted, Elvis only found time for a handful of dates in Tupelo, the West Coast, and Hawaii. "Jailhouse Rock" was performed live only a handful of times back then. It was resurrected, of course, for the *Comeback Special*. For Greil Marcus, Elvis delivers peak performances in the *Comeback*: "less songs than events— where anything could happen, where everything did."[494] The revamped version of "Jailhouse Rock" is astounding. A comparison with Elvis's earlier studio take is instructive. According to music critic Dylan Jones, what makes the 1957 recording amazing is that in places Elvis "sounds like he's coming to burn your house down."[495] If that is the case, then the unfeasibly ferocious redux that the singer unleashes during the *Comeback* sounds like *his* house *has* burned down—with all his family in it—and he is hell bent on retribution. To borrow from the French novelist Gaston Leroux, "his voice thundered forth his revengeful soul at every note."[496]

Elvis returned to "Jailhouse Rock" for the first of his Las Vegas shows, as he knew that the crowd would love it. He came back to it quite frequently after that—notably around 1973, 1976, and 1977—often pairing "Jailhouse Rock" with other rock 'n' roll classics like "Don't Be Cruel." It had sunk, by then, into the category of crowd-pleasing music that reflected a past era.

If Elvis had done nothing in his career other than recording this one hit record, he would still be understood as a significant artist.

6. "Always on My Mind" (from *Walk a Mile in My Shoes: The Essential '70s Masters*, 1995)

"When I was a child, ladies and gentlemen," said Elvis, accepting his Jaycees award in 1971, "I was a dreamer. I read comic books and I was the hero of the comic book. I saw movies and I was the hero in the movie."[497] Part of *the tao of Elvis*, part of his superhuman power, was that he could find and express emotions that seemed, *at least seemed*, way deeper than any ordinary man.

For such a signature song, "Always on My Mind" was a relatively late addition to Elvis's stellar catalog. Its story starts with the writer, Wayne Carson. Using Chet Atkins as a go-between, Carson supplied the avuncular country singer Eddy Arnold with his gentle 1966 hit "Somebody Like Me." He also penned Memphis rock band the Box Tops' uniquely gruff 1967 British Invasion–era hit "The Letter." On the phone to his wife, Carson talked apologetically about his habit of disappearing off with work. In 1988 he recalled saying to her, "Well, I know I've been gone a lot, but I've been thinking about you all the time." He added, "And it just struck me like someone had hit me with a hammer. I told her real fast I had to hang up because I had to put that into a song."[498] Sitting at his kitchen table in Missouri, he managed two verses in ten minutes, then put away the composition for a year. At American Sound Studio in Memphis, Carson invited Johnny Christopher to help him finish the number. He also seconded Mark James, who was tired by that point by his day's work in the studio. James helped the song lift toward the chorus and extended it too. He suggested ways to keep the different verses in check. The three men spontaneously finished the piece from there.

One of the first artists to address "Always on My Mind" was the Florida-born Gwen McCrae. She married George McCrae within a week of meeting him back in 1963; they had sung duets together for the Alston label by the end of the decade. George became her manager when she went solo. The funk soul diva released "Always on My Mind" as the B-side to her 1972 Columbia single, "He's Not You." The country singer Brenda Lee released a version as the A-side of her single for Decca the same year. Where McCrae's version had been soulful and gently majestic, Lee's quietly burst with pain and regret.

Elvis recorded "Always on My Mind" late in March 1972. The general tone of the three-day session at Studio C in Hollywood, despite being punctuated by "Burning Love," was more than a little maudlin; other songs included Kris Kristofferson's "For the Good Times," Paul Williams's "Where Do I Go from Here," and James Last and Carl Sigman's "Fool." After Felton Jarvis contacted Mark James looking for material, his publisher Irwin Schuster of Screen Gems Music in New York sent over a demo version.[499] The recording was completed in seven takes, with the first used as the master in the end.

The day after recording "Always on My Mind," the musicians returned to the studio for a "mock" session to be filmed as a rehearsal for MGM's feature documentary *Elvis on Tour*. At that point the new movie had the working title of *Standing Room Only*. Revealing footage of Elvis recording the song was eventually included on Malcolm Leo and Andrew Solt's 1981 feature documentary, *This Is Elvis*. What is interesting, however, was that "Always on My Mind" went missing in action from Elvis's live repertoire. For some reason, despite becoming a signature song over the years, it was not, as far as can be ascertained, performed in concert. Mark James felt that the Presley studio rendition was "a little too fast for a ballad."[500] Nevertheless, "Always on My Mind" was chosen as the B-side of Red West's "Separate Ways," a song that more directly reflected what the public knew, if anything, about Elvis's separation. The new single was released in November 1972. It went top twenty on the *Billboard* country chart and sold more than a million in the United States. RCA's decision to reverse the record for Britain, and promote "Always on My Mind," proved even more successful: The new A-side became a top ten hit. "Always on My Mind" has been featured on more than fifteen different compilation albums including Sony's *Voices: The Official Album of the 2006 World Cup*. The song was successfully covered by Willie Nelson and reinvented by the Pet Shop Boys. Now people see it as a central part of the Elvis canon—something that got there through popular demand rather than saturation marketing.

What is great about Elvis's version of "Always on My Mind" is that he plays it so straight, addressing the song with delicious and manly restraint. Despite an innate capacity to feel the emotional conflict in any material, he sings Carson, Christopher, and James's ballad in a way that escapes the stylized excesses of melodrama. The performance is exponentially more potent for it.

5. "Bridge over Troubled Water" (from *That's the Way It Is*, 1970)

One of Elvis's superhero qualities was his ability to effortlessly express emotions like colors of the rainbow. His most articulate defenders attribute one virtue to him that is rarely seen in modern performers: grace. Redeeming love expressed through care is the highest quality in Elvis Presley's lexicon, and, on the surface, perhaps the most surprising. If there is a single song that epitomizes Elvis's grace, then it is "Bridge over Troubled Water." Like "How Great Thou Art," Elvis used it as a means to communicate the pain and faith that shaped his life and defined his art. The most obvious window on the song's profound meaning is that it is an expression of social conscience: support for the worried, friendship for the lonely, help for the homeless. At base, beyond all those possibilities, however, is the comforting certainty of a spiritual presence. "Bridge over Troubled Water" suggests that only God seems big enough to shoulder our earthly suffering.

Elvis recorded a studio version of "Bridge over Troubled Water" on a pleasantly warm Thursday evening, 5 June 1970. Across its whole duration, the highly productive five-night Nashville session also featured "I've Lost You," "Heart of Rome," "I Washed My Hands in Muddy Water," "Love Letters," and "Patch It Up." Part of the session's magic was supplied by David Briggs, a Muscle Shoals musician, who—at that point, still in his late twenties and eight years younger than Elvis—offered a beautiful piano accompaniment. Wafting across the airwaves like mist, Simon and Garfunkel's angelic original stayed at the top of the *Billboard* charts for six weeks when it was released five months earlier. In that sense, it seemed quite daring for Elvis to record his own version, but, as his 1950s track record showed, he was never fazed by covering contemporary hits. After the *Comeback* and watershed recording experience at American Sound, for a few years he revived the practice and found fodder for his performances on stage. One of Elvis's influences in this era was the rousing sound of mainstream commercial folk.

What Art Garfunkel and Elvis Presley had in common was their fascination with the sound of 1940s and 1950s black gospel. The Swan Silvertones set a high standard with their spectacular, before-soul, harmony singing. Though Garfunkel's debt to the group is somewhat muted in

"Bridge over Troubled Water," echoes of the spiritual tradition are there in the song's theme and piano refrain.

While Simon and Garfunkel's version is undeniably passionate and powerful, there is, in its immense ethereality, still something bloodless about it. Drawing on the range of musical backing at his disposal, Elvis's "Bridge over Troubled Water," by contrast, sails with a colossal feeling of spectacle. The song's arrangement owes something to BJ Thomas's version, which came out two months before Elvis's trip to the studio.[501] Perhaps concerned to repeat the success he had at American Sound, the singer listened carefully to Thomas's recorded output. Another song that he covered from Thomas's *Everybody's out of Town* album was "I Just Can't Help Believing."

Elvis's musical team contained unsung heroes. One who has received greater recognition only recently is arranger Bergen White. The softly spoken arranger's father was a Baptist preacher; he learned to sing and read music in the choir. After graduating college, White became a teacher. When his income from helping with sessions exceeded his teaching salary, he switched to a career in Nashville and met Bill Justice, who had a hit on Sun with "Raunchy." White backed Justice at Hit Records, a company that churned out soundalike copies of chart material but used talented musicians like Charlie McCoy in the process. White soon became a jack-of-all-trades. Among other duties, he occasionally helped out the Jordanaires and first worked for Elvis when he substituted for Neal Matthews. Toward the end of the 1960s, White cut a deal with Monument Records and released a string of numbers, including his own 1970 Beach Boys–style "It's Over Now."

As a Music Row regular, Bergen White became friends with David Briggs and Norbert Putnam. When news of his talent spread, he was approached by musicians who wanted to add strings and horns to their studio sessions or augment live performances. The new vanguard of country artists like Kris Kristofferson and Tony Joe White regularly called on the arranger's services.

White carefully shaped the best of Elvis's 1970s concert staples. Not only did he arrange the horns on "Polk Salad Annie," he was also the horn player on "I Washed My Hands in Muddy Water." His arrangement of "Walk a Mile in My Shoes" remains absolutely outstanding. White even persuaded RCA to give him a label credit for his arrangements of "You Don't Have to Say You Love Me" and two other Presley singles.

His new billing was great for his reputation. Unfortunately, it was all over once Colonel Parker found out. The Colonel called the record company and stopped it using the credit. Nevertheless, White continued working for Elvis. He even helped with "Moody Blue."

One of White's greatest achievements was arranging "Bridge over Troubled Water" so that it would start sparse and build toward an epic finale, featuring violins, horns, and full backing vocals. Starting out in low key with spare keyboard backing, BJ Thomas's version gradually built toward an epic finale that was a tour de force. White's arrangement for Elvis followed suit, with a sound that was both full and majestic.

For pop professor Richard Middleton, Elvis's style was constantly "teetering on the edge of melodrama."[502] What is interesting is to compare Paul Simon's comment: "It was a great feeling when he sang 'Bridge over Troubled Water,' although he somewhat overdramatized the song—but that's how it really was [for him]." In other words, it was not so much that Elvis chose to present overblown interpretations—out of a sense of drama for their own sake or some unfortunate lack of taste—but rather he felt life's emotions on a grand scale. It is not hard to see that the many years since Gladys Presley died in 1958 were an extended experiment in love for Elvis, one that in some senses ultimately failed.[503] Singing was *both* a window on the magnitude of life's joy and pain for him *and* a technical achievement. Because "Bridge over Troubled Water" became an Elvis Presley staple, it helped to chart landmarks in the last act of his career: his 1970s live sets. At a September 1973 midnight show in Vegas, immediately after he'd sung "Bridge over Troubled Water"—in a moment that was not so unusual—he said, "That wasn't as good as I can do it; I'd like to do it again from the second verse." Afterward he added, "When I do something, I like to do it and get the sound as best I can or not at all."[504] Such was his drive to give his all and please the audience. On *That's the Way It Is*, seated in his rehearsal session, Elvis can be seen early on, reshaping the verse piece by piece. For the stage show, he delivers a solid performance, in slightly rueful "Danny Boy" mode. After he surrenders to the moment, his backing singers come in to support him for an absolutely towering finale. He then rocks into a slinky "Heartbreak Hotel" cut in the documentary with footage of Vegas's neon nightlife. Although the cut offered on the *That's the Way It Is* album took Elvis's initial studio outing and included a dubbed audience response at the end, many other takes of "Bridge over Troubled Water" have been released.

The specialist label Follow That Dream (FTD) has included the song on around twenty recordings so far, often commemorating specific live shows.

At the press conference before his Madison Square Garden concerts in June 1972, Elvis explained his set list: "It's a conscious thing. . . . I like to do a song like 'Bridge over Troubled Water' or 'American Trilogy' or something, then mix it up and do some rock 'n' roll or some of the hard rock stuff."[505] True to his word, when he played at the Garden, right in between "Hound Dog" and "Suspicious Minds," he sang a version of "Bridge over Troubled Water" with deep, slightly countrified vocals. The crowd was with him from the start, and by the end, it was astounded. In the 1972 feature documentary *Elvis on Tour*, he offered a version that began a little jittery and mannered but forged its way to brilliance, ending with JD Sumner's characteristically slurred low notes. "Bridge over Troubled Water" was not performed during *Aloha from Hawaii* or the 1977 CBS special, but it was revisited in the middle of what was to become Elvis's last concert, held at the Market Square Arena in Indianapolis. After "I Can't Stop Loving You," he launched into the song's pared-down beginning, cheerily improvising, "When tears are in your eyes, I will give you a scarf." By the song's end, he was back to a place of solemnity, carrying the full force of the climax.

Anyone who believes that mash-ups only began in the age of digital sampling should hear the bizarre version of "Bridge over Troubled Water" that Elvis performed in September 1973—released by FTD on the *Closing Night* album—where he sang the song's lyrics over the music of "Suspicious Minds." Despite being a throwaway, the combination actually worked. One mash-up that worked even better, though, was RCA's comparatively recent fusion of Elvis singing the lyrics while accompanied by the Royal Philharmonic Orchestra. The result is interesting: The Philharmonic's backing is predictably competent, smooth, and serene. It duets, in effect, with Elvis's own crisp vocals. To add a little character, a touch of Nashville guitar is added to the mix.

If Simon and Garfunkel sat listeners on a cloud and helped them float up to the heavens, Elvis gave them a ringside seat in the midst of the holy host and let them experience profound, cosmic majesty.

4. "Heartbreak Hotel" (from *Elvis Presley*, 1956)

Although "That's All Right" is often credited as a groundbreaking slice of rock 'n' roll, "Heartbreak Hotel" is also a unique record. There was, and is, nothing else like it. Beyond the South, the song let everyone know who Elvis was, that he had arrived. It was not his first-ever recording or first single, not even his first single for RCA (that was a reissue of "Mystery Train") or the first song he sung on national television ("Shake, Rattle and Roll / Flip, Flop and Fly" on the Dorsey show). To most people, however, it might as well have been all those things. They had never heard anything like it before.

"Heartbreak Hotel" was recorded on 10 January 1956 and released as a single less than three weeks later, complete with a picture of Elvis looking sullen and pouty on the cover. Excitement proper began on 11 February when he performed the song on *Stage Show* after "Blue Suede Shoes." Buoyed up by a response from the crowd, scissoring his legs, Elvis started bringing out the song's rock 'n' roll credentials during its instrumental break. He worked it again on subsequent *Stage Shows* and on his first engagement with Milton Berle.

"Heartbreak Hotel" was a number that nodded to jazz and winked at the blues but seemed to reject any easy genre categorization. It became Elvis's first million-seller, simultaneously topping *Billboard*'s pop, jukebox, country, and R&B charts.

It is not possible anymore to understand the impact of "Heartbreak Hotel" in its day. The record caused an explosion 'round the world, inciting John Lennon and his British peers to sally forth as fellow rock 'n' rollers. What were people hearing? "Heartbreak Hotel" is not an easily covered, rollicking fireball of a number like "Rock around the Clock" or "Tutti Frutti"—though many have tried. Neither is it too close to country music, even though Willie Nelson and Leon Russell managed to rework it as a country ditty in 1979.

"Heartbreak Hotel" paints an impressionistic sound-picture. On the cover of its EP, Elvis wears a high-collared raincoat. Despite its theme of feeling lonesome, it is not a record sung by a country boy; its singer is just someone with immense feeling.

The story of "Heartbreak Hotel" really begins with the blues. It is a rain-soaked, distinctly *urban* record with an aesthetic style that comes from the street; from the dead of night; from a state of traumatized desperation . . . from the same world as film noir. Where did Elvis go, emotionally, to find that place inside himself? It is as if he is saying to his audience that they might—just by lending an ear—establish the intimacy that is necessary to rescue him from a place of sheer desperation, from a loveless place, a place where nobody cares.

Mae Boren Axton was an English teacher who had already written hits for Ernest Tubb and Perry Como. She worked part-time as a publicist for Hank Snow's All-Star Jamboree Attractions. Bob Neal persuaded her to put Elvis on at the Gator Bowl in Jacksonville, Florida. When she saw one of her female students screaming at the young singer, she asked about his appeal. Her pupil exclaimed, "Oh, Mrs. Axton, he's just a great big, beautiful hunk of forbidden fruit!"[506] Mae Axton's links with Snow meant that she was able to liaise with both Colonel Parker and RCA. She suggested that she could deliver Elvis's first million-selling single. Her songwriting partner, Tommy Durden, read a story on the front page of the *Miami Herald* that said, "Do You Know This Man?" It was about the corpse of a well-dressed, middle-aged suicide victim discovered in a Miami hotel. Police could not identify the body, but a suicide note was found. It read, "I walk a lonely street." Durden thought it sounded like a line straight from the Delta. Axton figured that at the end of a lonely street, one might find a heartbreak hotel. After that, the song was written within an hour. Glen Reeves cut the demo in Nashville and made sure he copied Elvis's Sun style. Reeves's version was both more bluesy and also more country, more stylized and hicuppy. Elvis adored the song when he heard the demo. Its start bore a striking resemblance to "Hard Luck Blues," a 1950 hit for Roy Brown and his Mighty-Mighty Men. Axton offered Elvis a songwriting credit on "Heartbreak Hotel" if he would release it as his first RCA single; she said that she wanted to help him find the money to take his parents on vacation to Florida.

Elvis recorded "Heartbreak Hotel" on a Tuesday afternoon, just after capturing Ray Charles's "I Got a Woman" at RCA Studios in Nashville. It was his first session with RCA. Everyone was looking for a hit. Bill Black's sassy, walking bass line; Floyd Cramer's sublime piano fills; and Scotty Moore's slinky guitar licks all perfectly complemented the song's intoxicating premise. Elvis's vocal was recorded in a stairwell to give it that haunting reverb. The recording was an instant classic, way more than the sum of its parts.

It is a credit to the original that even the raw, yet goofy, version of "Heartburn Motel" Elvis offered when he taped the *Comeback Special* was not halfway as good. It was as if he forgot the devastating subtlety that made the song explode across the planet a few years earlier. He also forgot the lyrics.

Sam Phillips might have rejected "Heartbreak Hotel" as "a morbid mess," yet it's easy to see why it deserves a high place in any list of Elvis records.[507] The singer effortlessly pulled together a unique brew of suicidal melancholy and steamy sensuality; a combination, on the face of it, that is just so impossible to fathom.

Still a miracle in sound.

3. "Suspicious Minds" (from *Elvis' Gold Records Volume 5*, 1984)

When Elvis's microphone gave him trouble at a Vegas dinner show near the end of August 1973, he jokingly replaced the lyrics: "Let's not let a good sound die, we had it for three and a half weeks."[508] In "Suspicious Minds," Elvis could, without skipping a beat, gleefully present an existential meltdown *as the consummate show tune.* That, surely, was its magic—and precisely why the song deserves its place in any countdown of his best material.

For Elvis, the 1960s were generally lean years in terms of success on the singles chart. While his album showing was stronger, fourteen of the seventeen number one singles he had between 1956 and 1970 happened before 1961. "Suspicious Minds" struck a chord and was his first number one single since 1962's "Good Luck Charm." It was also the last pre-1977 number one of Elvis Presley's career on the *Billboard* Hot 100.

Toward the end of the first set of American Sound sessions in 1969, Elvis's friend Marty Lacker summoned up the courage to tell him that the best songwriters were no longer going to give up half of their publishing to Hill & Range as other famous acts could record their songs. He brought it home by saying, "They don't need you anymore."[509] Struggling to find decent material, Elvis was looking for something different. Songwriter Mark James had a group at the end of the 1950s named the Naturals. In Texas, the group had a hit called "Jive Note." Later, James was recruited as a house writer for American Sound, the creative force behind BJ Thomas's "Hooked on a Feeling" and other chart releases. When Chips Moman's business partner Don Crews asked James for some

Elvis material, he suggested a song that he had recorded a year earlier for Scepter called "Suspicious Minds." Moman had actually produced James's version. With the dramatic rhetorical questioning in one lyric line, the song was reminiscent, in part, of Brenda Lee's 1961 number "Emotions." Although the Scepter version of "Suspicious Minds" was a commercial failure, James decided Elvis might be able to succeed with it. He was right.

At first, Elvis was lukewarm. Joe Esposito helped him commit to the recording.[510] James felt a bit of an obstacle to Elvis's performance, so he did not come along when the singer covered his song in the studio. Elvis treated the Scepter version as a template, using the same musicians and arrangement. Such was the camaraderie at the studio that session player Bobby Wood gently showed Elvis where his vocal should begin on the track.[511] The song was recorded in eight takes made across three hours, with the singer stretching it out by repeating the final lyric lines over and over.

So what exactly did Elvis bring to "Suspicious Minds"? Mark James's version, which is introduced by a low-key organ vamp, offers vocals that are more plaintive and closer to the country tradition. It sounds comparatively jaded and sedate, despite the similarities. Elvis's version begins with a crisper sound: carefully picked guitar, stronger male lead and female backing vocals, and more percussion. When the breakdown happens partway into the track, it's so much more precipitous and dramatic, momentarily taking the song back to an almost 1950s weepy ballad style. The result is a heady cocktail of gusto and wistfulness. It spirals into a stomping finale that is absolutely exhilarating. The accompaniment alone could hold its ground as an instrumental, but what sends the song into orbit is Elvis's voice: there at the eye of the hurricane, in a way that is assertively masculine yet audibly sorrowful and cracking with raw emotion.

"Suspicious Minds" confronts listeners with the horror of an exasperated partner attempting to salvage his relationship in the face of its imminent collapse. He is utterly distrusted, but is he really to blame? Are his lover's innate insecurities sabotaging their happiness? While it might be easy to read James's number as an elegy to Elvis's collapsing marriage, that interpretation would ignore chronology and misread history. The song has its antecedents, as much as anywhere, in his previous *musical* work: numbers like "Suspicion" and the philandering role he played in the overstylized (and underrated) steamboat picture *Frankie and Johnny*. Nevertheless, according to *Telegraph* journalist Andrew Perry, "Suspicious Minds" was a song "whose lyrics of mistrust put a new Elvis on the world stage—one of vulnerability and depth. Indeed, this was a new kind of rock—adult-oriented, not kid's stuff."[512] Ironically, however, for various reasons, after the 1969 sessions, Elvis never worked at American Sound again.[513] He did, at least, hire back some members of the house band to help him find his groove when he later recorded at Stax. Nevertheless, fans can only speculate on the opportunities missed.

"Suspicious Minds" is often considered as Elvis's finest record. It's easy to hear why: It is the ultimate showstopper in an already devastating live arsenal. A few months after recording the song for Chips Moman, Elvis returned to concert performance with his first summer season in Las Vegas and unleashed his new weapon, even before it became a single. He fully exploited the tune on stage for its drama and spectacle, stretching the ending out further and further.

In the live show on *That's the Way It Is*, after a chaotic interlude wandering through the audience, Elvis gets back to sing "Suspicious Minds." When the time comes, he drops into a crouching position and inaugurates the dramatic break. As the song reaches its first astounding peak, Elvis shakes himself out, then drops down again, shifting his weight majestically from side to side like a praying mantis, limbering up before pursuing an even greater climax.

After Elvis Presley perfected a dramatic fade-out-then-in rendition of the song in Las Vegas, his regular RCA producer Felton Jarvis liked the live version so much that he added a famous "bump and fade" ending to mono and stereo mixes of the single, extending the record to beyond four minutes. When Elvis first heard the single version on his car radio, he snapped, "I know how this thing is supposed to sound, and this ain't it!"[514] Moman did not appreciate the new ending either. It foxed some radio DJs who were wrong-footed by the mix. Elvis's fans, however, loved "Suspicious Minds." Perhaps more than any other song, it became their anthem. Elvis also learned a lesson about sourcing his repertoire; at his June 1972 Madison Square Garden press conference, he said, "Anybody that writes a song, if they can get it to me, if it's good, I'll do it."[515]

2. "An American Trilogy" (from *As Recorded at Madison Square Garden*, 1972)

When Elvis first performed "An American Trilogy" in January 1972, he had already begun to disappear into his own legend. The Country Music Hall of Fame was founded in 1961. Elvis and the Colonel pledged $1,000 in 1963 to help fund a building for it. The exhibit opened four years later.[516] Elvis's birthplace in Tupelo had already been turned into a public museum. Memphis City Council renamed Highway 51 South, so that Elvis lived on Elvis Presley Boulevard. He was an icon and he knew it. His country, meanwhile, was in a state of disarray. Meredith Hunter's savage death at Altamont and the shooting of four students by the National Guard in Ohio ended the idealism of the counterculture era. The hope of the late 1960s was beginning to crumble. President Nixon entered office, saying, "The greatest honor history can bestow is the title of peacemaker."[517] His country remained in the midst of a messy and protracted war with Vietnam. It would not be long until Nixon's career came unraveled. Elvis, meanwhile, had become fixated by his mission to acquire a badge from the Bureau of Narcotics and Dangerous Drugs. In a handwritten letter to the director, he explained, "This country has been great to me and if I can ever help it out in some way I will wholeheartedly."[518] Before he met Nixon in the White House, he again pledged his support. On the flight to Washington, D.C., in a note addressed to the president, he said:

> The drug culture, the hippie elements, the SDS [Students for Democratic Society], Black Panthers, etc. do not consider me as their enemy or as they call it the Establishment. I call it America and I love it. Sir I can and will be of any service that I can to help the country out.[519]

Elvis's real mission to "help the country out" came to fruition in his music. "An American Trilogy" deserves a very high place in Elvis's top 100, not because it was a huge chart hit or even because it expressed his patriotism ("America the Beautiful" did that too), but rather the song conveys, in no uncertain terms, what it means to try and be a hero at a time when the word might seem hollow.

"An American Trilogy" is unique. Many great songs offer a perspective on what matters, emotionally, to a particular person. Very few depict the shared struggle of a nation so movingly. When Mickey Newbury first created the song in 1970, he combined "Dixie," "Battle Hymn of the Republic," and "All My Trials" into one number.[520] Elvis investigator Adam Victor neatly summarized the tune's etymology.[521] "Dixie," the unofficial Confederate anthem, was written by Daniel Miller in 1859. "Battle Hymn of the Republic" was a reworking of the folk classic "John Brown's Body" with new lyrics. It played at Robert F. Kennedy's funeral in 1968. "All My Trials," meanwhile, was a folk standard resurrected by 1960s protest singers. In their collective scope, the three songs expressed the complexity of America as a political project. The country was based on principles that were admirable. It was a democracy that idealized itself as a melting pot: abundant, inclusive, and open, theoretically, for all to join. Yet its reality was deeply flawed: built on appropriated land, slave labor, unjust market competition, and political corruption. As Newbury himself observed, "I'm talking as three different people but all are saying the same thing."[522] The owner of the Bitter End West club in Los Angeles told him not to perform the song there in November 1970, as there had just been a riot in Alabama when "Dixie" was played. Many decades later, it is hard to really understand how reactionary and inflammatory "Dixie" had been at the time, how many awkward phantoms it evoked.

Priscilla Presley heard Newbury's amalgam on the radio. She suggested to Elvis that it should be part of his set. Felton Jarvis had been Newbury's producer and got a copy to Elvis. After it became part of his repertoire in January 1972, he stuck with the song for three years straight, varying it only slightly, usually placing it late in the show to reflect its stature. Once the song concluded, Elvis would often introduce the flute player who took his solo in the piece.[523] Although the fans constantly celebrate their hero's monumental commercial success, what is perhaps more interesting is the way that Elvis adopted particular songs even when they were *not* proven hits because they resonated with his image and story. RCA reluctantly released "An American Trilogy" as a single in April 1972 and it utterly bombed, failing to make the top fifty, yet it is widely recognized as one of Elvis's most towering anthems. Few other songs, even in his catalog, are as epic, as poignant, as effortlessly complex, and as wide-reaching in their scope.

"An American Trilogy" is folk, Southern blues, gospel, and downhome country, but it is also Elvis showing cultural genius rarely paralleled except, perhaps, in figures such as William Shakespeare. His embrace of a popular form is not some kind of revenge of low culture.

Instead it includes everyone in the best of what humanity can say and do. "An American Trilogy" is not simply a melancholic song of the South or of the United States in general. It is a testament, not just to the superhuman talent of Elvis Presley, but to his innate understanding of compromised humanity. Like the best of Russian ballet, "An American Trilogy" directly conveys something about the human soul. The emotional tones expressed are, by turn, gently rousing, wistful, righteous, profound, heartbreakingly painful (in the sense of being beleaguered by responsibility), solemn, quietly regretful, and utterly overpowering. Its ending is shining and awesome, offering a musical vision on a truly immense scale.

"An American Trilogy" is not just about being American—and believing in the nation, for right or wrong—but about being human.[524] Part of the song's glory is that by seeming to lead the listener through the story of a nation, it actually presents the path of each human across his or her life: through the innocence, the strife, and, ultimately, through the majesty. The song allows its singer to get swept away in sound, surrendering to something completely different from the frenzied urgency of rock 'n' roll.

"An American Trilogy" marks Elvis's ascendance, not just into his own legend; its scope is larger still. Newbury's unique amalgam allowed him to portray the glory and pain of a nation in a way that was expressed for all to feel.

1. "If I Can Dream" (from *The Complete '68 Comeback Special*, 2008)

"If I Can Dream" is not Elvis's most popular or highest-selling record, but it deserves the top spot in any Elvis 100 quite simply because it is the song in which all the strands of his mission, all the reasons why he matters, come together in one monumental moment. Its full backstory does not begin with the *Comeback Special* producer Steve Binder, with Elvis bucking the Colonel's request for a conservative Christmas number, or even with Earl Brown's songwriting. It begins in 1964, when the African American sharecropper Fannie Lou Hamer testified to the Credentials Committee after being arrested for trying to register to vote in Mississippi. She explained that her guards said, "We are going to make you wish you were dead."[525] They made sure she was beaten and humiliated. Fannie Lou continued:

All of this on account of us wanting to register, to become first class citizens, and . . . I question America. Is this America, the land of the free and home of the brave, where we have to sleep with our telephones off of the hooks because our lives be threatened daily, because we want to live as decent human beings, in America?[526]

Hamer's heartbreaking speech is relevant because it directly asks America if it can any longer accept falling short of its humanitarian ideals. Whether Elvis saw her televised testimony or not, there are strong signs he cared. According to Jerry Scheff, "In some ways Elvis was more conservative, and in other ways he was very liberal. He wasn't someone that was following some political line, you know. He'd figure out for himself what he thought was right."[527]

A firm starting point for "If I Can Dream" is the fact that the highest aspects of Elvis's art began from his sense of human compassion. In private, he donated money to Martin Luther King Jr.[528] When King was assassinated in Memphis, a wave of shock and grief exploded across America. Elvis watched the funeral on television in April 1968 from his trailer on the set of *Live a Little, Love a Little*. His costar Celeste Yarnall recalled that he broke down in tears and cried on her shoulder. He sang "Amazing Grace," saying that he was shocked that King's shooting had happened in Memphis and that he wished he could have attended the funeral. The singer was heartbroken. "If I Can Dream" gave him a chance to do something about it.

After all the controversy over rock 'n' roll, Elvis spent a decade holding together the heart of the American mainstream. Somehow, the social changes he helped set in motion allowed him to retain his smoldering style *and* succeed as a family entertainer. At the time, the problem was that American culture and society was becoming increasingly divided, with generations and—to an extent—races in conflict. Having worked so hard to unite his audience, Elvis was understandably reluctant to take sides. Although Martin Luther King Jr. had initially disliked the vulgarity of rock 'n' roll, the preacher's colorblind wisdom struck a chord. He spoke from a place of reason that was somehow beyond racism. King had been a hero. Now he was gone. Although Elvis was saddened in private, there seemed nowhere apparent to register his concern within the remit of his *public* image. A sign was, however, needed. To secure mainstream acceptability, the civil rights movement needed endorsement from white leaders. With "If I Can Dream," Elvis Presley opened a door to social change through his music.

Things were already moving. Since rock 'n' roll started breaking down barriers, soul, Motown, Dylan, and the British Invasion had further awakened white interest in musical styles derived from the blues tradition. Three years before the *Comeback*, the Rolling Stones introduced Howlin' Wolf to the nation on *Shindig*. Such moments were about championing black performers as underdogs, about acting out equality in living form. Change had, so far, however, been confined to a new generation of progressive young whites. More than a decade after his rock 'n' roll heyday, Elvis represented something much bigger: Hollywood, family entertainment, social conformity. The challenge was to bring a push for equality to the mainstream, making it socially acceptable at the heart of conservative American culture. He could not have done it alone. After all, Elvis was not a songwriter.

Earl Brown's inspirational number was custom-written with Elvis Presley in mind. Born in Utah on Christmas Day 1928, the songwriter was nearly eight years older than Elvis. His father, Walter, led a successful swing band. As a child, Brown moved between American cities as they toured. He was a jack-of-all-trades, a mostly behind-the-scenes figure who specialized in providing music for family entertainment, as both a vocal arranger and writer of custom material. Brown carved out his career as a choral director on NBC's long-running late 1950s series *The Dinah Shore Chevy Show*.[529] He also sang on the series as part of the Skylarks, a mixed-sex, white vocal quintet. The Skylarks were refined and professional: a perfect ensemble that could provide slick, snappy, show business renditions of virtually any song they chose. They were a world away from the Southern sounds that Elvis was bringing to the mainstream. Almost a decade had passed since Brown's Dinah Shore days. He was as aware as anyone of the social ferment reflected in the horrific assassinations of Martin Luther King Jr. and Bobby Kennedy.[530] For the NBC show, Earl Brown was asked to supply special lyrics and vocal arrangements. The idea of doing a medley of spirituals was already one of his contributions. If NBC had any more doubts about Brown's role as choral director, he now had a chance to prove himself.

Steve Binder told Brown that since he had lived with Elvis for six weeks, he should be able to come up with something that expressed the singer's core beliefs. The director later explained, "I wanted to let the world know that here was a guy who was not prejudiced, who was raised in the heart of prejudice, but was really above all that."[531] He instructed Brown to come up with the greatest song of his life, a song with which Elvis could end the show. Earl Brown, however, told a slightly different story. Colonel Parker wanted to make sure that Elvis owned the publishing on any song. Brown had heard that Billy Strange or Mac Davis would create something and he would be asked to add the melody. Nothing happened. In the meantime, he took it upon himself to create something, a song that merged the style of "You'll Never Walk Alone" with the hopeful message of Sam Cooke's "A Change Is Gonna Come." If Elvis rejected it, Brown thought he could shop it to Aretha Franklin.

According to Binder, the *Comeback*'s original blueprint contained more than twenty Christmas songs, and only such songs.[532] The sponsor, Singer sewing machines, wanted a clean-cut, family-friendly Elvis Presley.[533] The Colonel had already forbidden "his boy" to finish the show by giving a closing speech that featured any personal beliefs. At most, Elvis would say, "Merry Christmas and good night."[534] Parker could not afford to lose face in front of his client. Relenting on the demand for a Christmas finish was out of the question.

The next morning at the television studio, Brown sang his composition to both Steve Binder and Bob Finkle with accompaniment from Billy Goldenberg on the piano. The songwriter heard Colonel Parker say from another room that it wasn't Elvis's kind of material. Recollections differ about what happened that day. Brown said that he was surprised to find Elvis standing in the doorway behind him, saying, "I'd like to try it, man."[535] In contrast, Binder claimed several run-throughs were performed in Elvis's dressing room, with Bones Howe present.[536] Howe had been a sound engineer on some of Elvis's early 1960s music. He was also Binder's business partner. Colonel Parker had already given Howe short shrift after he requested residual royalties. Goldenberg played the song to Howe, who called it a hit. Aware that the Memphis singer might not want to do anything resembling a straight Broadway ballad, Howe said, "You can do it with a real bluesy feel."[537] After several renditions, Elvis confidently announced, "We're doing it."[538] Whichever version of the story is correct, as soon as Elvis accepted "If I Can Dream," Billy Goldenberg erased his name from the lead sheet.[539] It was really *Brown's* understanding of what Elvis stood for, his own creativity and his interpretation.

On Brown's lyric sheet, in hope of a hit, Elvis wrote, "My boy, my boy—this could be the one!"[540] When he recorded a studio take of "If I Can Dream" at Western Recorders, he did it with a hand microphone in front of the whole orchestra. His intensity of commitment to the song was phenomenal. The three Blossoms were so moved by his performance that they cried. After the session, Goldenberg recalled, "He was on such a high; he was so involved and excited and emotionally charged—I don't remember anything in my life like that, frankly."[541]

Elvis invited Brown for a personal audience in his dressing room. He requested seven more songs, but unfortunately the writer became too busy with his television work to fulfill the request.

Popular music is an art of the moment, something that gives joy in its unfolding rather than at its end. Every replay of "If I Can Dream" brings its own pleasure, as Elvis gets swept up into the majesty of a number that lets him express the worth of his own legend. It proves that rock 'n' roll was only the beginning. There is nothing wrong with the playful, young singer of "Good Rockin' Tonight" or "Don't Be Cruel," but the person who performs "If I Can Dream" is light-years ahead: someone who has grasped his opportunity to achieve the impossible through the everyday miracle of song. The whole event drew Elvis into a world of seriousness that showed his talent was way beyond a matter of goofing around. As well as singing about his society, he was, in his urgent plea for change, discovering something immense inside himself. No wonder that Elvis found a new feeling of assertiveness and social conscience after performing the number. That he lost his way afterward does not diminish his achievement. It was the moment when he brought all his years of experience to bear. Elvis made Brown's song *his* anthem; the sheer power of his conviction and emotional force remains nothing short of astounding.

"If I Can Dream" allowed Elvis to express anguish and disappointment, to plead for Americans to put aside anger and segregation. The connection to race was no secret. As *Newsweek* said in 1969, the song "proclaims brotherhood according to the gospel of Martin Luther King."[542] Elvis was not just *entertaining*: Brown's anthem spoke of the values that made the singer and his country great. Presley's interpretation of Earl Brown's number put politics back into gospel and the hope back into the blues. It cut through the fog of the era and still acts as an inspiration. His performance squarely answered Fannie Lou Hamer by saying that, four years on, her country had not got there yet, but—even at the height of struggle—the dream was still possible. Everyone could still come together.

Here, more than anywhere, Elvis was a *soul* singer.

...AND 100 MORE

101. "I Just Can't Help Believin'" (*That's the Way It Is*, 1970).

102. "Milkcow Blues Boogie" (*For LP Fans Only*, 1959).

103. "I've Got a Thing about You Baby" (*Good Times*, 1974).

104. "Fairytale" (*Today*, 1975).

105. "Any Day Now" (*From Elvis in Memphis*, 1969).

106. "Just Because" (*Elvis Presley*, 1956).

107. "Love Me" (*Elvis' Golden Records*, 1958).

108. "You Asked Me To" (*Promised Land*, 1975).

109. "Proud Mary" (*On Stage*, 1970).

110. "I Don't Care If the Sun Don't Shine" (*The Sun Sessions*, 1976).

111. "Something" (*Aloha from Hawaii via Satellite*, 1973).

112. "Crying in the Chapel" (*How Great Thou Art*, 1960).

113. "Ready Teddy" (*Elvis*, 1956).

114. "I'm Leavin'" (*Elvis Aron Presley*, 1980).

115. "Separate Ways" (*Walk a Mile in My Shoes: The Essential '70s Masters*, 1995).

116. "Kiss Me Quick" (*Pot Luck*, 1962).

117. "A Hundred Years from Now" (*Walk a Mile in My Shoes*, 1995).

118. "It Ain't No Big Thing (But It's Growing)" (*Love Letters from Elvis*, 1971).

119. "Until It's Time for You to Go" (*Elvis Now*, 1972).

120. "Welcome to My World" (*Aloha from Hawaii via Satellite*, 1973).

121. "For the Heart" (*From Elvis Presley Boulevard, Memphis, Tennessee*, 1976).

122. "(There'll Be) Peace in the Valley (For Me)" (*Elvis' Christmas Album*, 1970).

123. "Just Pretend" (*That's the Way It Is*, 1970).

124. "Solitaire" (*From Elvis Presley Boulevard, Memphis, Tennessee*, 1976).

125. "It's Over" (*Aloha from Hawaii via Satellite*, 1973).

126. "(Let Me Be Your) Teddy Bear" (*Loving You*, 1957).

127. "Such a Night" (*Elvis Is Back!*, 1960).

128. "Stranger in My Own Home Town" (*From Memphis to Vegas/ From Vegas to Memphis*, 1969).

129. "I Forgot to Remember to Forget" (*A Date with Elvis*, 1959).

130. "Sweet Caroline" (*On Stage*, 1970).

131. "Softly As I Leave You" (*Elvis Aron Presley*, 1980).

132. "Patch It Up" (*The Other Sides—Elvis Worldwide Gold Award Hits Vol. 2*, 1971).

133. "It's Easy for You" (*Moody Blue*, 1977).

134. "I've Lost You" (*That's the Way It Is*, 1970).

135. "He Touched Me" (*He Touched Me*, 1972).

136. "Funny How Time Slips Away" (*Elvis Country (I'm 10,000 Years Old)*, 1971).

137. "Surrender" (*Elvis' Golden Records Volume 3*, 1963).

138. "Rock-A-Hula Baby" (*Blue Hawaii*, 1961).

139. "Make the World Go Away" (*Elvis Country (I'm 10,000 Years Old)*, 1971).

140. "My Boy" (*Good Times*, 1974).

141. "Blowin' in the Wind" (*Platinum: A Life in Music*, 1997).

142. "Tomorrow Night" (*Elvis for Everyone!*, 1965).

143. "I Really Don't Want to Know" (*Elvis Country (I'm 10,000 Years Old)*, 1971).

144. "GI Blues" (*GI Blues*, 1960).

145. "Release Me" (*On Stage*, 1970).

146. "Kentucky Rain" (*Worldwide 50 Gold Award Hits Volume 1*, 1970).

147. "I Gotta Know" (*Elvis' Golden Records Volume 3*, 1963).

148. "Long Black Limousine" (*From Elvis in Memphis*, 1969).

149. "I'm So Lonesome I Could Cry" (*Aloha from Hawaii via Satellite*, 1973).

150. "The Next Step Is Love" (*That's the Way It Is*, 1970).

151. "U.S. Male" (*Almost in Love*, 1970).

152. "After Loving You" (from *From Elvis in Memphis*, 1969).

153. "Hard Headed Woman" (*King Creole*, 1958).

154. "Mean Woman Blues" (*Loving You*, 1957).

155. "Good Luck Charm" (*Elvis' Golden Records Volume 3*, 1963).

156. "Danny Boy" (*Elvis Presley Boulevard, Memphis, Tennessee*, 1965).

157. "Lady Madonna" (*Walk a Mile in My Shoes: The Essential '70s Masters*, 1995).

158. "You'll Think of Me" (*From Memphis to Vegas/From Vegas to Memphis*, 1969).

159. "Lonesome Cowboy" (*Loving You*, 1957).

160. "She Thinks I Still Care" (*Moody Blue*, 1977).

161. "Up Above My Head" (*The Complete '68 Comeback Special*, 2008).

162. "She's Not You" (*Elvis' Golden Records Volume 3*, 1963).

163. "Snowbird" (*Elvis Country (I'm 10,000 Years Old)*, 1971).

164. "The Impossible Dream" (*Elvis: As Recorded at Madison Square Garden*, 1972).

165. "It's Midnight" (*Promised Land*, 1975).

166. "Words" (*From Memphis to Vegas / From Vegas to Memphis*, 1969).

167. "Return to Sender" (*Girls! Girls! Girls!*, 1962).

168. "It's Your Baby (You Rock It)" (*Elvis Country (I'm 10,000 Years Old)*, 1971).

169. "If You Talk in Your Sleep" (*Promised Land*, 1975).

170. "Crawfish" (*King Creole*, 1958).

171. "Harbor Lights" (*Elvis: A Legendary Performer Volume 2*, 1976).

172. "What Now My Love" (*Aloha from Hawaii via Satellite*, 1973).

173. "Your Love's Been a Long Time Coming" (*Promised Land*, 1975).

174. "White Christmas" (*Elvis' Christmas Album*, 1970).

175. "Wooden Heart" (*GI Blues*, 1960).

176. "Heart of Rome" (*Love Letters from Elvis*, 1971).

177. "The Girl of My Best Friend" (*Elvis Is Back!*, 1960).

178. "Clean Up Your Own Back Yard" (*Almost in Love*, 1970).

179. "For the Good Times" (*As Recorded at Madison Square Garden*, 1972).

180. "One-Sided Love Affair" (*Elvis Presley*, 1956).

181. "Your Cheatin' Heart" (*Elvis for Everyone!*, 1965).

182. "What'd I Say" (*Elvis' Gold Records Volume 4*, 1968).

183. "True Love Travels on a Gravel Road" (*From Elvis in Memphis*, 1969).

184. "O Come All Ye Faithful" (*Elvis Sings the Wonderful World of Christmas*, 1971).

185. "There Goes My Everything" (*Elvis Country (I'm 10,000 Years Old)*, 1971).

186. "Paralyzed" (*Elvis*, 1956).

187. "You're a Heartbreaker" (*For LP Fans Only*, 1959).

188. "Love Letters" (*Elvis' Gold Records Volume 4*, 1968).

189. "Only the Strong Survive" (*Elvis in Memphis*, 1969).

190. "If You Don't Come Back" (*Raised on Rock*, 1973).

191. "Blue Eyes Crying in the Rain" (*From Elvis Presley Boulevard, Memphis, Tennessee*, 1976).

192. "My Happiness" (*Elvis: The Great Performances*, 1990).

193. "Old Shep" (*Elvis*, 1956).

194. "Ghost Riders in the Sky" (*The Way It Was*, 2008). [1]

195. "I Got a Feelin' in My Body" (*Good Times*, 1974).

196. "Tweedlee Dee" (*Elvis: The First Live Recordings*, 1984).

197. "America the Beautiful" (*Elvis Aron Presley*, 1980).

198. "There's a Honky Tonk Angel (Who'll Take Me Back In)" (*Promised Land*, 1975).

199. "Three Corn Patches" (*Raised on Rock*, 1973).

200. "You'll Never Walk Alone" (*You'll Never Walk Alone*, 1971).

NOTES

INTRODUCTION

1. RCA Records/Legacy Recording's 2010 CD box set *The Complete Elvis Presley Masters* contains 711 original master recordings, plus various outtakes and alternate versions.

THE COUNTDOWN

1. "Gates of Graceland, Ep. 1—Peter Guralnick—Elvis in Vegas," YouTube video, 15:27, posted September 2015, https://www.youtube.com/watch?v= j1tmtbE0oeg.

2. David Ritz, ed., *Elvis by the Presleys* (London: Century, 2005), 136.

3. See James Burton's biography: http://www.james-burton.net/biography/.

4. The song appears listed as part of Elvis's personal collection on the 1996 *Virtual Graceland* CD-ROM set.

5. Georges Bataille, *The Accursed Share* (New York: Zone Books, 1988), 380.

6. Andy Warhol, *The Andy Warhol Diaries* (New York: Warner Books, 1989), 65.

7. On the 1996 *Virtual Graceland* CD-ROM set, Dion's LP is listed as part of Elvis's personal collection. Of course, however, the inclusion of a record in Elvis's collection *proves* relatively little beyond the fact that at some point he had probably heard the song in question. It is, nevertheless, worth noting when certain records were in his possession.

8. The next number Elvis recorded at the session was a country version of Lightfoot's "(That's What You Get) For Lovin' Me."

9. For a complete contrast to Peter, Paul and Mary's cover of "Early Mornin' Rain," readers should listen to the Grateful Dead's swinging version from the same year. Although its howling vocals hardly stand up, the breezy instrumentation presents San Francisco incarnate.

10. Paul Simpson, "Trains, Jet Plains and Morning Rain," *Elvis Information Network*, 2014, http://www.elvisinfonet.com/spotlight_elvis-if-youre-going-to-start-a-rumble.html.

11. As a show ballad, "Sylvia" is notable for seducing Brazilian fans when it was released as a single in their country.

12. Pino Donaggio was taught to play classical violin. In his twenties, he found commercial success as a balladeer. After that, he made a return of sorts to his classical roots, working as a film-score composer for directors such as Brian De Palma.

13. Vicki Wickham had previously worked behind the scenes producing the BBC pop series *Ready Steady Go!* Simon Napier-Bell went on to manage the pop group Wham!

14. Simon Napier-Bell, "Flashback: Dusty Springfield," *The Guardian*, 19 October 2003, http://observer.theguardian.com/omm/story/0,,1062873,00.html.

15. Napier-Bell, "Flashback: Dusty Springfield."

16. Elvis loved Prysock's stately voice and—according to the 1996 *Virtual Graceland* CD-ROM set—had the singer's 1957 Peacock Records single "Too Long I've Waited" (backed with "Bye Bye Baby") in his personal collection.

17. Trevor Cajiao, *Talking Elvis* (Gateshead, U.K.: Now Dig This, 1997), 213.

18. Cajiao, *Talking Elvis*, 210.

19. The database on Francesc Lopez's *Elvis Presley in Concert* website (http://www.elvisconcerts.com) suggests the song was performed during Elvis's shows at the Hilton on 25 and 29 March 1975, and even then in excerpted, throwaway form.

20. For a variety of reasons, every vast song catalog—even that of a musical genius—has a few lowlights. "Dominic" was a rustic ditty written by Sid Wayne and Ben Weisman that Elvis reluctantly sang to an impotent bull during the 1968 film *Stay Away, Joe.*

21. Often slightly misquoted, this line came from a 6 December 1980 interview that Andy Peebles did with Lennon and Yoko Ono for BBC Radio 1, two days before the ex-Beatle's untimely death. In context, it was about the press framing Lennon as having gone "underground" because he did not speak to them in the late 1970s: "When Elvis died, people were harassing me in Tokyo for a comment. Well, I'll give it you now: he died when he went in the army. You

know—that's when they killed him. That's when they castrated him, so the rest of it was just a living death."

22. Roy Orbison admired Gibson's style so much that he did a tribute album ten years later.

23. Tom Jones released a live album and single version of the song, too, soon after Elvis first recorded it.

24. Ernst Jørgensen, *Elvis Presley: A Life in Music. The Complete Recording Sessions* (New York: St. Martin's Press, 1998), 284.

25. Stamps-Baxter Music was founded on the partnership of the composer "Paps" Baxter and his Texan business partner, Virgil Oliver Stamps. Virgil and his younger brother Frank formed the famous Stamps Quartet in 1924, and three years later it became the first gospel quartet to record for a major label (RCA Victor). After World War II, Frank departed to form a rival publisher, the Stamps Quartet Music Company. JD Sumner, meanwhile, joined the Blackwood Brothers Quartet after two members died in 1954. Once James Blackwood purchased Frank's publishing company in the early 1960s, Sumner assumed management of the Stamps Quartet. After three years, Sumner left the Blackwood Brothers to sing with the Stamps. Following their long and productive engagement with Elvis, the quartet kept going and recently celebrated nine decades of existence as a professional outfit.

26. These included the All American Quartet (1949), Jimmy Jones (1957), the Harvesters (1962), the Tennessean Quartet (1963), and Duane Nicholson (1965). The last was the son of a First Assemblies of God preacher and only a year younger than Elvis. Fearing that it lacked the stage presence of other Southern quartets, his group the Couriers moved north to Pennsylvania and eventually became known nationally for promoting the Southern gospel style.

27. *Classic Albums: Elvis Presley*, television documentary, directed by Jeremy Marre (London: Eagle Rock Productions, 2001), DVD.

28. A key exception to this was Dusty Springfield, who brought her own production team in when she recorded at the studio.

29. Roben Jones, *Memphis Boys: The Story of American Studios* (Jackson: University of Mississippi Press, 2010), 217.

30. Interestingly, the country singer-songwriter's grandfather was reputedly a cousin of Tennessee Williams.

31. Hartford was quite a joker too: "Good Old Electric Washing Machine," which was also on the *Earthwords and Music* LP, is hilarious.

32. Jones, *Memphis Boys*, 221.

33. John Floyd, *Sun Records: An Oral History* (London: Avon Books, 1998).

34. Jørgensen, *Elvis Presley: A Life in Music*, 332.

35. Camille Paglia, *Sexual Personae: Art and Decadence from Nefertiti to Emily Dickinson* (London: Yale University Press, 2000), 165.

36. Eric Braun, *The Elvis Film Encyclopedia: An Impartial Guide to the Films of Elvis* (Woodstock, N.Y.: The Overlook Press, 1997), 183.

37. See: http://babyboomers-seniors.com/pdfs/jul07/articles/darwinporter.pdf.

38. The friendship between Elvis and Nick Adams continued until at least 1960, when Colonel Parker became godfather to Adams's daughter Allyson.

39. Jill Watts, *Mae West: An Icon in Black and White* (Oxford: Oxford University Press, 2001), 285.

40. Aberbach also attended the session where Jerry Leiber recorded the Drifters' "If You Don't Come Back," a song reworked much later at Stax by Elvis for his album *Raised on Rock*.

41. Bar Biszick-Lockwood, *Restless Giant: The Life and Times of Jean Aberbach and Hill and Range Songs* (Urbana: University of Illinois Press, 2010), 197.

42. The next track on *Elvis' Christmas Album* was Irving Berlin's "White Christmas." One story suggests that Berlin was incensed that a rock 'n' roll upstart like Elvis Presley could cover his distinctly refined material. However, Atlantic had already released a very groovy, swing version of "White Christmas" by the Drifters in November 1954. Its B-side, "The Bells of St. Mary's," is listed on the 1996 *Virtual Graceland* CD-ROM set, along with Bing Crosby's 1950 Decca version of "White Christmas"; Elvis had both renditions in his record collection. Shane Brown has contested the Berlin story. See Shane Brown, "Secrets and Lies: Getting to the Truth about *Elvis' Christmas Album*," *Elvis Information Network*, n.d., http://www.elvisinfonet.com/Spotlight-the-Truth-about%20Elvis-Christmas-Album.html.

43. Like the Sun number "Milkcow Blues Boogie," but in a different way, in its very musical structure the song demonstrates a chaotic transition in effect from the "safe" past of American popular music to the riskier, more vibrant world of the late 1950s.

44. Known as the fast-picking talent behind Red Foley's Decca 78rpm "Sugarfoot Rag," Garland went on to work with Elvis at RCA until he suffered a terrible car accident at the start of the next decade.

45. Steve Sullivan, *Encyclopedia of Great Popular Song Recordings, Volume 1* (Lanham, MD: Scarecrow Press, 2013), 302.

46. Jørgensen, *Elvis Presley: A Life in Music*, 317.

47. Bill Dahl, "Got It Covered," in *Vintage Rock Presents: Elvis Collector's Edition*, edited by Steve Harnell (London: Anthem Publishing, 2016), 107.

48. Elvis's comments can be heard on the 2008 Follow That Dream (FTD) collector label's two-disc version of the 1971 album *Elvis Country (I'm 10,000 Years Old)*.

49. Jerry Osborne, *Elvis: Word for Word* (New York: Gramercy Books, 2000), 43.

50. It is worth contrasting Presley pictures to the kitchen-sink dramas that came out in England. In the early 1960s, both raised issues of gender and class, but they could not have been more different.

51. Adam Victor, *The Elvis Encyclopedia* (New York: Overlook Duckworth, 2008), 219.

52. Film noir, for instance, epitomized the battle of the sexes. "(You're the) Devil in Disguise" was exactly what the hapless insurance salesman played by Fred MacMurray should have said to Phyllis Dietrichson—Barbara Stanwyck's unforgettable femme fatale in Billy Wilder's classic 1944 noir, *Double Indemnity*. Fictional characters like Norman Bates from Hitchcock's 1960 film *Psycho* registered the supposedly dark consequences of male distrust. Meanwhile, sociological shifts—including the rise of juvenile delinquency, the generation gap, permissive society, and growing divorce rate—could all be interpreted as collective expressions of failed intimacy and broken commitment. The point is that these things were way bigger than Elvis.

53. Ken Sharp, *Elvis Presley: Writing for the King—The Stories of the Songwriters* (London: FTD Books, 2006), 141.

54. Sharp, *Writing for the King*, 141.

55. Jay Spangler, "John Lennon Interview: Juke Box Jury 6/22/1963," *The Beatles Ultimate Experience*, 2011, http://www.beatlesinterviews.org/db1963.0622.jukebox.jury.john.lennon.html.

56. Spangler, "John Lennon Interview."

57. Joe Moscheo, *The Gospel Side of Elvis* (New York: Center Street, 2007), 63.

58. The Library of Congress has collected at least three thousand different performances of "Amazing Grace": http://memory.loc.gov/diglib/ihas/html/grace/grace-home.html.

59. "Lining out" is a form of religious folk singing in which the leader or "precentor" offers a sung version of the words for the congregation to echo, one verse at a time.

60. The Library of Congress keeps a handy time line of performances: http://memory.loc.gov/diglib/ihas/html/grace/grace-timeline.html.

61. Robert Matthew-Walker, *Elvis Presley: A Study in Music* (Tunbridge Wells, U.K.: Midas Books, 1979), 89.

62. Erik Lorentzen et al., *Ultimate Elvis* (Oslo: KJ Consulting, 2014), 1390.

63. Sharp, *Writing for the King*, 380.

64. Rather like "That's All Right," for example, this Pomus and Shuman song has been labeled in different ways in different places, sometimes as "Marie's the Name (His Latest Flame)" and "(Marie's the Name of) His Latest Flame." Del Shannon's version was simply called "His Latest Flame." I am using the com-

mon title that was listed on the actual pressing of Elvis's 45rpm RCA single release.

65. Other examples include "Judy" from 1961, "Mary in the Morning" and "Sylvia" from 1970, plus "Sweet Angeline" from 1973.

66. Ironically, in more recent years, indie rock bands like the Residents and the Smiths have taken up "(Marie's the Name) His Latest Flame" and performed it in their own ways.

67. One exception to Elvis's aversion to playing "(Marie's the Name) His Latest Flame" in concert occurred in Las Vegas, on 3 September 1971, when he offered a brief throwaway snatch at his midnight show.

68. Robert Hilburn, "When the Chairman Met the Returned King," *Los Angeles Times*, 25 January 2004, http://articles.latimes.com/2004/jan/25/entertainment/ca-hilburn25.

69. Peter Guralnick, *Careless Love: The Unmaking of Elvis Presley* (London: Little, Brown and Company, 1999), 44.

70. As well as Scotty, DJ, and the Jordanaires, the Nelson Riddle Orchestra backed this unique double act performance. Riddle was a New Jersey native who had been inspired by the Boston Symphony Orchestra. He worked with Capitol for a decade, arranging music for stars like Nat King Cole and having instrumental hits of his own. One of his biggest was "Lisbon Antigua," which contained some open-throated, Jordanaires-style harmonies. Riddle went on to work with Ella Fitzgerald. His arranging skills can be heard on the wonderfully jazzy and dynamic 1966 theme tune for the TV show *Batman*.

71. It is interesting to note that Bill Johnson's Sun single "Bobaloo" was released in the same month that Elvis recorded and released "Stuck on You." While the records are not carbon copies, they seem in quite a similar style. According to a list that came in the 1996 *Virtual Graceland* CD-ROM set, Elvis had the Johnson record in his collection, but to say any more is a matter of speculation.

72. Jørgensen, *Elvis Presley: A Life in Music*, 122.

73. Jack Kerouac, *On the Road* (London: Penguin, 2000), 185.

74. McFarland, who was apparently known for his eccentric lyrics and wild ways, went on to work with Aretha Franklin.

75. Sharp, *Writing for the King*, 120.

76. Sharp, *Writing for the King*, 120.

77. Adam Victor claims that Sinatra telephoned Elvis. Guralnick and Jørgensen say he sent a "get well" card. Victor, *The Elvis Encyclopedia*, 472; Peter Guralnick and Ernst Jørgensen, *Elvis Day by Day: The Definitive Record of His Life and Music* (New York: Ballantine Books, 1999), 353.

78. Using his mother's name (Anne Orlowski) as a pseudonym, Gene Pitney, who began as a songwriter, co-wrote "Rubber Ball" alongside Schroeder. The

pair had business ties too; Schroeder persuaded Pitney to launch himself as a performer and consequently managed his career.

79. The single's other side, "I Let Her Get Away," is listed on the 1996 *Virtual Graceland* CD-ROM set as belonging to Elvis.

80. Lorentzen et al., *Ultimate Elvis*, 799.

81. Jørgensen, *Elvis Presley: A Life in Music*, 262.

82. David Neale, *Roots of Elvis* (New York: iUniverse, 2003), 120.

83. That particular version was posthumously released in 1997 on the twentieth-anniversary box set, *Platinum: A Life in Music*.

84. The piano fill intro was used a decade earlier on Elvis's take of the Blackwood Brothers' "In My Father's House," which appeared on the album *His Hand in Mine*.

85. Andrei Tarkovsky, *Sculpting in Time: Reflections on the Cinema* (London: Faber & Faber, 1989).

86. Kathy Westmoreland, *Elvis and Kathy* (Glendale, Calif.: Glendale House, 1987), 229.

87. Ken Burke and Dan Griffin, *The Blue Moon Boys: The Story of Elvis Presley's Band* (Chicago: Chicago Review Press, 2006), 62.

88. Ken Sharp, "Interview with Mike Stoller Legendary Songwriter," *Elvis Australia*, 23 July 2015, http://www.elvis.com.au/presley/interview-with-mike-stoller.shtml.

89. Sharp, "Interview with Mike Stoller Legendary Songwriter."

90. Beverly Ross was credited on "Dixieland Rock" as Rachel Frank. She also co-wrote "Lollipop" with Julius Dixon. Early in the year when Elvis recorded the *King Creole* soundtrack, the Chordettes released "Lollipop" as a single. According to the 1996 *Virtual Graceland* CD-ROM set, that Cadence Records release was in his collection. Working with Sam Bobrick—who went on to become a successful television scriptwriter and playwright—Ross penned another song taken up by Elvis in 1960, "The Girl of My Best Friend."

91. Among other staff who deserve a mention here is the Paramount music director Walter Scharf. The prolific conductor adapted music for five Elvis features starting with *Loving You*. His role in Elvis's movie soundtrack recordings merits further attention.

92. Claude Demetrius and Fred Wise were both experienced songwriters. Born in Maine, Demetrius moved to New York and had great success in the 1940s writing for the energetic Louis Jordan. His songs for Elvis already included "I Was the One" and "Mean Woman Blues." Together with Aaron Schroeder, he wrote "Santa, Bring My Baby Back (To Me)," which appeared in 1957 on *Elvis' Christmas Album*. Wise, meanwhile, was most known for Buddy Kaye's cutesy late 1940s hit, "A—You're Adorable."

93. As an interviewee on Jeremy Marre's documentary, *Classic Albums: Elvis Presley*, Jørgensen suggested that Elvis's early 1956 New York studio sessions had an edge.

94. The Germans obviously thought so: Their pretender to the throne, the schlager singer Ted Herold, did a passable job of re-creating "Dixieland Rock" in his own language a year after the initial RCA release.

95. Revaux and Thibaut also became known as writers for singer Michel Sardou.

96. The Anka songs are listed as residing in Elvis's personal collection on the 1996 *Virtual Graceland* CD-ROM set.

97. Elvis *may well* have had Sinatra's reprise single of "My Way" in his collection, as the song appeared in the list offered by the 1996 *Virtual Graceland* CD-ROM set.

98. Published by Ballantine Books, *Elvis: What Happened?* was a 1977 commercial biography written by three of Elvis's former employees (Red West, Sonny West, and Dave Hebler) with the help of tabloid reporter Steve Dunleavy. Subtitled "a shocking, bizarre story," it weighed in somewhere between a wake-up call and cash-in. Never before had the singer's personal failings been discussed so publicly. In a letter, Elvis described it as "gossip put out as a book." Red West et al., *Elvis: What Happened?* (New York: Ballantine, 1977); Osborne, *Elvis: Word for Word*, 325.

99. Ace Collins, *Untold Gold: The Stories behind Elvis's #1 Hits* (Chicago: Chicago Review Press, 2005), 146.

100. Collins, *Untold Gold*, 143.

101. The Blue Moon Boys was the name sometimes given to Elvis's band when they played live. It may have been used as early as October 1954. Since both "Blue Moon of Kentucky" and "Blue Moon" were recorded by then, the name could have come from either song. Jørgensen, *Elvis Presley: A Life in Music*, 17.

102. "A Big Hunk o' Love" was recorded two and a half years after Elvis praised the talent of Jackie Wilson during the famous Million Dollar Quartet session. In the years just after the 1958 single was recorded, Sid Wyche went on to pen several hits for the black singer.

103. The quartet's burbling bass notes seem pitched here between the Coasters, who released Leiber and Stoller's "Yakety Yak" a year earlier, and the Marcels, who created a doo-wop arrangement of "Blue Moon" that would set new standards two years later.

104. The end of "Move It" is almost certainly a direct tribute to Elvis's style. The record's B-side, "Schoolboy Crush," was a Schroeder composition and had previously been released by country singer Bobby Helms.

105. The live performance of this number can be heard on RCA/Legacy's three-CD set *A Boy from Tupelo: The Complete 1953–1955 Recordings*. A similar introduction was used during the closing night show at the New Frontier Hotel in Las Vegas, 6 May 1956. Existing sources cannot, however, affirm that "I Got a Woman" was actually played during that show. Osborne, *Elvis: Word for Word*, 26.

106. Rapper Kanye West played with the gender theme when he sampled part of "I Got a Woman" for "Gold Digga," which was released in 2005.

107. Elvis played "I Got a Woman" at Eagles' Hall in Houston on New Year's Day, 1955, and recorded it at a session that happened between 30 January and 4 February that year. http://www.keithflynn.com/essential_lists/02-1955.html; http://www.keithflynn.com/recording-sessions/50_index.html.

108. Duke Records was started in Memphis by Bill Fitzgerald and the WDIA program director David Mattis. In 1952, Don Robey bought up the label and moved it to Houston, Texas, where he ran it alongside his other concern, Peacock Records. Peacock specialized in gospel. Duke focused on R&B—including artists such as Bobby "Blue" Bland and Johnny Ace.

109. Interestingly, in what may well be a simple mistake, *Elvis Encyclopedia* author Adam Victor suggested the song that inspired Charles was "My Jesus Is All I Need." Certainly, the Calvary Tabernacle Singers released a song called "Jesus Is All I Need" on Mercury in 1950. See Victor, *The Elvis Encyclopedia*, 248.

110. Biszick-Lockwood, *Restless Giant*, 201.

111. Jørgensen, *Elvis Presley: A Life in Music*, 300.

112. Francesc Lopez's *Elvis Presley in Concert* website suggests that "I Got a Woman" was played at more than half of the 1,147 post-1968 shows listed. Since Lopez has not been able to locate track listings for all the shows included, the actual number is almost certainly higher. http://www.elvisconcerts.com.

113. The Christmas feel of "Amen" may have been inspired by Marv Meredith's 1960 instrumental "Salvation Rock," which riffed on "Amen" in a snazzy, easy listening style, complete with jingle bell accompaniment.

114. This is speculation; the only Otis Redding track listed in Elvis's personal record collection on the 1996 *Virtual Graceland* CD-ROM set was "Mr. Pitiful," a number that formed the A-side of a Volt Records single from 1965 and also appeared on the 1968 Atco Records EP *Otis Redding in Person at the Whisky a Go Go*. "Amen," meanwhile, came out as the A-side of a 1968 Atco single and also appeared on the posthumous 1968 Atco LP compilation *The Immortal Otis Redding*.

115. Matthew-Walker, *Elvis Presley: A Study in Music*, 80.

116. Arved Ashby, *The Pleasure of Modern Music: Listening, Meaning, Intention, Ideology* (Martlesham, U.K.: Boydell & Brewer, 2004), 57.

117. Ashby, *The Pleasure of Modern Music*, 58.

118. Ocie got his nickname because his name was O. C. Smith.

119. "Little Green Apples" was written by Bobby Russell. Columbia backed it with Ocie's version of Vern Stovall and Bobby George's "Long Black Limousine." Elvis took on a different Russell number ("Do You Know Who I Am?") and tried "Long Black Limousine" at American Sound a few months later—possibly indicating that Ocie's music was on his radar. Ocie's April and June 1969 soul singles were both Mac Davis numbers too: "Friend, Lover, Woman, Wife" and "Daddy's Little Man." The latter was, evidently, based on a broadly similar topic to "Don't Cry Daddy." In return, Ocie endorsed Mac's solo album.

120. Listed in the 1996 *Virtual Graceland* CD-ROM set.

121. Charles White, *The Life and Times of Little Richard: The Quasar of Rock* (London: Pan Books, 1985), 68.

122. White, *The Life and Times of Little Richard*, 64.

123. Bumps Blackwell said that his family called a meeting to check whether he had "turned" when he started working with Richard. See White, *The Life and Times of Little Richard*, 64.

124. In his book on Elvis's TV appearances, Allen Wiener speculates, "It is possible that he wanted to do 'Heartbreak Hotel' but it was rejected during rehearsal for some reason." Allen Wiener, *Channeling Elvis: How Television Saved the King of Rock 'n' Roll* (Potomac, Md.: Beats & Measures Press, 2014), 16.

125. Biszick-Lockwood, *Restless Giant*, 200.

126. The exception was when Elvis opened his 30 August 1957 show in Spokane, Washington. See: http://www.keithflynn.com/essential_lists/06-1957.html.

127. Osborne, *Elvis: Word for Word*, 275.

128. Lamar Fike, "More Feedback on Elvis Coming to London," *Elvis Information Network*, 24 April 2008, http://www.elvisinfonet.com/index_april08.html.

129. Freddy Bienstock recalled that at least twenty of the girls were more than satisfied during Elvis's ten-day stay. Sharp, *Writing for the King*, 381.

130. Lamar Fike was unmissable and portly in stature. He originally met Elvis as early as 1954. In 1957, he became part of the inner circle and was with the Memphis singer for the next two decades, often acting as the punch line to Elvis's humor. Ironically, Fike later helped Albert Goldman get inside interviews for his infamous Presley biography. In fairness, though, he may not have known quite what Goldman had planned. Lamar Fike also did much to support Elvis's career, not least by working as an intermediary for Hill & Range.

131. Sharp, *Writing for the King*, 70.

132. Sharp, *Writing for the King*, 70.

133. Sharp, *Writing for the King*, 78.

134. Sharp, *Writing for the King*, 70.

135. Lorentzen et al., *Ultimate Elvis*, 602.

136. The medley version of "Little Sister" was performed, for instance, on Elvis's 12 August 1970 and 3 September 1971 midnight Las Vegas shows (the former of which can be seen on *That's the Way It Is*).

137. Shuman's first solo album, "My Death" from 1969, was named after his cover of Jacques Brel's song. A year earlier, he also produced an off-Broadway tribute to the famous Belgian chansonnier.

138. Matthew-Walker, *Elvis Presley: A Study in Music*, 69.

139. In 2009, the DJ Moby released a funky yet strangely ambient version of "Run On," which featured a sample of Bill Landford and attempted to address the song's complex genre career.

140. Many writers think Elvis was inspired by the Golden Gate Quartet's version of "Run On," "God's Gonna Cut You Down." He was certainly a fan of the group. Charlie Hodge nudged him to record their standard "I Will Be Home Again" by giving him a Golden Gate Quartet record, which might well have been the album *That Golden Chariot*. A German EP pressing on the Fontana label, F76806, also contained "God's Gonna Cut You Down." In January 1960, Elvis and Charlie also sang backstage with the Golden Gate Quartet when they met in Paris. Guralnick and Jørgensen, *Elvis Day by Day*, 144.

141. The 14 March 1960 *Life* magazine piece is quoted in Ben Cosgrove's *Time* story. See Ben Cosgrove, "Return of the King: When Elvis Left the Army," *Time*, 8 February 2014, http://time.com/3638949/return-of-the-king-when-elvis-left-the-army/.

142. When Hoyle and Bowles claimed "Working on the Building" in the 1930s, it may well have been for the purpose of copyrighting sheet music.

143. This comes from 1 Corinthians verse 3:10.

144. Jørgensen, *Elvis Presley: A Life in Music*, 142.

145. For another spirited African American version of the song, check out Dr. C. J. Johnson's stomping mid-1970s take on Savoy Records.

146. Cornel West, *Black Prophetic Fire* (Boston: Beacon Press, 2014).

147. Victor, *The Elvis Encyclopedia*, 590.

148. The 1996 *Virtual Graceland* CD-ROM set lists four Blackwood Brothers numbers in Elvis's record collection, including this one.

149. In 1948, J. E. Mainer's Mountaineers offered a sweetly picked country version of "I'm Working on a Building" in the same vein as the Carter Family. Bill Monroe covered the Carters' version in 1954. Their real inheritor, though, was John Fogerty, who released a rousing take on his 1973 post-Creedence album, *The Blue Ridge Rangers*. https://secondhandsongs.com/topic/9645.

150. Jerry Schilling, *Me and a Guy Named Elvis: My Lifelong Friendship with Elvis Presley* (New York: Gotham Books, 2006), 186.

151. Nigel Goodall, "Interview with Elvis Presley: The 1972 Madison Square Garden Press Conference: June 9, 1972," *Elvis Australia*, 8 June 2011, http://www.elvis.com.au/presley/interview-with-elvis-presley-the-1972-press-conference.shtml.

152. Goodall, "Interview with Elvis Presley."

153. Bruno Tillander, *The World Knows Elvis Presley, but They Don't Know Me* (Stockholm: Premium, 2014), 254.

154. Goodall, "Interview with Elvis Presley."

155. Jerry Hopkins, *Elvis* (London: Open Gate Books, 1972), 350.

156. Western Swing is well known as one of several precursors to rock 'n' roll; Bill Haley, for instance, served his apprenticeship in Western Swing bands and reshaped Big Joe Turner's "Shake, Rattle and Roll" using elements of that style.

157. A bootleg version of the first show was released by TCB Records as *Las Vegas Dinner Show* in 1992; then Straight Arrow put out a slightly better recording called *Faded Love* in 2010. The Lake Tahoe version was released on FTD's 2003 CD *Takin' Tahoe Tonight*.

158. Albert Hand, "How to Kill Elvis by Inches," *Elvis Monthly* 5, no. 4 (1964): 2.

159. Sharp, *Writing for the King*, 395.

160. Dylan Jones, *Elvis Has Left the Building: The Day the King Died* (London: Overlook Duckworth, 2014), 274.

161. Jones, *Elvis Has Left the Building*, 274.

162. Lorentzen et al., *Ultimate Elvis*, 784.

163. Elvis struggled in Las Vegas playing at the New Frontier Hotel there from 23 April to 5 May 1956.

164. Tipping its hat to the Trashmen's insane "Surfin' Bird," "Elvira"—from 1966—contained a moment of "papa-oom-papa-mow-mow" scat singing.

165. Sharp, *Writing for the King*, 220.

166. This can be heard on the second disc of FTD's 2013 two-CD rerelease of the classic 1969 album *From Elvis in Memphis*.

167. Sharp, *Writing for the King*, 220.

168. Scotty said this on Jeremy Marre's documentary, *Classic Albums: Elvis Presley*.

169. Burke and Griffin, *The Blue Moon Boys*, 36.

170. Osborne, *Elvis: Word for Word*, 53.

171. Pierce's luck changed two years later when Elvis recorded his Wayne Walker co-write, "How Do You Think I Feel." See Martin Torgoff, *The Complete Elvis* (London: Virgin Books, 1982), 199.

172. Peter Carlin, *Paul McCartney: A Life* (New York: Touchstone, 2009), 22.

173. John Broven, "Roy Brown Part 2: Hard Luck Blues," *Blues Unlimited*, 1977, http://www.rocksbackpages.com/Library/Article/roy-brown-part-2-hard-luck-blues.

174. The reference to "mighty men" is biblical in origin. Both 1 Samuel verse 14:52 and 1 Chronicles verse 11:10, for instance, talk about "the mighty men whom David had."

175. Kays Gary, "Elvis Defends His Low Down Style," *Charlotte Observer*, 27 June 1956, 1B.

176. Broven, "Roy Brown Part 2."

177. Broven, "Roy Brown Part 2."

178. A copy of the *Billboard* review is posted here: http://www.boija.com/skivor/sun_singles_0.htm.

179. As is well known, Lansky Brothers of Memphis was Elvis's preferred clothing store. He wore many garments from the shop, especially in his early years as a professional musician.

180. The Lubbock radio performance became part of RCA's 1992 release *The King of Rock 'n' Roll: The Complete '50s Masters*.

181. Elvis had Turner's 1956 Atlantic single "Corrine, Corrina" (backed with "Boogie Woogie Country Girl") in his collection: http://www.scottymoore.net/records.html.

182. Morgan Ames, "Presley: The Product Is Sex," *High Fidelity*, April 1969, 104.

183. Ames, "Presley: The Product Is Sex," 104.

184. Michael Bertrand, *Race, Rock, and Elvis* (Urbana: University of Illinois Press, 2000), 164.

185. "Rock 'n' Roll: Return of the Big Beat," *Time* 94, no. 7 (1969): 57.

186. *The Elvis I Knew*, television documentary, directed by Dale Hill (Decker Television and Video, 1994).

187. Julie Burns, "His Latest Flames," in *Vintage Rock Presents: Elvis Collector's Edition*, edited by Steve Harnell (London: Anthem Publishing, 2016), 103.

188. "Lawdy Miss Clawdy" was among the records that Elvis asked Scotty Moore to transfer to tape in January 1968: http://www.scottymoore.net/records.html. The other Price records listed on the 1996 *Virtual Graceland* CD-ROM set are "Oooh-Oooh-Oooh" (1952), "What's the Matter Now?" (1953), and "Happy Birthday Mama" (1962).

189. Marc Weingarten, *Station to Station: The History of Rock 'n' Roll on Television* (New York: Pocket Books, 2000), 151.

190. Weingarten, *Station to Station*, 152.

191. Greil Marcus, *Mystery Train: Images of America in Rock 'n' Roll Music* (London: Omnibus Press, 1977), 139.

192. Paul Simpson, *The Rough Guide to Elvis* (London: Rough Guides, 2004), 243.

193. Ritz, *Elvis by the Presleys*, 102.

194. After Elvis scored a number one hit with "In the Ghetto," Davis started his own career as a performer on Columbia Records. He delivered a signature, plodding, country funk version of "A Little Less Conversation" at the end of 1970 for his second album, *I Believe in Music*.

195. The "Elvis vs. JXL" remix benefited from promotion by Nike's multimillion-dollar advertising campaign. Its "Secret Tournament" television commercial featured a set of top soccer players competing to mark the FIFA World Cup, which took place that year in South Korea and Japan.

196. On a joking 1970s live version of "Fever," Elvis took the line even further and talked about cats being born to give chicks "acne."

197. Most drummers now use a "match" grip, but DJ Fontana employed a "conventional" grip in his classic performances, with his left hand across the toms and snares. When he came back from the Korean War, Fontana worked in a popular after-hours club. The place featured comedians and singers, as well as dancers. It was there that he learned to accent bumps and grinds in the way that he later did for Elvis. See Burke and Griffin, *The Blue Moon Boys*, 56. *Billboard* ran a regular burlesque column in the early 1950s; it mentioned that the Stork Club and the Beverley in Shreveport both played host to dancing girls.

198. Anne Nixon, "Elvis Said . . . ," in *Elvis Special 1976*, edited by Albert Hand (Prescot, U.K.: World Distributors, 1976), 65.

199. Tragically, when Welch visited Rostill's home studio that same month, he discovered his bandmate had suffered a lethal electric shock.

200. See: http://www.keithflynn.com/essential_lists/concerts-1977.html.

201. Around a decade earlier, Columbia promoted Craddock as the next teen angel with songs like "Heavenly Love." He had a smash in Australia with "Boom Boom Baby" but left the music industry for a few years and returned to North Carolina. In the mid-1960s, Date Records—an old Columbia subsidiary that once specialized in rockabilly—reopened with a roster of new talent that included Martine. When Craddock returned to the recording business, he signed to the tiny Cartwheel label, scoring a country hit by covering Tony Orlando and Dawn's "Knock Three Times." After he moved to ABC, Craddock recorded "Rub It In" and established Martine's hit-making reputation.

202. Craddock had a follow-up hit that year with Leiber and Stoller's "Ruby Baby," a punchy doo-wop number the Drifters first released on Atlantic back in 1956. During the *Jailhouse Rock* sessions, Elvis briefly entertained Mike Stoller at the Beverly Wilshire Hotel and he sang along to the Drifters' version when it came on the radio. See Ken Sharp, "Leiber and Stoller: The Masters behind the

Masters," *Elvis Australia*, 21 June 2004, http://www.elvis.com.au/presley/leiber-and-stoller-elvis-presley.shtml.

203. Sharp, *Writing for the King*, 375.

204. Stevens was a country performer who recently scored his own hit with the traditionally styled "Misty."

205. According to cousin Billy Smith, Elvis laughed when JD Sumner hit the low note on "Way Down."

206. Sharp, *Writing for the King*, 377.

207. David Paulson, "Songwriter Layng Martine Recalls Writing 'Way Down,' Elvis' Last Hit," *The Tennessean*, 7 May 2016, http://www.tennessean.com/story/entertainment/music/2016/05/07/songwriter-layng-martine-recalls-writing-elvis-last-hit/83975104/.

208. Bob Dylan, *Dylan on Dylan: The Essential Interviews* (London: Hodder, 2007), 212.

209. Guralnick, *Careless Love*, 560.

210. Guralnick and Jørgensen, *Elvis Day by Day*, 159.

211. "Swing Down Sweet Chariot" was included during the afternoon and evening shows at the Ellis Auditorium in Memphis, 25 February 1961, and another concert a month later at the Bloch Arena in Honolulu: http://www.keithflynn.com/essential_lists/07-1960-61.html.

212. From the liner notes of the 2009 *I Believe: Gospel Masters* CD box set.

213. From the liner notes of the 2009 *I Believe: Gospel Masters* CD box set.

214. Alain Locke, *The New Negro* (New York: Albert and Charles Boni, 1925).

215. In the *Comeback Special*, it seems likely that "Motherless Child"—a number that Elvis may have known from the Golden Gate Quartet's early 1950s or Mahalia Jackson's late 1950s renditions—was chosen specifically to evoke aspects of the Harlem Renaissance, quietly framing the black community as America's "motherless child," deprived of its dignity by slavery and searching for better treatment in the civil rights era. To that end, a solitary black male dancer lyrically interpreted a brief version sung by Darlene Love of the Blossoms on the show. Coupled with "If I Can Dream," such muted messages were about as much as Steve Binder and Elvis could comfortably say while courting the gamut of popular support within the American family mainstream. After all, Binder had already provoked controversy when he made the NBC TV special *Petula*, a show that aired in the spring of 1968; Petula Clark, a white female singer, had physically touched Harry Belafonte on camera during the pair's duet performance of a war protest song.

216. The 1959 Newport Folk Festival LP contained an equally animated version by Odetta, but it is less likely that Elvis heard it.

217. Mike Eder, *Elvis Music FAQ* (Milwaukee: Backbeat Books, 2013), 184.

218. Biszick-Lockwood, *Restless Giant*, 211.

219. Sharp, *Writing for the King*, 57.

220. Sharp, *Writing for the King*, 57.

221. "Don McLean – 'You Gave Me a Mountain,'" YouTube video, 6:13, posted June 2009, https://www.youtube.com/watch?v=ZCa96u09J-o.

222. "Don McLean – 'You Gave Me a Mountain.'"

223. "Don McLean – 'You Gave Me a Mountain.'"

224. "Don McLean – 'You Gave Me a Mountain.'"

225. Osborne, *Elvis: Word for Word*, 288.

226. Lorentzen et al., *Ultimate Elvis*, 1630.

227. *The Elvis I Knew*, television documentary, directed by Dale Hill (Decker Television and Video, 1994).

228. Elvis had long been an admirer of Tubb and had met him when auditioning for the *Grand Ole Opry* in Nashville in the fall of 1954.

229. As if not to be outdone, MGM released another version in 1950 focused on some rich vocals by its black baritone Billy Eckstein.

230. Joe Botsford, "'Elvis Tops . . . Rock 'n' Roll Here to Stay' Says Winterhalter," *The Milwaukee Sentinel*, 27 June 1958, part 3, 6.

231. Botsford, "Elvis Tops," 6. Ironically, Winterhalter and his orchestra backed the Turtles—not the 1960s group—in a version of "Mystery Train" that RCA released in December 1955.

232. The 1996 *Virtual Graceland* CD-ROM set includes Hugo Winterhalter's "Blue Christmas" in its list of Elvis's records. In 1950, RCA released a 10-inch pressing of Hugo Winterhalter's Orchestra and Chorus performing the song with a rendition of Irving Berlin's "White Christmas" on the flip side.

233. Kirkham went freelance in the mid-1950s after almost a decade working for Nashville's WSM. Program director Jack Stapp hired Anita Kerr as a composer and ensemble leader, and Kirkham came in to sing with her. During the period, Stapp also set up the Tree publishing operation, which eventually became Sony/ATV music publishing. After "Gone" and "Don't," Kirkham's career kept on a high—she worked alongside not only Elvis but also a range of other singers. Her haunting soprano is audible, for instance, behind Brenda Lee's 1960 classic "I'm Sorry"; she also had a hand in Bobby Vinton's 1963 cover of "Blue Velvet." Elvis owned the Clovers' 1955 version—its B-side "If You Love Me (Why Don't You Tell Me So)" is listed on the 1996 *Virtual Graceland* CD-ROM set. He might well also have known about Arthur Prysock's typically gentle, wonderfully ghoulish 1951 version of "Blue Velvet."

234. "Millie Kirkham Remembers Her First Recording Session with Elvis Presley," YouTube video, 6:33, posted February 2013, https://www.youtube.com/watch?v=f-dOk5wSVzI.

235. Jørgensen, *Elvis Presley: A Life in Music*, 96.

236. Jørgensen, *Elvis Presley: A Life in Music*, 96.

237. Banking on the repeated profit potential of its Christmas hits, the record company also repackaged "Blue Christmas" as a 45rpm the next year, this time backing it with "Santa Claus Is Back in Town."

238. Understandably, however, "Blue Christmas" was dropped from NBC's summer 1969 repeat broadcast of the *Comeback*.

239. Greil Marcus, "The Little Theatre," *'68 Comeback Special* Deluxe Edition DVD, directed by Steve Binder (1968; New York: Sony-BMG, 2004), liner notes, 4.

240. It is interesting to note that Elvis had a kind of proto-feminist answer record to Jim Reeves's late 1959 number "He'll Have to Go" in his record collection: Jeanne Black's 1960 release "He'll Have to Stay." The song appears on the list published in the 1996 *Virtual Graceland* CD-ROM set.

241. "It Hurts Me" was a co-write with Charlie Daniels (of "The Devil Went Down to Georgia" fame). Byers's husband, Bob, also claimed to have written the Elvis numbers but avoided a credit for contractual purposes.

242. Matthew-Walker, *Elvis Presley: A Study in Music*, 72.

243. Jerry Ragovoy and Bert Burns's "32 Miles out of Waycross" seemed to get retitled as "Mojo Mama" by Jerry Wexler and Bert Burns, who took the credit on both Pickett's and Don Varner's versions. Ravogoy and Burns then sued Edwin Starr over "25 Miles."

244. Gillian Gaar, *Return of the King: Elvis Presley's Great Comeback* (London: Jawbone Press, 2010), 63.

245. Osborne lists this live performance as 1 August 1969, but surviving recordings start from the 3 August 1969 dinner show. Osborne, *Elvis: Word for Word*, 214. Intonation has been added on "Memphis" to reflect how Elvis said it.

246. Osborne, *Elvis: Word for Word*, 224.

247. Since he made some slight changes to lyrics, Muddy Waters also tried to claim credit as a songwriter of "Got My Mojo Working." A court case rightly found in Preston Foster's favor.

248. The "Birthday Cake" staple was worked by blues man Big Bill Broonzy as "Keep Your Hands Off Her" (on Mercury in 1949), country singer Skeets McDonald as "Birthday Cake Boogie" (on Fortune Records in 1950), and another country performer, Billy Hughes, as "Take Your Hands Off It" (on 4 Star Records from 1951). Jerry Lee Lewis also performed a characteristically energetic take at the very start of the 1960s, which was released later on various compilations of his Sun work. Dahl, "Got It Covered."

249. Imperial and Nashboro also distributed later pressings.

250. The CBS Trumpeteers' "Milky White Way" is mentioned in the list on the 1996 *Virtual Graceland* CD-ROM set.

251. The arrangements on both sides of Little Richard's "I've Just Come from the Fountain" single were credited to the multitalented George Goldner, a 1940s music impresario who, over the next few years, moved into rock 'n' roll from the dance club scene and Latin music and then had an R&B phase. By the end of the 1950s, he had started several small labels and discovered some of the best young doo-wop hit makers.

252. "Elvis Presley as Remembered by Bill Medley," YouTube video, 9:44, posted June 2010, https://www.youtube.com/watch?v=-QDjdSyfJFs.

253. Neale, *Roots of Elvis*, 104.

254. Joe Tex's "C.C. Rider" was the B-side to "A Woman's Hands," which was a song listed on the 1996 *Virtual Graceland* CD-ROM set as being in Elvis's personal record collection.

255. The phrase "a machine for living in," which was used to define the function of a modernist dream house, came from Le Corbusier's 1923 manifesto, *Towards an Architecture*.

256. The pace is brisk, for instance, in Roy Brown's "Good Rocking Tonight" and even more so in "Hurry Hurry Baby" from 1953.

257. Glen Spreen was a talented arranger and member of the American Sound team. He was asked to write live arrangements when Elvis ventured back to Las Vegas in 1969, and he continued in that role until 1972. Spreen had been responsible for arranging the Masqueraders' recording of "Steamroller Blues." When he was asked to re-create it for Elvis's show, he refused, later citing the prominence of "screech trumpet" in the Vegas sound and the Colonel's pettiness.

258. Paul Richardson, "Glen Spreen Interview: Part 1," *Elvis: The Man and His Music* 110 (2015): 24. "James Taylor – Steam Roller Blues (Live Acoustic)," YouTube video, 4:18, posted September 2010, https://www.youtube.com/watch?v=TT7tWlHp3WA.

259. "James Taylor – Steam Roller Blues (Live Acoustic)."

260. Jørgensen, *Elvis Presley: A Life in Music*, 97.

261. Collins, *Untold Gold*, 101.

262. Collins, *Untold Gold*, 144.

263. David Troedson, "Jerry Reed and the Importance of Elvis Presley's Guitar Man Sessions," *Elvis Australia*, 28 March 2015, http://www.elvis.com.au/presley/jerry-reed-and-elvis-guitar-man-sessions.shtml.

264. Sharp, *Writing for the King*, 181.

265. Depending on the source, it was either producer Felton Jarvis or Chet Atkins's secretary Mary Lynch who made contact with Jerry Reed, although of course Lynch could have sought Reed out at Jarvis's behest. Despite her reservations in 1965 about Jarvis taking over the producer role, she eventually married him. She also suggested, and hired, Elvis's gospel backing for the *How Great Thou Art* session in May 1966.

266. One source of inspiration for the opening riff from "Guitar Man" may have been Stick McGhee's number "Drinkin' Wine Spo-Dee-O-Dee": a jump blues classic that came out just after World War II on Harlem Records and was later reworked by Jerry Lee Lewis.

267. A version of "Guitar Man" featuring the "What'd I Say" ending was released in 1993 on *From Nashville to Memphis*, a five-CD set of 1960s masters.

268. Purchased by Elvis early in 1967, the Circle G ranch is located in Horn Lake, Mississippi—the relatively isolated retreat gave him an opportunity to escape his working life and have outdoor fun with his friends. See Shara Clark, "Home on the Circle G," *Memphis: The City Magazine*, 8 August 2016, http://memphismagazine.com/features/elvis-circle-g-ranch-home/.

269. Matthew-Walker, *Elvis Presley: A Study in Music*, 76.

270. Sharp, *Writing for the King*, 182.

271. Nick Keene, "For the Billionth and the Last Time: Lifting the Lid on the King's Record Sales," *Elvis Australia*, 11 March 2016, http://www.elvis.com.au/presley/one-billion-record-sales.shtml.

272. Keene, "For the Billionth and the Last Time."

273. Sharp, *Writing for the King*, 126.

274. Julie Burns, "Elvis and His Italian Inspirations," *Italy Magazine*, 9 August 2011, http://www.italymagazine.com/featured-story/elvis-and-his-italian-inspirations.

275. Simpson, *Rough Guide to Elvis*, 256.

276. Victor, *The Elvis Encyclopedia*, 296.

277. Two years before Elvis recorded his version, the comedian Harry Einstein had a heart attack and fell into Milton Berle's lap at a Friars Club dinner. The emcee ordered Tony Martin to sing "There's No Tomorrow" to distract the audience. Harry Einstein's heart attack was fatal. Martin became a pallbearer for the unlucky comedian's funeral.

278. Wally Gold, a sax player who had recently worked with Boston's the Four Esquires, also penned Lesley Gore's famous "It's My Party." He ended his career, unfortunately, outside the music field as a travel agent.

279. Sharp, *Writing for the King*, 126.

280. Jørgensen, *Elvis Presley: A Life in Music*, 126.

281. Elvis writer Paul Simpson, who interviewed many of the inner circle, claimed that sound engineer Bill Porter offered to splice together different endings, but Elvis said, "I'm going to do it all the way through or I'm not going to do it." However, Lorentzen et al. claim that the end of take two was spliced onto take four, with percussion and piano overdubbed two days later. See Simpson, *Rough Guide to Elvis*, 257; Lorentzen et al., *Ultimate Elvis*, 469.

282. Barry Scholes, "The Amazing Success of 'It's Now or Never,'" in *Elvis Special 1964*, edited by Albert Hand (Norwich, U.K.: Worldwide Distributors, 1964), 48.

283. Barry White, *Love Unlimited: Insights on Love and Life* (New York: Broadway Books, 1999), 22.

284. Osborne, *Elvis: Word for Word*, 319.

285. Elvis's preference for "It's Now or Never" also made commercial sense, as it had been his best seller. Goodall, "Interview with Elvis Presley."

286. Nixon, "Elvis Said . . . ," 68.

287. Braun, *The Elvis Film Encyclopedia*, 103.

288. Elvis, of course, put his stamp on "What Now My Love": first, by making a home-taped version in Hollywood around 1966, then adding it to his shows in the summer of 1972 before performing a definitive version in January 1973 for the *Aloha* engagement. According to the 1996 *Virtual Graceland* CD-ROM set, Elvis also owned a 45rpm copy of Mitch Ryder's dramatic and spooky version of "What Now My Love" (unfortunately dated now by its backing), which came out in 1967 on songwriter Bob Crewe's aptly titled DynoVoice label. Ryder had a hit the previous year with the rip-roaring soul number "Devil with a Blue Dress On."

289. It is hard to be certain here, of course. Elvis was well aware of the Everly Brothers. The songs he had of theirs in his record collection—as listed on the 1996 *Virtual Graceland* CD-ROM set—were "All I Have Tt Do Is Dream" (1958), "That'll Be the Day" (1965), and "I Don't Want to Love You" (which was the flip side of "Bowling Green" from 1967).

290. An exception was 26 January 1970, when he sang the song after "Long Tall Sally."

291. The low tones on Olivia Newton-John's original of "Let Me Be There" were reportedly supplied by Mike Sammes, who was active from the 1950s onward in his vocal group, the Mike Sammes Singers. The group worked on TV shows and recordings for Tom Jones and many other artists.

292. Matthew-Walker, *Elvis Presley: A Study in Music*, 81.

293. Adam Victor suggests that Elvis may have heard "Power of My Love" as early as 1966. Victor, *The Elvis Encyclopedia*, 406.

294. Apart from inclusion of the Sun classic "When It Rains, It Really Pours" and a sincere but slightly doleful cover of Chuck Berry's "Memphis, Tennessee," the LP *Elvis for Everyone!* was perhaps more notable for its unfortunate cash register picture sleeve than its music.

295. Sharp, *Writing for the King*, 143. Giant, Baum, and Kaye tried to chart similar territory to "Power of My Love" with "Animal Instinct," an addition to *Harum Scarum* that borrowed from Bob & Earl's "Harlem Shuffle." Unfortunately, their achievement came nowhere close.

296. Elvis reprised "One Night" for his 1970s engagements, though it featured much less in his live set between 1973 and 1976.

297. Marcus, "The Little Theatre," 4.

298. Robert Matthew-Walker, *Heartbreak Hotel: The Life and Music of Elvis Presley* (Chessington, U.K.: Castle Communications, 1995), 83.

299. Paul Simpson, *Elvis Films FAQ* (Montclair, N.J.: Applause, 2013), 225; Ritz, *Elvis by the Presleys*, 136.

300. Osborne, *Elvis: Word for Word*, 316.

301. This first take of "And I Love You So" can be heard on *Elvis Today*, the FTD label's 2005 extended reissue version of Elvis's 1975 studio album *Today*.

302. No wonder, then, that Jimmy Ellis—who later offered a unique masked tribute to Elvis—recorded "And I Love You So" as part of a medley, the same year that his hero addressed the song. A full version appeared on the 1989 album *Orion Sings Elvis, Volume II*.

303. Gaston Leroux, *The Phantom of the Opera* (London: HarperCollins, (2011 [1909]), 136.

304. Jørgensen, *Elvis Presley: A Life in Music*, 340.

305. Stephen Miller, *Kristofferson: The Wild American* (London: Omnibus Press, 2009).

306. One influence on Elvis recording "For the Good Times" may have been Ray Price's cover of the number, which became a single for Columbia in 1970. According to the 1996 *Virtual Graceland* CD-ROM set, Elvis had the disc in his collection.

307. The B-side, "If You Love Me (Why Don't You Tell Me So)," appears on the list of Elvis's personal records featured on the 1996 *Virtual Graceland* CD-ROM set.

308. This original release included a comma in the title, making it "Bossa Nova, Baby."

309. Alan Lorber was a significant composer, arranger, and writer of his era, specializing in genre fusions. After working as a station programmer for New York's WMCA, he helped Neil Sedaka and a number of other artists achieve their potential.

310. Bruce Pegg, *Brown Eyed Handsome Man: The Life and Hard Times of Chuck Berry* (Abingdon, U.K.: Routledge, 2002), 130.

311. Pegg, *Brown Eyed Handsome Man*, 142.

312. Lorentzen et al., *Ultimate Elvis,* 1506.

313. Osborne, *Elvis: Word for Word*, 276.

314. Richard Middleton, "All Shook Up?" in *The Elvis Reader*, edited by Kevin Quain (New York: St. Martin's Press, 1992), 7.

315. David Adams, "Interview with Steve Binder, Director of Elvis' '68 Come-back Special," *Elvis Australia*, 8 July 2005, http://www.elvis.com.au/presley/interview-steve-binder.shtml.

316. Osborne, *Elvis: Word for Word*, 213.

317. Ironically, Elvis revisited some of the style and theme of "MacArthur Park" when he recorded the less ornate ballad "The Next Step Is Love" in June 1970.

318. Weingarten, *Station to Station*, 157.

319. Victor, *The Elvis Encyclopedia*, 329.

320. It was not unusual for numbers that missed the top of the hit parade to become part of Elvis's canon. Consider, for instance, "Viva Las Vegas" and "An American Trilogy."

321. Marc Myers, "Bill Medley on Phil Spector," *Jazzwax*, July 2012, http://www.jazzwax.com/2012/07/bill-medley-on-phil-spector.html.

322. Another big production number from this period that Elvis owned in his record collection was Jackie DeShannon's "I Can Make It with You," as listed on the 1996 *Virtual Graceland* CD-ROM set.

323. Ritz, *Elvis by the Presleys*, 205.

324. Elvis may have worn the gorilla mask a few times in 1971, for example for both his Vegas midnight show on 13 February and his Lake Tahoe show from 1 August.

325. This performance of "You've Lost That Lovin' Feelin'" appeared on the 1972 RCA LP *Elvis: As Recorded at Madison Square Garden*.

326. Peter Guralnick, *Last Train to Memphis: The Rise of Elvis Presley* (London: Abacus, 1994), 77.

327. Guralnick and Jørgensen, *Elvis Day by Day*, 15.

328. The Washington-based Eagles were, of course, no relation to Don Henley and Glenn Frey's rock group, which did not form until 1971.

329. The pair also wrote "I Beg of You," which was released as the B-side to "Don't" in January 1957. Charlie Singleton extended the appeal of two Bert Kaempfert instrumentals when he added lyrics: Kaempfert's "Moon over Na-ples" became "Spanish Eyes"—which was released on Elvis's 1973 LP, *Good Times*—and "Beddy Bye" transformed into the Frank Sinatra classic "Strangers in the Night."

330. "Tryin' to Get to You" was likely first studio recorded between 30 Janu-ary and 4 February 1955: http://www.keithflynn.com/recording-sessions/50_index.html.

331. The Eagles' version of "Tryin' to Get to You" is listed on the 1996 *Virtual Graceland* CD-ROM set as part of Elvis's collection, so he probably had their Mercury single.

332. Mark Bego, *Cher: If You Believe* (Lanham, Md.: Taylor Trade, 2004), 47.

333. Alan Hanson, "Love Me Tender: A Signature Elvis Presley Recording," *Elvis History Blog*, July 2012, http://www.elvis-history-blog.com/love-me_ tender.html.

334. Simpson, *Elvis Films FAQ*, 44.

335. "Interview with Elvis Presley: The 1969 Press Conference: August 1, 1969," *Elvis Australia*, 12 January 2008. http://www.elvis.com.au/presley/ interview_with_elvis_presley_the_1969_press_conference.shtml.

336. Collins, *Untold Gold*, 206.

337. Sharp, *Writing for the King*, 195.

338. Hopkins, *Elvis*, 350.

339. Simpson, *Rough Guide to Elvis*, 273.

340. Simpson, *Rough Guide to Elvis*, 273.

341. Jones, *Memphis Boys*, 209.

342. Osborne, *Elvis: Word for Word*, 225.

343. Ritz, *Elvis by the Presleys*, 144.

344. Jørgensen, *Elvis Presley: A Life in Music*, 271.

345. Susan Doll, *Elvis for Dummies* (Hoboken, N.J.: John Wiley & Sons, 2009), 188.

346. Collins, *Untold Gold*, 208.

347. Ellen Willis, "Elvis in Vegas," in *Ellen Willis: Out of the Vinyl Deeps*, edited by Nona Willis Aronovitz (Minneapolis: University of Minnesota Press, 2011), 179.

348. Willis, "Elvis in Vegas," 180.

349. "Joey Dee & The Starliters – 'Hey Lets Twist' Movie," YouTube video, 2:56, posted August 2015, https://www.youtube.com/watch?v=4r2hsc-yTk4.

350. Victor, *The Elvis Encyclopedia*, 358.

351. The main lyrics of "Worried Man Blues" may go back even further into the blues tradition—some sources suggest to the black musicians Esley Riddle or John D. Fox.

352. Simpson, *Rough Guide to Elvis*, 236.

353. Long after "Mystery Train" was released, British Invasion bands were inspired by Pat Hare's heavy style of electric blues playing.

354. Scotty said this in Jeremy Marre's documentary, *Classic Albums: Elvis Presley*.

355. Peter Guralnick, *Sam Phillips: The Man Who Invented Rock 'n' Roll* (London: Weidenfeld & Nicolson, 2015), 151.

356. Guralnick, *Sam Phillips*, 256.

357. Sharp, *Writing for the King*, 70.

358. It has been speculated that when writing "Big Boss Man," Al Smith and Luther Dixon were inspired by Charley Jordan's old blues standard "Stack o' Dollars." Jordan's neatly picked introduction, however, bears relatively little

similarity to the number. Sleepy John Estes's 1930 version for Victor, Poor Jim and Dan Jackson's 1934 interpretation on Melotone Records, and Big Joe Williams's 1945 rendition for Columbia all came a bit closer to the Smith-Dixon composition—even so, there is still significant difference.

359. Jim O'Neal and Amy Van Singel, *The Voice of the Blues: Classic Interviews from* Living Blues *Magazine* (New York: Routledge, 2002), 329.

360. "Pa pa Oom Mow Mow" had, of course, been a big novelty hit in 1962 for the Rivingtons.

361. Robert Christgau, "Rock 'n' Roll: Elvis in Vegas," *Village Voice*, 4 September 1969, 29.

362. The "Blue Bird" section of the *Comeback* was Steve Binder's bid to present a gifted, everyman guitarist who achieves the American dream, gets tempted by the distractions of life on the road, and then decides to turn his back on the whole crazy, corrupt, and hollow world of commerce. All this was done in stylized form, through musical numbers. Maurice Maeterlinck's 1908 stage play *The Blue Bird* was Binder's inspiration. In a sense, the "Blue Bird" section therefore represents Binder's take on Elvis's own story, reflected through myth and archetype.

363. Garth Cartwright, "Luther Dixon Obituary," *The Guardian*, 11 November 2009, https://www.theguardian.com/music/2009/nov/11/luther-dixon-obituary.

364. In the June studio session, "Let Yourself Go" was actually recorded straight after "Nothingville" and *before* "Big Boss Man."

365. Elvis included "Big Boss Man" in his stage shows, particularly in 1974 and 1975. Those concert performances could not muster the *white heat* of its *Comeback* incarnation.

366. Favius Friedman, *Meet Elvis Presley* (New York: Scholastic Book Service, 1973), 7.

367. Victor, *The Elvis Encyclopedia*, 97.

368. Though he did not work with Elvis in person, Dennis Linde overdubbed some of the singer's 1970s material. He added the guitar intro to "Burning Love" on 27 April 1972. He also provided backing vocals and bass parts for live material that appeared on the *Moody Blue* album.

369. "Burning Love" was a regular feature in Elvis's 1975 and 1976 live sets.

370. Linde also released his own version that year. He had *character*, in the John Fogerty mold, as a vocalist, but his own take of the song was relatively pedestrian; his vocals gave it almost all its color.

371. David Ritz, Jerry Leiber, and Mike Stoller, "Hound Dog," *New York Times*, 12 June 2009, http://www.nytimes.com/2009/06/14/books/excerpt-hound-dog.html.

372. Ritz, Leiber, and Stoller, "Hound Dog."

373. Ritz, Leiber, and Stoller, "Hound Dog."

374. Ritz, Leiber, and Stoller, "Hound Dog."

375. Sharp, "Interview with Mike Stoller Legendary Songwriter."

376. Another pre-1968 version of "Saved" was performed by Billy Fury & the Gamblers; Fury's version sounds peculiarly English, carefree, and sedate.

377. Elvis performed "Tweedlee Dee" several times on his early 1955 *Louisiana Hayride* sets. The song's writer was Otis Blackwell's collaborator Winfield Scott, who went on to write "Return to Sender."

378. These discs are included in a list of Elvis's personal records on the 1996 *Virtual Graceland* CD-ROM set.

379. Jørgensen, *Elvis Presley: A Life in Music*, 217.

380. "Up Above My Head"—which Elvis recorded immediately *before* "Saved" at the same Western Recorders session—was originally released on Decca in 1949 by the irrepressible Sister Rosetta Tharpe. (While there is some overlap between Tharpe's and Elvis's gospel catalog—notably "(There'll Be) Peace in the Valley" and "Milky White Way"—others also recorded versions of those songs.) "Up Above My Head" was revived the next decade when Frankie Laine and Johnnie Ray belted it out as a forthright duet that achieved a place in the UK top thirty for Philips. In 1964 the song went even higher in the U.S. adult contemporary charts when it was performed by the bearded, avuncular trumpeter Al Hirt. Elvis's nicely flowing version was close to Hirt's—though minus the jazz horn—since it emphasized female vocal gospel backing. Another tune sometimes credited with a minor moment in the *Comeback* medley—as it may have been recorded in the middle of "Saved"—was keyboardist Tommy Wolfe's brief instrumental "Preach for the Sky." Information about both Wolfe and his tune seems missing from Ernst Jørgensen's definitive 1998 book, *Elvis Presley: A Life in Music*, and remains a bit sketchy. Keith Flynn's relatively comprehensive sessions website says Wolfe was present playing keyboards during the Western Recorders session on 22 June 1968: http://www.keithflynn.com/recording-sessions/680622.html.

381. This holy laughter is faintly spooky; more reminiscent of the kind of thing that happened in the 1990s Toronto Blessing and other such events than of Elvis's natural laughter—as anyone who has heard the laughing live version of "Are You Lonesome Tonight?" will know.

382. Jørgensen, *Elvis Presley: A Life in Music*, 250.

383. Jørgensen, *Elvis Presley: A Life in Music*, 250.

384. Osborne, *Elvis: Word for Word*, 103.

385. Sharp, *Writing for the King*, 20.

386. Elvis was not an experienced electric bass player at the time so this was remarkably intuitive.

387. Like the Leiber and Stoller hit before it, "C'mon Everybody" also became a rocking staple. Elvis never recorded the Cochran hit—he left that to punk.

Instead, he released a less edgy song of the same name by Joy Byers as part of a 1964 soundtrack EP for *Viva Las Vegas*.

388. Marcus, "The Little Theatre," 4.

389. It is interesting to note here that Reed's gently liberated performances were shaped by his alcoholism.

390. In the same years as the *Comeback*, Reed rode high on the bill of the American Folk Blues Festival.

391. The song is listed as part of Elvis's collection on the 1996 *Virtual Graceland* CD-ROM set.

392. Listed on the 1996 *Virtual Graceland* CD-ROM set.

393. An associated influence on "Baby What You Want Me to Do" may have been a second Jimmy Reed recording—"Too Much"—which came in the wake of Doggett's style. According to the 1996 *Virtual Graceland* CD-ROM set, Elvis owned a copy of the late 1962 Vee-Jay release.

394. "Gates of Graceland—Elvis' Record Collection," YouTube video, 22:47, posted April 2016, https://www.youtube.com/watch?v=JaItl4lJFWw.

395. Guralnick, *Careless Love*, 596.

396. Jørgensen, *Elvis Presley: A Life in Music*, 398.

397. Roy Hamilton's "Hurt" (backed with "Star of Love") was one of the vinyl records that Elvis asked Scotty Moore to transfer to tape early in 1968: http://www.scottymoore.net/records.html.

398. Timi Yuro's first name was actually Rosemary.

399. Liberty broke Julie London, Eddie Cochran, and Henry Mancini back in the mid-1950s and then underwent a renaissance in the new decade with Bobby Vee.

400. Osborne, *Elvis: Word for Word*, 42.

401. Depending on the source consulted, it was Al Stanton or Aaron "Goldie" Goldmark. Sharp, *Writing for the King*, 32; Collins, *Untold Gold*, 70.

402. Sharp, *Writing for the King*, 65.

403. Robert Palmer took the slow and deliberate approach to its logical conclusion in his muscular and strangely compelling cover version of "All Shook Up."

404. Herm Schoenfeld, "Jocks, Jukes and Discs," *Variety*, 27 March 1957, 50.

405. This quote, which comes from the 24 August 1969 midnight show, introduces a live version of "All Shook Up" that is included on the first of two CDs accompanying Ken Sharp's excellent 2006 FTD book, *Elvis Presley: Writing for the King—The Stories of the Songwriters*.

406. Rob Bowman, *Soulsville, USA: The Story of Stax Records* (New York: Schirmer Trade, 2003), 304.

407. "Interview with 'Aloha from Hawaii' director and producer, Marty Pasetta," YouTube video, 13:11, posted May 2015, https://www.youtube.com/watch?v=mKHcHAXne_g.

408. When Andy Williams recorded his own rather languid version of "I'll Remember You," his haunting vocal was backed by a Mantovani-style string section.

409. The studio version of "Memories," recorded a little later, had the same lush instrumentation as "I'll Remember You" and is, to some extent, a sister song.

410. Milton Erickson, *My Voice Will Go with You: The Teaching Tales of Milton H. Erickson* (New York: Norton, 1982).

411. The Hilltoppers were named after a local college football team.

412. The last song Elvis ever sang at home was Fred Rose's "Blue Eyes Crying in the Rain." Columbia had released Roy Acuff's rendition on a 10-inch shellac disc three decades earlier. The Hilltoppers included a reworking on their eponymous 1953 EP.

413. This was one of the singles Elvis wanted Scotty to transfer to tape in January 1968: http://www.scottymoore.net/records.html.

414. Osborne, *Elvis: Word for Word*, 145.

415. The Hilltoppers' "To Be Alone" is listed on the 1996 *Virtual Graceland* CD-ROM set as being part of Elvis's personal record collection.

416. According to song historian David Neale, the start of the spoken-word section of "Are You Lonesome Tonight?" was inspired by Jaques's speech to Duke Senior in Act II, Scene VII of William Shakespeare's famous play *As You Like It*: "All the world's a stage, And men and women merely players."

417. Elvis's RCA label mate, Jaye P. Morgan, also released a classic but unsuccessful single version of "Are You Lonesome Tonight?" a year before his own. Morgan's golden, string-ballad rendition echoed Patti Page's 1950 Mercury Records hit "Tennessee Waltz" in tone. It definitely belonged to the pre–rock 'n' roll era.

418. "Cowboy Joe Babcock Sings His 'Washed My Hands in Muddy Water': Viva! NashVegas® Radio Show 9-1-12," YouTube video, 4:44, posted September 2012, https://www.youtube.com/watch?v=cszY1jWWQoU.

419. Elvis had already showed more than a passing interest in Charlie Rich's music. In his singles collection, according to the 1996 *Virtual Graceland* CD-ROM set, he had three of Rich's 1960 Philips's numbers: "Lonely Weekends," "On My Knees," and "Gonna Be Waiting" (the flip side of "School Days"). He also seemed to echo their style in his 1961 recording "What a Wonderful Life." Another of Rich's singles, "Mohair Sam," was released by Smash Records in the summer of 1965, backed with "I Washed My Hands in Muddy Water." Elvis certainly knew about the A-side, as he was practicing it on electric bass when the Beatles popped over to visit his home that August.

420. Just like Hill & Range organized the publishing to keep Elvis loyal by giving him a cut, so he would sometimes record songs by other musicians who

were present at his sessions; he had to like the song, of course, but he also knew that any release would be a source of income for the writer.

421. Scotty Moore could not recall the Blue Moon Boys jamming the song. No Sun tape has ever surfaced. However, Sam Phillips tended to record over unused performances to save the cost of raw master tape.

422. Coben also wrote "Nobody's Child," which became a hit in the 1960s for Hank Williams Jr. It was also performed by Tony Sheridan when the Beatles were his (otherwise named) backing band. The lucky Sheridan went on to perform regularly with Elvis's former rhythm section from 1978.

423. One later Coben record was Mac Wiseman's name-dropping 1969 novelty country number, "Johnnie's Cash and Charley's Pride."

424. Collins, *Untold Gold*, 222.

425. Jimmy Bowen was a skilled songwriter and pianist in his own right. He coproduced an album for Kenny Rogers and the First Edition in 1968 called *Ruby, Don't Take Your Love to Town*.

426. Initially released in 1992, *Elvis: The Lost Performances* is a compilation of outtake footage from *Elvis: That's the Way It Is* (1970) and *Elvis on Tour* (1972) found during a 1986 vault inspection. *Elvis: The Lost Performances*, directed by Denis Sanders, Robert Abel, and Pierre Adidge (1992; Burbank, CA: MGM/Warner Home Video, 1999), VHS.

427. Biszick-Lockwood, *Restless Giant*, 219.

428. Vee Gee, "Elvis 'Queer Disc' No. 8 *Blue Suede Shoes*," *Elvis Monthly* 81 (1965): 10.

429. Nik Cohn, *WopBopaLooBop A LopBam Boom* (St. Albans, U.K.: Granada, 1973), 26.

430. Biszick-Lockwood, *Restless Giant*, 199.

431. Jørgensen, *Elvis Presley: A Life in Music*, 37.

432. It's likely that young Elvis broke a string—a frequent occurrence during his exuberant performances.

433. David McGhee, "Carl Perkins: Original Cat," in *Rockabilly—The Twang Heard 'Round the World: The Illustrated History*, edited by Michael Dregni (Minneapolis: Voyageur Press, 2011), 53.

434. Quoted from the Sun Records biography for Carl Perkins: http://www.sunrecords.com/artists/carl-perkins.

435. Cohn, *WopBopaLooBop*, 26.

436. Sharp, *Writing for the King*, 382.

437. The song was later released by RCA as an album track on Elvis's eponymous first LP as a splice of takes two and four. Jørgensen, *Elvis Presley: A Life in Music*, 12.

438. Osborne, *Elvis: Word for Word*, 6.

439. Osborne, *Elvis: Word for Word*, 72.

440. Burke and Griffin, *The Blue Moon Boys*, 14.

441. Ninian Dunnett, "Elvis and Me, the Night Rock 'n' Roll Was Born," *The Scotsman*, 9 March 1999, 22.

442. Guralnick, *Last Train to Memphis*, 95.

443. *Classic Albums: Elvis Presley*, television documentary.

444. Ray Connolly, "Sam Phillips Plus Johnny Cash, Carl Perkins and Roy Orbison," *Radio Times*, September 1973, http://www.rayconnolly.co.uk/pages/journalism_01/journalism_01_item.asp?journalism_01ID=56.

445. Elvis's was probably quoting the hard-partying, R&B-playing Tennessee DJ Bill "Hoss" Allen. Burke and Griffin, *The Blue Moon Boys*, 42.

446. Hopkins, *Elvis*, 73.

447. Jørgensen, *Elvis Presley: A Life in Music*, 15.

448. Connolly, "Sam Phillips Plus Johnny Cash."

449. Lorentzen et al., *Ultimate Elvis*, 35.

450. Matthew-Walker, *Heartbreak Hotel*, 167.

451. Zaret's real name was Hyman Harry Zaritsky.

452. Spector was a friend of Doc Pomus and likely produced some of the demos sent to Elvis. He also claimed that he liaised with Elvis's publishers, the Aberbachs, and had some consequent involvement in Elvis's early 1960s material. Such claims are contested. Other sources suggest that Spector tried to contribute to the *Blue Hawaii* soundtrack but was stopped by his business connections with Leiber and Stoller. See Sharp, *Writing for the King*, 281; Biszick-Lockwood, *Restless Giant*, 225.

453. "Elvis Presley as Remembered by Bill Medley," YouTube video, 9:44, posted June 2010, https://www.youtube.com/watch?v=-QDjdSyfJFs.

454. According to the list on the 1996 *Virtual Graceland* CD-ROM set, Elvis had Hamilton's "You'll Never Walk Alone" in his personal record collection. The 1954 single was backed with "I'm Gonna Sit Right Down and Cry (Over You)."

455. Ritz, *Elvis by the Presleys*, 231.

456. Osborne, *Elvis: Word for Word*, 234.

457. From the interview with Myrna Smith. Starring Yaphet Kotto and Anthony Quinn, Shear's feature also had an impressive Bobby Womack soundtrack. See Lorentzen et al., *Ultimate Elvis*, 1638.

458. According to Lisa: "When my father would take me on the road I'd practically live with the Sweet Inspirations. . . . I felt like they helped raise me." Ritz, *Elvis by the Presleys*, 202.

459. Sharp, *Writing for the King,* 252.

460. Jørgensen, *Elvis Presley: A Life in Music*, 292.

461. Osborne, *Elvis: Word for Word*, 226.

462. Cleothus Hardcastle, "The Back Pages Interview: Jerry Leiber and Mike Stoller," *Rock's Back Pages*, 30 June 2001, http://www.rocksbackpages.com/Library/Article/the-backpages-interview-jerry-leiber-and-mike-stoller.

463. Taken from http://www.elvisconcerts.com.

464. Serene Dominic, *Burt Bacharach, Song by Song: The Ultimate Burt Bacharach Reference for Fans, Serious Record Collectors, and Music Critics* (London: Omnibus Press, 2003), 66.

465. Michael Spörke, *Big Mama Thornton: The Life and Music* (Jefferson, N.C.: McFarland, 2014), 25.

466. Hardcastle, "The Back Pages Interview."

467. Scotty Moore said Elvis asked him to transfer the single to tape in January 1968: http://www.scottymoore.net/records.html.

468. Just to confuse matters, Festival Records used the Teen Records name again at the end of the decade, assisted by the Elvis-style New Zealand rocker Johnny Devlin.

469. Bernie Lowe went on to co-write "(Let Me Be Your) Teddy Bear" for Elvis with the comedy scriptwriter Kal Mann and made a fortune promoting Chubby Checker on the Cameo-Parkway label.

470. Jørgensen, *Elvis Presley: A Life in Music*, 48.

471. Nixon, "Elvis Said . . . ," 67.

472. Jørgensen, *Elvis Presley: A Life in Music,* 51–55.

473. Spörke, *Big Mama Thornton*, 106.

474. Spörke, *Big Mama Thornton*, 106.

475. *The Elvis I Knew*, television documentary, directed by Dale Hill (Decker Television and Video, 1994).

476. Don Cusic, *The Sound of Light: A History of Gospel and Christian Music* (Milwaukee: Hal Leonard, 2002), 185–86.

477. See: http://www.blackwoodbrothers.com/history.htm. Victor, *The Elvis Encyclopedia*, 241.

478. Trevor Simpson, "Elvis Presley—*How Great Thou Art*," in *Vintage Rock Presents: Elvis, a Celebration*, edited by Rik Flynn (London: Anthem Publishing, 2017), 58.

479. After Elvis's version of "How Great Thou Art," the Blackwood Brothers used it again on their 1973 Camden album that took its name from the song and on the end of the 1975 Skylite album, *Hymns of Gold*.

480. Simpson, "Elvis Presley—*How Great Thou Art*," 52.

481. *Beyond Elvis's Memphis*, directed by Mike Freeman (Memphis: Arts Magic, 2007), DVD.

482. Jørgensen, *Elvis Presley: A Life in Music*, 212.

483. Dave Marsh, *Elvis* (London: Omnibus Press, 1992 [1982]), 158.

484. The Imperials particularly struck a chord with a contemporary-sounding 1967 Christian music album called *New Dimensions*.

485. Unfortunately, Jake Hess soon had to bow out of the Imperials for health reasons. Doyle Blackwood's son Terry replaced Hess and sang lead in the Imperials from 1967 to 1976. Hess lived long enough to sing with the Statesmen at Elvis's funeral in 1977 and survived for almost another three decades.

486. Jørgensen, *Elvis Presley: A Life in Music*, 212.

487. The initial version of "How Great Thou Art" took a Grammy in 1967, while a live version from *Elvis Recorded Live on Stage in Memphis* achieved it 1974. "He Touched Me" secured Elvis's other Grammy in 1972. All three of these awards were in the Best Sacred Performance category, which was renamed as Best Inspirational Performance from 1972 onward. NARAS (National Academy of Recording Arts and Sciences, Inc.) also delivered a Bing Crosby Lifetime Achievement Award to Elvis in his Las Vegas dressing room in August 1971.

488. Arjan Deelen, "Interview with Jerry Scheff," *Elvis Australia*, 1 January 2016, http://www.elvis.com.au/presley/interview-jerryscheff.shtml.

489. Collins, *Untold Gold*, 86.

490. Simpson, *Rough Guide to Elvis*, 254.

491. Simpson, *Rough Guide to Elvis*, 253.

492. One of the discs that Elvis had in his personal collection, as listed on the 1996 *Virtual Graceland* CD-ROM set, was Dale Wright's Fraternity Records single "She's Neat." It sounds quite similar to "Jailhouse Rock" and was released around the same time.

493. Collins, *Untold Gold*, 89.

494. Marcus, "The Little Theatre," 4.

495. Jones, *Elvis Has Left the Building*, 267.

496. Leroux, *Phantom of the Opera*, 134.

497. Osborne, *Elvis: Word for Word*, 232.

498. David Colker, "Wayne Carson Dies at 72; Songwriter Penned Hits 'Always on My Mind' and 'The Letter,'" *LA Times*, 23 July 2015, http://www.latimes.com/local/obituaries/la-me-wayne-carson-20150724-story.html.

499. It is possible that Red West may also have given Elvis a tape of the song.

500. Sharp, *Writing for the King*, 217.

501. Eder, *Elvis Music FAQ*, 197.

502. Middleton, "All Shook Up?" 6.

503. Elvis's charity concerts for the USS *Arizona* memorial and Kui Lee Cancer Fund are well known, but what is less remembered is that on 13 May 1973, in the midst of his divorce settlement, he performed a special 3 p.m. Lake Tahoe Mother's Day afternoon show in Gladys's honor, with all the proceeds going to the Cardiac and Intensive Care wing of the Barton Memorial Hospital. She was always on his mind.

504. Anne Nixon and Richard Harvey, *King of the Hilton: Memories of Elvis Presley's Las Vegas* (Cheadle, U.K.: A&R Publications, 2014), 64.

505. Goodall, "Interview with Elvis Presley."

506. Sharp, *Writing for the King*, 11.

507. Guralnick, *Sam Phillips*, 283.

508. Nixon, "Elvis Said . . . ," 64.

509. Jones, *Memphis Boys*, 212.

510. Jones, *Memphis Boys*, 212.

511. Trevor Simpson, "Bobby Wood: An Exclusive Interview with Elvis' Friend, Session Musician and Songwriter," *The Elvis Mag* 90 (2015): 18.

512. Andrew Perry, "From Elvis in Memphis: When Elvis Presley Found His Soul," *Daily Telegraph*, 14 August 2009, http://www.telegraph.co.uk/culture/music/rockandpopfeatures/6016795/From-Elvis-In-Memphis-when-Elvis-Presley-found-his-soul.html.

513. Moman procured "Suspicious Minds" from its writer for his own publishing company. Once Hill & Range knew about Elvis recording the song, its representatives pressured the producer to give up some of the publishing income stream. Chips stood his ground but did not endear himself to the Colonel or the Aberbachs. Elvis was thrilled to have more hits, but later he reportedly became upset when he found that Chips had produced "The Sidewalks of the Ghetto" by the hippie group Eternity's Children. It was released just a month after "In the Ghetto" and appeared to replicate the theme of Mac Davis's number.

514. Ritz, *Elvis by the Presleys*, 144.

515. Goodall, "Interview with Elvis Presley."

516. Hopkins, *Elvis*, 316.

517. Richard Perlstein, *Nixonland: The Rise of a President and the Fracturing of America* (New York: Scribner, 2010), 358.

518. Osborne, *Elvis: Word for Word*, 234.

519. Osborne, *Elvis: Word for Word*, 240.

520. Newbury did not record "An American Trilogy" until the next calendar year. Elektra released it as a single in October 1971 to mark the arrival of his *Frisco Mabel Joy* LP. Dennis Linde and Charlie McCoy helped Newbury with the album.

521. Victor, *The Elvis Encyclopedia*, 16.

522. Sharp, *Writing for the King*, 302.

523. Nixon and Harvey, *King of the Hilton*, 65. For *Aloha*, Gabe Baltazar offered this solo.

524. Elvis marked his nation's bicentennial by regularly including "America the Beautiful" in his shows from December 1975 through the following year. He also owned a copy of Ray Charles's 1976 recording of it, according to the 1996 *Virtual Graceland* CD-ROM set.

525. Andrew Himes, *The Sword of the Lord: The Roots of Fundamentalism in an American Family* (Seattle: Chiara Press, 2011), 43.

526. Himes, *The Sword of the Lord*, 43.

527. Deelen, "Interview with Jerry Scheff."

528. Larry King, "Interview with Joe Esposito," *Elvis Australia*, 1 November 2016, http://www.elvis.com.au/presley/interview-joe-esposito.shtml.

529. At one point in the series, Dinah, Dean Martin, Joey Bishop, and *Wyatt Earp* actor Hugh O'Brian performed their own version of "All Shook Up."

530. Brown quoted King's famous August 1963 "I Have a Dream" speech directly in "If I Can Dream." Just over two weeks before "If I Can Dream" was recorded, television newscasts of RFK's killing brought Elvis's rehearsal of *Comeback* material to a halt. According to Steve Binder, "There was just something weird that evening and I just sensed something had gone wrong. Then we spent the whole night basically talking about the Kennedy assassination, of both Bobby and John [Kennedy]." See Adams, "Interview with Steve Binder."

531. Guralnick and Jørgensen, *Elvis Day by Day*, 241.

532. Hopkins, *Elvis*, 336.

533. Hopkins, *Elvis*, 337.

534. Hopkins, *Elvis*, 336.

535. Sharp, *Writing for the King*, 200.

536. Guralnick, *Careless Love*, 309.

537. Alanna Nash, *The Colonel: The Extraordinary Story of Colonel Tom Parker and Elvis Presley* (London: Aurum, 2003), 240.

538. Guralnick, *Careless Love*, 309.

539. Weingarten, *Station to Station*, 153.

540. Sharp, *Writing for the King*, 202.

541. Weingarten, *Station to Station*, 152.

542. "Return of the Pelvis," *Newsweek*, 11 August 1969, 83.

. . . AND 100 MORE

1. Featuring rehearsal material from 15 July 1970, *Elvis: The Way It Was* is a release from the specialist label Follow That Dream (FTD) designed to commemorate the thirtieth anniversary of Denis Sanders's 1970 feature documentary, *Elvis: That's the Way It Is*.

BIBLIOGRAPHY

Adams, David. "Interview with Steve Binder, Director of Elvis' '68 Comeback Special." *Elvis Australia*, 8 July 2005. http://www.elvis.com.au/presley/interview-steve-binder.shtml.
Ames, Morgan. "Presley: The Product Is Sex." *High Fidelity*, April 1969, 104.
Ashby, Arved. *The Pleasure of Modern Music: Listening, Meaning, Intention, Ideology*. Martlesham, U.K.: Boydell & Brewer, 2004.
Bataille, Georges. *The Accursed Share*. New York: Zone Books, 1988.
Bego, Mark. *Cher: If You Believe*. Lanham, MD: Taylor Trade, 2004.
Bertrand, Michael. *Race, Rock, and Elvis*. Urbana: University of Illinois Press, 2000.
Beyond Elvis's Memphis. Directed by Mike Freeman. Memphis: Arts Magic, 2007. DVD.
Biszick-Lockwood, Bar. *Restless Giant: The Life and Times of Jean Aberbach and Hill and Range Songs*. Urbana: University of Illinois Press, 2010.
Botsford, Joe. "'Elvis Tops . . . Rock 'n' Roll Here to Stay' Says Winterhalter." *The Milwaukee Sentinel*, 27 June 1958, part 3, 6.
Bowman, Rob. *Soulsville, USA: The Story of Stax Records*. New York: Schirmer Trade, 2003.
Braun, Eric. *The Elvis Film Encyclopedia: An Impartial Guide to the Films of Elvis*. Woodstock, N.Y.: The Overlook Press, 1997.
Broven, John. "Roy Brown Part 2: Hard Luck Blues." *Blues Unlimited*, 1977. http://www.rocksbackpages.com/Library/Article/roy-brown-part-2-hard-luck-blues.
Brown, Shane. "Secrets and Lies: Getting to the Truth about *Elvis's Christmas Album*." *Elvis Information Network*, n.d. http://www.elvisinfonet.com/Spotlight-the-Truth-about%20Elvis-Christmas-Album.html.
Burke, Ken, and Dan Griffin. *The Blue Moon Boys: The Story of Elvis Presley's Band*. Chicago: Chicago Review Press, 2006.
Burns, Julie. "Elvis and His Italian Influences." *Italy Magazine*, 9 August 2011. http://www.italymagazine.com/featured-story/elvis-and-his-italian-inspirations.
———. "His Latest Flames." In *Vintage Rock Presents: Elvis Collector's Edition*, edited by Steve Harnell, 98–103. London: Anthem Publishing, 2016.
Cajiao, Trevor. *Talking Elvis*. Gateshead, U.K.: Now Dig This, 1997.
Carlin, Peter. *Paul McCartney: A Life*. New York: Touchstone, 2009.
Cartwright, Garth. "Luther Dixon Obituary." *The Guardian*, 11 November 2009. https://www.theguardian.com/music/2009/nov/11/luther-dixon-obituary.
Christgau, Robert. "Rock 'n' Roll: Elvis in Vegas." *Village Voice*, 4 September 1969, 29–33.
Clark, Shara. "Home on the Circle G." *Memphis: The City Magazine*, 8 August 2016. http://memphismagazine.com/features/elvis-circle-g-ranch-home/.
Classic Albums: Elvis Presley. Directed by Jeremy Marre. London: Eagle Rock Productions, 2001. DVD.

Cohn, Nik. *WopBopaLooBop A LopBam Boom*. St. Albans, U.K.: Granada, 1973.

Colker, David. "Wayne Carson Dies at 72; Songwriter Penned Hits 'Always on My Mind' and 'The Letter.'" *LA Times*, 23 July 2015. http://www.latimes.com/local/obituaries/la-me-wayne-carson-20150724-story.html.

Collins, Ace. *Untold Gold: The Stories behind Elvis's #1 Hits*. Chicago: Chicago Review Press, 2005.

Connolly, Ray. "Sam Phillips Plus Johnny Cash, Carl Perkins and Roy Orbison." *Radio Times*, September 1973. http://www.rayconnolly.co.uk/pages/journalism_01/journalism_01_item.asp?journalism_01ID=56.

Cosgrove, Ben. "Return of the King: When Elvis Left the Army." *Time*, 8 February 2014. http://time.com/3638949/return-of-the-king-when-elvis-left-the-army/.

Cusic, Don. *The Sound of Light: A History of Gospel and Christian Music*. Milwaukee: Hal Leonard, 2002.

Dahl, Bill. "Got It Covered." In *Vintage Rock Presents: Elvis Collector's Edition*, edited by Steve Harnell, 104–7. London: Anthem Publishing, 2016.

Deelen, Arjan. "Interview with Jerry Scheff." *Elvis Australia*, 1 January 2016. http://www.elvis.com.au/presley/interview-jerryscheff.shtml.

Doll, Susan. *Elvis for Dummies*. Hoboken, N.J.: John Wiley & Sons, 2009.

Dominic, Serene. *Burt Bacharach, Song by Song: The Ultimate Burt Bacharach Reference for Fans, Serious Record Collectors, and Music Critics*. London: Omnibus Press, 2003.

Dunnett, Ninian. "Elvis and Me, the Night Rock 'n' Roll Was Born." *The Scotsman*, 9 March 1999, 22.

Dylan, Bob. *Dylan on Dylan: The Essential Interviews*. London: Hodder, 2007.

Eder, Mike. *Elvis Music FAQ*. Milwaukee: Backbeat Books, 2013.

Erickson, Milton. *My Voice Will Go with You: The Teaching Tales of Milton H. Erickson*. New York: Norton, 1982.

Fike, Lamar. "More Feedback on Elvis Coming to London." *Elvis Information Network*, 24 April 2008. http://www.elvisinfonet.com/index_april08.html.

Floyd, John. *Sun Records: An Oral History*. London: Avon Books, 1998.

Friedman, Favius. *Meet Elvis Presley*. New York: Scholastic Book Service, 1973.

Gaar, Gillian. *Return of the King: Elvis Presley's Great Comeback*. London: Jawbone Press, 2010.

Gary, Kays. "Elvis Defends His Low Down Style." *Charlotte Observer*, 27 June 1956, 1B.

Gee, Vee. "Elvis 'Queer Disc' No. 8 *Blue Suede Shoes*." *Elvis Monthly* 81 (1965): 10.

Goodall, Nigel. "Interview with Elvis Presley: The 1972 Madison Square Garden Press Conference: June 9, 1972." *Elvis Australia*, 8 June 2011. http://www.elvis.com.au/presley/interview-with-elvis-presley-the-1972-press-conference.shtml.

Guralnick, Peter. *Last Train to Memphis: The Rise of Elvis Presley*. London: Abacus, 1994.

———. *Careless Love: The Unmaking of Elvis Presley*. London: Little, Brown and Company, 1999.

———. *Sam Phillips: The Man Who Invented Rock 'n' Roll*. London: Weidenfeld & Nicolson, 2015.

Guralnick, Peter, and Ernst Jørgensen. *Elvis Day by Day: The Definitive Record of His Life and Music*. New York: Ballantine Books, 1999.

Hand, Albert. "How to Kill Elvis by Inches." *Elvis Monthly* 5, no. 4 (1964): 2.

Hanson, Alan. "Love Me Tender: A Signature Elvis Presley Recording." *Elvis History Blog*, July 2012. http://www.elvis-history-blog.com/love-me_tender.html.

Hardcastle, Cleothus. "The Back Pages Interview: Jerry Leiber and Mike Stoller." *Rock's Back Pages*, 30 June 2001. http://www.rocksbackpages.com/Library/Article/the-backpages-interview-jerry-leiber-and-mike-stoller.

Hilburn, Robert. "When the Chairman Met the Returned King." *Los Angeles Times*, 25 January 2004. http://articles.latimes.com/2004/jan/25/entertainment/ca-hilburn25.

Himes, Andrew. *The Sword of the Lord: The Roots of Fundamentalism in an American Family*. Seattle: Chiara Press, 2011.

Hopkins, Jerry. *Elvis*. London: Open Gate Books, 1972.

"Interview with Elvis Presley: The 1969 Press Conference: August 1, 1969." *Elvis Australia*, 12 January 2008. http://www.elvis.com.au/presley/interview_with_elvis_presley_the_1969_press_conference.shtml.

Jones, Dylan. *Elvis Has Left the Building: The Day the King Died*. London: Overlook Duckworth, 2014.

Jones, Roben. *Memphis Boys: The Story of American Studios*. Jackson: University of Mississippi Press, 2010.

Jørgensen, Ernst. *Elvis Presley: A Life in Music. The Complete Recording Sessions*. New York: St. Martin's Press, 1998.

Keene, Nick. "For the Billionth and the Last Time: Lifting the Lid on the King's Record Sales." *Elvis Australia*, 11 March 2016. http://www.elvis.com.au/presley/one-billion-record-sales.shtml.

Kerouac, Jack. *On the Road*. London: Penguin, 2000.

King, Larry. "Interview with Joe Esposito." *Elvis Australia*, 1 November 2016. http://www.elvis.com.au/presley/interview-joe-esposito.shtml.

Locke, Alain. *The New Negro*. New York: Albert and Charles Boni, 1925.

Leroux, Gaston. *The Phantom of the Opera*. London: HarperCollins, 2011 [1909].

Lorentzen, Erik, et al. *Ultimate Elvis*. Oslo: KJ Consulting, 2014.

Marcus, Greil. *Mystery Train: Images of America in Rock 'n' Roll Music*. London: Omnibus Press, 1977.

———. "The Little Theatre." *'68 Comeback Special* Deluxe Edition DVD. Directed by Steve Binder. 1968. New York: Sony-BMG, 2004. Liner notes.

Marsh, Dave. *Elvis*. London: Omnibus Press, 1992 [1982].

Matthew-Walker, Robert. *Elvis Presley: A Study in Music*. Tunbridge Wells, U.K.: Midas Books, 1979.

———. *Heartbreak Hotel: The Life and Music of Elvis Presley*. Chessington, U.K.: Castle Communications, 1995.

McGhee, David. "Carl Perkins: Original Cat." In *Rockabilly—The Twang Heard 'Round the World: The Illustrated History*, edited by Michael Dregni, 46–55. Minneapolis: Voyageur Press, 2011.

Middleton, Richard. "All Shook Up?" In *The Elvis Reader*, edited by Kevin Quain, 3–12. New York: St. Martin's Press, 1992.

Miller, Stephen. *Kristofferson: The Wild American*. London: Omnibus Press, 2009.

Moscheo, Joe. *The Gospel Side of Elvis*. New York: Center Street, 2007.

Myers, Marc. "Bill Medley on Phil Spector." *Jazzwax*, July 2012. http://www.jazzwax.com/2012/07/bill-medley-on-phil-spector.html.

Napier-Bell, Simon. "Flashback: Dusty Springfield." *The Guardian*, 19 October 2003. http://observer.theguardian.com/omm/story/0,,1062873,00.html.

Nash, Alanna. *The Colonel: The Extraordinary Story of Colonel Tom Parker and Elvis Presley*. London: Aurum, 2003.

Neale, David. *Roots of Elvis*. New York: iUniverse, 2003.

Nixon, Anne. "Elvis Said . . ." In *Elvis Special 1976*, edited by Albert Hand, 64–68. Prescot, U.K.: World Distributors, 1976.

Nixon, Anne, and Richard Harvey. *King of the Hilton: Memories of Elvis Presley's Las Vegas*. Cheadle, U.K.: A&R Publications, 2014.

O'Neal, Jim, and Amy Van Singel. *The Voice of the Blues: Classic Interviews from Living Blues Magazine*. New York: Routledge, 2002.

Osborne, Jerry. *Elvis: Word for Word*. New York: Gramercy Books, 2000.

Paglia, Camille. *Sexual Personae: Art and Decadence from Nefertiti to Emily Dickinson*. London: Yale University Press, 2000.

Paulson, David. "Songwriter Layng Martine Recalls Writing 'Way Down,' Elvis' Last Hit." *The Tennessean*, 7 May 2016. http://www.tennessean.com/story/entertainment/music/2016/05/07/songwriter-layng-martine-recalls-writing-elvis-last-hit/83975104/.

Pegg, Bruce. *Brown Eyed Handsome Man: The Life and Hard Times of Chuck Berry*. Abingdon, U.K.: Routledge, 2002.

Perlstein, Richard. *Nixonland: The Rise of a President and the Fracturing of America.* New York: Scribner, 2010.

Perry, Andrew. "From Elvis in Memphis: When Elvis Presley Found His Soul." *Daily Telegraph,* 14 August 2009. http://www.telegraph.co.uk/culture/music/rockandpopfeatures/6016795/From-Elvis-In-Memphis-when-Elvis-Presley-found-his-soul.html.

"Return of the Pelvis." *Newsweek,* 11 August 1969, 83.

Richardson, Paul. "Glen Spreen Interview: Part 1." *Elvis: The Man and His Music* 110 (2015): 18–25.

Ritz, David, ed. *Elvis by the Presleys.* London: Century, 2005.

Ritz, David, Jerry Leiber, and Mike Stoller. "Hound Dog." *New York Times,* 12 June 2009. http://www.nytimes.com/2009/06/14/books/excerpt-hound-dog.html.

"Rock 'n' Roll: Return of the Big Beat." *Time* 94, no. 7 (1969): 57.

Schilling, Jerry. *Me and a Guy Named Elvis: My Lifelong Friendship with Elvis Presley.* New York: Gotham Books, 2006.

Schoenfeld, Herm. "Jocks, Jukes and Discs." *Variety,* 27 March 1957, 50.

Scholes, Barry. "The Amazing Success of 'It's Now or Never.'" In *Elvis Special 1964,* edited by Albert Hand, 47–48. Norwich, U.K.: Worldwide Distributors, 1964.

Sharp, Ken. "Leiber and Stoller: The Masters behind the Masters." *Elvis Australia,* 21 June 2004. http://www.elvis.com.au/presley/leiber-and-stoller-elvis-presley.shtml.

———. *Elvis Presley: Writing for the King—The Stories of the Songwriters.* London: FTD Books, 2006.

———. "Interview with Mike Stoller Legendary Songwriter," *Elvis Australia,* 23 July 2015, http://www.elvis.com.au/presley/interview-with-mike-stoller.shtml.

Simpson, Paul. *The Rough Guide to Elvis.* London: Rough Guides, 2004.

———. *Elvis Films FAQ.* Montclair, N.J.: Applause, 2013.

———. "Trains, Jet Plains and Morning Rain." *Elvis Information Network,* 2014. http://www.elvisinfonet.com/spotlight_elvis-if-youre-going-to-start-a-rumble.html.

———. "Interview with Legendary Songwriter Mike Stoller." *Elvis Australia,* 23 July 2015. http://www.elvis.com.au/presley/interview-with-mike-stoller.shtml.

Simpson, Trevor. "Bobby Wood: An Exclusive Interview with Elvis' Friend, Session Musician and Songwriter." *The Elvis Mag* 90 (2015): 8–19.

———. "Elvis Presley—*How Great Thou Art.*" In *Vintage Rock Presents: Elvis, a Celebration,* edited by Rik Flynn, 52–59. London: Anthem Publishing, 2017.

Spangler, Jay. "John Lennon Interview: Juke Box Jury 6/22/1963." *The Beatles Ultimate Experience,* 2011. http://www.beatlesinterviews.org/db1963.0622.jukebox.jury.john.lennon.html.

Spörke, Michael. *Big Mama Thornton: The Life and Music.* Jefferson, N.C.: McFarland, 2014.

Sullivan, Steve. *Encyclopedia of Great Popular Song Recordings, Volume 1.* Lanham, MD: Scarecrow Press, 2013.

Tarkovsky, Andrei. *Sculpting in Time: Reflections on the Cinema.* London: Faber & Faber, 1989.

Tillander, Bruno. *The World Knows Elvis Presley, but They Don't Know Me.* Stockholm: Premium, 2014.

Torgoff, Martin. *The Complete Elvis.* London: Virgin Books, 1982.

Troedson, David. "Jerry Reed and the Importance of Elvis Presley's Guitar Man Sessions." *Elvis Australia,* 28 March 2015. http://www.elvis.com.au/presley/jerry-reed-and-elvis-guitar-man-sessions.shtml.

Victor, Adam. *The Elvis Encyclopedia.* New York: Overlook Duckworth, 2008.

Warhol, Andy. *The Andy Warhol Diaries.* New York: Warner Books, 1989.

Watts, Jill. *Mae West: An Icon in Black and White.* Oxford: Oxford University Press, 2001.

Weingarten, Marc. *Station to Station: The History of Rock 'n' Roll on Television.* New York: Pocket Books, 2000.

West, Cornel. *Black Prophetic Fire.* Boston: Beacon Press, 2014.

West, Red, Sonny West, and Dave Hebler as told to Steve Dunleavy. *Elvis: What Happened?* New York: Ballantine, 1977.

Westmoreland, Kathy. *Elvis and Kathy.* Glendale, Calif.: Glendale House, 1987.

White, Barry. *Love Unlimited: Insights on Love and Life*. New York: Broadway Books, 1999.

White, Charles. *The Life and Times of Little Richard: The Quasar of Rock*. London: Pan Books, 1985.

Wiener, Allen. *Channeling Elvis: How Television Saved the King of Rock' n' Roll*. Potomac, MD: Beats & Measures Press, 2014.

Willis, Ellen. "Elvis in Vegas." In *Ellen Willis: Out of the Vinyl Deeps*, edited by Nona Willis Aronovitz, 178–81. Minneapolis: University of Minnesota Press, 2011.

INDEX

ABOUT THE AUTHOR

Mark Duffett is a reader in media and cultural studies at the University of Chester. His interest in Elvis Presley began in the mid-1990s, when, after a brief spell working for Sony Music, he embarked on a PhD looking at the relationship between the singer and his fans. Since then, Duffett has become widely recognized as an expert on popular music and media fandom, a role cemented by the publication of his book *Understanding Fandom* (2013). He has edited two books and various journal special issues in his research area and published many academic chapters and articles. He has presented papers in conferences at Oxford University, la Sorbonne Nouvelle, and many other universities, as well as being specially invited to speak at international events in Rotterdam and Moscow. Duffett's research has been featured in the *New York Times*, *Rolling Stone*, and BBC World Service.